CAMP 7

Hauser stare[illegible]
wall topped [illegible] guard in the
watchtower w[illegible] over the parapet, lolling there like a rag-doll. Hauser came to life with a jerk. He sprinted across the grass, made a grab for the top of the wall and hung there with his legs dangling. In an instant, he pulled himself up and threw his left leg across the parapet—he seemed to roll over the barbed wire in one continuous movement. Then he dropped to the ground on the far side of the wall and was lost from view.

Escape from Camp 7 was not only a punishable offence; it was also an admission of guilt . . .

Available in Fontana by the same author

Who's in Charge Here?
The Revolt of Gunner Asch
Gunner Asch goes to War
Officer Factory
The Night of the Generals
What Became of Gunner Asch?
The 20th of July
The Wolves
Undercover Man
Death Plays the Last Card

HANS HELLMUT KIRST

Camp 7 Last Stop

Translated by J. Maxwell Brownjohn

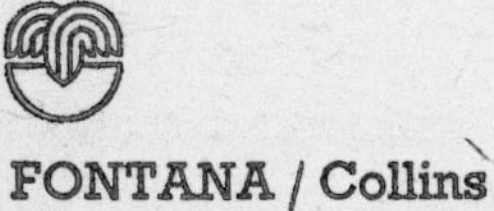

FONTANA / Collins

Originally published in Germany under the title
Letzte Station Camp 7
First published in Great Britain by Wm. Collins 1969
First issued in Fontana Books 1971
Second Impression April 1971
Third Impression August 1971
Fourth Impression April 1973

Printed in Great Britain
Collins Clear-Type Press London and Glasgow

Camp 7 – 'Civil Interment Camp No. 7' – was set up by members of the United States Army in July 1945 and located in the former school of mountain warfare at Garmisch-Partenkirchen. Roughly four thousand internees passed through it in the course of a single year. They were allotted a serial number and an additional coding such as ST (Security Threat), BL (Black List), WC (War Criminal), AA (Automatic Arrest). They belonged to a variety of age-groups and professions. The one thing common to them all was a reputation for being dangerous Nazis. Some of them were just that.

H.H.K.

Ted Harte, the chief CIC officer, strolled down the corridor of the former German army barrack block, heading for his office. He whistled as he went, unmelodiously but with great volume and persistence.

He always whistled the same tune—*Camptown Races*. None of his colleagues would have recognized it if he had not impressed on them that he never whistled anything else. Harte emitted these strident and provocative sounds every morning before embarking on his duties in Civil Internment Camp No. 7.

The recital ceased abruptly as soon as he opened the door to his office. He paused in the doorway for a moment and studied the girl who was laying out the mail on his desk—a slim, blue-eyed blonde who had been picked for the job with extreme care. She was supposed to be an incentive to greater effort.

'Morning,' said Harte, slamming the door behind him.

'Good morning,' said the secretary.

Harte chuckled contentedly. Sylvia Meiners looked annoyed, much to his delight. He brought off the same childish little coup every morning. His shrill whistling irritated her and she showed it, but that was just about the only private emotion he had ever detected in her. She obviously didn't like him, which was understandable. Her manner towards Captain Keller, the camp commandant, was a good deal friendlier, which was also understandable. Apart from that, she just worked. She was a fast worker, too—accurate, painstaking and reliable.

'The commandant wanted you. He's gone to see the trial commissioners. He was annoyed, by the way. You're half an hour late again.'

'What do you mean, half an hour?' Ted Harte laughed nonchalantly and tossed his uniform cap on to the window-sill. 'I'm precisely fifty minutes late, and that's still too early for my liking.'

'There are some important items on the agenda.'

Harte sat down behind his desk. 'Don't talk nonsense, Sylvia—anyone would think you were Keller's pet parrot. Nothing around here is important. Four thousand inmates, and every one with a memory like a sieve and half a dozen assorted alibis. How the hell am I and my six interrogators expected to find out what really goes on inside their thick German skulls?'

Sylvia eyed him keenly as he flicked through his mail. 'Captain Keller wants the job done quickly and thoroughly.'

'Either quickly or thoroughly—he can't have both. The only way I'll get results is to botch the job, and that's just what I won't do.'

'There are four thousand men locked up in here, Mr Harte.'

'I didn't lock them up, Fräulein Meiners.'

'No, but the slower you work the longer they stay inside.'

Ted Harte gave an amused glance at the secretary he shared with Captain Keller. 'Do you know why I picked you? Because of your blue eyes, that's all. You look so gloriously Germanic. I find that stimulating in the extreme. One look at you and I know exactly what country I'm in.'

'Why do you needle me all the time?'

'Because I need a top-notch secretary, not an angel of mercy. Stop dishing out advice. I'm a member of a victorious army, and that makes me impervious to reason. Ask any of the Nazis cooped up in here.'

Sylvia bit her lip and said nothing. Her only response was to deposit a sheaf of newspaper cuttings on his desk. 'Articles about the camp,' she explained. 'Hot off the press—six of them in the past week.'

Harte glanced through them calmly and then laughed aloud. 'Who says fairy-stories have had their day? These pieces are a joke. Why not have a good laugh?'

'But you will get them to put the record straight, won't you?' Sylvia said. 'None of this is true—in fact most of it is sheer lies.'

'My dear Fräulein Meiners, we subscribe to freedom of the press in America. Human rights don't always take priority, least of all here in Germany. Cheap journalists get a completely free hand, but so do responsible ones. Besides, internment camps are all the rage at the moment. The war's been over three months and heroes are going out of fashion. The world is starting to count its dead and look for scapegoats. Well, here they are.'

'But not everyone in this camp is guilty—not legally.'

'I'm aware of that. I studied law myself, much as I sometimes regret it. We have four thousand suspects locked up in here, and the other camps probably house several hundred thousand more. There must be a few hundred criminals among them.'

'But these measures are indiscriminate—you know that perfectly well. I'm surprised a person like you can accept such a situation without doing something about it.'

'If you only knew just what I do think, Sylvia . . . You and I were born and bred in Germany. You stayed put and I was kicked out. We're both German. My American citizenship doesn't alter that, but we're two completely different people. Hasn't it ever occurred to you that there may be two Germanys?'

Harte decided to spare her further argument. He had other worries. An article in *Tiger Club* had aroused his interest:

'*. . . in the old days, a German barracks which rang to the sound of jack-boots. Today, the only sound to be heard in camp is the shuffling footsteps of men who gambled on conquering the world and lost . . .*'

'*. . . a model of American efficiency and organization . . .*'

'*Criminals of every type can be found here. Most of them are thugs and murderers. Their records read like an account of the Spanish Inquisition . . .*'

There was a similar article in *Stars and Stripes*:

'*Lofty snow-capped peaks, gazing down silently on a picture of American efficiency and discipline . . .*'

'*Notices in English and German warn the visitor that all access to the area is prohibited . . .*'

The *Thundering Herd*, another American army newspaper, spoke of '*infantrymen guarding the crazy dregs of the former Nazi regime.*'

'*Heel-clicking is one of the characteristics common to most of the prisoners. When the German ex-soldier who cleans Captain Keller's office every day turns up for duty he clicks his heels, stands at attention, and refuses to start work until the captain nods.*'

Harte tossed the cuttings on to the second large desk in the office. 'Captain Keller will revel in these effusions,' he remarked. 'He's a born conqueror.'

'Is that your only reaction, Mr Harte?' Sylvia Meiners eyed

him reproachfully. 'They publish a collection of biased and unscrupulous stories, and all you do is make jokes?'

'You've got very beautiful eyes,' Ted Harte said gravely. 'I'm aware of them but I refuse to be over-impressed by them—that's one of my good resolutions. Here's another: whenever I hear a German in today's Germany talking about decency and fair play I get suspicious, so you can cut out the attacks of sensitivity. This internment centre isn't a concentration camp. The internees get bigger rations than the civil population and we haven't beaten anyone to death yet.'

Sylvia Meiners walked over to the commandant's desk and started to tidy his papers with single-minded attention. She seemed to have forgotten all about the CIC officer.

Harte busied himself with the morning's mail. It was always the same—letters from internees' wives, demands, requests, veiled threats, promises, barely disguised bribes. Some of the letters opened with the words '*If you have a spark of decency . . .*'

'I don't have a spark of decency,' Harte muttered without looking up.

'No need to broadcast the fact,' remarked Sylvia.

Harte glanced at her in surprise. She sounded amused. More than that, there seemed to be a hint of warmth and familiarity in her tone. Deciding that he must be mistaken, he hurriedly picked up the German camp commandant's daily report. It read:

> '3753 *Internees* (*previous day's total:* 3754; *one death by pneumonia*).
> *Of whom:* 38 *in sick-bay,*
> 12 *in solitary confinement.*
> *Number of amputees ascertained as instructed. Total:* 69.
> *Internees below the age of* 18*:* 10.
> *Internees over age of* 60*:* 204.'

Harte scribbled the word 'Balls' in the margin of the report and underlined it several times. Then he dropped the sheet of paper on Keller's desk.

'I asked you to make some inquiries in Frankfurt last week,' he said, leaning back in his chair. 'Do you remember? I wanted to find out what had happened to an old school-friend of mine—my only school-friend.'

Karl-Georg Zaunitz, a policeman's son . . . As useful with his fists as Harte himself, and equally respected on that account by his class-mates. The two youngsters had sacrificed an entire month's pocket-money at the Café Central for a glimpse of Ilse Benjamin, their first great love.

Sylvia bent over the commandant's desk, apparently searching for something.

'Did you get a reply?'

'Yes. It came in yesterday.'

'Well, what's old Zaunitz doing these days? Where is he?'

Sylvia did not look at Harte. 'He's in an internment camp.'

Harte rose silently and walked over to the window. A ration detail was trudging past, carrying pails of stew. He ran his eyes along the stockade and noted the guards leaning negligently over the parapet, tommy-guns ready. They didn't look as if they expected to use them.

He did not speak for a long time.

'A teletype message from Dachau,' said Sylvia. 'Colonel Cord urgently needs the file on Hauser. Captain Keller wants you to give the case top priority.' Still Harte did not speak. He propped his right hand against the window-frame as though in need of support.

'That's the third message about Hauser,' she went on, 'the fourth, actually, if you count the general directive about urgent cases. Captain Keller says . . .'

'All right,' Harte said brusquely. 'Stick it on my desk. I'll handle it, but in my own way. These damned internees make me sick. If there's a cure for that kind of sickness, I'm going to find it.'

Internee Manfred Hauser stood beside the barbed-wire fence at the rear of the camp and stared down the track that wound among the corn-fields. He had been standing there for a long time.

It was going to be a hot day, one of those days which made the blood sluggish and dulled the brain. That didn't apply to him, though. He was immune to weather conditions.

Hauser had stationed himself beside the fence and stared

down the track from nine o'clock onwards every morning for the past two weeks. He was waiting. Waiting was the principal pastime of all internees. Few of them knew exactly what they were waiting for, but Hauser did.

The bulky man was wearing an SS uniform without badges of rank. Insignia, epaulettes and sleeve badges had been neatly removed. The jacket was carefully brushed and free from stains. There was even a suggestion of a crease in the thick trousers, and the sturdy shoes had been polished with spit. Hours went by and days turned into weeks, and still Hauser stood there, waiting. He showed no signs of fatigue.

Perched on a near-by stone was Internee Mangel. He had laid a rough wooden board across his knees and was drawing. Mangel had been a lieutenant-colonel on the General Staff and was an authority on the railway systems of South-East Europe. One of Harte's interrogation officers had put an ample supply of paper at his disposal. At present, Mangel was reconstructing the Jugoslavian railway network from memory, firmly concentrating on strategic factors.

'What are you waiting for all the time, Herr Hauser?' Mangel asked, but Hauser brushed the question aside.

'I'm not in the mood for small-talk,' he retorted, and continued to stare down the track.

Mangel frowned at his companion's lack of tact. He wagged his head reprovingly. 'You ought to find yourself a hobby, Herr Hauser—something to take your mind off things. It's no good rotting in idleness.'

'You're all right,' Hauser said rudely. 'You haven't got a mind to rot. That's why you feel so at home here.'

Ex-Lieutenant-Colonel Mangel glanced up from his railway lines. He was not offended, just a little taken aback. 'There's no need to use that tone,' he observed mildly.

'Then stop pestering me the whole time,' Hauser snapped. 'I don't mix with shits who play ball with the Americans. Make a note of that and pass it on to the others.'

Mangel did not reply. His horsy face registered uneasiness. Joining two parallel lines by means of fine cross-strokes, he turned them into a main track—a double track forming one of the arteries of his railway network. Efficient rail transport was the prime requirement of any smooth-running military operation and balm to any military commander's soul, but people like Hauser couldn't be expected to understand such things.

The man had been standing there waiting for two weeks, on and off. What for? For a woman—his wife, perhaps? Anything was possible in detention camps, as the colonel well knew. He had once written a paper entitled *Human Behaviour under Stress*. Consequently, he was familiar with the sexual aspects of an unnatural mode of existence of this kind. Women could move mountains. Perhaps Hauser was waiting for the one who had just come into view—a walking fashion-plate of the type favoured by junior officers.

Hauser breathed heavily as he watched his wife approach. What a woman! She looked just as she had three months before, when he was arrested in their bedroom and hauled off to the internment camp—just as she had three years earlier, when he married her. Their wedding had been the culmination and crowning glory of an unforgettable spell of leave.

So the ball of paper he had managed to throw to a farm-hand two weeks ago while on an outside working party had reached its destination . . . Good man, that farm-hand—you could still rely on some people in Germany. His wife had received and understood the message, and now, here she was.

She walked past Hauser, who thought he detected a faint smile on her face. Barbed wire separated them and two watch-towers manned by American soldiers overlooked them from some distance away. The guards were dozing at their posts.

His wife's head moved almost imperceptibly in a covert nod. Hauser felt her eyes on him and gripped the barbed wire. He opened his mouth and whispered her name, 'Brigitte!'

Brigitte walked on for another few yards, then halted with her back to him. She raised one arm as though consulting her watch. Then, very deliberately, she pulled off a bracelet, held it up to the light for a brief moment, and slipped it into her pocket. That done, she turned and looked at him.

He shook his head, slowly but decisively. His meaning was plain. It was as if he had said, 'No, not the bracelet.'

Brigitte walked on again. Her steps slowed after another hundred yards. The sentries became aware of her. One of them waved a packet of cigarettes in her direction while the other leant over the parapet and offered her canned food—half a dozen cans. Having appraised her figure with an expert eye and found it flawless, he generously raised his bid.

Hauser compressed his lips and stuck out his square chin. The hand gripping the barbed wire trembled a little.

Brigitte sauntered back and glanced up at the guards as though by accident. Gracefully, she raised a hand in greeting and approached the wire.

'Try anything!' Hauser muttered, frozen-faced. 'Anything!'

'Hey, you!' called one of the guards in the tower. His voice was high-pitched, almost shrill. A shot rang out and a small puff of dust spurted beside Brigitte's feet.

Hauser did not move, but Brigitte backed off a couple of paces. The guard roared with laughter as if he had just told a particularly good joke and made another gesture of invitation.

Ex-Lieutenant-Colonel Mangel of the General Staff looked up indignantly from his diagram. 'Go away!' he called. 'We can't afford to antagonize these people. Have a little consideration for us.'

Brigitte moved off unhurriedly, pursued by admiring glances.

She hadn't changed, thought Hauser. The set of her head, the way her hips moved, the long slender legs—everything was just the same. He hoped she wouldn't do anything stupid with the bracelet, but then, she always knew what she wanted and did what he asked of her.

He left the barbed-wire fence and walked over to Mangel. After scrutinizing the railway expert's diagram for some time he said slowly, as if to himself,

'A neat job, Colonel, but absolutely no use to you or anyone else. Know what you should be drawing? A detailed plan of this camp. If there are any gaps in the security system we ought to plot them for future reference.'

'I don't understand you,' replied Mangel. 'We have to take things as we find them. There's no point in resorting to violence.'

'That may be your attitude,' Hauser countered scornfully. 'It isn't mine. You simply haven't grasped our position, but don't worry—we'll drum it into you yet, you and those like you. This is still Germany, in case you'd forgotten.'

Captain Keller strode into his office like an actor making an entrance. He was tall and slim, and his uniform fitted immaculately. Hollywood could not have supplied a finer candidate for the leading role in an army recruiting film.

'I'm surprised you bother to turn up at all,' he said to Harte.

'Quite frankly, so am I.' Harte leant back in his chair and ostentatiously propped his legs on the desk. 'This country makes me either yawn or puke—both at once, sometimes, and that's quite an achievement, you've got to admit.'

Keller went to the window and leant out. 'Come here a minute,' he said. 'I've got a new attraction to show you.' He lit a cigarette and beckoned Harte over.

Harte got up laboriously and joined Keller at the window. 'It better be good,' he said. 'Your attractions usually leave me cold.'

Keller gave a good-natured chuckle, then tossed his lighted cigarette out of the window. It described a wide arc and landed in the forecourt, which was being swept by a party of internees.

The cigarette had scarcely touched the ground before two internees hurled themselves at it. They collided and tried to jostle one another out of the way. A third man bent down, scuttled nimbly over to the smouldering butt, and picked it up.

'I got that from Sergeant Popper,' explained Keller. 'It's his favourite trick. He's even trained a major-general to retrieve like a gun-dog, and they say there's a prince in Block C who holds the camp record.'

Harte returned to his desk without speaking. 'Got anything to drink?' he asked.

Keller frowned. 'At this hour?'

'I feel sick,' Harte said. 'This country turns my stomach. My father was a front-line soldier in the First World War—won himself an Iron Cross First Class. What was he, Keller, an idealist or an idiot? Come to that, what are we—liberators or bear-baiters?'

'The climate here doesn't suit you, Ted.' Keller sounded a little hurt. 'Before you get another attack of moral indigestion, may I remind you that we're dealing with men who burnt millions of people like coal?'

'You say that, Keller, but do you always bear it in mind—whatever you're doing?'

'Yes, sir!' Keller replied firmly. 'I don't have any half-baked ambitions to be a psychologist and I refuse to be side-tracked.

These mental acrobatics of yours have been getting me down lately.'

'Listen,' said Harte. 'Every card-carrying Nazi must have five or six corpses to his credit, statistically speaking. We have four thousand of them in here, but at least three thousand are just as innocent or guilty as you and me.'

'What do you mean?'

'There are three sorts, Keller. One group was for it and another against it. The rest stood aside and watched, the way America did for a while. We didn't know any better. We just looked on from the other side of the Atlantic, but how often do we admit it?'

'Nonsense!' snapped Keller. 'Utter nonsense, Harte. I tell you quite frankly, I don't like the way your mind works.'

'And I don't like the way you're running things. This is a detention centre, not a concentration camp. I hated Nazi Germany as much as anyone, but I sure as hell don't want to feel ashamed of America.'

'You've been drinking,' Keller said, 'drinking at this hour of the morning.'

'And you're drunk, Keller—drunk with war and propaganda. Okay, make with that bottle. Let's get blind so we don't have to see straight.'

Harte produced a glass from his desk drawer and held it out to Keller, who filled it slowly, almost ceremoniously.

'When I got to America,' Harte continued, taking a pull, 'I worked as a wholesale cattle-dealer, first in Nevada, then in California. It was a straightforward process: X equals demand, Y equals supply, Z equals price. But this business here! I'm no saint, Keller. I'm itching for revenge—anyone with my background would—but I also want the results I deliver to be as impartial as possible. How do I reconcile those two things?'

'You're a poor Jew,' Keller said, unmoved. 'Try and reconcile yourself to that.'

Ted Harte was a senior interrogation officer in the CIC or Counter Intelligence Corps. Frank Keller was an infantry captain whose appointment as commandant of a civil internment camp had come as a complete surprise to him and was presumably due to his knowledge of German. Ted had been assigned to him, together with six other interrogation officers. The two men had known each other for some time. They belonged to the same army corps and had worked together during the Battle of the Bulge.

Keller was a true-blue second-generation American. Eighteen months at a German university, where he studied political economy, had left him with the certainty that Europe could teach him little. America was decades ahead in the field of practical economics. He was proud of his native land, its people and way of life, and prouder than ever now that the Old World had wallowed in blood, filth and brutality. The sight of the Stars and Stripes waving from a flag-pole made his heart beat higher.

Harte found it more difficult to muster exalted sentiments of this type. He was an American too—an American of some years' standing, according to his papers—but before that he had been a 'lousy immigrant'.

Germany was to blame for that. Barely a dozen years earlier, he had been declared a stateless person because of the shape of his nose. His father's former comrades-in-arms stuck him in a concentration camp, but he escaped and fled to America. Now the tide of war had washed him back to Germany.

So there they both were, settling a debt to humanity and ushering in a new age. They were liberators, and if that entailed depriving a few people of their liberty for a start—well, that was the sort of age it was.

They didn't live badly themselves. A private villa had been allocated to them and their office would have done credit to Madison Avenue. Its main features were a pair of gleaming leather arm-chairs and two magnificently directorial desks laden with dog-eared files. The desks stood close together, which was important in view of the directive which stipulated that camp commandant and senior interrogation officer should 'co-ordinate' their activities. The phrase had a splendid ring, but it might equally have meant: keep an eye on the cake and make sure the other man doesn't cut himself an extra slice. The aim was to prevent fiddling, corruption and petty tyranny. The military authorities seemed blind to the possibility that two men could happily fiddle in unison.

So much for the prettier side of the coin.

Down below in the former school of mountain warfare, like a sluggishly fermenting mass, lived almost four thousand men.

They included ambassadors, generals, senior civil servants, judges, government officials, and a few hundred dubious characters who were classified as ST, or potential threats to security.

Four thousand men, men who had once commanded hundreds of thousands of soldiers, organized convoys of prisoners, passed sentences, directed special operations, undertaken diplomatic missions, or systematically warped the human mind: the élite of Nazi Germany.

Now they slouched around the camp, lounged against walls or stood by the barbed wire. What went on inside their heads? What were they hatching? What had they really done?

Seven interrogation officers and a couple of dozen assistants had four thousand dossiers to compile. Mountains of lies, distortions and evasions could be expected, and there were some internees who would not wait for the touch of the noose on their neck.

'How about getting started on the job?' Keller asked.

'What job?'

'The Hauser case has got to be settled.'

'How?'

'You're in charge of interrogation, not me.'

'Right. You're the commandant. By all means give me orders, but make them reasonable. Telling me to untangle the Hauser case is like ordering me to turn night into day. Even I have my limitations.'

Harte felt Keller give him a searching stare as he slowly drained his glass. His own eyes rested on Sylvia. He decided that he liked the shape of her mouth, but her lips were not for him, worse luck. Women who looked like Sylvia were out of his league. She might be a marvellous secretary but she was a German. The fact that her record was clean made no difference.

Keller said: 'The inmates of this camp are under suspicion of having committed war crimes.'

'With all due respect, Captain, that isn't exactly news to me. However, suspicions have to be substantiated.'

'Exactly, Harte. That's your job.'

Harte studied the rim of his glass thoughtfully but made no reply. Sylvia Meiners interrupted her work to stare at him.

'How do you intend to proceed?' Keller's tone was studiously correct.

Harte pushed his glass away with an abrupt gesture and looked up. 'I'm sick to death of this filthy job. What a lousy, miserable, idiotic race the Germans are! The Nazis knocked the stuffing out of them and now they whimper: we didn't know a thing. All right, they know now, and what do they do about it? Lynch their Nazis? Like hell they do! They send them food parcels and leave us to wash their dirty linen.'

Keller merely shrugged his shoulders. 'Get used to the idea, Ted. You're an American now, remember? Do your job and stop sentimentalizing about the past. Okay, what's with Hauser?'

'I've found a DP who's ready to testify against him.'

'Then I advise you to get cracking. It's time we came up with some definite results.'

The German commandant of Civil Internment Camp No. 7 was Karl Reiter, an army captain. Although an internee like all the rest, he had been assigned to this important post by Keller on Harte's recommendation.

Reiter was supposed to be no more than a recipient of orders —a 'channel of command', as the camp regulations phrased it. He was responsible for internal discipline and the implementation of orders conveyed to him by the American commandant. The middle-man between Captain Keller and Hauptmann Reiter was the provost-marshal, Sergeant Popper, a bullying humorist whose favourite victims were German ex-generals.

'Are this camp and the men interned here subject to the Geneva Convention, the Hague Convention and the Habeas Corpus Act?' Reiter had asked on being offered the appointment.

'No,' Keller told him. 'But if you don't want to be German camp commandant I can easily find someone else.'

Reiter took the job. Before his appointment he had been one of the inmates of Room 29, Block C. The room senior of 29C was and continued to be ex-Lieutenant-Colonel Mangel, the acknowledged railway expert who had served with the German High Command.

Mangel had the reputation of a trustworthy officer and

gentleman whose words it was wise to heed. Unlikely as it sounded, what he told Reiter on this occasion merited acceptance at face value.

Mangel informed Reiter about Hauser and his odd behaviour beside the barbed wire. The incident clearly required investigation. Under prevailing circumstances, any unauthorized conduct spelled danger for the whole camp. Discretion was the order of the day.

'Just what one would expect of Hauser,' Mangel concluded. 'He's worse than a bull in a china shop.'

Reiter nodded. 'Knowing the man as I do, I couldn't agree more. If there's any trouble with the authorities we'll all suffer, and that must be avoided at all costs.'

Reiter, who was permitted to move freely within the camp, set off for Block C at a rapid pace. He was always in a hurry because the extent of his daily duties was prodigious, but his pace grew even brisker when he scented trouble.

Reiter wore an arm-band which informed everyone that he bore the title 'German Camp Commandant'. This arm-band was white, and the American guards were familiar with it. Other selected internees—Reiter's aides and associates, the German camp police, doctors and medical orderlies—wore arm-bands of a darker shade. They too could move about the camp, though only within certain strictly defined boundaries. Reiter alone could go anywhere any time.

Reaching Block C, he picked his way through the swarms of internees who were sitting, lounging, or strolling in the quadrangle, some chatting and others plunged in gloomy silence. He climbed the stairs to the first floor, turned right, and made for the door of Room 29.

He opened the door and peered into the room.

The view was obscured by crudely constructed two- and three-tiered bunks. These shelves for the storage of human beings jutted into the middle of the room. Between them stood two scarred and filthy tables of clumsy design, and pushed beneath the latter were a number of benches, stools and crates. Cubes of bread threaded on string were hanging in the window to dry. A sickly smell of sweat and decaying food assailed Reiter's nostrils.

There were only five or six people in the room. The rest

were presumably sitting outside in the midday sun, feeding on its warmth. Unlike food, sunlight was not rationed.

'Is Hauser here?' Reiter asked.

'You mean Herr Hauser, I presume,' said Internee Laffrentz, formerly a senior administrative adviser in the Ministry for the Eastern Territories. Laffrentz set great store by ranks and titles, particularly his own.

Reiter shrugged. 'Very well. Is Herr Hauser here?'

Laffrentz stuck out his still substantial paunch. 'We insist on proper treatment—even from you, if you still value our trust and co-operation. But perhaps you don't care about anything except keeping in with the Americans.'

'All right, all right,' Reiter said, controlling himself with an effort. 'My job's difficult enough as it is. I don't want any additional complications.'

'What the hell do you want?' Hauser asked, craning resentfully over the edge of his bunk. He had appropriated the top bunk nearest the window. It was the best in the room because it allowed the occupant to regulate the flow of fresh air.

'May I have a word with you?'

'If you must.'

Hauser, who had been resting on his trousers to preserve their creases, pulled them on over his underpants. He slipped into his uniform jacket and buttoned it carefully. Having flicked a speck of dust off his sleeve, he said, 'Well?'

'Perhaps it would be better if we went outside,' Reiter ventured.

'What's all this?' demanded Laffrentz. Are you keeping secrets from us?'

'Of course not,' said Reiter.

'Then sit down and give us the pleasure of your company. It's high time the German camp commandant remembered that he used to live in this room.'

'I hadn't forgotten, I assure you,' Reiter told him good-naturedly. 'I've got so much on my mind these days, that's all.'

'That's no reason for you to fill all the jobs in the cookhouse with people from other rooms. A lot of us regard that as a slur on our integrity.'

'Go easy!' said Mangel, glancing up from his diagram. He was a stickler for the conventions, especially in these surroundings. 'Let's not forget who we are, gentlemen.'

'All right, what do you want?' Hauser made a curt gesture of invitation. 'I'm listening, but make it snappy.'

Reiter sat down. Laffrentz sidled nearer with an air of interest. Mangel, who was evidently reluctant to be distracted, went on drawing. The other occupants of the room behaved as if the whole thing had nothing to do with them.

Reiter seemed to be having some difficulty in finding the right words. At last he said, 'Look, it's like this. The Americans have got us by the short hairs, whether we like it or not. In our position, all we can do is sit it out. You ought to accept that and behave accordingly.'

'Is that so?' Hauser said stiffly. 'Sit it out, did you say? Do you seriously mean it, or are you preaching the gospel according to Captain Keller?'

'Yes, just what do you mean, Herr Reiter?' Laffrentz edged nearer still. 'Are you throwing in the towel? Have you forgotten where you are—where you belong?'

Reiter drew himself up. 'There's no point in riling the Americans unnecessarily. They don't treat us badly on the whole, but I've got to know one or two of them pretty well lately. If they had their way, they'd really put the screws on us.'

'What makes you think so?' Hauser asked brusquely. 'You do your best to keep them sweet, God knows.'

'I do my job, that's all.' Reiter was slightly affronted but took care to conceal the fact. 'My duty is to represent the interests of my fellow-internees.'

Hauser's voice took on a bullying note. 'All this talk about duty is just so much hot air. An errand-boy, that's all you are. Well, that's your affair, but don't expect us to believe you play the Americans' game for our sake.'

Reiter's pallid face became a fraction paler. 'Be that as it may,' he said with unmistakable menace, 'good order and discipline are essential in this camp, and I won't tolerate any attempt to undermine them. In our position, the wisest policy is to adapt ourselves to prevailing conditions as skilfully as possible.'

'I shit on that sort of policy!' barked Hauser. 'If you insist on crawling to the Americans, crawl up their asses and stay there—the sooner the better—but leave me and my kind in peace.'

'Hear, hear!' Laffrentz said firmly. 'If you only became German camp commandant with an eye to the main chance we can do without you, Herr Reiter. It's obvious you've forgotten who your friends are. I'm told the food distribution job is still open. Why haven't you picked one of us? I'd be glad to offer my services.'

'Really, Herr Laffrentz!' Mangel remonstrated from his corner. 'This is hardly the time . . .'

'Come on, let's go outside,' Reiter urged Hauser. 'It's impossible to exchange two sane words in here.'

'So it's secrets after all!' Laffrentz cried indignantly. 'Always the same backstairs gossip!'

Reiter opened the door. After a moment's hesitation, Hauser followed him into the corridor. They went and stood by the open window, where they stared out at the hot summer day.

'I'll be quite candid,' said Reiter. 'I know you're trying to make contact with the outside world. That could mean trouble for all of us. Increased restrictions, room searches, water cuts, extra parades—that sort of thing.'

'So Mangel talked,' Hauser observed impassively. 'He's as bad as an old washerwoman, that man. No wonder we lost the war, with degenerate windbags like him on the General Staff.'

'Herr Mangel and I had a chance conversation in the course of which he happened to mention your attempts to communicate with someone through the wire. Quite seriously, Herr Hauser, we can't afford to make trouble of any kind.'

'I'll give you some good advice, Reiter. Hear no evil, see no evil, speak no evil. And now get going.'

'I've got some advice for you too. Keep clear of the wire in future and I'll gladly forget what I've been told. Otherwise . . .'

'Otherwise what?'

'Well,' said Reiter, using his forefinger to excavate some dust lodged in one corner of the window-frame, 'if you make trouble I shall take counter-measures. I know one or two things about you, don't forget.'

'Is that a threat?'

'No, a warning. I'm responsible for four thousand men, and I won't have them endangered by one individual.'

Hauser squared his shoulders. 'So you know one or two things about me,' he said slowly. 'Good, why not? Here's something else you ought to know. If anyone produces incriminating evidence they'll wonder how he came by it. Maybe he was there too, they'll say—maybe he's implicated himself.'

'I wouldn't put anything past you, Hauser. You'd send a score of innocent men to the gallows if you thought it would save your neck for another ten minutes.'

'Be sensible, then. Keep your trap shut and you keep your job. If you want to stay healthy, mind your own business.'

Ted Harte proposed to teach Captain Keller a lesson on the dubious nature of their joint activities.

In front of him stood Slembeck, allegedly a DP or Displaced Person. Once a peace-loving Pole, Slembeck had been hauled off to a forced labour camp by the Nazis. Now he was all for the Americans, or so he said. He said so time and time again in the identical words, wearing an air of extreme probity. He was a short, thick-set man with a face like a carp, but there were occasions when a strange gleam came into his eyes.

Harte's aim was to lean on Slembeck a little and so prove to Keller that a conviction could not be based on any old testimony. Perjury was positively normal these days. Decency and personal integrity were at a premium and the price of human life was low.

'So you want to help us get at the truth,' Harte began, striving to sound affable.

'Of course, sir,' Slembeck assured him with an ingratiating smile. 'That's why I'm here.'

'Which particular brand of truth do you want to help us find?'

The little man gave a start of surprise. Then he said in a faintly resentful voice, 'Well, you'll have to tell me exactly what you're after. I'm anxious to help, but mind-reading isn't my strong point.'

Although well on the way to unseating his star witness, Harte felt distracted. Sylvia Meiners was submitting various documents to Keller at the next desk. She explained each item in an undertone, obviously so as not to disturb Harte. Her hair, her thick and glossy hair, brushed the captain's shoulder as she bent over him.

Harte was irritated by the sight. He had put his feet up on

the desk, less to demonstrate his Americanized manners than as an aid to concentration, but Sylvia's presence distracted him. He fiddled with a match-box, tossed it aside and picked up a pencil instead, but it was no use—his nerves were on edge.

'So you'd definitely recognize him again, Slembeck?'

Slembeck nodded eagerly. 'Anywhere!'

Harte temporarily forgot to put any more questions. He strained his ears to catch the whispered exchanges between Sylvia Meiners and Captain Keller. They seemed to be concerned exclusively with official matters. He turned back to Slembeck and pondered his next question.

At that moment Sylvia gave a stifled laugh, evidently at some quip of Keller's. Eyeing them sourly, Harte decided that they looked like a still from a romantic film. It was a blissful spectacle.

Sylvia giggled.

'Must you?' Harte demanded loudly.

Sylvia stared at him wide-eyed. 'Sorry,' Keller said, 'we didn't mean to disturb you.'

The captain bent over his papers and Sylvia sat down at her desk with her back to Harte. Her shoulders twitched a little. Was she still laughing? And Keller? He appeared to be immersed in his work, but he was bound to be listening hard. All right, Harte told himself, let him hear something for once.

'So you're quite positive you're not mistaken?'

Slembeck nodded confidently. 'I don't know if he called himself Hauser in those days, of course. After all, a lot of water has flowed under the bridge since then. It was him that did it, though, I'm dead certain of that.'

'What exactly did he do?' Harte broke in. 'What can you actually prove against him?'

Slembeck's enthusiasm waned a little. He felt that Harte had turned on him—forced him on to the defensive. Damn this pseudo-American with his insistence on the whole truth! Why didn't he say precisely what he wanted?

'Prove? Come with me to Mlawa, Mr Harte. I'll dig up the bodies and hold them under your nose. The Nazis butchered the bailiff with an axe. The manor house was a pile of rubble by the time they'd finished. They sent the whole place up in flames.'

Harte looked totally unmoved. He picked up a paper-knife and started to play with it.

'That's all very well, Slembeck,' he observed. 'What do you mean, though—the Nazis butchered, looted, burnt, and so on? Did you actually see this SS officer, Hauser, kill the bailiff with his own hands?'

Slembeck did not reply. He stared at Harte as though it was the first time he had ever seen someone wearing an American uniform bare of regimental insignia. Then he glanced helplessly at Keller, but Keller was leafing through some papers.

'Well, Slembeck, why don't you answer? Was it definitely Hauser and nobody else?'

Still no reply.

'Did Hauser loot the manor house personally? Did he swing an axe or set fire to the place, or was he a chance spectator who just stood there and watched? Is it possible that you've confused him with someone else? What if Hauser alleges that he wasn't in Poland at all during the time in question? Well, what then?'

Silence.

Looking round, Sylvia Meiners saw that Harte's eyes were slightly narrowed. His usually boyish and friendly face had gone hard. He looked dangerous. Keller was watching Slembeck in silence.

Slembeck suddenly blurted out, 'But he did . . .' He hesitated, drew a deep breath, and relapsed into silence again.

'Well, what did he do?' Harte demanded after a brief pause.

Slembeck was visibly disconcerted. His eyes darted back to Keller, seeking help, but Keller's face had become a frozen mask. Harte strove to see if Keller and Sylvia were exchanging glances. He was reassured to note that they were both watching him.

'Tell me,' said Harte, 'why did you stop short just then? You were going to say something. What was it? What was it about—money, women, or what?'

Slembeck had recovered his composure and was looking furious. 'You're always confusing the issue, Mr Harte. I tell you the way it was but you don't believe me. Who will you believe, then? This Hauser fellow? I can swear to what I've told you. I can't produce photographs or a gramophone record of what happened, but I'm prepared to swear that Hauser was there. That's all you need, isn't it? Isn't that what you're after?'

Deliberately, Harte began to clean his nails with the paper-knife. 'So Hauser was there,' he mused, exploring the recesses of his left thumbnail. 'That means you were there too, Slembeck.'

The Pole grew even more enraged. 'There's a hell of a difference!'

Harte looked regretful. 'You set yourself up as a prosecution witness, Slembeck. It remains to be seen how effective you'd be in the box. What I need is water-tight evidence—something tangible, let's say.'

'Isn't my testimony good enough for you?'

'No.' Harte's tone was sorrowful. 'You overrate yourself, Slembeck. Do you know what might happen if you testified that Hauser had committed war crimes? Hauser might allege, in his turn, that you acted as his informer or were implicated yourself—even that you belonged to his organization. You being the only prosecution witness, he wouldn't hesitate to swat you like a fly. Think it over carefully and then come back and see me again.'

Slembeck stood there turned to stone, not knowing what to say. He couldn't believe his ears. He had just delivered the goods and Harte had rejected them.

Harte tossed the paper-knife on to the desk and started to leaf through a file. He said casually, 'All right, Slembeck, you can go.'

As soon as Slembeck had closed the door behind him, Keller got up. His expression was grave. 'I have to have a serious talk with you, Harte. This just won't do. I can't tolerate your methods.'

Harte rose stiffly to his feet. 'I'd remind you that we're not alone,' he said curtly.

Keller looked astonished. 'Since when has Sylvia's presence worried you?'

'Fräulein Meiners could work just as well next door. She ought to try it more often.'

'She doesn't worry me.'

'So I've noticed.'

Sylvia had also risen. She looked first at Keller, then at Harte. Her eyes lingered on the CIC officer for a few moments. Then she left the room without a word.

'She worries me,' said Harte.

Sergeant Popper, the provost-marshal, had assembled his pet internees, to wit, a party consisting of five German generals. These privileged individuals had the honour of sweeping the gymnasium under his personal supervision. In return, they received certain extras.

'All together, boys!' Popper adjured them from the comfort of a chair. 'One, two, one, two!'

The generals plied their brooms industriously. The work was not arduous, especially as the provost-marshal diluted it with relaxing conversation. What was more, it earned them a bowl of soup at midday. Only working internees were entitled to this. The others were limited to bread and coffee for breakfast and evening repast of oatmeal, semolina or noodle soup.

'Come here, boys!' the sergeant called gaily.

They gathered around him with their brooms at the order. Popper surveyed them with vague benevolence. Then he pulled out a pack of cigarettes.

'Hitler,' he announced, 'was a moron.'

The generals confirmed this. Three openly declared that Popper was right and were rewarded with two cigarettes. The other two, a former corps commander and an army chief of staff, made no response. Their silence was correctly interpreted as a sign of agreement. They received one cigarette each.

'Light up,' Popper said graciously.

The internees smoked greedily and with relish, avoiding each other's eyes. The provost-marshal watched them with the gleeful air of a child watching the antics of a mechanical doll.

'Okay, boys,' he said. 'We've established that Hitler was a moron.'

'A half-baked amateur, you could certainly say that,' observed one of the generals, a former divisional commander whose Knight's Cross now reposed in the camp's personal effects store. 'A bungling megalomaniac.'

'You mean that?' asked Popper.

'Certainly.'

'In that case,' Popper said with satisfaction, 'you took orders from a moron. Looking at you, I can well believe it. And now get sweeping. It's about time you did some honest work.'

The American sentry casually opened the gate leading to the inner compound. He put his hand to his helmet in a negligent salute as Keller and Harte passed through, then slammed the gate behind them.

The captain and his chief CIC officer had left the outer precincts where the administration block stood and were now strolling along the main camp thoroughfare. On their right were the three accommodation blocks which housed the internees, on their left the work-areas, store-rooms and cookhouses.

Harte glanced over his shoulder. Sure enough, he could see Sylvia standing at the office window.

'Is she watching us?' asked Keller.

Harte did not reply. Of course she was watching them. She could see them walking down the road from up there—see Keller's athletic figure and smartly tailored uniform, and, beside him, a smaller, slightly stooped man with his jacket unbuttoned and a uniform cap perched carelessly on his head.

'Strange girl, Sylvia,' mused Keller. 'She really seems to have fallen for one of us. I hadn't noticed before—always thought she was a professional virgin. Maybe I ought to take a closer interest in her. Or would you like to instead? You only have to say—I'm well taken care of. My score-card looks pretty good these days, what with the mayor's wife and her two daughters.'

There was no response. Harte's head just drooped a little lower than usual.

Small parties of internees passed them. They marched in file, each commanded by a member of the German camp police. 'Squad!' came the order. 'Eyes left!' No doubt about it: this was not only Germany but a German barracks.

'Halt!' called Keller.

'Halt!' barked the camp policeman. His charges automatically halted, eyeing the two Americans.

The camp policeman stood stiffly at attention with his hands clamped to his sides. 'Eight men from Block B reporting for sick parade. sir!' he announced loudly and succinctly.

Keller scrutinized the emaciated figures in front of him—

skin stretched taut over bone, dull grey faces, lustreless eyes. One or two of them stared at him unashamedly as if he were a man from Mars.

'Carry on,' said Keller.

'Quick march!' commanded the policeman, and the squad continued on its way. The men's shoes scuffed the concrete road in unison.

Keller stared after them. Thoughtfully, he said to Harte, 'If they had the chance they'd tear us to pieces like mad dogs.'

'Do you expect them to love us?'

'Me?' replied Keller, stressing the word. 'I'm quite aware that this isn't a kindergarten.'

Facing him: searchlights, barbed wire, watch-towers, loaded machine-guns. In his pocket: a Browning automatic with the safety-catch on and eight rounds in the magazine. Beside him: Harte, clearly dissatisfied with every order which he, Keller, thought fit to give. All around him: internees.

Other squads passed the two Americans, none of them more than eight men strong. Camp regulations decreed that no 'organized body' of internees should exceed ten. As a precautionary measure, the German commandant had reduced this maximum by two.

Keller stopped every squad he met. He stared keenly at the men as they stood there in their worn and crumpled clothing, half-sickened by the sweetish smell that drifted in his direction. The faces he tried to memorize looked spiteful and malevolent. They were Nazis—stinking, unkempt, unwashed Nazis. His shouts of 'Halt!' took on an increasingly waspish note.

Keller was the type of man who feels unhappy without at least one bath a day. He doused his face in astringent shaving-lotion after every shave. His shirts were soft—some of them silk—and his principal item of baggage was a capacious dressing-case.

The captain's flamboyant taste in clothes had earned him quite a reputation in his unit, and he was proud of it. He knew that his men laid bets on how he would turn out every morning—in brown shoes or black, tie or silk scarf, special green tunic or battle-dress, riding-crop in hand or *New York Times*.

Keller owed his flawless German accent to his immigrant grandfather, a highly qualified chemist. Grandfather Keller entertained German friends, read German books, loved German food and drank German beer. The same went for his son, Keller's father, a senior chemist employed by du Pont. Keller's mother also spoke German.

It was not easy to overcome a thing like that, and Keller had found it an effort to shake off his background. He was American, though, that was for sure—American to the core. No childhood memories could be allowed to obscure that.

Then, by the grace of God, came the war, and with it a chance to show America what he was made of and prove to himself that he had finally overcome his youthful complexes. Keller demonstrated his courage even before he was promoted captain. He commanded his infantry company with verve and initiative. The establishment of Camp 7 was a tribute to his outstanding talent for organization.

General Thomas had bestowed a high decoration on him and Colonel Cord trusted him implicitly. Keller felt satisfied that these marks of esteem were well deserved. He had never let Thomas down and he would do his utmost to see that he never let Colonel Cord down either. He owed it to himself and to America, which had assigned him a part in cleaning up Nazi Germany.

Keller found the bustle of activity on the camp road too brisk, too hard to supervise. 'Like a goddamned fair-ground,' he grumbled. 'This isn't a camp, it's a recreation centre.'

Harte said, 'Let them wander round the place. It makes a change for them. They only get crazy ideas if they're cooped up in their cages the whole time.'

'Maybe, but too much sight-seeing could give them a few pegs to hang their crazy ideas on. I know there aren't any gaps in our security system, but we don't have any concentration camp experience—no electrified barbed wire or guards with itchy fingers. The Nazis beat us hands down in that respect.'

'I'd call that a point in our favour,' Harte said drily.

Reiter, the German commandant, hurried towards them. He sketched a salute and requested permission to speak, but Keller cut him short.

'I don't like all these organized promenades, Reiter. Eight men off to see the doctor, six detailed for potato-peeling in the cookhouse, seven going for firewood, another eight loading trash-cans—and all in the ten minutes I've been standing here. It's too much. Slow it down and work more methodically, otherwise I'll start drawing my own conclusions.'

Reiter attempted to explain. 'Things are much quieter in camp as a rule, sir, but at this hour of the day . . .'

Keller made a curt gesture of dismissal which reduced Reiter to silence. The German muttered a few inaudible words, delivered another sketchy salute, and strode off.

'Obstinate bastard,' said Keller.

Harte shook his head. 'A method man. If we didn't have him this place would be like hell's kitchen.'

'I don't like it,' Keller said sharply, giving Harte a challenging glare. 'I don't like anything I see around here.'

'Apart from Sylvia.'

'At least Sylvia can be relied on. She does her job. She doesn't sabotage my efforts, like some other people I know.'

'Who, for instance?'

Keller snorted indignantly. 'What has Sylvia got to do with these rest-cure methods you're so hot on using—or encouraging, at least? Why drag Sylvia into it, anyway? Are you trying to side-track me?'

'Who's sabotaging things round here, Keller?'

'Okay,' Keller said with sudden decision, 'if you really want to know what's on my mind, I'll tell you.'

'I'm listening.'

'The fact is, I don't get the impression that you're doing a particularly successful job here,' Keller said, almost coldly. 'You were assigned to me as an interrogator but you spend the whole time preaching.'

Harte gazed at him sadly. 'Is that an official reprimand?'

'A statement of fact, Harte, nothing more at this stage. However, I'm in charge of this place. I bear sole responsibility so I determine the methods used here. I want my views to be respected—without question.'

Keller had drawn himself up to his full height. He allowed a party of internees carrying crates to pass him unchallenged.

'So I'm not doing a successful job here in your opinion,' Harte said, filling his pipe. 'What's your definition of a successful job—delivering the maximum number of war criminals for retribution or producing as much valid evidence as possible?'

He lit up, settled the pipe in one corner of his mouth, and exhaled a cloud of smoke.

'For weeks now,' Keller began quietly, 'Colonel Cord of the judge-advocate's department in Dachau has been asking for solid proof of Hauser's guilt. From the sound of it, he's the missing link in an important chain. Why don't you come up with the evidence they need?'

'Because it's incomplete.'

'Then complete it, for God's sake!'

Harte stared through the clouds of smoke from his pipe at the barbed wire that enclosed the internees like a cage. There they were, doomed to balance the books of history. Scape-goats would be needed as long as the world endured. Maybe there really were some to be found this time, but not at any price.

He looked at Keller. An athletic young man, a happy child-hood spent among friends, a spell at a German university, European travel, expensive luggage, a shiny car, a wallet stuffed with dollars and the right kind of passport—in short, an American. If it weren't for the war, the world would be his oyster.

Then he looked at himself. Sharp, shrewd, politically aware, holder of an honours degree from Frankfurt. His world had suddenly collapsed in 1933. He was beaten up and consigned to a concentration camp, escaped, starved his way to America, where he swept roads, tried to sell vacuum cleaners, radios and cars, and finally worked as a cattle-dealer among farmers who, like him, had once been German. Then they put him into uniform. It was time to pay his debts.

Harte sucked at his pipe.

At last he said, 'You're not only remote from Germany, Keller—you're too remote. All you do is look at the map and see what's written across this part of our weird and wonderful world. You know a lot of facts and figures, but do you know people? Every human being who lives here has a very personal destiny. You only studied here. I was beaten unconscious several times in this country, but it hasn't destroyed the things I love about it. You'd better get used to the idea.'

Keller drew a deep breath. The gentle summer breeze wafted the stench of an open latrine to his nostrils. He walked off in disgust, followed by Harte.

After a brief pause, Keller said, 'I just don't get it. Did they beat this Germanic sentimentality into you in the concentration camp? Was that when you caught this philanthropic bug of yours? I've always found it highly original until now, but it's beginning to get me down.'

Harte removed the pipe from the corner of his mouth and said very gravely, 'I wouldn't want anyone to go through that again.' Quietly, he added, 'Not anyone.'

'Even if he deserved it?'

'Nobody deserves what happened to us, least of all because of his convictions. It isn't possible to punish a man for his beliefs—even Churchill says so.'

'I couldn't care less what criminals believe,' Keller said harshly. 'They're criminals. That's good enough for me.'

Brigitte, the wife of Internee Hauser, headed for the main entrance.

Brigitte had just emerged from the White Horse, where she had—as her husband would have put it—washed down the little shooting incident beside the barbed-wire fence. Brandy was exorbitantly expensive these days, but she felt fortified.

She had inspected her face in the mirror of her compact while making up—critically and at rather greater length than usual. She found her appearance wholly acceptable. Her eyes reminded people of Marlene Dietrich, and she knew it.

She wondered, as she carefully outlined her lips, if it mightn't have been better to choose a slightly brighter shade of lipstick, but decided that it would be wiser not to appear too conspicuous. And so, armed for the fray, she slowly approached the gate of Civil Internment Camp No. 7.

Brigitte had many requirements but few assets. She wanted her husband back. He knew how to live and what to do in order to live well. She also wanted the White Horse, the biggest and best hotel in the district, and would happily have swapped it for the small inn near Mittenwald which her parents had left her. That was her dearest ambition. The moment was not inauspicious, either, since the White Horse was without a legal proprietor. It was there for the asking. She wondered what she had to do to get it.

Nobody gets something for nothing, she told herself. It was no use offering money—money was almost valueless. What else? All she owned was a little jewellery and her body. She doubted if that would be enough.

Her thoughts turned to the bracelet which her husband had brought back from the wars, a platinum bracelet thickly encrusted with sparkling blood-red stones—rubies. It must represent a fortune, if only because of its intrinsic value. There was no knowing how much a collector would pay for it. An asset like that might well be worth a dream or two.

Unfortunately, the bracelet was the one asset her husband didn't want her to realize. His response to her implied question that morning couldn't have been plainer.

Why, she wondered?

The American sentry had stationed himself in front of the gate and was standing there with his hands on his hips, grinning amiably. Brigitte could see that he liked her looks. She wasn't surprised.

'Well, hello, baby,' said the sentry.

'Hello.' Brigitte approached him with a friendly smile. He had a smooth, round, good-natured face. A tuft of sandy hair escaped from under the lip of his steel helmet. He had tilted it to the back of his head, either because of the heat or so as to see better.

'Who are you looking for, baby?' asked the sentry. 'Me?'

'Can I come in?'

'Sorry, no civilians admitted.' The sentry gave an apologetic shrug. 'Internees aren't allowed visitors.'

'I haven't come to see an internee. I'm looking for Fräulein Meiners.'

'Ah,' said the sentry, 'you mean Sylvia.'

Brigitte raised her eyebrows. So the Americans called her Sylvia, did they—or was that the sentry's privilege? She wondered if the girl who had written her the letter was a communal American possession or simply a general favourite. Some women inspired liking rather than lust, so she had heard.

'All right,' she said, 'I'd like to see Sylvia.'

A few minutes later Brigitte found herself face to face with Sylvia Meiners. She didn't look like a camp-follower or the boss's girl-friend. Far from putting on airs, she behaved in a reserved, almost diffident fashion. All the same, she held a key job and she wasn't physically unattractive.

'You wrote to me,' Brigitte said politely.

'Yes, on behalf of Mr Harte.'

Sylvia felt a little disconcerted. She hadn't been expecting a woman of this sort. The few internees' wives who had managed to obtain an interview with Harte had all been typical post-war products, at least outwardly. All looked careworn and sullen; some grovelled unashamedly, and a few clung stubbornly to their pride.

The Hauser woman was quite different.

How had Harte come to invite her here? Did he know what she looked like? What was he after? Since when had he taken an interest in such women? More than that, since when had he taken an interest in women generally?

'What sort of man is he, this Mr Harte?' Brigitte inquired.

'He's the chief interrogation officer.'

'I know, it said so in the letter. I'm more interested in the sort of person he is.'

'I've no idea,' Sylvia said brusquely. 'How should I know? I only work here.'

Abruptly, she turned her back and busied herself with the papers on her desk.

The inmates of Room 29, Block C, were waiting for their midday meal. They sat on stools or on the edge of their bunks, food-bowls within easy reach, and stared into space—apathetically, for the most part. Hauser had stretched out on a bench with his head pillowed on his folded arms and was contemplating the ceiling. Baron von Hagen, an ex-ambassador of the Greater German Reich, who regarded this bench as his private preserve, stood beside the window overlooking the yard and stared out impassively.

At the big table in the corner sat Mangel, the railway expert. His diagrams reposed on his bunk, carefully wrapped in newspaper. He now had in front of him a ladle, a wooden measuring-stick, and a slide rule. Mangel was in charge not only of Room 29 but also of Corridor 2, Block C, and one of his duties was to dole out food to the hundred men in his care.

Before long the first pail of food reached Block C. Mangel's technique was to plunge his measuring-stick—devised and calibrated by himself—into the exact centre of the contents. Having thus established the total quantity of stew available, he used his slide rule to divide it by the number of mouths to feed. He now knew how far to fill the ladle so that each man got as fair a share as possible.

'It's our turn for left-overs today,' observed Internee Laffrentz, the corpulent civil servant. 'Left-overs' consisted of what remained after the distribution, which was never very much. Turning to Mangel, Laffrentz went on, 'Make sure you leave a decent helping for each of us.'

Mangel shook his head. 'I go strictly by the book.'

'What about Room 24?' Laffrentz whined. 'Ten days ago they got almost a whole extra ladleful and a nice big helping of the solid stuff. We've never had more than a half-portion—watery muck, what's more. It isn't fair.'

'Can't you find another topic of conversation?' Baron von Hagen demanded reprovingly from the window. 'Can't you think about something else for a change?'

'No,' said Laffrentz. 'Rations are far too important to be left to an expert on railways. Colonel Mangel can't handle the job by himself. He needs someone to stir the food while he's dishing out. That's another aspect of fair distribution.'

'And you're the man to do it?'

'Of course I am. Say we were first in line, just for the sake of argument. In that case, I'd stir the hell out of the contents of the pail so that the bits floated to the top. If we were last, I'd only stir gently so that there'd be some meat left at the bottom—for us!'

'Herr Laffrentz,' Hauser said, still staring fixedly at the ceiling, 'kindly shut up. If all you can do is figure out how to stuff your belly, you belong in a sty. Why not concentrate on how we're going to get out of here?'

Laffrentz relapsed into aggrieved silence. The other men in the room made no comment. They continued to wait. There was no point in taking sides either way—it only wasted time and frayed the nerves.

The ceiling above Hauser's head was grey, grimy, and covered with a network of fine cracks. He shut his eyes. A pale blue glow seemed to descend on him—blue as the quilt in his bedroom at home. He could picture Brigitte lying beneath it, naked.

It had all started during his first war-time leave, after the defeat of Poland. In search of relaxation, he had booked a room at her parents' inn in the mountains—only a few miles from this godforsaken internment camp.

They hadn't taken their eyes off each other the first evening. 'Come for a stroll?' he suggested later on, when the other guests had gone up to bed. 'With you?' she replied. 'Any time.' And they had gone out into the summer night. It was dawn when they returned, tired and silent but happy.

Brigitte stopped work early the second evening. She sped upstairs to her room almost automatically, as though propelled by an irresistible force. So did he.

They lay together until late next morning. Brigitte locked the door and refused to appear for work. 'I'd like you to be there when I come back,' he told her, and she replied, 'Don't worry, I'll always be there for you.'

They got married at once. It was an idyllic time made more idyllic by the discovery that they suited each other in every respect. They both committed adultery regularly and without scruple while they were apart but swapped experiences and laughed about them when he came home. Their reunions always ended in bed.

Still lying on the hard bench, Hauser screwed up his eyes. What lousy times these were, and what a woman Brigitte was! For all the barbed wire that separated them, she seemed so close he could almost touch her—feel the arms that had clung to him, the thighs that had received him, the fingers that had clawed his flesh. But he was cut off from all that by a barbed-wire cage.

Baron von Hagen called from the window, 'The next ration detail has arrived. This time it's our turn.'

There was immediate pandemonium. The room emptied rapidly. Mangel, measuring-stick, ladle and slide rule in hand, hurried on ahead of the rest.

Only Hauser lingered behind. He stood there for a moment, brooding on his fate. No decent food, no women, nothing to drink—no Brigitte. Another ten yards and he could have touched her, another few steps and he could have felt her breath on his cheek. If it weren't for that barbed wire—that goddam barbed wire . . . He cursed the camp, cursed the Americans, pondered for the umpteenth time how to escape.

Then he picked up his tin bowl and strode out into the

corridor, elbowing his room-mates out of the way. They stood aside with scarcely a protest. Hauser was Number One.

Captain Frank C. Keller, commandant of Camp 7, and Ted Harte, his chief interrogation officer, made a habit of lunching together in the officers' mess at District Headquarters. The internment camp was not the only military establishment in the small mountain resort. In addition to the camp garrison, the American units stationed there included a tank battalion, two field hospitals, a supply depot, and three motor transport companies.

The former town hall, which had become the official headquarters of the Commander of Occupational Forces, was presided over by a Major Forsell. Forsell was allegedly related to half the officers in the US Army, though only those of influential rank. Almost opposite the town hall stood what used to be the best inn in town but had now been commandeered as the officers' mess.

Just before one o'clock every day, Keller and Harte gathered up their papers, called out 'Lunch!' waved to Sylvia, and climbed into their jeep. Usually, Keller drove while Harte whistled a medley of the latest hits, all of which sounded like *Camptown Races*. On reaching the mess they stormed the bar and downed a couple of drinks. After that, they ate.

Today, however, the jeep roared swiftly through the narrow streets with their picturesque half-timbered houses. Keller stared straight ahead. Harte sat beside him, looking blank. Keller said nothing and Harte did not whistle.

There was virtually no conversation during lunch. They wolfed their food more quickly than usual and gulped their coffee, cursing under their breath because it was too hot.

Finally, they lit up—Keller a cigarette and Harte a cigar. Leaning back in their chairs with legs extended, they surveyed their surroundings.

Everyone who lunched in the mess was in a hurry, and few people ever finished what was on their plates. Mountains of untouched food were borne off by the mess waiters and emptied into trash-cans.

Before long, the two men were alone. It was Keller who broke the silence.

'Funny girl, Sylvia,' he mused. 'Ultra-German in a way. I'd

scarcely noticed her before. Sure, I thought she was a nice little thing, but nothing out of the ordinary. That's what I thought, as I say, but when you take a closer look . . .'

Harte, who had been listening to this monologue with outward indifference, said, 'All the same, there's an army directive which says Germany is a defeated hostile power—that we're here to occupy the country, not liberate it. It isn't altogether true, of course, but it does affect Sylvia's status, especially as she's working for us. She's off limits, Keller, even though she wasn't a Nazi.'

'Well, I'm going to take a closer look at her,' Keller said, undeterred. 'She isn't really my type—in fact you could call her virgin territory from my point of view—but that's just what appeals to me. Makes me feel like an explorer.'

'All forms of fraternization are banned,' Harte insisted. 'That even goes for German kids,' he added, but Keller had not exhausted his subject.

'Sylvia isn't the kind of woman who excites me, exactly. This lousy country doesn't seem to produce any really exciting women. I've already experimented with a whole series—generals' daughters, waitresses, civil servants' wives, maids, so-called society women—none of them made the grade. They're too goddamned willing. Sylvia promises to be an exception.'

Harte interrupted him. 'You ought to have a word with that fire-eating Forsell. He's instructed the mess waiters to destroy all scraps. It's an outrage, when there are people starving outside. Do something about it, Keller. You're an expert on justice.'

Keller waved the remark aside. 'Major Forsell happens to be the nephew of a four-star general—you know that.'

'Sure I know,' said Harte. 'If he weren't, he'd probably be washing dishes, not sitting behind a mahogany desk.'

'That's beside the point. Forsell's an influential man. The fact that he's no genius is secondary. I have to co-operate with him, and that means we both do. It's not only logical, Harte. It has its advantages too. For instance, today he called his four-star uncle, who was spending the morning in Dachau.'

'Ah!' Harte pulled at his cigar and exhaled a cloud of smoke. 'And I suppose Colonel Judge-Advocate Cord was standing at the general's elbow, and Colonel Judge-Advocate

Cord hinted that the commandant of Camp 7 wasn't doing his job—wasn't producing enough evidence to enable him to bombard Washington with glowing reports of how many war criminals he's sent to the gallows. Am I right?'

'More or less,' replied Keller, shifting slightly in his chair. 'They're tired of waiting—everyone is. In other words, you're to speed up the Hauser investigation.'

Harte looked down at his cigar, which had developed a cone of snow-white ash. Delicate skeins of smoke drifted to the ceiling.

'My dear Keller,' he said, addressing his cigar, 'I shall conduct my inquiries as I think fit. As long as I remain in charge of the Hauser case, I'm the one who determines what methods are used to complete it.'

In other words,' said Keller, 'you refuse to carry out the instructions of the Dachau tribunal?'

'The tribunal can't instruct me to produce evidence, it can only make a request. I won't submit any evidence until I'm satisfied that it's watertight.'

Keller lit a fresh cigarette from the glowing butt of his old one. He took a deep drag, blew the smoke past Harte's head and stared after it. At length he said slowly,

'What if I take you off this particular case?'

'Is that an order?'

'No, just a suggestion.'

Harte made no immediate response. He rose, brought another ash-tray from the next table and set it down in front of him. Every one of his movements might have been designed to gain time.

'Good,' he said finally. 'Very good.' After another pull at his cigar, he added, 'Why not?'

He leaned back comfortably in his chair. 'If I were a hypocrite I could solemnly proclaim that I was obeying an order. To be honest, your suggestion comes as a relief. I'll overlook the fact that it offends me.'

'I'm sorry, Harte.'

'You're sorry? No, no, Keller, don't be sorry yet. Wait till you come to the unpleasant part. There's a dividing line between doing one's duty and committing a crime. I've always wondered where it lay. Do you feel capable of putting your finger on it? Have you got the guts to distinguish between honest men and murderers, idiots and idealists, genuine belief and criminal subservience?'

Keller stood up. He went to the hat-rack and took down his cap, his expression clearly conveying what he thought. Harte was a poor bastard with a chip on his shoulder. He just couldn't live down his unfortunate background.

'What do you expect us to do?' Keller demanded. 'Fight force with philosophy? These men were ruthless, Harte. Well, I'm going to give them a dose of their own medicine, lean on them for a change, show them what it feels like.'

'You call that the dawn of a new age?'

'No, the end of an old one. I won't hesitate to lean on them hard, either—very hard.'

'All right, go to it,' Harte said. 'Why not start with Sylvia? Show her and her friends what a conquering hero can do. I'm curious to see how far you get.'

'Gentlemen,' Baron von Hagen said courteously, 'thank you for putting in an appearance.'

His five fellow-internees had appeared with alacrity. Their American-issue camouflage suits made them look like headmasters, bank managers, civil servants or regional museum curators in fancy dress. They were all, in fact, ex-ambassadors.

The camp's records listed thirty-six senior and middle-ranking members of the diplomatic service. Block C housed seventeen, five of them former ambassadors to countries in South-East Europe. Having made contact shortly after their internment, they now held regular councils of war.

'Gentlemen,' said His Excellency Herr von Weisänger, ex-ambassador to Rumania, 'I take the liberty of reverting to our discussion of yesterday, in the course of which it was proposed that we should expand our little circle. I'm against the idea. We must co-ordinate our activities first—at the highest level, so to speak. Other reliable people can be brought in gradually at a later stage.'

After being debated for some time, this suggestion was finally adopted. All expressed their views at considerable length in a resolutely cordial and harmonious atmosphere.

These ambassadorial conferences took place in the first-floor corridor of Block C between the lavatory door and the window overlooking the road. Weighty resolutions had already been passed, e.g. that a sharp distinction be drawn between ex-members of National Socialist agencies abroad and former representatives of the Central State Security Bureau, also between members of the diplomatic corps and former military administrators of foreign territory, whether occupied, liberated, or 'protected'.

'Speaking for myself,' declared Herr von Kernitz-Weibel, who had served in Budapest, 'I repeatedly took exception to certain policy decisions and protested against them in the most vigorous terms. I recall a meeting two years ago in Vienna at which I poured scorn on our so-called Foreign Minister, Herr von Ribbentrop.'

'So did we all!'

The ex-ambassadors nodded enthusiastically. They could vouch for one another—yet another point in their favour. They swapped reminiscences and devised felicitous phrases for use in their defence.

'There'll be time enough for that later,' Baron von Hagen said, a trifle nervously. 'I have a far more urgent matter to raise. The Americans are focusing their attentions on a certain Herr Hauser, whose name may be familiar to you gentlemen in connection with a special operational group formerly active in Eastern Europe.'

'In that case, we must cover ourselves at once!'

'Precisely—I mean, that is a problem which demands full and concerted discussion.'

Sylvia Meiners was sitting behind Ted Harte's desk. She was sitting in his chair, confronted by his papers and the small white china elephant which he used as a paper-weight.

The little white elephant seemed to be eyeing her with a faintly ironical grin. Sylvia raised her eyebrows and grimaced back at the china figure.

She started to tidy Harte's papers—documents relating to Hauser, reports from his team of interrogators, folders containing denunciations. There were two such files, one devoted to letters which incriminated existing internees and the other to those which denounced men still at liberty.

Sylvia stacked newspaper cuttings, letters and pamphlets in

neat piles. There was abolutely nothing of an intimate nature, no personal correspondence, no snapshots, no private jottings. Her brow wrinkled at this surprising discovery.

Sylvia's thoughts were interrupted by the telephone bell. She picked up the receiver and was told to hang on for a long-distance call from Dachau. Colonel Cord wanted to speak to Camp 7.

The judge-advocate's voice came reverberating down the line. Sylvia, long inured to Cord's telephonic tirades, could almost predict what he was going to say.

'I'm surprised to hear there's still no action at Camp 7,' boomed the colonel. 'Very surprised. Things can't go on this way. Tell Keller and Harte that—especially Harte. I'm in urgent need of certain papers and you're the supplier. If you can't deliver the goods I'll have to shop around elsewhere. Know what I mean, Miss Meiners? If the boss is no good, the whole firm stinks. Point that out to Keller and Harte—especially Harte.'

'I'll do that, Colonel,' Sylvia replied, and started to hang up. This time, however, Colonel Cord departed from his normal routine.

'Know something?' he said. 'I get the feeling my pep talks go in one ear and out the other. I suppose your bosses are enjoying their afternoon siesta.'

'Captain Keller and Mr Harte never take a siesta,' Sylvia assured him.

'Maybe not, but they're half asleep most of the time,' Cord grumbled. 'Well, I'm going to put a firecracker under them. I'll be with you in two hours. I propose to inspect the camp and have a talk with those two boy-friends of yours. Goodbye!'

'Goodbye, Colonel,' said Sylvia. She hung up hastily and put an immediate call through to the mess.

'So what?' was Harte's casual response to the news of Cord's impending visit.

'What would you like me to do?'

'We've still got two hours—three, probably. The colonel's a slow mover. The commandant and provost-marshal are responsible for his reception. For a start, tell Sergeant Popper to get the camp ready for inspection. Is that all you called about?'

'Don't you ever take me seriously, Mr Harte?'

'Ah,' he said, 'I follow. You'd like to speak to someone who does take you seriously—Captain Keller, for instance. Touché?'

Sylvia slammed the receiver down furiously and pushed the telephone away.

'Idiot!' she muttered.

Sergeant Marty Popper resented the interruption of his siesta, but there was nothing he could do. As provost-marshal, he was responsible for internal security and for the housing, feeding and clothing of internees—officially, that was. In practice, he functioned as a glorified messenger-boy to Captain Keller, who was thirsting for promotion.

Popper resolved to sacrifice part of his siesta in the national interest. He gave orders that the German camp commandant was to report to him immediately.

A quarter of an hour later Reiter appeared on the balcony where Popper lay sprawled in a deck-chair, listening to the radio and imbibing vast quantities of Coca-Cola.

The sergeant barely moved. Without looking up, he raised a limp hand in greeting, then gestured to a near-by stool.

Reiter sat down and waited, looking eager to please.

Popper twitched his right eyebrow a fraction. Reiter, who interpreted the signal at once, turned the radio down a little.

'Smoke?' said Popper.

'Thanks,' said Reiter. 'I also drink Coca-Cola.'

'Help yourself.' The sergeant shifted laboriously in his chair so as to see Reiter better. 'There's another inspection coming up,' he drawled.

Reiter lit a cigarette. 'When?'

'This afternoon, in two hours' time. Some colonel from the J.A.-G.'s department.'

Reiter nodded. He understood. He always understood Popper. The two men had more in common than met the eye. They were born soldiers—soldiers who had found out for themselves what really went on inside an army. There was no dodge they didn't know, no command procedure they hadn't mastered, no problem they couldn't solve. They might belong to different nations but they spoke the same language. The rites, conventions and principles of the soldier's craft were universal.

'What will he want to see?' asked Reiter.

'The man's a colonel,' said Popper.

'And a lawyer.'

'A God-fearing man,' amplified the sergeant. 'If there hadn't been any Crusades, he'd have invented them.'

Reiter thought for a moment. 'We might arrange a Bible-reading class.'

'Good,' said Popper. His brain was obviously working overtime. 'Get the camp choir to sing *O God Our Help in Ages past*.'

'By all means,' said Reiter. 'It might also be a good thing if the internees were allowed a shower. Cleanliness always makes a good impression.'

Popper raised his head. 'Smart bastard,' he said with approval. 'Trying to put one over on me, are you?'

Reiter grinned back at him. 'The colonel won't have any complaints,' he replied, dexterously opening his third bottle of Coca-Cola.

Popper sank back in his deck-chair. Reiter was doing a little horse-trading. He guaranteed a first-class inspection and asked for showers in return—showers for four thousand men, with water and fuel in short supply.

'The internees could find the fuel,' Reiter added. 'There's plenty of timber around here.'

'You'd just love that, Reiter, wouldn't you?' Popper knew exactly what the suggestion entailed: larger outside working parties, additional transport, increased surveillance, bigger rations. That was all he needed! It wasn't child's play, keeping the place on an even keel. If these Germans only knew how few guards there were and how little they relished the idea of restraining four thousand men, some of them hardened killers . . .

Reiter emitted a friendly, almost familiar chuckle. Satisfied that the sergeant was thinking hard, he helped himself to two cigarettes.

'Take the whole pack,' said Popper.

Reiter hesitated. 'And the showers?'

'Approved.'

'Thank you,' Reiter said. 'The inspection will be a success.'

'I know.' Popper moved his right hand a fraction.

Reiter obediently turned the radio up to full volume and withdrew on tiptoe.

The jeep drove through the main entrance and braked sharply to a halt in front of the administration block.

Keller leapt out, followed more slowly by Harte. The sentry greeted them with an amiable grin and the usual negligent salute. Harte jabbed the man gently in the ribs as he passed and the grin turned into a smothered laugh.

Keller hurried upstairs and along the corridor to his office, briefly noting that there were a number of women sitting on chairs at the far end of the passage. Sylvia Meiners was waiting for him in the outer office.

'Who are those females?' he demanded.

'Visitors, Captain.'

'Send them away. Visitors aren't allowed. They never have been, as a general rule, and from now on they're banned by order. Internment means isolation—tell them that. I'm sorry, but that's how it is.'

'Colonel Cord telephoned.'

'I know. Has Popper been informed?'

'He has, Captain.'

Keller smiled at her. 'Congratulations, reliable as ever,' he said.

'Thank you, Captain.'

'We ought to celebrate some time,' he said. 'When are you free?'

Harte appeared in the doorway. 'Who's that outside in the passage, Sylvia?'

'Four women. All internees' wives.'

'I rather gathered that.' Casually, he added: 'Is Hauser's wife among them?'

'Yes, just as you requested, Mr Harte.'

Keller, who had retired behind his desk, glanced up in surprise. 'What's that? I'd appreciate an explanation, Fräulein Meiners.'

Sylvia looked slightly at a loss. She put a hand to her forehead and brushed a lock of hair aside. Keller thought she looked more than usually attractive when she was perplexed and made a private resolution to perplex her more often.

Sylvia said: 'Weren't you informed, then?'

'No, he wasn't,' Harte cut in. 'Not even camp commandants know everything that goes on in their sphere of command. This is a case in point. All right, Sylvia, talk. Let Captain Keller in on it.'

'Frau Hauser lives in the area. I sent her a note telling her that her husband was interned here and hinting that it might be possible to obtain some news of him.'

'Where did you get this crazy idea?' demanded Keller.

'From me,' Harte said. 'As you so forcefully pointed out just now, crazy ideas are a speciality of mine. What's more, it was I who gave orders for a few of the women waiting outside the gate to be admitted. The idea was to get Frau Hauser in here without attracting too much attention.'

Keller fidgeted nervously with his papers. 'What do you hope to achieve?'

'Nothing, now. I'm not heading this investigation any longer—it's your case. Maybe the lady will loosen up when she sees you.'

Keller frowned. 'What has Hauser's wife to do with his war crimes status?'

Harte gathered all the documents on the Hauser case into a pile and carried them over to Keller's desk. 'I've made inquiries about this woman. From the sound of her, she may know a good deal. She's dangerous. Why shouldn't she become a danger to her husband—or herself, for that matter? It's just a question of giving her a nudge.'

'I don't know,' Keller said uncertainly.

To their surprise, Sylvia Meiners joined in the conversation uninvited. 'It wouldn't be standard procedure. It would be highly irregular.'

'I'll tell you something else irregular,' Harte said. 'You, sticking your nose in.'

'Why shouldn't she?' snapped Keller. 'She's our personal assistant.'

'How personal can you get?'

Keller glared at him irritably. 'What's going on around here? Have we got a job to do or haven't we?'

'All I want to know is this,' Harte said. 'Are you going to see Frau Hauser?'

'Let her wait.'

'Quite right, Keller, let her wait. Let her go on waiting until you decide what you can afford to gamble without endangering your position—until you've consulted your sidekicks. Don't rush things. The internees have plenty of time—they can rot, for all you care—and the army has plenty of time because it won the war.'

Sylvia was astonished to see Harte so agitated. It was a novel experience. She wouldn't have thought him capable of such an emotional reaction. In an attempt to defuse the atmosphere, she said, 'By the way, we've received some information about Slembeck.' She proffered the file to Harte, but he waved it aside.

'In the future, anything to do with the Hauser case goes to Captain Keller.'

Sylvia's astonishment increased. She handed the file to Keller without a word and returned to her desk, where she listened intently to what was going on behind her back.

Keller flicked through the file and said, 'Aren't you interested in knowing about Slembeck?'

'Officially, no.'

'And unofficially?'

Harte's tone was indifferent. 'Anything special?'

'A Polish information bureau reports as follows: Slembeck, Johann, alias Jan, son of a foreman employed on the main Patocki estate near Mlawa. Claims to be a Pole, but probably comes from West Prussia and was only employed in Poland. After the estate was looted by German troops or SS units Slembeck worked in Germany, probably under duress. Some members of the Patocki family managed to escape by abandoning all their personal possessions. That's all.'

'Just a minute,' said Harte. 'What did these personal possessions consist of?'

'The usual. Antique furniture, pictures, furs, and so on.'

'What about jewellery?'

'Jewellery as well.'

'Any valuable pieces?'

'Several rings and a pearl necklace—nothing out of the ordinary except for a platinum bracelet set with stones.'

'What sort of stones?'

'Rubies—a lot of them. Pretty big ones, too.'

Keller closed the file and laid it on his desk. 'Anyway, there's nothing in this report which directly incriminates Slembeck. Looks as though your suspicions were unfounded. No reason why we shouldn't use him as a material witness.'

Harte fidgeted with a ruler. 'A platinum bracelet has great intrinsic value, Keller. And if it's studded with big red rubies, it may be worth a small fortune. Find the bracelet and you'll really have something to go on. Slembeck's testimony won't be enough to convict Hauser by itself—after all, what's a verbal allegation worth? You've got to have evidence, preferably tangible.'

Harte sliced the air with his ruler. 'Take any ten witnesses, Keller, and I guarantee you each of them will be prompted by a different motive. The first testifies out of revenge, the second envy, the third hatred. The fourth bores everybody with his high-flown notions of justice, the fifth acts out of patriotism, the sixth is impelled by greed, the seventh by an urge to assert himself, the eighth by self-interest, the ninth sends a man to the gallows out of ignorance, and the tenth keeps mum for fear of perjuring himself. Verbal evidence is malleable stuff, though. It can be beaten out of people, beaten into them, beaten into any required shape or form.'

The ruler was pointing straight at Keller now. 'On the other hand, a demonstrably stolen article of jewellery coupled with evidence or a sworn affidavit that Hauser and the jewellery were both there when the murder and looting occurred . . . That would give your case a firm foundation—firm enough to build a gallows on.'

'You're too imaginative for your own good,' retorted Keller. 'What basis do you have for these wild conjectures of yours? You see problems everywhere. I only see facts, and goddamned unpleasant ones at that. You go on looking for proof of something which has been proved to the hilt already. The whole world knows what Germany's capable of.'

'To me, what you call the whole world is an agglomeration of prejudices. A hundred thousand identical uniforms don't make a hundred thousand identical human beings. There were several million registered members of the Nazi Party, but there were some philanthropists amongst them. I could even quote you a few butchers in the SS who'll find two or three Jews willing to testify in their favour when the time comes. What are you planning to do—play God Almighty? Try it and you'll come unstuck.'

'I know what I'm doing,' Keller insisted.

Harte slammed his ruler on the desk. 'That's what Hitler always said, but it didn't mean he wasn't talking out of the back of his neck.'

Some internees lay on their bunks after lunch. Others, whose beds consisted of pallets which were not laid out on the floor until nightfall, sat hunched over tables. They pillowed their heads on their arms and sought oblivion in sleep.

The midday meal had to be digested—a thin gruel of potatoes, oats and water boiled to the point of amalgamation, slopped into tin bowls, and devoured.

It was the hour of vague and nebulous visions. The women, friends, victims, liquor-bottles and heaped plates of a lifetime passed in endless array across closed eyelids. Bodies lay limp with arms extended. Heads felt like hollow drums filled with putrid vapour.

Laffrentz was snoring with his mouth open. Mangel lay like a fallen statue. Baron von Hagen had carefully spread a handkerchief over his face. No one ever knew whether he was asleep or awake. The chief meteorological adviser to the German High Command had rolled into a ball, hedgehog-fashion, and was making a faint purring noise.

'He was a strict vegetarian,' Arthur Wammenberg declared with emotion. He was speaking, as usual, about the Führer. 'He didn't begrudge us meat, though—any amount.'

'Must you?' protested Mangel, but Wammenberg—known in camp as 'Hitler's butler', though he was really the Führer's ex-chef—had the bit between his teeth.

'Even vegetarian dishes lend themselves to subtle preparation—with oil, for instance. Italian olive oil is best. It not only promotes digestion but possesses high nutritional value.'

Wickler, an architect, rose without a word and walked over to Wammenberg. He pulled him to his feet, said 'Out!' in a low but menacing voice, and propelled him towards the door with a well-aimed kick in the pants.

A member of the German camp police appeared in the doorway and looked round the room.

'Does someone named Hauser bunk here?' he demanded. Without waiting for an answer, he went on, 'Hauser, you're wanted for interrogation.'

Hauser silently climbed out of his bunk.

The occupants of the room were awake in an instant. 'All the best,' Mangel called cheerily. Baron von Hagen gave the SS officer a nod. The meteorologist stared mournfully into space and Wickler sent Hitler's butler on his way with another kick.

'Don't let them trick you,' said Laffrentz. 'They're a clever bunch.'

Even the former Foreign Office interpreter, who normally kept himself to himself, peered out of his burrow. 'I hope you get Harte. He doesn't seem a bad man.'

Hauser ignored every word, every gesture. They were windbags, all of them. He strode out, slamming the door behind him.

The policeman trotted ahead, anxious not to keep the Americans waiting. They didn't know the meaning of the word patience. Speed was their god and '*Mak snell!*' their favourite expression. It was wise to bear that in mind.

Being a camp policeman was a distinction which brought certain advantages in its train. While on duty, a camp policeman had access to various restricted areas including the cookhouse, where scraps of food were always to be found. This particular policeman had only been a local Party official and belonged to the AA or automatic arrest category, hence his eligibility for the job.

'Hurry it up, can't you?' he called to Hauser.

Hauser made his way down the worn and dirty stairs at a snail's pace, still half asleep. The first thing that met his eye as he emerged from Block C was barbed wire.

Barbed wire!

There had been a photograph when he was a boy—a roll of barbed wire, and behind it the steel-helmeted figure of his father, a captain in the army reserve. Field-grey uniform, belt and holster, ribbon of the Iron Cross Second Class in buttonhole, Iron Cross First Class on chest, eyes alight with faith in final victory . . .

The photograph had hung above his father's desk for years. He had been manager of a factory which produced hardware

—household articles to begin with, then field kitchens, mess-tins and eating utensils. He remained a soldier all his life, every move governed by an imaginary drill manual. Father, the head of the family, issued orders. Everyone else—mother, son, servants. employees, wartime comrades of inferior rank—obeyed.

The tall fence enclosing the factory premises was topped with barbed wire. Father stood there with a stop-watch. 'Are you ready? Move!'—and he, the obedient son, scrambled over, dropped down on the other side, and called, 'Half-time!' Another climb in the opposite direction, and he landed at his father's feet. Father checked time and meted out praise or censure. If he tore his clothes on the barbed wire the performance didn't count and had to be repeated. 'I'll make a man of you yet!'

There was more barbed wire on the fence bordering the paddock at his uncle's farm, where one of the maidservants had pushed him into the grass and wrestled with him. Blue sky, hot sun, sweating bodies, a revolting sense of lassitude afterwards, and a richly contented woman's voice purring, 'You're quite a man . . .'

His father again, 'Your school report stinks. Two weeks' house arrest this vacation. School work to be completed between 1400 and 1800 hours every day. 1800 to 1900 hours, physical training.' And then, when he finally managed to elude the Old Man for the sake of a girl, it meant scaling yet another fence topped with barbed wire.

Keep fit, prove yourself, be a man . . . It became fun in the end. It was sport. Violent rough-and-tumbles followed with his father acting as referee. Then came his first duel, and the moment when his opponent's cheek suddenly gaped like a split plum and poured blood. His father congratulated him proudly.

Then the Waffen SS. War, blood and fire. More barbed wire, this time for enemies of the State or others afflicted with criminal tendencies. More brawling and women. Barbed wire festooned with articles of clothing, sometimes human beings.

Then the war's end. Old barbed-wire fences dismantled and replaced with new. There was money to be made in barbed wire—it stood to reason.

'Do me a favour,' said the policeman. 'The Yanks are waiting for you.'

'What the hell do you think you are,' Hauser retorted, 'a sheep-dog? I'll be with your American pals soon enough.'

He had been through a lot, seen a lot—too much to be thrown off balance easily. He'd been brought up the hard way, and they'd find him a tough nut to crack. Anyone could be locked up—that was nothing new—but for him it was just an interlude. Things would straighten themselves out in due course. Meanwhile, grin and bear it. Who could prove anything against him, anyway? They'd have their work cut out.

He knew the ropes. He had commanded a camp of his own, once. Twenty thousand faceless names on a list, and he hadn't even known if the numbers tallied. You simply couldn't check things like that. Nothing could be checked. It was all old hat to him. He was the one with the practical experience, not these slipshod, decadent, over-fed Americans.

Yes, he knew the ropes all right. Anything that couldn't be proved was simply alleged and the allegation corroborated by so-called witnesses. Witnesses could always be found, but they wanted payment. That was easy: first lock them up and then release them. That was payment enough. In return, they told you all you wanted to hear and testified against anyone you wanted to incriminate.

It wouldn't work with him, though. He knew the trade secret and was ready to exploit it without scruple. He wanted Brigitte back at all costs. From the moment of seeing her again that morning he had known exactly what his next objective was.

They reached the gate which separated the camp proper from the administration block. A lanky American was leaning against a post, smoking. Hauser eyed him with contempt. Americans weren't soldiers, just civilians in uniform. Their sort of patriotism could be bought with a fat wad of dollar bills.

'Name?' demanded the sentry.

'Hauser,' replied the policeman, 'AA 505 Internee Hauser, reporting for interrogation.'

The American consulted his clip-board. 'Okay,' he said. '*Komm! Mak snell!*'

Harte closed the file in front of him and slowly rose to his feet.

'I have to go out in a hurry,' he told Sylvia as he left the office. 'To the canteen, in case Captain Keller wants to know. I could be an hour, maybe more.'

There was a full-length mirror outside in the corridor. Harte paused and scrutinized himself closely. He frowned and shook his head.

'Don't you like your looks, Mr Harte?' asked a voice behind him.

Harte did not turn round. 'No,' he said firmly. 'I can't say I do. Do you?'

Sylvia Meiners, who had followed him outside on impulse, ostensibly to fetch something, did not answer at first. Then she said, 'Since when did my opinions matter?'

'Keller listens to you.'

'You aren't Keller.'

Harte swung round abruptly. 'No, thank God.'

'You sound proud of the fact.'

He moved towards her. Two steps were enough to bring them face to face. 'What are you really trying to do, Fräulein Meiners—sabotage this department?'

'Our department, Mr Harte. I work here too.'

'Captain Keller is your direct superior, not me.'

'But you picked me for the job.'

'That's beside the point,' Harte said. 'And now kindly excuse me. I have to visit the main gate before I go to the canteen.' He turned and started down the passage towards the head of the stairs.

'We're going the same way,' Sylvia said, keeping pace with him.

Harte descended the stairs slowly, avoiding her eye. He could hear her light tread beside him, so close that he could detect her breathing. Suddenly he stopped and turned to face her with one hand resting on the banisters. His outstretched arm barred her path.

'What do you really want to know about me, Fräulein Meiners? What's behind this sudden interest of yours?'

Sylvia regarded him gravely but there was a gleam of mischief in her eyes. 'I wanted to talk to you, that's all.'

'All right, talk,' he said curtly.

'It's very hot today,' Sylvia said. The sparkle in her eyes became more pronounced.

'Have some ice-water.'

'It was very hot yesterday, and it'll probably be just as hot tomorrow.'

'Ice-water helps.'

'Hot weather makes people tired,' she said. 'It makes them sluggish and saps their energy. Colonel Cord sets a lot of store by energy.'

'My dear girl,' Harte said irritably, 'Colonel Cord isn't coming here today to check on our work, so you can keep your broad hints to yourself. He's simply giving himself a nice afternoon out at government's expense, and just so he won't get bored he's going to inspect some internees.'

'I had a cat once,' Sylvia said. 'It ate mice.'

'Cats are like that.'

'Yes, but when it was full it went on eating mice out of sheer habit, just for something to do.'

'Cord's no cat and we aren't mice. Anyway, even if we were, he'd find us a hard mouthful to swallow.'

Sylvia smiled at him. 'I didn't mean to annoy you, Mr Harte.'

'What was the idea, then?'

'I only wondered if you were tired—if you found the heat tiring.' She paused for a moment, then added candidly, 'I was wondering if you really had handed over the Hauser case to Captain Keller. After all, he isn't an interrogation officer.'

'No, but he's in charge here. The camp commandant can do what he likes. I've no right to stand in his way. If he messes things up the responsibility won't be mine.'

'But you'd feel responsible,' Sylvia said firmly.

Harte shook his head. 'Nonsense, you don't know me. I lay no claim to a clear conscience, iron self-discipline, a strong sense of integrity—any of those things. I'm just a very ordinary human being. I may have been through a lot of unpleasantness and spent a lot of time thinking about it, but that's no recommendation.'

'Is there anything I can do to help?'

'Yes, get out of my sight or come for a walk with me, leave me in peace or get drunk with me. Just do something—anything, as long as it gives me a clear picture of you, you understand?'

He turned suddenly and clattered downstairs.

Outside in the forecourt he drew several deep breaths and mopped his brow. It was a hot day, he told himself. A very hot day.

Internee Hauser approached him under escort. 'Good afternoon, Mr Harte,' he said in a loud breezy voice.

'Heil Hitler,' Harte retorted.

Hauser feigned a hearty laugh. 'We could have used people like you, Mr Harte. I was always opposed to kicking decent types out of Germany just because they didn't toe the line. From the long-term point of view, anti-Semitism was a ridiculous policy—a political boomerang.'

'Keep talking if it amuses you,' Harte said. He glanced back at the entrance and the first-floor windows but could not see Sylvia anywhere.

Hauser, who felt confident that he had summed Harte up in the course of their numerous interviews, adopted a condescending tone. 'Our leaders got rid of a lot of good men—men with brains. Take Thomas Mann, Einstein, Remarque, Kortner, Piscator, Jaspers . . . We ought to have hung on to them, not bounced them. That was the biggest miscalculation of all. I warned against it time and time again—I expect some of my friends still have letters from me to that effect. I always said we had more than enough brawn. Brain-power, that's what we were short of. A few hundred men like you, Mr Harte, and we'd have pocketed Europe for good.'

Harte listened with a faint smile. He made it a principle to give the Hausers of this world plenty of rope. It was a convenient way of getting to know them thoroughly.

'Interesting,' was his only comment. 'Carry on. I enjoy listening to you.'

Harte's mild manner had confused Hauser at first and aroused his misgivings. It took him some time to get used to it. The man was clever, true enough, but it became more and more apparent that he was incapable of decisive action. He was hobbled by his superiors and by what was laughably known as public opinion, swamped by decrees, laws and directives, tripped up by Roosevelt's puerile four freedoms. The Western Allies didn't subscribe to the authoritarian principle. Everyone had his say, with the result that smart fellows like Harte were hamstrung by sheer democracy.

'Well, Mr Harte, what's your good news? Were you going to tell me that I'm due for release at last?'

'I don't have anything to tell you, Hauser—not for the moment, at least. Captain Keller will be handling your case on his own from now on.'

'That's all I needed,' Hauser said resentfully. 'Does that mean the whole business starts from scratch again? How much longer do I have to wait for a decision?'

'Don't tell me you're getting impatient, Hauser. You may not have to wait much longer.'

Hauser pondered the latest development with some uneasiness. The fact that his case had been transferred might mean that they were going to lean on him. Keller was an arrogant, cold-eyed bastard. Hauser wondered if he would bend the rules but decided that it was unlikely.

Harte said, 'I'd welcome the change if I were you. It's an easy way of getting rid of me, so consider yourself lucky.'

Hauser fought down his misgivings. 'You're a considerate man. Mr Harte. I mean that, but don't take it as a compliment. Your delaying tactics have cost me several weeks of freedom.'

'Don't be too sure,' Harte replied. 'There may come a time when you look back on them as several extra weeks of life.'

Hauser started. He tried, as he had so often done in the preceding weeks, to detect some clue in Harte's face, some hint of brutality, decadent stupidity, predatory cunning—even ingenuous good nature or smiling resignation, but it was no use. The man was inscrutable.

'I'm used to your little jokes, Mr Harte. They've never made me laugh yet, but they don't worry me either.'

'All the better. In that case you won't mind seeing the last of me. Goodbye, Hauser.'

Harte stared after Hauser as he was escorted through the gate, then made his way to the guard-house and picked up the telephone. He asked for his office.

Sylvia answered.

'Are you very annoyed with me?' he asked.

'Very,' she replied. She sounded quite gay.

'That's all right then.' Harte smiled to himself. 'I'm off to see Gernsbach.'

'Good,' said Sylvia. 'Very good,' she added, as though conferring a pat on the back.

Harte rang off, still smiling.

No doubt about it, Gernsbach was the person to speak to. As head of the de-Nazification department, Gernsbach kept his ear even closer to the ground than Harte did himself. He picked up the phone again and made another call to his office.

'Tell me, Sylvia, what are you doing this evening?'

She did not answer for a moment. 'I don't know yet.' There was another pause. 'I'll think it over and let you know later—maybe.'

Rolf Gernsbach was painting.

The canvas glowed with luminous violet and the red of port by candlelight. A figure composed of bold, almost mathematically drawn planes was silhouetted against an endless expanse, solitary yet overwhelmed by the vague dreamlike shapes which hovered round it.

Gernsbach inspected his handiwork with disfavour, gripping the brush in his right hand like a truncheon. Rage gnawed at him. The colours refused to catch fire. He glared at the canvas. If that was all he could produce, he was finished. He ought to stop painting and take up interior decoration.

Or was there something else he ought to do? What about making capital out of politics? Why not enlarge the scope of what he had undertaken out of personal conviction and turn it into a gold mine? Nothing could be easier. His office was in the administration block of Camp 7, and the sign on the door read: SPECIAL BRANCH—ROLF GERNSBACH.

Here, Gernsbach carried out de-Nazification procedures, checking on the recent careers and property acquisitions of persons resident in the town and its environs. All local trustees and solicitors were at his beck and call.

He had lived in the district for fifteen years, knew the countryside and the people who inhabited it. He had learned to love and fear them—sometimes to hate them too. His one crime, a heinous one, had been his style of painting. It was not only misguided, but, in Third Reich terminology, degenerate. Neighbours who spent their evenings at the same Gasthof and allowed their daughters to dance with him had wrested the brush from his hand, substituted a shovel, and dressed him in concentration camp uniform. Constructive work for Germany, they called it.

Then, when it was all over and he was doing his best to forget, he received a visit from a man named Harte. 'We need you,' Harte told him. Gernsbach had hesitated and done his best to refuse, but Harte managed to talk him into it. 'Your abilities are of secondary importance,' Harte had said. 'The main thing is, you weren't a Nazi.'

'I never got a chance to become one,' Gernsbach replied.

Harte's chuckle had an infectious warmth. 'Now's your chance to make up for lost time.'

That was how Rolf Gernsbach came to take over the Special Branch office. He did so on one condition: no regular office hours. He insisted on painting whenever the mood took him, and Harte had readily acceded to his request.

The trouble was, he couldn't paint any more. He couldn't bear to look at what he had painted. Years in a concentration camp had left his hands unsteady, vitiated his talent, destroyed his capacity for self-criticism.

Gernsbach closed his eyes. He was tired, drained of courage, fire, creative energy. At thirty-nine he was an old man—twice as old as his years. He was burnt out and exhausted. He had dug sewers and communal graves, carted corpses and human excrement until he dropped in his tracks. A victim of his age? Not at all! Just a gutless wonder who lacked vigour, application, concentration—all the things that really mattered.

He had shown promise, at least to begin with. At school he learnt little but knew everything. His comments during Bible class were calculated to induce a state of acute embarrassment in his teacher. After only three drawing-classes he proclaimed that the art master was nothing but a glorified photographer.

He worked like a demon at art college. His few friends called him a genius, his many enemies a madman. He was gay and overbearing, often intemperate and seldom respectful, but he believed in his work.

Manet he characterized as the first brush-wielding sensualist of real genius. Böcklin's painting he was bold enough to describe as sublime idiocy. Rembrandt reduced him to reverent silence. Van Gogh made him burn with excitement. The sight of some etchings by Käthe Kollwitz filled him with abject misery. 'I can't draw,' he burst out. 'What's the use unless you can draw like that?'

Years of unremitting work followed. He retired to the

mountains for the sake of privacy and took a cottage outside a village between Garmisch and Mittenwald. Few women ever interrupted his activities. Women were models, just as the world itself was his model.

By 1932, when he was twenty-six, art dealers were starting to tick his name in exhibition catalogues. 'Rolf Gernsbach is ten years ahead of his time,' one critic wrote. 'Where will he be in another ten years?' Exactly ten years later he was wielding a shovel in a concentration camp, starving, saying nothing, eternally drawing shapes in the sand, in the snow, on latrine walls, on burial-mounds.

He never quite gathered how people had come to regard him as an opponent of National Socialism. Politics didn't interest him. He painted: the rest could do what they liked as long as they let him paint. Then a State cultural tribunal pronounced him a 'degenerate dauber'. The local edition of the *Süddeutscher Beobachter* called him a 'wretched, debased, un-German defiler of canvases, a parasite who battens on our noble German cultural heritage'. He promptly called the writer of the article an imbecile. He did so in public and before several witnesses, three of whom denounced him in writing for uttering an 'unpatriotic and seditious remark'.

The rest was simple: three years in a concentration camp, two years' probationary service with a penal battalion, an unsuccessful attempt to escape, entered on his record-sheet as 'desertion', and then more concentration camp. He stayed there until Germany's collapse, for some the bitter end, for others a happy ending.

Now he was a free agent. He could do as he pleased. He could even paint again, but he was failing miserably. A fresh start meant a return to the old, oppressive, agoraphobic solitude which had stimulated his imagination but made him ache for someone to cling to.

And yet this time he could conceive of people who might give him the stability he craved. There was Ted Harte, for one. Harte was the perfect potential friend—prickly, critical, richly endowed with the compassion of those who know what torment can be, but incapable, for that very reason, of wholehearted love. Only a woman could supply that—a woman like Sylvia Meiners.

The buzzer sounded. Gernsbach smoothed his hair back and

massaged his damp face for a few moments. Then, squaring his shoulders, he went to open the door. Ted Harte was standing outside.

'Mind if I disturb you, Gernsbach?'

'You won't disturb me,' Gernsbach replied. 'I'm past being disturbed by anyone.'

Harte's smile was mildly ironical. 'So far above the world of art?'

'So far beneath it,' Gernsbach retorted, waving his visitor into a chair.

Harte sat down on a worn and lumpy sofa and surveyed his surroundings: an easel and canvases, a table, a few chairs, hessian curtains and dirty window-panes. Gernsbach's studio verged on the primitive even though he could have lived in the height of luxury. At least three dozen confiscated Nazi villas in the neighbourhood were earmarked for people like him.

'Do you paint portraits?'

Gernsbach shook his head. 'I don't paint anything,' he said. 'All I do is mess up acres of canvas. Anyway, why portraits? Don't tell me you're eager to see yourself hanging in a gallery somewhere—Harte, the conquering hero of Camp 7?'

'You're sour today, Gernsbach. What's on your mind? Having de-Nazification trouble?'

'No.'

'Really not? All the better. Let's talk about painting, then. I don't know much about it—in fact I don't know anything about it, to be frank, but at least I know what I'd like to see on canvas. That's something, isn't it?'

'It's a great deal.' Gernsbach joined Harte on the sofa. 'What did you have in mind?'

'The way I look at it, a good artist doesn't paint things—he paints what's inside them. Not reality but truth, not a face but the soul behind it. Correct?'

Gernsbach stretched his legs. 'You've got a point,' he said indifferently. To him, theoretical speculation was little more than a trivial game indulged in by frustrated artists. Nothing could be neatly pigeon-holed, hard as official or self-appointed art critics strove to do so. The key-word was tolerance. Without tolerance, even the realm of art became a battlefield.

'What sort of truth are you looking for, Harte?'

'I'm not after a single truth. There are lots of them, I suspect. For instance, what goes on inside the people we've locked up? What are the people we work with really like? Where should we start looking for a potential truth—in other words, a truth which we hope exists?'

'Who do you want to put under the microscope? Take care, the truth can be a big disappointment sometimes. Who's worth the gamble, in your opinion?'

'Well, one possible candidate might be Sylvia Meiners.'

'Ah,' said Gernsbach, 'that's intriguing.'

'Why?'

Gernsbach smiled faintly. 'Because it shows I was right about you. You've a talent for seeing through people—an instinct, if you like. You know a great deal and keep most of it to yourself. I've watched you, Harte. You try to explore people—help them too, if possible, even though you do your best to hide the fact. You've got all the makings of an anonymous benefactor. In less troubled times, you might have been a priest.'

'You overestimate me,' Harte said, slightly taken aback. He hadn't expected this sort of reaction. 'You may be a good friend, Gernsbach, but you aren't a great judge of human nature. Me a do-gooder? What gave you that ludicrous idea?'

Gernsbach's smile broadened. 'To the best of my recollection, you were only present two or three times when I came to see Sylvia on official business, but you spotted my interest in her at once. I saw you watching us together.'

Harte sat up abruptly and shook his head as though to clear it. At length he said, 'I certainly didn't see myself as a matchmaker.'

'I never thought you did, but I'm happy to take the hint. I promise I'll make the most of your suggestion. It's a good one—in fact the more I think about it the better it seems. It could put me on the right track again. Will you help me?'

'You mean with the portrait?'

Gernsbach laughed briefly and fell silent for a while. 'It really was a bright idea of yours,' he mused, after an interval. 'You don't think she'd mind sitting for me?'

'No idea—I don't know enough about her. You'll have to ask her yourself.'

It was a long time since Gernsbach had felt such a surge of happiness. Gazing at his visitor with gratitude, he felt that

Harte was waiting for something. 'How about you?' he asked.

Harte emerged from his reverie with a jerk. 'What do you mean?'

'I understand,' said Gernsbach, confident that he knew what was going on in Harte's mind. 'You refuse to be thought of as a do-gooder. You prefer to keep everything on a rational, down-to-earth basis. All right, let's strike a bargain.'

'What do you mean?' Harte repeated.

'You claim you didn't come here today just on my account. I'll accept that, if it makes you happy. What can I do for you in return?'

Harte pulled himself together. 'Look,' he said eventually, 'if you really want to do me a favour, tell me everything you know about a woman named Hauser, Brigitte Hauser. You ought to know her—she lives in your area. Her parents own a small inn somewhere in the neighbourhood, if I remember right.'

Gernsbach raised his eyebrows. 'What do you want, an official report?'

'No,' Harte replied with a smile. 'This is more in the nature of a private inquiry, otherwise I'd have sent you an official request for information.'

Gernsbach shook his head almost imperceptibly. 'You really mean that? You have a personal interest in this woman.'

'Certainly, since I'm not allowed to take an official interest in her at this stage—but you probably won't understand that.'

Gernsbach didn't understand at all. He did his best to brief Harte impartially, difficult as he found it in this particular instance. Brigitte Hauser, née Zehntner, was known to him. Well known. She was a woman who got herself talked about—not the sort of woman you could overlook.

'If you have any dealings with her, Harte, dealings of any kind, be careful.'

'They must be giving Hauser a real going over,' observed Internee Laffrentz. 'It's three o'clock, which means they've been at him for two hours already. That ought to soften him up, the impudent swine. I wouldn't like to be in his shoes, but then my conscience is clear—pure as driven snow. I sat behind a desk in Berlin the whole time. A senior administrative adviser only does what his head of department instructs him to do—no more and no less. My boss can take the responsibility.'

'What if your boss has disappeared?' Wickler, the architect, flipped back the edge of his blanket and scratched himself. 'What'll you do then?'

'No problem there. My departmental chief was responsible to a Second Secretary, and the Second Secretary to a First Secretary. Right at the top of the tree came the Minister, and he's in prison at Nuremberg. Know what that means, Herr Wickler? It means I'm insured in quadruplicate. Nothing can happen to me. I just shuttled papers back and forth—never handled a gun in my life.'

'So what?' retorted Wickler. 'Why use a gun when you can throttle people with red tape?'

'What about you? What did you do?'

'I built all kinds of things, Herr Laffrentz, war memorials and cenotaphs included. When your turn comes I'll be glad to design a mausoleum for you—free of charge, too.'

'What about the harbour installations at Tobruk—they were yours', weren't they? You built them for the Afrika Korps.'

'And for the British and the Americans!' Wickler smiled proudly. 'Field-Marshal Montgomery spoke very highly of them—it said so in an army newspaper.'

'What!' Laffrentz exclaimed in outrage. 'Don't tell me you're hoping for a medal from the Allies!'

'Yes, and the freedom of Marseilles,' Wickler replied gleefully. 'Part of the dockyard quarter was dilapidated and infested with vermin. It was blown up and burnt on my instructions—with the willing co-operation of my French colleagues, of course.'

'For God's sake don't say things like that!' pleaded the meteorologist. 'Those are war crimes you're talking about.'

'Steady, gentlemen,' said Mangel, who uttered the same warning cry about once every ten minutes. 'I should like to stress, yet again, that everything which is said in this room must remain strictly between ourselves.'

Room 29 Block C gradually emerged from its midday torpor. The internees found it inadvisable to sleep for more than two hours in the middle of the day or they could not sleep a wink at night. This was a proven fact. Better to mooch around during the day than toss in your bunk all night, oppressed by dark thoughts and utterly at the mercy of the sound and scent of your slumbering neighbours.

'Sometimes,' mused Arthur Wammenberg, 'the Führer got me to play him a tune on my piano accordion. He was very musical.'

'I can be very musical too,' growled the architect, raising his rear end menacingly.

'Steady, gentlemen!' Mangel remonstrated.

Laffrentz looked round for a possible source of conversation. Baron von Hagen was playing chess with himself. The meteorologist was absently working on a sketch which was meant to represent Copernicus. Another internee was drying bread. Yet another, the Foreign Office interpreter, was converting empty tins into ash-trays—a pointless occupation, since few internees had anything to smoke. Two men, a taciturn tank manufacturer and a lieutenant with peculiarly glassy Hitler Youth eyes, were assiduously unravelling a tangle of string which they had found on a rubbish-dump. Wickler was the only one who showed any inclination to help Laffrentz while away the time.

'Tell me, Herr Laffrentz, why do you always say Herr Hauser and never Standartenführer Hauser?'

'It's a question of tact,' Laffrentz replied.

'How does tact come into it?'

Laffrentz did not seem to grasp the implication of this remark at once, but Mangel stepped into the breach.

'It's like this, Herr Wickler. There are temporary titles and permanent titles. Some designations are earned and others conferred for a limited period. With us in the army everyone makes a clear distinction between rank and appointment. Take me, for instance. Staff Lieutenant-Colonel is a permanent rank, but I was also Director of Operations, Subsection Transport, South-Eastern Command. That was a temporary appointment, not a substantive rank linked to my name.'

'Very interesting,' said Wickler, 'but very confusing too. Some military ranks don't seem to fit your pattern—SS ranks, for example. Strange how everyone has dropped them since the collapse. Wouldn't it be simpler and less confusing if we addressed each other by our surnames?'

'Christian names,' interjected the lieutenant with the Hitler

Youth gaze. 'Christian names are customary in times of stress.'

'I'm only holidaying here,' said Wickler, and added curtly, 'I don't bandy Christian names with everyone but I'm no stickler for formality either. Personally, I prefer to be addressed as Herr Wickler.'

'I'm with you up to a point,' Mangel said amiably. 'On the other hand, I must admit that I don't find your suggestion altogether satisfactory. "Herr" on its own is a convention, but the insertion of a rank or title classifies a man. It automatically denotes his status within an organization.'

'At Supreme Headquarters,' ventured the meteorologist, whose name was Trost, 'when it was my job to brief our military leaders on the state of the weather, I was entitled to use the rank of administrative adviser.' He almost choked with pride. 'The Chief of the General Staff didn't advise the Führer—I mean, Hitler—to launch his attack on Russia until I had predicted favourable weather conditions on the Eastern Front.'

'I had my promotion to departmental supervisor virtually sewn up,' proclaimed Laffrentz. 'The war was too quick for those lazy bastards in our personnel department, worse luck. I'd have been a Second Secretary by now, considering my length of service and excellent record, but then I never was a yes-man.'

'In that case, perhaps you'd better address me as Board of Works Supervisor in future,' Wickler suggested with a grin. 'That was the title they gave me when I was building the flak barracks at Schongau.'

Laffrentz made no comment. The lieutenant, whose record as a National Socialist Guidance Officer had aroused American suspicions and earned him a 'Security Threat' coding, uttered a ringing plea for solidarity.

'We must close ranks and stand shoulder to shoulder,' he concluded.

'Don't talk crap, man,' the grizzled tank manufacturer said soothingly.

'Gentlemen, gentlemen,' Mangel interposed, 'I really must ask you to observe the conventions, if nothing more.'

The meteorologist, who had just inserted a faint shadow behind the left ear of his Copernicus sketch, coughed discreetly. 'Baron von Hagen was an ambassador. As such, he's entitled to be addressed as Your Excellency. Is that a title or an appointment? Do we refer to him as His Excellency or plain Herr von Hagen? What do you say, Your Excellency?'

'Gentlemen,' Wickler said with finality, 'my wife calls me Jupp. My subordinates called me "sir" before the surrender and "Nazi pig" afterwards. My platoon sergeant at the training depot—I rose to the rank of lance-corporal, by the way—always addressed me as "you there!" Take your pick.'

Hauser sat and waited.

He had been waiting for two hours. It was one o'clock when they brought him in. Now the clock was striking three.

The room was a cell, an interrogation cell—obviously a novelty dreamed up by these uniformed American gangsters. The walls were whitewashed, the floor-boards worn and dirty. High up at the far end of the room was a small aperture which served as a window, and facing it a stout wooden door. The only furnishings were a stool, a table and a chair. Nothing else.

Hauser sat with his back to the door. It was quiet outside in the corridor. The door had a spy-hole like a police cell. It could be that he was being observed as he sat there with his back to the door. It could also be that the guard posted outside was leaning against the wall, dozing, or that he had parked himself comfortably in a chair. Anything was possible.

There was the sound of brisk footsteps, and the door, which had no handle on the inside, opened.

The American guard swiftly palmed his lighted cigarette as Captain Keller went into the cell and locked the door after him.

Hauser rose without haste. He made it a rule on such occasions to show no fear but avoid provocation. No arrogance, just easy self-assurance and an air of optimism. A faint smile helped too.

Keller nodded curtly as he brushed past Hauser on his way to the table. He deposited a file on it with a crisp smack, then sat down.

Hauser slowly followed suit. The faint smile persisted but a wary look came into his eyes.

Keller took out a propelling pencil and adjusted the lead. Opening his file, he started to leaf through it in silence.

Hauser decided to start the conversation himself—brusquely, so as to demonstrate how cocksure he felt. He said, 'I hope you're going to settle things at last.'

Keller briefly interrupted his business with the file. He forced himself not to look up. 'As far as I'm concerned,' he said, 'yours is an open-and-shut case.'

'All the better,' Hauser commented genially. 'That means I'll be transferred to a proper POW camp.'

'To the war crimes tribunal at Dachau, more like.' The words were uttered in a businesslike tone, without particular emphasis.

'What?' Hauser exclaimed with dignity. 'You don't think I'm a war criminal, do you?'

'That's exactly what I do think.'

Hauser hesitated. Then he said, 'That won't get you very far. There's a lot of difference between believing something and producing the evidence to support it.'

'What makes you think I can't?'

Keller looked up. For the first time, just for a fraction of a second, their eyes met. Then they looked away. Keller studied his fingernails and Hauser stared at the floor. The German drew a deep breath.

'What you said just now—you don't believe it yourself. You must be aware of the differences that existed in Nazi Germany, Captain. Very few of the men who wore our uniforms were assigned to special units, and I wasn't one of them. I was a member of the Waffen SS—a common-or-garden soldier. That's no crime. I belonged to a combat unit. Spent the whole war on active service from beginning to end. Infantry, that was me. No mopping-up behind the lines, no guarding concentration camps, no internal security duties at home. Just fighting, honest-to-God fighting. No decent man has ever shirked military service since history began. I don't care if you're talking about the ancient Greeks or peace-loving Americans—the same applies the whole world over. I was a plain ordinary soldier, and I challenge you to prove otherwise.'

Quietly, without an edge to his voice, Keller asked, 'Do you know Mlawa?'

Hauser did not turn a hair. He was prepared for any question, that one included. 'Yes, I know Mlawa,' he replied calmly. 'From the map.' After a brief pause, he added, 'Why, what about it?'

'Do you know the Patocki estate?'

'I'm not a farmer or a tourist,' Hauser retorted. 'I told you—I'm just a soldier.'

Keller sat back, tapping the file with his pencil. 'The Patocki estate,' he said, as though delivering a prepared statement, 'was looted and burned in 1939.'

'Sorry to hear it, of course, but these things happen in wartime—so I'm told.'

'We have witnesses.'

'Witnesses to what? Anyone can dig up witnesses so long as he holds the whip-hand—the Nazis proved that over and over again. I always deplored their methods and I can prove it. You're not proposing to take a leaf out of their book, are you?'

Keller screwed up his eyes slightly as though he, not Hauser, were looking into the sunlight that streamed through the window aperture. 'We happen to have some witnesses who don't need processing in advance.'

Hauser's confidence returned. Keller would have to do better than that. 'Congratulations,' he said. 'In that case all you need do is rely on your witnesses and make sure their stories stand up in court.'

'You seem very sure of yourself.'

'I put my faith in American justice.'

'So you can, Hauser. You can bank on a scrupulously fair hearing followed by a legally unobjectionable sentence. It shouldn't be too hard to manage both those in your case. We have an eye-witness who can confirm beyond all doubt that the looting, arson and murder at Mlawa were your sole responsibility.'

Hauser looked unimpressed. 'Haven't you ever heard of false statements?' he said sarcastically. 'They exist, take it from me. People perjure themselves for a variety of reasons. Would you like me to give you a lecture on the subject?'

Keller ground his palms together. Hauser's effrontery was almost more than he could take. He had been prepared for a lot of things, but none of these ruthless Nazi bastards had ever dared to treat him like this before.

'Hauser,' he said softly and with barely concealed menace, 'you misjudge your position.'

Hauser ignored Keller's menacing undertone. He was feeling relatively pleased with himself. It wasn't so easy to play cat and mouse with him—he knew all the answers. 'And you misjudge my motives,' he said, trying to sound reasonable. 'I'm merely objecting to being described as a war criminal. That's my privilege.'

'I very much doubt if that is your privilege.'

Keller pushed the file aside with an abrupt gesture and leant forward, looking straight at Hauser. 'I don't have to tell you that there are lots of ways of securing a conviction. Getting a man to confess is the safest. It isn't the most difficult, either.'

Hauser pricked up his ears at last. He knew this sort of hint from personal experience. It was a guaranteed prelude to threats on a massive scale. 'You're not planning to squeeze a confession out of me, are you?' he asked.

'No, just itching to subject you to the methods you used on other people. It would be fascinating to see how you react to them.'

Looking into Keller's grim face, Hauser thought he detected a hint of curiosity. He felt a momentary urge to hurl himself at the man and send him crashing against the wall, but dismissed the idea as pointless. Not without an effort, he asked, 'What precisely does that mean?'

Keller got up. 'Nothing, yet. It's just a thought.' He paused for a moment, staring down at his prisoner. 'You're a tough man, Hauser. Your nervous system's intact and your powers of resistance seem to be unimpaired, but there's no reason why that should be a permanent state of affairs. Consult your own experience. How long would it take a greenhorn, an amateur like me, to reduce you to a gibbering wreck? I'd say about ten hours.'

This was what Hauser had been afraid of—what he had seen coming for the past ten minutes. Keller was quite capable of turning such a threat into reality. You could see it in his glacial eyes and menacing air of calm. If this was rage it was rage of the ice-cold variety.

Ten hours? It would be child's play to break him well within that time. You had to know the proper methods, of course. As a general rule it took about half an hour to induce a state of shock. After that, a few buckets of cold water followed by a spell in the hot-box. Another twenty minutes' expert treatment, and the subject was a lump of flesh without a mind of his own. Then came more water, preferably from high-pressure hoses. Next. the subject was trampled under foot, special attention being paid to the abdomen and kidneys. The main thing was to avoid finishing a man off too quickly. His brain must be allowed to go on functioning—just. Therefore, keep away from his head. Ten hours? Child's play!

'I wouldn't put anything past you,' Hauser said, breathing heavily.

Keller perched on the table with one hand in his trousers pocket. 'We're starting to talk the same language.'

Hauser made a weary gesture. 'But you're wrong.'

'Let's try it and see,' Keller suggested.

'You're not wrong about my powers of resistance,' Hauser said, shaking his head. 'It's what you're accusing me of that's absurd. My conscience is clear.'

Keller swung his left leg like a pendulum. 'What if it makes no difference to me whether or not you think your conscience is clear? What if I'm determined to get your confirmation of certain statements, right or wrong?'

Hauser's hand tightened on the edge of his stool. His stomach felt empty. He hadn't eaten enough, he thought inconsequently. This would never have happened with Harte. He had come up against some Americans in his time, but Keller put them all in the shade.

He said, 'So my life's at stake.'

'Don't be melodramatic. All I want is a confession.'

'Oh, yes!' Hauser retorted bitterly. 'Oh, yes, but if I give you a confession I'll automatically be branded as a war criminal. That's as good as putting a rope around my own neck.'

'Sure,' Keller replied implacably. 'You've had it either way. On the other hand, I would point out that under our law a full voluntary confession is generally regarded as grounds for leniency. You might bear that in mind.'

'I'm not going to bank on that,' said Hauser. 'I've got a few cards to play first.'

'What cards?' demanded Keller.

Hauser did not answer. He rose to his feet, dwarfing the American by almost half a head even though his shoulders were slightly bowed.

Keller eyed him with composure.

'How much time are you giving me?' Hauser asked.

'I intend to wrap up your case by tomorrow at the very latest,' Keller replied calmly. 'That gives you twenty-four hours—less ten. You know what those ten hours are reserved for . . .'

The glaring sunlight streamed through the window aperture and stabbed unmercifully at Hauser's eyes. It illuminated Keller from behind, turning his face into a vague and shadowy blur.

'Is that the only practical course of action that occurs to you, Captain?'

'I don't see any other.'

Seated at his desk again a few minutes later, Keller squinted into the sunlight and thought. A little about himself, more about Hauser, mostly about America. It was quiet in the office. The camp choir could be heard practising hymns and folk-songs in the distance.

The door opened and Sylvia Meiners came in with some papers under her arm. She went over to the filing-cabinet and stood on tiptoe to reach the 'A' drawer. Watching the girl contemplatively, Keller was reminded of his decision to take a closer interest in her. It was Ted Harte's fault for putting the idea into his head.

He inspected Sylvia from behind. She had tilted her head back slightly, and her long, silky, smoothly brushed hair hung down to her shoulders. He got up and walked towards her across the thick pile carpet. Sylvia swung round suddenly.

'Come to help with the filing, Captain?' she inquired. Her tone was not over-friendly.

Keller made no reply. He did not stop until they were a few inches apart. Sylvia backed away but was brought up short by the filing-cabinet. Her eyes narrowed.

Keller bent over her. 'How would an afternoon off appeal to you?'

'It wouldn't,' Sylvia replied.

'What do you say we take a car, drive off somewhere and forget this lousy dump for a couple of hours? Would you like that?'

'No,' said Sylvia. 'I've got work to do.'

Keller leant against the filing-cabinet with one arm on either side of her. He said, 'Don't be like that.'

Sylvia dropped the files she was holding and pushed him away with both hands. He laughed and released her, looking slightly disconcerted.

'It's very hot in here,' she said, trying to smile.

'Hot as hell.'

'Shall I get you some ice-water, or would you prefer a cold shower? It's very humid today—look at the heat-haze on those mountains. That explains a lot of things.'

Keller said, 'Come off it.' He stood there irresolutely for a moment or two longer, then turned and went back to his desk. 'You're only a woman like all the rest.'

'You can cut out the "only", Captain,' Sylvia said defiantly. 'Besides, I'm here to work. Correct me if I'm wrong.'

'All right, Fräulein, all right. Forget it.'

Sylvia could still feel the filing-cabinet pressing into her back. 'Anything else, Captain? Any official instructions?'

'Yes, tell the German camp commandant I want to see him. Stay in the room when he comes and make a note of everything we say.'

'Certainly, Captain.'

'Where's Mr Harte?'

'I've no idea.'

'When did you see him last?'

'About half an hour ago.'

'What was he doing?'

'Telephoning.'

'Who to? What about?'

Sylvia stared full at Keller with a mixture of surprise and resentment. She wasn't used to being cross-examined, so she made no immediate response. She waited with something like curiosity to see if Keller would repeat his question.

'I asked you who he was phoning and why.'

'Mr Harte was speaking to a jeweller,' Sylvia replied coolly. 'He wanted some information about the value of a platinum bracelet set with rubies the size of a thumbnail.'

'Remarkable,' said Keller, sitting up straight. 'So our mutual friend is interested in the current price of platinum and rubies, is he?'

'I don't know if he's interested, Captain. I merely heard him mention the subject. It was only a routine inquiry, I'm sure.'

'That remains to be seen,' Keller said drily. 'Is the Hauser woman still outside?'

'I didn't tell her to go away. She had lunch somewhere in town and came back.'

'Good. I want to speak to her, but not for the moment.'

'Very well, Captain.'

Keller frowned. Sylvia Meiners was a strange girl—strange and unapproachable. She was obviously one of those people who like to draw a veil over their private lives, who don't like anyone to know what is going on inside them.

'Know what, Sylvia? You spend too much time on paper-work and too little on yourself. You suffer from the occupational disease of the small-town bureaucrat. The Germans are absolutely incapable of drawing a line between business and pleasure.'

'We haven't had much opportunity.'

'That's typical. You aren't open-minded enough. You cling to narrow, outmoded codes of behaviour. You've forgotten how to breathe freely. You're a mass of inhibitions—a typical Prussian local councillor's daughter. That's what your father was, wasn't he?'

'Yes, until nineteen thirty-three. Local councillor and Socialist member of the Reichstag.'

She could see her father as she spoke—a short, rather corpulent man who drove himself hard, making notes at the dinner table, reading newspapers or listening to reports while he ate. He was seldom at home and spent most of his time on the move. Conferences, assemblies, inaugural ceremonies, celebrations, meetings—all for the country he loved. For years, his conversations with her had consisted of little more than 'Good morning, Sylvia' or 'Good night, Sylvia'—little more than that for years on end. She looked Keller in the eye.

'Yes, I suppose you could call him a small-town bureaucrat. They arrested him in 'thirty-three—quite automatically, since he belonged to the wrong party—and put him in a concentration camp. They were pretty innocuous in those days, concentration camps. My father stayed inside for fourteen months before they released him. He did a spell as a car salesman and then became a representative for a small firm which manufactured beer-taps—it belonged to an ex-minister. His subsequent jobs included pipe-laying, mat-making and sticking paper bags together.'

As she spoke, she could picture the night in 1933 when her father came home for the last time, trembling with agitation. 'Mother,' he called—he always addressed his wife as 'Mother' —'what's going to become of us? They'll murder us all!' And she, Sylvia, had been standing in the doorway in her nightie, a frightened little girl of ten. Thanks to the icy blast whistling past her from the hall window, which was wide open, she had gone down with pneumonia a few hours later.

'He probably earned a good salary,' Keller said. 'Auto-agencies pay well as a rule. Anyway, then came 'thirty-nine and a chance to fight for Adolf Hitler and the Third Reich.'

'You could put it that way,' Sylvia replied. 'He even became a wartime officer. His last rank was major. In August 'forty-four he was re-arrested, quite by chance. His name happened to be on a list found in Colonel Stauffenberg's office.'

'I know the form. The Nazis pulled in everyone who was in the least bit suspect, and today the whole of the rest of Germany is trying to get in on the act—claim credit for a single ray of light in a thousand years of darkness. There weren't much more than a hundred men involved, but just ask our four thousand internees what they were doing on July 20th, 1944; A thousand of them will tell you they were involved and another thousand will assure you that they were secret sympathizers. The other two thousand will deplore the fact that they knew nothing about the plot but swear blind that, if they had known, they'd have joined in. That's the general attitude.'

'My father died in a concentration camp at the beginning of 'forty-five, during an air-raid.'

'An American air-raid, I suppose. Is that what you were going to say, Fräulein Meiners?'

'Yes.'

She could see the clay urn and the note that came with it. Funeral expenses totalled 246 marks 30 pfennigs and were to be remitted to the appropriate State fund within four weeks from the date of receipt. 'They say the urns sometimes don't contain human ashes at all,' her mother told her. 'Any old ash will do. Say they have eighty-four urns and eighty-four accompanying letters to send: it doesn't matter which urn goes with which letter or what's inside.'

'Hard times,' said Keller. 'They're over now, though. You ought to stop brooding about them all the time. The fact that you were a local big-wig's daughter doesn't mean a thing now.'

'I've never had much time for local big-wigs but my father meant a great deal to me, even though I hardly knew him. You can't ignore family ties, Captain.'

'You're very young still, Fräulein Meiners, but I don't think you're naïve. Tell me something: what would you do if you owned a platinum and ruby bracelet?'

'I don't own such a thing and never will.'

'Who knows? Anyway, it was only a hypothetical question. Well, what would you do with an article of value like that?'

'Hide it, probably.'

'Correct,' said Keller. 'That's exactly what I thought you'd say. People who own valuable jewellery today don't flash it around—they hide it. The problem is, where?'

As soon as Reiter's presence had been announced Keller got up from behind his desk. He ensconced himself in one of the massive leather arm-chairs, casually crossed his legs, and gave Sylvia Meiners a nod.

'Don't forget, get everything down on paper—everything, however unimportant it may seem to you. Okay, now send Reiter in.'

Reiter entered, closing the door noiselessly behind him. Just inside the office he halted, brought his heels together—still noiselessly—and stood there with his arms at his sides, elbows slightly bent and outstretched fingers just touching his trousers seams. It was a pose which combined deference with dignity, respect with self-respect.

Keller never failed to marvel at Reiter's stance. The precision with which he reproduced it every time was remarkable.

Reiter waited until he was addressed. Keller was familiar with this part of the ritual too. The German commandant didn't cringe but he wasn't a rebel either. He was a born subordinate with a single streak of individuality: he occasionally had some ideas of his own.

'Well, what's new?' inquired Keller. 'Any requests or suggestions?'

Reiter hesitated for a moment. He couldn't gauge the mood of the man in the arm-chair. It was not clear whether he ought to bring out his suggestions now or reserve them for a more auspicious occasion. He decided that it would be safer to fall back on ritual.

'Nothing special to report,' he announced.

'Cut out the clichés,' Keller told him kindly. 'I didn't give you the commandant's job so you could bombard me with small-talk. Co-operation—that's what I want from you. I hope you appreciate that.'

Reiter nodded and produced a sheet of paper from his armband. Keller's secretary was sitting there with pencil poised, presumably about to take notes, so the interview must be an official one. Consequently, he must do what was expected of a German camp commandant under prevailing circumstances.

'In my view,' he began, 'isolation of individual accommodation blocks is pointless. It should be discontinued.'

Keller slowly uncrossed his legs and settled himself even deeper in the arm-chair. 'Why pointless? Why discontinue it?'

'The camp is divided into three blocks,' Reiter pursued, 'A, B, and C. Each of them is separated from the other two by barbed wire, but the inmates of Block A can converse through the wire with those in Block B, and—indirectly, since Blocks B and C are in similar contact—with those in Block C. In practice, therefore, the isolation of individual groups of internees is inoperative.'

'Oh, and what do you suggest?'

'That isolation should be officially discontinued.'

Keller drew in his legs abruptly and leant forward. 'Wrong, Reiter, dead wrong. You're way off the target. Isolation is part of a deliberate policy. The only answer is to make it work by adopting much tougher measures.'

Reiter found this suggestion highly unwelcome. He had managed to get a whole series of restrictions lifted or relaxed by patient and unhurried spadework, and Keller had seldom raised any objection. He wondered what had got into the man.

'Tougher measures?' he said slowly, as though doubting his own ears. 'Are you proposing to go back to square one?'

The arm-chair creaked as Keller shifted his weight. 'Yes,

why not? There are plenty of indications that stricter measures are urgently called for. You know me, Reiter. I'm not small-minded as a rule, but I've no intention of letting your boys take me for a ride. Anyone who tries it will be sorry.'

He fitted his fingertips together and gave the German a benevolent smile.

'Let's not quibble, Reiter. You speak of tougher measures. I'd prefer to talk about tightening security, and my version is the one that counts around here. Is that clear?'

Reiter nodded, pondering darkly on the growing ferment of dissatisfaction inside the camp. He was not particularly popular, even with his former room-mates—no German commandant could hope to be popular, though there were plenty of contenders for the job. Every day brought new problems in its train. His special skill consisted in dodging them and turning them to good account.

'I'm afraid the internees could get far more restive than they are now,' he said cautiously.

'For your information,' Keller replied, quite unmoved, 'internment isn't meant to be a rest-cure. Your boys can get as restive as they like—I couldn't care less—but actual disturbances are another matter altogether. If unrest developed into rioting the number of internees might decrease sharply without anyone being released.'

Reiter digested this in silence. 'What exactly are you afraid of?' he asked at length.

'All kinds of things—mutiny, organized passive resistance, a mass escape. There are enough pointers in that direction. However, you will inform the internees that any attempt to mutiny or escape will be taken as an admission of guilt. Innocent men don't run for it, they stand trial with a clear conscience.'

Keller had risen and was pacing up and down. His voice grew louder. 'To minimize the chances of escape, the following regulations will come into force immediately: no internee may approach within three yards of the wire. Clearly defined boundary lines are to be marked out by the internees within twenty-four hours and instructions regarding them issued within the same period. A progress report on the subject to be submitted to me personally—by you at 1200 hours tomorrow. Calling across the fence prohibited from now on. Guards will be instructed to open fire without warning if this regulation is disobeyed. Type that out in the form of a standing order, Fräulein Meiners, and send Hauptmann Reiter a copy. Any other comments, Reiter?'

Keller interrupted his pacing and paused beside the window. Turning his back on the German, he surveyed the internment camp spread out beneath him—Camp 7, his private kingdom.

Reiter cleared his throat. 'I can't help feeling that our position has deteriorated.'

'You're right,' Keller replied curtly. 'It has.'

'Are these new measures permanent, or may we regard them as a temporary expedient?'

Keller slowly turned to face him. Just as slowly, he said, 'That will depend on the internees' conduct, not on me.' He smiled suddenly as though something funny had occurred to him. 'Germany is renowned for its discipline, Reiter. Make sure you maintain it here. There may come a time when your lives depend on it.'

He turned back to the window and leant against the frame. 'It's quite possible that these restrictions will be lifted before long. It's even possible that I shall abolish the ban on communication between individual blocks and grant some other privileges as well. Anything is possible, but all in good time.'

'May I point something out?' Reiter asked cautiously. 'A large proportion of the internees are innocent beyond question. Many are only technically implicated and others have been falsely denounced. Your measures will penalize innocent men as well as guilty.'

'Innocent men?' Keller drew himself up and stared intently at Reiter. 'You dare to try that tack with me, after all that's happened? Does a man have to murder women and stick children in gas-ovens to be guilty? Everyone who knew something and said nothing is guilty. Everyone who turned a blind eye rather than acknowledge the truth is guilty. They're all guilty—even the honest, stupid, uninformed spectators of your country's murderous performance. You'll be telling me next that there's no difference between a massacre and a Mass.'

Reiter did his best to appease Keller, looking pained and surprised. 'I don't deny that this camp contains a few men who joined in without scruple.'

'A few? A sizeable number, you mean! It took thousands of killers to dispose of millions of victims. This camp contains a prize collection of them—diplomats who officially sanctioned the deportation of Jews, generals who tolerated executions which infringed international law, ministry hacks who helped to put their bosses' murderous directives into effect, doctors who carried out lethal experiments on racially inferior victims, patriotic poets who dulled and anaesthetized the brains of the masses. You call them innocent?'

Keller's angry outburst was cut short. He gave Reiter a searching stare. 'If you like,' he said quietly, 'let's call this camp a hen-house with only a handful of foxes loose inside.' He thrust one hand deep into his pocket as though to convey indifference, then added casually, 'The only thing that puzzles me is why you chickens don't turn on them.'

Reiter, genuinely at a loss for an answer, did not reply. Instinct told him that this was not the time or place to trot out the 'companions-in-misfortune' theory which was so rife in camp. It was the Americans' own fault if they ran their heads against a brick wall. They had welded guilty and innocent into a makeshift community by putting a few potential war criminals and numerous unwitting victims of circumstance in the same boat.

Keller leaned against the window-frame. 'Do you know a man named Hauser?' he asked softly.

'Yes,' Reiter replied, without realizing what his answer portended.

'You see,' Keller went on calmly from the window, 'Hauser is one of the people who make these restrictions unavoidable. Why don't you stop sitting on the fence? If you know Hauser you must know something about him.'

Reiter said nothing.

'Can you supply me with some information about Hauser? If not, do you know someone who could?'

Reiter still said nothing.

'Where did he serve? What operations did he take part in? Is there a list somewhere with his name on it? Why don't you answer, man? These are questions which need answering, and fast.'

Reiter was utterly at a loss. He wondered how best to react. Ought he to look shocked, amused, interested, indignant? In the end he shook his head blankly and said, 'What do you expect me to say?'

Keller turned away. 'I expect nothing, Reiter—nothing at all, except possibly a modicum of intelligence, a sense of duty or a vague instinct for self-preservation. You're in charge of four thousand internees. I put you in charge of them because I had confidence in you. All I ask myself is, why should four thousand men have to suffer just because a few of their number move heaven and earth to escape the consequences of their own actions? That's my only point. Have I made myself clear?'

'Yes,' said Reiter, bowing his head almost humbly, 'I think I understand.' Then he left the room.

Keller walked over to the map which occupied almost the entire rear wall of his office. It was a detailed plan of Camp 7.

On the right, black, bulky and heavily shaded, the three double blocks which housed the internees; on the left, a number of hatched rectangles: two cookhouses, an elongated hall, and three barnlike buildings used as store-rooms and workshops; between them, like a snake, the camp road. At the bottom of the map, outlined in green, Keller's administration block, containing interrogation rooms, the de-Nazification department run by Rolf Gernsbach, two rooms reserved for the standby squad, the American guard-rooms, a teletype-room, and, next to that, a switchboard and radio-room. All these premises were manned predominantly by American personnel assisted by a handful of carefully selected German civilians.

Keller's eyes roved thoughtfully over the maze of red lines, squares and circles. Red denoted security installations: barbed wire, watch-towers, electricity cables, fields of fire, and the mined areas taken over from the Nazis. The Nazis knew how to lay man-traps.

Keller was not entirely happy with Camp 7's security system, for all that. Fields of fire did not overlap effectively at every point and a minor shortage of guards would create dangerous gaps in the cordon. He needed another forty men or so to ensure that not even a mouse could get in or out of camp unobserved.

Sylvia Meiners interrupted his train of thought.

'About your interview with the German commandant, Captain—shall I make a finished copy of the minutes and put them on record?'

'Of course.'

'But you told me to take down everything that passed between you and Hauptmann Reiter.'

Keller paused in his study of the map. His eyes came to rest on a watch-tower whose field of vision was partly obscured by a protruding section of wall. 'Everything?' he repeated slowly.

It was only then that he grasped the significance of her question. As though to himself, he said, 'Some people are unobservant—they're no use to me. Other people hear far more than is good for them—they can be dangerous if they don't have the knack of forgetting quickly.'

'So how much of what I took down still stands?'

'Only my direct instructions. Put them in the report and delete the rest. That goes for your memory as well as your shorthand pad.'

Sylvia tore several sheets off her pad and walked over to him, holding them between her thumb and forefinger. Their hands brushed as she gave them to him.

Keller forced himself not to look at her. He glanced at the sheets, tore them into little pieces and dropped them in an ash-tray. Then he set fire to them and watched them burn.

'Fräulein Meiners,' he said, 'have you ever wondered why you're here?'

'Not because of the high salary or special privileges. At the risk of annoying you, I work here out of principle.'

'Much as I appreciate your idealistic motives,' Keller said as he returned to his desk, 'you're working in a contemporary species of prison, not a parsonage. You ought to bear that in mind.'

'I've borne it in mind from the outset.' Sylvia eyed him appraisingly. 'I've even tried to understand your methods, but I sometimes feel that you and Mr Harte use some pretty tough techniques. You may find you lose by them.'

'Lose?' Keller made a dismissive gesture. 'What are we likely to lose? If you're talking about loss of life, people died like flies in Nazi concentration camps. We haven't killed anyone here so far. If you mean loss of confidence, forget it.

Criminals don't inspire confidence in me and never have. This is a damned tough job, and one's reactions have to be just as tough.'

He picked up the phone. 'Get me Mr Harte,' he said with a sidelong glance at Sylvia, who did her best to look uninterested.

'Hello. Harte. I'm told you've been making inquiries about that bracelet. Did you get anywhere? You did? Good. Well, what would a thing like that cost?' He listened intently, then laughed—a little grimly, or so it seemed to Sylvia. 'You don't say! I agree, Ted. Anyone who can lay hands on that sort of loot is worth a closer look.'

He hung up slowly and turned to look thoughtfully at Sylvia. Then he went over to the map again and stood there, unmoving.

'Shall I ask Frau Hauser to come in now?'

'Yes, I'll deal with her personally.'

Sylvia left Keller and went into the outer office, her official place of work. She shared the room with a sergeant who was known to everyone, herself included, as 'ABC'. She didn't know his real name.

ABC was Captain Keller's special orderly. He rarely had anything to do but, being devoid of ambition, did not bemoan the fact. ABC spent his time reading comic-books. From time to time he burst out laughing, wiped imaginary tears from his eyes and groped for a hip-flask of whisky. Then he went on reading. His supreme form of exertion was to take a pair of scissors and cut out a pin-up girl, which he would carefully tuck away in an already bulging wallet.

'Any idea where Mr Harte is, ABC?' Sylvia asked.

'He didn't clock out with me,' replied the sergeant, looking round vaguely.

'The scissors are on the typewriter table.'

'Thanks,' said ABC. He began snipping away happily. 'I didn't ask where Harte—sorry, Mr Harte—was going, but if you want me to look for him I'll find him in fifteen minutes flat. Detective work's a speciality of mine.'

'Thank you, ABC.'

As soon as the sergeant had gone Sylvia picked up the phone and asked the switchboard operator if she knew where Harte was.

'With Herr Gernsbach,' said an indifferent voice.

'Please put me through.'

Gernsbach answered almost at once.

'Sylvia Meiners here, Herr Gernsbach. Forgive me for disturbing you.'

'Not at all, Sylvia. Nice to hear your voice. I was just talking about you, as a matter of fact.'

'About me? Who to?'

'Ted Harte, of course. Who else?'

'Oh, I see.' Sylvia sounded a little embarrassed.

'What can I do for you? You know I'm always at your service, on duty or off. I'd even be prepared to show you my pictures, and that's saying something. But perhaps you weren't calling me at all. Did you want to speak to Harte?'

'Yes, please,' Sylvia replied, adding hurriedly, 'And many thanks for the invitation. I'd be very interested to see some of your work.'

A moment later she heard Harte's voice, serene and slightly sarcastic, 'Is something on fire? My filing-cabinet, I hope.' There was a pause. 'Have you thought over my suggestion?'

'Mr Harte,' Sylvia said, 'did you know that security precautions are to be tightened up?'

Harte did not reply for a moment. Then he asked, without a trace of sarcasm, 'On whose orders?'

'Captain Keller's. He said so just now, during an interview with Reiter. What can we do?'

'Nothing,' Harte said after a brief pause. 'Absolutely nothing. It's a matter for the commandant alone—nothing to do with me.'

'But you know perfectly well that the reintroduction of harsher measures would be unwise—possibly even dangerous. You said so yourself a few days ago, in my presence. Are you really going to stand by and do nothing?'

'Count me out of this, Fräulein Meiners. It's nothing to do with me—or you, for that matter. I was just asking Gernsbach to explain how you turn a patch of canvas into an oil-painting. That's a far pleasanter and more fascinating subject—less risky, too. Kindly don't distract me. In fact stop distracting me in general unless you can think of a more enjoyable way of doing it.'

There was little activity in the wash-room. Today was shower-day, and on shower-days hardly any internees felt like toiling over their laundry in the airless basement. Refreshed by their showers, they were mostly lolling in the sun, sitting in their rooms or strolling about, deep in meditation.

Not so the inmates of Room 29. Theirs was the only room in their half of the block to miss a shower because the water had run out just before their turn came. They had marched off to the basement wash-room, almost to a man, and were now gathered round the capacious cement trough, outwardly calm but inwardly fuming. Any outsider who tried to use the wash-room was hustled outside with the words, 'Full up! Come back later!' Meanwhile, they worked off their fury at the missed shower by pummelling their soiled clothes.

'It's a downright disgrace, depriving us of our shower,' Laffrentz griped. 'Provocation, that's what it is. It's an assault on our dignity, a barefaced infringement of human rights. We mustn't take it lying down.'

'You make personal hygiene sound quite ideological,' Wickler said. 'I suppose you judge a man's character by the smell of his feet.'

Mangel gloomily inspected some new holes in his under-pants. 'I never cease to marvel at the way some people get worked up over trifles. Small-minded is the expression I'd use.'

Laffrentz slapped his wet socks down on the edge of the trough and propped his paunch delicately against the side. 'What the hell do you mean by that?'

'The Americans have got us by the short hairs. All we can do is try to maintain a little poise and dignity. We're being held here under duress, and there's nothing we can do about it.'

'Yes there is.'

'What, exactly? Be more specific.'

'It's our misfortune,' Laffrentz declared weightily, 'to have a German camp commandant who spends his whole time crawling up the Americans' backsides.'

'No danger of that in your case,' interposed Wickler. 'There isn't an asshole big enough to accommodate you.'

Everyone laughed. Even Laffrentz was shrewd enough to take the architect's remark in good spirit, but his expression clearly conveyed that if anyone could do the job that man was

Laffrentz: organizer and dominant personality, comrade-in-arms and realist. He'd stir things up all right!

'No laundry in the trough yet!' he warned. 'It's got to be fuller than that before we can rinse properly.'

Wickler grinned. 'Just as you say, Commandant.'

'What do you think, Hauser?' inquired Laffrentz.

Hauser, who was mechanically kneading a pair of socks with his large beefy hands, did not look up at first.

'I took the liberty of asking your opinion, Herr Hauser.'

'About what?'

'The whole situation.'

Hauser stared round contemptuously. 'Shit!' he said, and went on kneading.

'My sentiments exactly,' Laffrentz declared with a gratified smile. 'The present German camp commandant is a great disappointment.'

'Herr Reiter was a room-mate of ours,' Mangel put in. 'Kindly remember that.'

'So what? What have we got out of it? How many jobs has he put our way? How many of us work in the cookhouse? Who's looking after the rations? Who's in charge of food distribution? Not us!'

'So that's the trouble,' said Wickler. 'The wrong people are doling out the grub, and our friend here feels specially qualified to take over.'

Laffrentz looked round defiantly. 'Why not? Room 29 wouldn't lose by it.'

'Nor would you.'

'Things would be fairer than they are now, I can assure you,' Laffrentz said. 'The present commandant sells himself for bars of chocolate and plenty of kip. He guzzles Coca-Cola like water. He smokes American cigarettes and wolfs white bread while we waste away.'

'Your co-operation would cost the Yanks more, I suppose?' Wickler said, still grinning, and dabbed his hands in the water.

'Take your paws out of there!' snapped Laffrentz. 'You'll make the rinsing water dirty in advance. As for your foul insinuations, keep them to yourself. You don't appreciate the extent of my community spirit.'

'You have my fullest confidence, Herr Laffrentz,' said

Arthur Wammenberg. 'You think like our Führer in these matters. He always laid great emphasis on the power of personality.'

'Which is one reason why we're here,' said Wickler.

Surprisingly, Baron von Hagen permitted himself an ambassadorial dictum. 'History,' he announced, 'has a big belly—it digests everything.'

'Ah, digestion!' sighed Wammenberg. 'Digestion is very important. Ours would improve considerably if only the menu could be livened up—with salads, say. Take watercress, dandelion leaves and nettles . . . I'd lay on tons of greenstuff if I was in charge of the cookhouse. What do you say, Herr Laffrentz?'

'You're welcome to the job,' Laffrentz replied magnanimously.

'Everyone round here seems open to bribery,' Wickler said with a provocative grin. 'All that varies is the price.'

'As for me,' Mangel said sharply, every inch the staff lieutenant-colonel, 'I firmly reject such an imputation.'

The architect laughed. 'What's the matter? Who said anything about you? People like you don't need bribing. You toe the line without question, regardless of who's giving the orders. Your sort come cheaper than any other.'

Mangel preserved an outraged silence. Trost shook his grey head reproachfully. Baron von Hagen wondered absently how the wash-room would look if it had wrought iron window-frames filled with amber glass. Wammenberg snorted indignantly, the Hitler Youth lieutenant ground his teeth, and even the Foreign Office interpreter looked depressed.

Hauser continued to knead his bundle of wet clothes grimly. Without looking up, he said, 'They do what they damn well like with us. They treat us like shit. They think they've got us just where they want us. They bank on us acting just like we are now—shooting our mouths off and doing bugger all.'

'Everything has its price,' Laffrentz said impatiently. 'The trouble is, we can't pay—or won't. Anyway, why should we? We don't have any dollars or sterling, furs or jewellery, sexy wives or desirable daughters. These are stinking awful times, gentlemen. I worked twelve years for the Third Reich. Now I'm taking a breather. The Americans can't pin anything on me, so why should I make them a present of my little nest-egg? You don't think I'm going to spend the rest of my days sweeping the streets, do you? I'm not that stupid!'

Hauser had straightened up and was staring at Laffrentz. 'You think the Americans could be bribed?'

'Of course!' sneered Laffrentz. 'You don't imagine they came here out of the goodness of their hearts, surely? Like hell they did! They mean to make something out of it. The Russians are pig-headed, the French like amusing themselves, the English are happy if they can do business, but the Americans . . . Gangsters, the lot of them! Ransom money, that's what they're after. It's downright extortion, what they're doing here. The German people have got to be made to suffer, but no Yank is averse to making a profitable little deal on the side.'

'You think so?' Hauser said.

'Of course! How many dollars is a human being worth? Ten thousand? Don't you believe it! They wouldn't offer five hundred marks a nose for our Jews in the old days, so ten times that much ought to be more than enough for one of us today. Try waving a few thousand dollars under Keller's nose some time. What do you think would happen? Simple! He'd pronounce you an innocent man—give you it in writing, even. Money talks, Hauser, and so does real estate. Transfer some real estate to him or one of his relations. Hang some jewellery round the neck of his ever-loving wife or girl-friend, whichever. Provide a nice-looking piece for his bed, either as a bonus or in part payment, and you'll soon find out!'

'Shut up!' Hauser snapped furiously. 'That's enough!'

Laffrentz dropped his laundry into the trough. 'Rinsing, commence!' he ordained.

Brigitte Hauser was waiting in the outer office. She observed everything that went on around her. Nothing, however trivial, escaped her notice.

The Americans would not have been pleased to learn how much Brigitte had found out in the few hours since her enforced sojourn in the outer office began. She now knew the commandant's daily schedule. She knew where his private residence was and where he usually ate his meals, had learned some of his idiosyncrasies and observed the way he treated other people. He was a self-assured man, but very much a man.

She had overheard two conversations of minor importance through the open door. She had also managed to steal a glimpse of the plan of Camp 7, from which it appeared that her husband must be housed in Block C. Communication through the wire between Block C and the outside world was relatively awkward. It would be far easier to maintain contact via the window of Cookhouse No. 2. A track led past it, close enough to enable written messages in bold lettering to be deciphered without difficulty.

Captain Keller came out of his office. He stood there, a tall slim figure, muscular but relaxed, and stared round the room. His eyes came to rest on her.

After a well-judged pause, he asked, 'Are you Frau Hauser?'

'Yes.'

'You wanted to speak to me?'

Brigitte straightened slightly and gazed up at him. 'If possible,' she said, 'yes. I'd like that very much.'

'It isn't customary,' Keller said. 'I never grant interviews to internees' wives and I wouldn't be justified in making an exception in your case.'

Brigitte started to smile. Two alluring dimples appeared at the corners of her mouth and her eyes narrowed like those of a contented cat.

'No exceptions?' she said.

'Not officially.'

'And unofficially?'

'I'm going into town to have coffee and do a few errands,' Keller said. 'You can come part of the way with me if you like. But only if you like.'

'By all means.'

Brigitte rose at once. She was a head shorter than Keller Her gleaming crown of auburn hair only came up to his shoulder. She looked him full in the face as though they had known each other a long time. It was a long, steady look.

'All right,' she said. 'What are we waiting for?'

He opened the door for her and they went downstairs and across the courtyard. The gate opened with a clang and the sentry gave a casual salute. Glancing at the man, Keller saw that he was actually grinning.

Not without reason, Keller thought good-humouredly. The sentry's grin was benevolent—even admiring. Some woman, it said. And: some man, the Captain. Got good taste, knows his way around. Wouldn't mind being in his shoes . . .

Keller could sympathize with thoughts of this kind. There was a worldly beauty about the woman beside him, with her poise, her slightly full but shapely breasts, her gliding walk, her half-demure, half-wilful air. It gave him a thrill of excitement just to walk beside her.

'Well.' he said. trying to sound businesslike. 'what was it you wanted to know?'

'My husband is in your camp.'

'I know. SS Standartenführer Hauser. I know all about him and his past record. No need to fill me in on that. What else?'

'May I speak to him?'

'I'm sorry. It's out of the question.'

'Even for a short time—enough time to ask him a few questions?'

'Not even a minute.'

She studied his profile: the lock of hair escaping from his cap. the straight brow, the slightly jutting nose, the full lips, the hint of vigour in the square jaw. An attractive man, but lacking in brute masculinity. A magazine-cover American.

'Can't I speak to my husband under any circumstances?' she asked. 'Wouldn't you make another exception?'

Keller avoided her eye. All he could think of to say was, 'Are you so eager to see him? Why should I break my own regulations for your sake?'

Brigitte gave a low laugh. Surprised, he turned his head and saw that she was watching him. Their eyes met for a moment. Then he looked away.

The road ran straight for over half a mile. The trees on either side were trimmed as evenly as if they had been aligned with a tape-measure. Benches affording a view of the mountains were spaced out at hundred-yard intervals. There were few houses. The town itself, a cluster of half-timbered buildings, was still a quarter of a mile away. No traffic, scarcely a soul to be seen. Just the two of them.

'Let's sit down,' suggested Keller.

Without further prompting, she walked to the next bench and sat down in the exact centre. Wherever he chose to sit he would be close to her.

'I'm not dying to see him,' she said almost indifferently, as though to herself. 'It isn't that. I've got other worries. I was married in the middle of the war, you see. We only had a few weeks together—maybe thirty days in three years. I ask you, what was I supposed to do with myself for the other thousand days and nights. You certainly couldn't call our relationship a grand passion.'

'What was it, then?'

'My parents died during the war. They left me a small hotel near here—the Crown. It's more of an inn, really. However, I've now got a chance to acquire a far larger place right here in town—the White Horse. It's going begging.'

Keller detached his gaze from the vista of mountains, trees and meadows in front of him. He looked down at Brigitte's feet, her supple legs, the small firm hand that rested on her curving thigh, close beside him and well within reach.

'Is that what you wanted to discuss with your husband?' he asked suspiciously. 'I thought he was a soldier, not a businessman.'

'I have to know what his prospects are. As his wife, I'm dependent on him—that is, as long as we're still married. That's why I wanted some information from you.'

Keller studied his shoes, then hers. She crossed her legs and leaned towards him with a faint smile.

'Information?' he drawled. 'What, for instance?'

'Whether my husband will be transferred to a prisoner-of-war camp. Whether I can count on him being released in the foreseeable future or whether he's regarded as a war criminal.'

'Nothing's settled yet, Frau Hauser. However, I take it you'd like to know if your husband will be at your service again before long—or however you care to put it.' He smiled wryly. 'Perhaps it is a grand passion after all.'

Brigitte gently shook her head. 'Put it another way,' she said. 'If my husband—my present husband—isn't classified as a war criminal, there's no objection to my buying the White Horse. As the wife of a war criminal I'd never obtain the necessary permit. That's my problem.'

'You want this permit so badly?'

'I'd do anything to get it.'

He leaned forward. 'Anything?'

Her eyes widened and her lips parted a little She sank back with her arms limp at her sides.

'I'd do anything,' she repeated, 'anything within reason.'

'Let's go,' he said after a pause. 'This needs discussing more fully, but first I'm going to buy you that coffee.'

'My dear Gernsbach,' said Ted Harte, studying the portfolio of sketches on his knee, 'you can say what you like but you'll never convince me. Painting is a perfectly good profession. Why don't you make a proper business out of it?'

Gernsbach, who was sitting beside him, said, 'You don't find my work convincing?'

'That isn't the point and you know it. Let's assume that I like what you turn out. Let's even assume that I'm crazy about your pictures. Okay, so I'd like to buy some, but I can't. All good things have a price-tag, but you're living in a country where there's no market for your kind of art and won't be for quite a while. So you can't sell. You paint, but you'll starve for a long time to come.'

'All the same, I paint.'

'You're a strange man, Gernsbach.' Harte shook his head and turned over another sheet.

'Why strange?'

'You may be an outstanding painter for all I know. All I know for certain is that one or two people think you're an odd-ball.'

Gernsbach burst out laughing. 'Is that all? I'm used to far worse than that. They called me morbid, degenerate and un-German, and I took it as a compliment.'

Harte picked up another sheet and scrutinized it closely. 'What about Sylvia Meiners?' he asked suddenly. 'How much do you know about her?'

'As little as you do, I imagine.' Gernsbach gave the CIC officer a new sketch to look at—a rugged vista of mountains and forest captured with a minimum of lines and planes. 'You have to study a thing thoroughly before you can reproduce its essentials. If I painted Sylvia I'd have to get to know more about her, and I'd like that.'

'Ask her to sit for you.'

'You think she would? She's a very sensitive person—anyone can see that.'

Harte smiled. 'An operation of this kind needs careful planning. I suggest you invite her over this evening. I'll come too, as a sort of chaperon.'

'Excellent,' Gernsbach said. 'Let's make it a social occasion. We'll talk about everything under the sun—America and the Germans included—but not a word about art.'

Harte found himself staring at a pencil-sketch which looked as if it had been dashed off in a hurry. It showed a huge rectangular chamber scattered with bundles of rags—human beings with deep cavities in their skulls where the eyes should have been. Eyes! There seemed to be myriads of them, non-existent yet riveted on the beholder.

Harte avoided Gernsbach's inquiring gaze. 'Agony,' he said, 'agony and torment. Is that all you have to offer?'

'What else is there in this modern age of ours?'

'Laughter, Gernsbach. Even death has its humorous side. You ought to read the Old Testament.'

'I've forgotten how to laugh.'

'In that case, how can you bear it all?'

Gernsbach reached for the portfolio and hugged it to his chest. 'Let's talk about something else. Tell me, if it isn't another side of the same subject, why I'm supposed to be an oddball.'

'With pleasure.' Harte subjected Gernsbach's studio to an appraising stare. 'You're not wealthy, yet you're temporarily in charge of assets worth millions of marks. All Nazi-owned property in the district, whether government, municipal or private, passes through your hands. It's worth millions, as I say, but none of it has rubbed off on you.'

Gernsbach looked dumbfounded. 'You really think I'd . . .' He paused, struggling for words. 'What do you take me for?'

'An ordinary human being,' Harte replied. 'After all, what could be more natural? The Nazis destroyed your health, livelihood and self-confidence. Health is irreplaceable and self confidence takes time to regain, but there's a new livelihood staring you in the face. Why not help yourself?'

'You're tempting me,' mused Gernsbach. 'Why? What's the object?'

There was a gentle tap at the door. Gernsbach crossed the studio and opened it.

'Could I have a word with you?' someone asked in a low voice.

'Sorry,' said Gernsbach. 'I've got visitors.'

'That's all right!' called Harte. 'It's my old friend Slembeck

—ask him in. I can't wait to hear what he wants to discuss with you.'

Slembeck, hovering in the doorway, bowed in Harte's direction. 'I wouldn't want to intrude,' he said deferentially. 'I'll come back another time.'

'No false modesty,' Harte insisted. 'Come in, Slembeck. We've been waiting for somebody in your price-range.'

'All right,' Gernsbach said. 'come in.'

Slembeck took a few diffident steps into the room. 'It isn't important,' he pleaded. 'There's no urgency, either. I just happened to be passing.'

Harte grinned as he noted the brilliant yellow vest. sky-blue shirt, blue-striped suit and well-shined brown shoes.

'You look positively seductive, Slembeck. Pity you've never taken that much trouble with me. Come here—I want to see if you're wearing perfume.'

Gernsbach pulled up a chair and Slembeck sat down, looking uncomfortable.

'I only wanted a little information,' he said awkwardly.

'I have an office,' Gernsbach told him. 'It's in the administration block at Camp 7.'

Harte laughed. 'Herr Slembeck knows that. I imagine he also knows that I check your visitors' list every day—that's why he wanted a word in private. All right, give him what he wants. Don't let me disturb you.'

Harte got up and stationed himself by the window with a number of Gernsbach's drawings, holding them up one by one as though searching for the angle which would show them in the best light. He seemed to be wholly engrossed.

'Right,' Gernsbach said briskly. 'What can I do for you?'

'Nothing important. I really didn't mean to intrude. I'll gladly come back another time.'

'You're here now, so you might as well tell me.'

Slembeck wiped his sweating palms on his trousers. 'Well,' he said, glancing covertly at Harte, who was studying one of Gernsbach's sketches at arm's length, 'well, it's like this: suppose, just for the sake of argument, that someone appropriates something belonging to someone else.'

'That's theft.' Gernsbach's tone was businesslike. 'A matter for the police.'

'That isn't what I meant,' Slembeck said hesitantly. 'I was thinking of a Nazi who seized foreign property in wartime.'

'In cases like that, documentary proof of ownership has to be produced.'

'What if there isn't any?'

'In default of documentary evidence, witnesses will do.'

'And if witnesses come forward, is the property returned to its original owner?'

'Yes.'

'That's all I wanted to know,' Slembeck said, getting up.

'Come off it!' Harte called from the window. 'That isn't all you wanted to know, not by a long shot.'

'You're wrong, Mr Harte. That's all the information I need, believe me.'

'Believe you, Slembeck? You must be joking! However, this hypothetical case of yours intrigues me. Who is the original owner involved? You, Slembeck? If so, what sort of property have you lost? Money, articles of value—jewellery, maybe?'

Slembeck shied like a frightened horse. 'You misjudge my motives, Mr Harte. I was just making some inquiries for a friend.'

'How charitable of you! What's the name of this friend? Not Slembeck, by any chance?'

Finding no other way out of his predicament. Slembeck went over to the attack. He said, 'I'm not under interrogation, am I?'

'No,' Harte replied, 'not by me. Captain Keller has taken over the Hauser case.'

'I don't understand. The Hauser case doesn't come into this.'

'Doesn't it? You mean you've got more than one iron in the fire, Slembeck? Be careful you don't burn your fingers.'

Slembeck turned to Gernsbach. 'Thank you for the information.'

'You're welcome.'

Ignoring Harte, Slembeck bowed and made headlong for the door.

'Strange fellow,' said Gernsbach, when he had gone.

'Not at all,' Harte replied. 'He strikes me as the height of normality. Absurdity is the norm these days—it's time you accepted that.'

'What was he really after? Do you know?'

'What do you think he was after? A little investment for the future, I imagine. Some people get cleaned out and others cash in. War costs money. The important thing is to find somebody to foot the bill. Every war throws up a mass of parasites who are anxious to profit by it.'

'You're very cynical, Harte.'

'I may be cynical, my dear Gernsbach, but you err on the gullible side. My advice is, be careful. I know you mean well, but good intentions don't make a man mistake-proof. To err is human, they say. All well and good, but we're living in an age when mistakes can be inhuman—fatal, even. It pays to guard against them. And now give me something to drink. I'm parched.'

Baron von Hagen summoned his 'esteemed colleagues', as he called them, to the second ambassadorial conference of the day. Having turned out punctually and at full strength, they were now assembled in their usual place between the window and the lavatory door, expectant but a trifle uneasy.

'Gentlemen,' the Baron said gravely, 'there are one or two problems which would seem to merit our urgent consideration. I take it we all agree that we owe it to our own good name and that of the Foreign Service to abide by the truth?'

This was promptly confirmed by Herr von Kernitz-Weibel, late of Budapest. 'Of course. The widespread tendency to regard all internees as companions in adversity, irrespective of guilt or innocence, is a metaphysical aberration which, in the final analysis, yields no benefit—least of all to Germany.'

Ambassador von Weissänger, formerly of Bucharest, nodded emphatically. 'We are unanimous in rejecting any taint of suspicion. Not only are we guiltless; we were avowed and outspoken opponents of the regime. That is the point which we must ram home.'

'We haven't dissociated ourselves clearly enough from some of the more undesirable elements in this camp,' declared His Excellency, Herr von Wangenheim, erstwhile ambassador to Prague, Ankara and Sofia, in that order.'

'Is it to do with that man Hauser?' demanded Kernitz-Weibel. In response to a discreet nod from the Baron, he went on crisply, 'There's no reason whatsoever why we should shield certain individuals from the consequences of their own—hm, indiscretions. The SS and the Foreign Office belong to two different worlds. Failure to state our position with sufficient clarity would be not only suspect but dangerous.'

'I move that we define our position in detail,' said Herr von Weissänger. 'Certain distinctions have to be drawn. We must impress that on the American authorities at the earliest possible opportunity. We owe it to Germany—and ourselves, of course.'

Brigitte Hauser was sitting opposite Captain Keller in one of the side-rooms in the American officers' mess. A mess waiter had silently served coffee and left the room without so much as a nod from Keller. They had the place to themselves.

'I'd be glad to help you, Frau Hauser,' Keller said, pulling his heavy arm-chair a few inches nearer Brigitte's. 'The only thing is, I don't know what practical form my help would have to take—not yet, anyway.'

Brigitte Hauser put her cup down on the small table at her elbow. 'I'm grateful to you for taking an interest in my case at all, Captain. Somehow, I feel sure you'll find a way to help me. My courage is returning, thanks to you.'

'Let me think,' Keller said, drawing on his cigarette. 'In the first place, it would help you if your husband was cleared, but I can't clear him without prejudicing myself and the case against him.'

'Are you implying that he may be a war criminal?'

'He is one. I'm sure of it.'

'That's that, then,' Brigitte said bitterly. 'I can say good-bye to all my plans.'

Keller raised a restraining hand. 'There are other alternatives. You could always divorce him.'

'Yes, but it would take far too long. I'd lose any chance I might have had of acquiring the White Horse, and that would be the end of my little dream.'

She gazed at him with a mixture of hope and despair. He wanted something. Not her, or not only her—she could sense that. He wanted something else as well, but what?

Keller ground his cigarette out in the ash-tray. 'Well,' he said slowly, 'that doesn't exhaust the list of alternatives.'

'What else did you have in mind?'

'You could still get your permit even if your husband was

classified as a war criminal. We shouldn't find it too hard to come to some arrangement. I get the feeling we understand each other pretty well, you and I.'

Brigitte leant forward. Involuntarily, he dropped his gaze to the hollow between her breasts, then looked up quickly. He saw that she was breathing fast. She said softly, 'You'd really do that for me?'

Keller reached for another cigarette. 'It might be possible, under certain circumstances. I'm in command of the internment camp, but I can also influence anything to do with de-Nazification in this locality. The office which deals with these matters is only a few doors from my own, as you may know. I could virtually arrange what you have in mind with a stroke of the pen, so why shouldn't I?'

Without moving, Brigitte said, 'I'm grateful to you, if only for raising my hopes.'

'Whether or not I can fulfil them will depend on a number of things.'

'You can count on me in every respect. Tell me quite frankly, what must I do?'

Keller deliberately laid his cigarette aside. Brigitte could see that he had come to a decision, and it hadn't taken him long. That was what she liked about him—he knew exactly what he wanted. It made things easier. Dealing with him wasn't difficult, especially as she found him far from unattractive as a man.

'Tell me,' she repeated.

'You need a permit,' Keller said. 'All right, you can have one, but I want something in return.'

'What?'

'A platinum and ruby bracelet.'

Silence descended on the room, a long, oppressive silence. Brigitte slowly straightened in her chair, then sank back again. She said, 'Give me a cigarette.'

Keller opened his case and got up. He bent over her, resting one hand on the arm of her chair. She took a cigarette without looking at him, and he lit it for her.

Keller remained bending over her as she drew on the cigarette, hard. He shut his eyes for a moment as though trying to collect his thoughts. Then he said slowly,

'Am I to take it that your husband didn't give you a platinum and ruby bracelet? If not, can you at least tell me where it is?'

Brigitte looked up at him. To get a better view of his face she sank even deeper into the chair and—coincidentally, it seemed—spread her legs a little. That was temptation enough, at least for the moment. She was not going to give something for nothing.

Seeing her stretched out beneath him, Keller thought she looked magnificent—lovelier than many of the women he had known in the past. If it weren't for their business relationship he would fall hopelessly in love with her—he knew that for sure. Fortunately, the common sense on which he prided himself still prevailed.

'A strange idea of yours,' Brigitte said at last. 'Worth considering, though. Would you care to come and see me this evening? We could have a more detailed discussion—about that and other things. All right?'

'All right. Seven suit you?'

'Fine. About the permit, Captain—I think you can make the necessary arrangements in advance.'

Colonel Cord, the judge-advocate, reached Camp 7 at 1615 hours.

Sergeant Popper had been waiting for Cord in his capacity as provost-marshal with the main guard drawn up behind him. He advanced on the big limousine, saluted, and was privileged to shake the colonel's hand.

Meanwhile, the switchboard had quickly notified all interested parties. Waiting at the outer gate were Ted Harte, Keller, and Lieutenant Colman, Keller's deputy, who was only too happy to be left in total idleness and resented the intrusions of officialdom. The inner gate was manned by Reiter, the German commandant, and two camp policemen who acted as runners when required.

'What about a drink in my office, Colonel?' suggested Keller. 'I prescribe a B and B after a long drive like that.' Keller was a great believer in the restorative effects of brandy and Benedictine, a beverage which Cord knew and appreciated.

'Later,' said the colonel, looking round intently. 'Business before pleasure.'

'Just as you wish, Colonel,' Keller replied, and led the way to the inner gate.

'Another thing,' said Cord. 'I'm afraid I'll have to leave right after the inspection. We won't be able to have dinner together.'

'Sorry to hear that, Colonel,' Keller and Harte said simultaneously. They managed to keep a straight face, which was no mean feat in view of their delight at this welcome news.

'The General is expecting me this evening,' Cord explained.

'Sorry to hear that, Colonel,' Lieutenant Colman chimed in belatedly. Colman was more or less indifferent to what the colonel did. His sole ambition was a quiet life, and he normally fulfilled it in the bar of the officers' mess.

Reiter, waiting at the inner gate, came to attention.

'Internee Reiter,' Keller said by way of introduction, 'the German camp commandant.'

'Aha!' said Colonel Cord. He nodded graciously and waved his right hand in the region of his cap.

Reiter at once realized that this was meant to be a salute. He bowed—not too deeply because there were internees watching, but low enough to satisfy the colonel.

'Any complaints?' Cord asked in English. Keller interpreted with alacrity.

'The food is insufficient,' Reiter said bluntly.

Keller did not look at him. 'The rations could be more plentiful,' he translated.

'This isn't a recreation centre,' said Cord.

'This isn't a recreation centre,' Keller said in German.

Reiter grew bolder. 'There's a list of guard duty instructions posted up in the watch-towers which refers to internees as murderers.'

Keller translated. 'He wants to know if it's true that all internees are classified as murderers.'

Cord made an indignant gesture. 'That is complete and utter nonsense!'

Keller to Reiter, 'Cut the bullshit.'

Cord was angry. His bland face became empurpled and several beads of sweat appeared on his brow, though these might have been attributable to the heat. He set off down the main camp thoroughfare.

Harte caught hold of Reiter's sleeve and drew him aside. 'Be careful,' he said in a low voice. 'Don't forget, it usually pays to keep quiet.'

'But if I'm asked something?'

'If you're asked, answer the way you're expected to.'

Voices were raised in four-part song as the inspection party made its way between Blocks A and B. The colonel paused to listen, nodding with approval.

'I sang second bass at the military academy,' he said. 'Good basses were always in demand. Hear that? Those second basses aren't up to much.'

Sergeant Popper flashed a look at Reiter, Reiter nudged one of the camp policemen, and the camp policeman took off at the double. The tour of inspection proceeded, methodically and according to plan.

First came the sick-bay, where it just so happened that clean linen was being distributed, then a basement room where a Bible class was in progress, then a dormitory smelling of fresh wax polish.

'Not bad,' said Colonel Cord, 'not bad at all.'

'Would the Colonel care to visit the gymnasium?' inquired Popper. 'I'm trying out some new re-education methods there.'

Harte frowned at Keller, but Keller was politely concentrating on Cord. Lieutenant Colman strolled casually along behind, followed by Reiter.

In the gymnasium, Popper's troupe of performing generals was hard at work. All seven were busy cleaning windows in time to the strains of an accordion. Arthur Wammenberg, Hitler's ex-chef, was seated on a chair playing *Who's Afraid of the Big Bad Wolf?*

Popper explained the set-up with a touch of pride. The colonel looked impressed and asked to be introduced to the internees. One by one, carefully rehearsed by Popper in advance, they announced their name, rank, number, appointment, and political allegiance. e.g.,

'Reinhagen, Major-General, No. 2878, Chief of Staff—opposed to Hitler.' Or,

'Hassfurth, Lieutenant-General, No. 3127, Corps Commander—no view on the subject of Hitler.'

Cord seemed genuinely astonished. 'Quite remarkable,' he conceded, and hurried outside. Here he removed his cap and fanned copious quantities of fresh air into his lungs.

Then he said to Reiter, 'The impressions I have gained here today will have a bearing on the future treatment of internees.'

Keller's translation was, 'The internees will soon see what sort of impression they've made on the Colonel.'

Reiter remained rigidly at attention and stared after the party as it headed for the administration block, Cord in the lead flanked by Keller and Harte, Colman and Popper bringing up the rear.

Cord drew Harte aside with a fatherly air. 'You go on ahead, Frank,' he told Keller. 'Take the lieutenant and the sergeant with you. Ted and I have a couple of things to discuss.'

'Listen, Ted,' he said when they were alone. 'I don't have to tell you how highly we rate you at Dachau. You're one of our most efficient interrogators. In other words, we rely on you implicitly.'

'With all due respect, Colonel, come to the point.'

Cord gave an indulgent smile. 'We want a thorough job done, my boy, but we also want results. Time waits for no man, and neither does the war crimes tribunal.'

'I'm doing all I can, sir,' Harte replied curtly. 'However, working here is anything but a picnic. It's like wrestling in mud. Perhaps the worst feature is that I—I, of all people—have to protect Nazis who are guilty as hell but legally innocent. That's life, though. At the moment, I can't see the wood for the trees.'

Cord's smile became even more indulgent. 'My dear Ted, don't tell me you're going soft on us. We'll give you all the backing you need—you have my personal guarantee of that. Who's making difficulties? Keller? If so, tell me. A man like Keller wouldn't present any problem. If he's obstructing the course of justice, out he goes—on his ear. A substantiated report from you is all we need.'

Harte was surprised and incensed, but before he could get a word out the colonel had walked off and was on his way into the administration block.

Slowly, he and his entourage climbed the stairs. They processed down the corridor and entered the outer office. Here, Cord made a bee-line for Sylvia.

'You must be Fräulein Meiners,' he said, pumping her hand vigorously. He gave her a benevolent stare, then turned to Harte and Keller and said, 'You boys have mighty good taste, I'll say that!'

Sylvia smiled and the colonel emitted a booming laugh. 'Now hear this, little lady,' he said, putting an avuncular arm round her. 'It's good to see you here. People like you are at a premium these days. I hope you'll stay with us for a long time. If you have any problems, just phone me. Don't hesitate to call me any time.'

Keller had meanwhile concocted some of his notorious B and Bs. They raised their glasses, and Cord said, 'To the vital work you're doing here, my friends. I want you to know how proud I am of all your efforts. I know I expect a lot of you, but I also know you won't let me down.'

They drank in silence.

'Right,' said Cord. 'And now, I propose to have a few words with the Captain here. I'll see you other gentlemen again before I go.'

A minute later, Cord and Keller were alone.

'Listen, Frank,' Cord said in his most paternal tone, 'just exactly what are your problems here? What's the trouble?'

'Nothing we can't handle, sir,' Keller replied evasively.

'What's wrong, then? Who's throwing in the monkey wrench—Ted Harte?'

Keller hesitated. 'The material we have to deal with isn't easy—in fact it's extremely complex.'

'I know all that. I also know that your organization is first class, Frank—and I congratulate you. Nothing's perfect, of course. Sergeant Popper indulges in ridiculous little games, but he can afford to, with a lousy rich father and an uncle on the presidential staff. No, what worries me is the interrogation set-up. Harte and his team are half asleep. I need full documentation on Hauser, Frank, and I need it fast. That man has become a kind of key-figure. Once we've nailed him we'll be able to untangle a heap of cases.'

'We're doing our best,' Keller said. 'One thing I can promise you, Colonel: I'm going to make it my personal business to settle Hauser for good.'

'Do that, my boy,' Cord said heartily, clouting Keller hard on the shoulder. 'If you have any problems, just call me. Anyone who obstructs the course of justice gets slung out on his ear—and it doesn't matter if his name is Ted Harte. A substantiated report is all that's required.'

'Another B and B, sir?'
'With pleasure.'

The first of the outside working-parties returned to Camp 7 shortly after 1700 hours.

Only the so-called 'soft cases' were allowed to work outside camp. Among these were leaders of local farming associations, junior civil servants, heads of local Party branches, and service officers up to and including the rank of captain.

Outside duties provided a much-coveted change of scenery. For some weeks now, Reiter had been permitted to send out fatigue parties for the following purposes: street-cleaning, auxiliary duties with American units, and the repair of the ice stadium, once an arena for Olympic competitors but now the headquarters of a commissary unit.

All these occupations offered a reasonable prospect of bonuses in the form of extra food. The smuggling of letters was also possible despite strict checks and searches. The normal fee for this type of postal service was one midday ration. On special occasions, e.g. when the fatigue party was commanded by a small, wiry American corporal with the face of an ex-prize-fighter, the fee went up by half a bread ration. The technical term for this supplementary charge was 'danger money'. Each outside working-party transported ten or fifteen letters at a time.

The composition of working-parties varied almost daily. There were few exceptions to this rule, but one of them was the ex-local Group Leader of Immenstadt, Strauss by name and a holder of the Party's Gold Badge. He spent every afternoon cleaning the lavatories of the American officers' mess, where his work enjoyed universal esteem.

Strauss had recently been favoured with the friendship of Internee Laffrentz. Laffrentz felt drawn to Strauss because he kept his ear to the ground, was a man of wide experience, and had, on his own submission, built up a network of useful contacts.

It was now late afternoon, and Laffrentz was as usual waiting for the return of the outside working-parties. At long last the heavy trucks roared through the main gates and pulled up in the courtyard facing the administration block. There, an

American soldier called the roll and handed the internees over to the German camp commandant, who divided them into three groups according to their block of origin.

German camp police then escorted the internees along the road to the entrances which led to the inner courtyard of each barrack block. A final roll-call was taken before they were allowed to dismiss.

'Well,' said Laffrentz, 'how did it go, Strauss?'

Strauss gave him a confidential nod. 'Like clockwork.'

'I bet it did,' Laffrentz said, and gratified the Local Group Leader by patting him familiarly on the shoulder.

Strauss, a small emaciated man with a furrowed face and tortoise-like neck, prided himself on his friendship with Laffrentz, the senior civil servant who should really have been a first secretary, if not a minister.

'Did it pay off?' Laffrentz inquired.

'Of course,' said Strauss. 'I stashed away a dozen or more cigarette butts and two bars of soap today, not to mention a hundred sheets of paper for letters. I could ask a mark a sheet.'

'You deserve every pfennig, Strauss.'

'You'll get your cut, of course.'

'Forget it. Keep the stuff yourself.'

'No, go on—have some.'

'All right, Strauss, anything to please you. I wouldn't want to hurt your feelings.'

Strauss peered round cautiously. The yard was swarming with internees. 'Come inside,' he said. 'No need for everyone to see what we've got.'

More internees were standing around in the main corridor, so they retired to the latrines, which were almost always empty at this hour.

When they were facing the latrine wall, Strauss felt in his trouser-pocket and brought out a handful of butts. He also produced a few sheets of toilet paper.

'You really shouldn't,' said Laffrentz, grabbing them.

'Here, take this piece of soap too.'

Laffrentz took it. 'I won't forget this in a hurry, Strauss. You know what real friendship means. It's a rare commodity these days'

Otherwise engaged, they preserved a lengthy silence. Then Laffrentz said,

'How did things go apart from that?'

Strauss snorted. 'How do you think? Lots of activity as usual. I tell you, these Yanks live like the lords of creation. All they do is eat and drink—the whole lavatory was plastered with puke. And as for women! I'd like to see what goes on there at night, considering what happens in broad daylight.'

'Really?'

'I'm telling you!'

'German women, Strauss?'

'Of course, what do you think? It's like a cattle auction, I tell you.' He buttoned his fly and walked to the window. 'They practically stand in line—three or four to every American. Talk about a stampede!'

Laffrentz joined him at the window. 'You don't say! No dignity, eh?'

'Depraved bitches! They ought to have their heads shaved, the way they did after '14-'18, during the French Occupation. That was standard practice, so I've heard.'

'Of course. People still had a healthy sense of patriotism in those days. These modern women forget themselves in droves—they're scared stiff of not getting a man. The Allies took care of that by mowing down millions of our boys, and damned short-sighted they were. There'll come a day when they need us, and what happens then? How are they going to stamp out international Communism without our help?'

'Tell me something, Laffrentz. You know that big tall chap, the SS officer who bunks in your room?'

'Hauser, you mean?'

'If you say so—I don't know his name. Was that his wife, the woman who went by this morning?'

Laffrentz eyed the little man inquiringly. 'What woman?'

'She walked past on the other side of the wire. Hauser, or whatever his name is, stood there in a trance. Then she made some kind of signal to him and one of the Yanks fired into the ground.'

'What of it? That happens a couple of times a day.'

Strauss leant against the window-sill and stared down into the yard. 'But the woman—was she Hauser's wife?'

'No idea.'

'Pity,' said Strauss. 'I'd like to know for sure.'

'Why?'

'Well, I saw her again this afternoon.'

'You don't say? Squatting on one of your lavatories?'

'Of course not. She was in the officers' mess with a Yank, and not just any old Yank, either. It was Keller, no less.'

Laffrentz slowly stiffened. 'You actually saw Hauser's wife with Keller?'

'I told you—I don't know for sure, but it may have been.'

'What did she look like?'

Strauss thought hard. 'Difficult to say, really. All dolled up, and pretty expensively at that. Lots of make-up and red hair the colour of copper—looked like a high-class whore. Not what you'd call busty exactly, but well upholstered in the right places.'

'How did she behave?'

'How do you think she behaved? How do any of these whores behave? They were all alone in a sort of side-room, the two of them. Keller looked like the cat that swallowed the cream when he came into the lavatory afterwards. I tell you, it's a long time since I saw a man so pleased with himself. Who wouldn't be, with a woman built like that? Hey, Laffrentz, where are you off to?'

'Sorry, Strauss,' Laffrentz said hurriedly, 'I've got to pay a quick visit to Room 29. Urgent business.'

Lieutenant Colman, deputy camp commandant of Camp 7, took an exalted view of the world. He was at least six feet six inches tall. The car he was driving with his usual panache skidded sharply to a halt in front of the house.

Keller, who was sitting behind, said, 'Go get Gernsbach.'

When Gernsbach emerged a few minutes later he was surprised to find the captain ensconced in his official car, a gleaming and luxuriously appointed eight-cylinder Cadillac. The car was a tribute to Keller's excellent connections. Vehicles of this size were normally reserved for generals.

Keller opened the door invitingly. 'You must forgive me for spoiling your afternoon off, Herr Gernsbach. I need you in your capacity as head of the de-Nazification department.' He shook hands.

'Glad to be of service, Captain.'

Keller moved over and Gernsbach got in beside him. He realized that it was an honour to be allowed to sit in the car at all. Keller rarely consented to share it with anyone. The fact that he was doing so now, and doing so with such studied affability, must mean something. Gernsbach wondered how much the ride would cost.

'Okay, Colman.'

'Where to?' asked Colman, without turning round.

'Back to camp, of course.'

Sitting beside Keller, Gernsbach felt the American sink back against the soft upholstery. 'It's a source of regret to me that I see so little of you,' the Captain said amiably. 'We've hardly had a chance to get to know one another personally. It's a shame, but I imagine you're always busy, either at the office or in your studio.'

Gernsbach nodded. 'I miss out on a lot of things. It's time I made up for lost opportunities.'

The unevennesses of the road surface were almost imperceptible. The Cadillac simply absorbed them, transforming the road into an eiderdown.

'Anyway,' Keller said, 'I'm glad people like you still exist. They have rarity value, certainly in Germany today.'

Strange, thought Gernsbach. Keller, who generally confined himself to issuing orders, was making conversation. He never discussed his personal views or private life with anyone of junior rank, let alone a German. Gernsbach wondered why he was doing so now.

The car glided through the streets of the small town, heading for the camp. The Zugspitze stood out clearly against the shimmering summer sky, but only Gernsbach appeared to notice it.

'Do you know the White Horse, Herr Gernsbach?'

It was an abrupt and unmistakable return to their usual business relationship. Keller had once more become the man to whom Gernsbach's department was subordinated.

'Of course, Captain. The White Horse comes within my sphere of responsibility. Are you interested in it?'

'What sort of place is it?'

Gernsbach was obviously glad to be back on solid ground at last. 'The White Horse is the biggest and best hotel in town. It was "Aryanized" in 'thirty-six. The proprietor received compensation. My job is either to appoint a trustee or arrange a sale.'

'So the original owners are . . .' Keller made a graphic chopping motion with his right hand.

Gernsbach nodded. 'Dead—the old story. No traceable heirs, so we shall have to dispose of the place as we think fit, under present circumstances.'

'Any prospective purchasers?' asked Keller.

'Several, including two I could recommend. One of them . . .'

'It's all right, Herr Gernsbach,' Keller said with finality. 'I've already made a decision about the White Horse.'

Gernsbach seemed quite prepared to accept this. 'You have?' he said politely.

Keller raised his voice as though to drown the monotonous hum of the car. 'Yes. Kindly prepare a deed of sale or transfer —whatever you call it. The White Horse is to be handed over to its new proprietor right away, if not tomorrow, then within the next few days. I'm relying on you to arrange it. That's why I'm driving you to your office.'

'I understand,' replied Gernsbach. 'I'm at your service any time, Captain. It shouldn't take longer than a couple of days to carry out your wishes—I mean your instructions. Who is the new proprietor to be?'

'Frau Brigitte Hauser.'

Colman swung the car round a sharp bend. Keller slid gently towards Gernsbach, who sat there stiff as a ramrod.

Gernsbach said, 'You don't mean the wife of Manfred Hauser, the ex-SS regimental commander interned here?'

The car was now racing along the dead straight avenue which linked the town with the former barracks.

'Precisely,' replied Keller.

Gernsbach drew a deep breath. His right hand tightened on the grab-handle. After a pause, he said, very slowly and distinctly, 'I have to inform you, Captain, that it would be impossible for me to carry out your instructions. They not only conflict with military government regulations but infringe the dictates of common sense.'

The main gate was flung open and the car swept into the courtyard, where it drew up smoothly in front of the administration block. Colman switched off but continued to lounge behind the wheel.

Keller's voice broke the silence. 'You can leave questions of responsibility to me, Herr Gernsbach. I represent the military government here. The dictates of common sense, as you call them, don't enter into it.' Keller sounded wholly impersonal now, like someone issuing instructions through a megaphone.

He opened the car door. 'After you,' he said. 'Go to it, and remember I expect quick results.'

Gernsbach climbed out mechanically. He felt an impulse to tackle Keller again and state his arguments more clearly, but the American cut him short.

'This is a straightforward issue, Gernsbach. I know exactly what I'm doing. I'm in a better position to judge certain matters than you are, don't forget. I'm also in possession of certain facts which are quite unknown to you. Finally, not to beat about the bush, what I say goes around here. The responsibility rests with me.'

Keller pulled the car door shut and sat back. Gernsbach stood there forlornly for a moment, then took a hesitant step towards the car.

'By the way, Gernsbach,' Keller called, 'you really must try and have a bit more faith in us. We aren't here to make the Germans' dreams come true. You may have been a political prisoner, but that doesn't give you a monopoly on anti-Fascism, so don't think it does.' He turned to Colman. 'You can drive me home now, Lieutenant. I have to change.'

The Cadillac's engine came to life. Colman spun the wheel and the car shot out of the gate again like an arrow.

Helplessly, Gernsbach stared after the car and its occupants until they were engulfed by a plume of dust. Then he bowed his head as if he wanted to erase the picture.

The expanse of grass between Blocks B and C was barely half the size of a football field and divided into two equal sections by barbed wire.

This was where the internees strolled, sat, or lounged in small groups. Although sizeable in itself, the recreation area was hardly spacious enough for several hundred men. Consequently, traffic regulations were fairly strict. Sedentary souls sat in the corners, idlers lounged in the central area or along the sides, and those of a more active disposition strolled in a circle, clock-wise, like the audience at an open-air band concert.

The recreation ground was always packed during the pre-supper period. Crowds of internees surged across the trampled grass, shoulder to shoulder, chattering like starlings. It was an ideal transhipment point for rumours, a source of evening conversation, a stock exchange where the price of vague conjecture touched a new low every day: Hitler was still alive and had been convicted of mass murder; ministers would be treated as accomplices, generals as accessories. How could they safeguard their position? Who would help whom?

Laffrentz was disappointed to find Room 29 almost empty. Still in quest of Hauser, he emerged on to the narrow path leading to the recreation ground and surveyed the scene.

The first person he saw was Staff Lieutenant-Colonel Mangel, who was circling the dusty grass in conversation with Baron von Hagen. Behind them he caught sight of Wickler, and beside him Trost, erstwhile meteorological adviser to the High Command.

Mangel was saying, 'There can be no doubt that our military setbacks in Russia resulted from the inadequate development of lines of communication, in particular the railway network. The doubling of the railway construction battalions—as I personally recommended in a memorandum dated February 1940—would in itself have enabled us—with the aid of the indigenous population, of course—to convert all main lines to the German gauge and reconstruct them on a double-track basis as well.'

Baron von Hagen nodded. 'I doubt if sufficient reserves of manpower were available. We were, if I may so put it, biologically over-extended.'

'In other words,' interposed Wickler, 'we were done for even before the first shot was fired.'

'Meteorologically speaking,' said Trost, 'the Russians had an unfair advantage over us. They were inured to the cold.'

'In my considered opinion,' Mangel said, 'the root of all our troubles was a dual one: appallingly bad management and faulty judgment. The General Staff always acted as an executive body, never as the direct source of command which it should have been. If only the bloated Luftwaffe had been cut by a fifth or even a sixth, it would have enabled us to boost the performance of the communications network—particularly the railways—by almost a hundred per cent. And that, in my opinion, would have tipped the scales.'

Laffrentz hurriedly insinuated himself into the group. 'Does anyone know where Herr Hauser is?'

'No, but you'll probably find him beside the back fence. That seems to be his favourite spot these days.'

'What do you want with Hauser?' asked Wickler. 'Why don't you leave him be? The poor bastard looks completely deranged.'

'There are certain things he ought to know,' Laffrentz declared firmly. 'Friendship forbids me to keep the truth from him.'

'When you talk about friendship,' Wickler said, 'I get suspicious.'

Mangel left the procession of strollers, beckoning to the others to follow. They did so automatically. Laffrentz at once became the centre of an attentive circle of internees from Room 29.

'Gentlemen,' he said, 'however much of a burden they are, some responsibilities cannot be evaded.'

'Especially not when they give you a chance to make trouble,' said Wickler.

'It might be advisable if you gave us something concrete to go on,' suggested the Baron, 'some facts, Herr Laffrentz. Hints won't get us very far.'

Deep lines of sorrow etched themselves into Laffrentz's podgy face. He panted a little, like a man under great strain.

'I'm not happy about Hauser,' he said eventually. 'He's all tense and wound up—hasn't got himself fully under control. I find that disturbing, gentlemen. Most men in his position would feel desperate, but not in a way that might endanger others. Hauser's different. His kind don't give up so easily—they're hard as nails. Do you know what I'm scared of in his case? An act of desperation, that's what! He'll do something stupid and land us all in trouble.'

'And you believe you know why he's behaving in this way?' Mangel asked.

'It's clear as daylight,' Laffrentz said firmly. *'Cherchez la femme*, as usual. Women are capable of anything.'

'Kindly explain yourself.'

'There's nothing to explain. His wife is fooling around with the Yanks, that's all. A typical broken marriage—happens every day. It's all bound up with the stability of the dollar and the law of supply and demand.'

'I don't believe it,' Mangel said. 'I saw Hauser's wife this morning. She tried to contact him as she went by.'

Laffrentz waved this aside. 'I know. One of the guards supplied a bit of local colour by firing into the ground. She waved bye-bye and went off to join her Yankee boy-friend. And who do you think the lucky man is? I'll give you three guesses. No, gentlemen, you might as well give up. It's Captain Keller, no less. They've been seen together, and very friendly they looked. I have that on the authority of a reliable witness.'

'Better forget it as quickly as possible, Herr Laffrentz. It isn't a suitable topic of conversation.' Mangel started to turn away.

'Why should I forget it?' Laffrentz demanded. 'Keeping quiet would be a mistake. Our mutual friend Hauser needs to be told. He's all upset and uncertain at the moment. If we tell him the truth it'll calm him down.'

To everyone's surprise, Baron von Hagen appeared to accept this line of reasoning. 'If things really are as Herr Laffrentz says, and if conclusive proof exists, it might be better to acquaint Herr Hauser with the facts as tactfully as possible rather than conceal them from him. In my experience, procrastination and concealment can have disastrous repercussions. There is Herr Hauser, by the way. He's sunning himself in that corner over there.'

'Excellent,' said Laffrentz. 'Let's go and tell him.'

'Discreetly, though, if I may suggest. Delicacy is essential.'

'Leave it to me,' Laffrentz told the Baron. 'Delicate matters are a speciality of mine.'

He turned and elbowed his way through the dawdling throng, followed by the others.

Hauser was sitting on the ground with his craggy chin almost resting on his knees and his legs drawn up close to his body. His head jutted forward, his eyes were tight shut, his features rigid. He looked like a dead man.

Laffrentz stationed himself in front of Hauser flanked by the other inmates of Room 29. Finding himself suddenly in shadow, Hauser opened his eyes. He blinked a couple of times and closed them again, then opened them wide and surveyed the baggy-suited delegation with hostility.

'Are we disturbing you?' Laffrentz inquired.

'Yes.'

'We only wanted to tell you to stop worrying about your wife. There's no need.'

Hauser frowned. 'What's it got to do with you?'

'She's not worth it. The whole thing's finished—over and done with.'

Hauser rose to his full height, dwarfing the portly Laffrentz.

'What are you driving at?'

'These things happen.'

'What things?'

'You're making it difficult for us as well as yourself, Herr Hauser. After all, she's only human. She was seen this afternoon with Keller—Captain Keller. They're obviously on intimate terms, but that sort of thing happens all the time these days. It's more or less inevitable, isn't it?'

'Who are you talking about?'

'Your wife, of course.'

Hauser took a step forward so that he almost collided with Laffrentz's protruding paunch.

'I don't know what you're hinting,' he said, in a low, menacing voice, 'but my wife is my business. She's got nothing to do with you.'

'Easy, easy!' Laffrentz protested, retreating a step. 'We only wanted to help.'

'That's a laugh! Stop pestering me with your filthy gossip, Laffrentz. What the hell do you know about what goes on outside? You're a lousy stinking trouble-maker, like a lot of other people in here.'

Then, almost musingly, as though to comfort himself, he said, 'Maybe everything has to be this way. Who knows what's really behind it all—who can tell why these things happen?' Hauser turned his broad back on his fellow-internees and strode off through the crowd. He was quickly hidden from view.

'In my opinion, Laffrentz,' Wickler said, 'you're a fat, nosy, interfering pig—and that's putting it mildly.'

Sylvia Meiners generally finished work at about six o'clock. Her final job was to check whether any department was working later than usual. Keller always liked a report on the subject the following morning, complete with reasons.

The duty officer supplied her with the requisite information. All departments had signed off with the exception of 'Special Branch,' the de-Nazification department. Apparently, Herr Gernsbach was still at work on a special assignment.

Sylvia telephoned Gernsbach. 'Have you got much left to do? Perhaps you'd like to cancel this evening. Harte called me earlier—gave me an invitation from you. Is that right? Good, of course I'll come, as long as you promise to show me lots of your pictures.'

She replaced the receiver thoughtfully. Gernsbach sounded worried, but then the camp was a worrying place. She locked the filing-cabinets, covered her typewriter, and looked round the office. Everything was locked, just as regulations prescribed. The files had been safely tucked away for the night—a few dozen files for four thousand internees.

She went out into the passage. The rays of the setting sun fell softly on the whitewashed walls. With a sudden sense of oppression, she hurried down the passage and knocked on the door marked SPECIAL BRANCH—ROLF GERNSBACH. She walked in without waiting for a reply.

The room was bare of pictures and almost empty. Rough grey curtains flanked the windows. In one corner stood a safe, against the walls a massive filing-cabinet, and in the centre a desk, behind which Gernsbach was sitting. Sylvia sat down on the single chair facing him.

'What's the matter?' she asked. 'You look worn out. What's worrying you—please tell me.'

'Captain Keller has instructed me to hand over the White Horse to Frau Brigitte Hauser—Brigitte Hauser! Well, does that mean anything to you?'

Sylvia looked at Gernsbach. There was a touch of helplessness in his expression. It was an intelligent face, but full of doubt and melancholy. She wondered how anyone could have entrusted such an onerous job to a man of his type.

'Do you follow me, Sylvia?'

'I think so,' she replied.

'Then you'll realize that I can't go on. This is where I pull out.'

'Resign, you mean?'

'Yes, I can't see any alternative. It's pointless my continuing to work here under these circumstances.'

Sylvia glanced at the open filing-cabinet. The drawers were overflowing with papers. 'If you leave here, Herr Gernsbach, someone else will be put in your place—someone who'll supply Captain Keller with all the papers he wants and ask no questions.'

'Let him,' said Gernsbach. He pushed the White Horse file brusquely across the desk. 'He can take the responsibility for this kind of dirty work, that's the important thing. I know I can't.'

'What did you think this de-Nazification business would entail?' Sylvia asked. 'Did you imagine you'd simply have to sit behind a desk, stretch your legs and sign papers just like that—no fuss, no complications?'

'We're doing our level best, Sylvia, you know that. You also know the snags. Nazis are already bobbing to the surface again and we can't do anything to stop them. However, this directive from Keller has just about finished me off. Everything seems to be losing its point.' He looked full at her. 'Everything,' he repeated.

'You're tired now, but you can still put up a fight. Germany has an account to settle and we're the only ones who can do it. You can't expect the Americans to take the job off our hands or be more German-minded than we are. Anyway, Keller isn't America. You know exactly what you want. Go for it—in spite of Keller, if necessary.'

Gazing into her wide, unclouded eyes, Gernsbach found them even more attractive than before. He leaned across the desk.

'You've got a lot of character, Sylvia—a lot of courage, too, but there's one thing you mustn't overlook. Germany is down and out. We may have a chance—a slim one—but we're done for unless we can rely on outside help.'

'You're not done for, Rolf. Far from it. Everyone gets tired and wants to give up sometimes, but the feeling doesn't last. Anyway, do you know what Keller really has in mind?'

'His instructions seem plain enough to me.'

Sylvia looked down at the file on Gernsbach's desk. She put out a hand and rested it on the red cover. Gernsbach watched her slender fingers slowly push the file in his direction.

'You ought to discuss this with Ted Harte,' she said. 'Be absolutely frank with him. I have a feeling he may understand. Whatever happens, try to make your objection stick, even if it means antagonizing Keller. He isn't your last resort, after all. Are you going to let yourself be beaten by a woman like Frau Hauser?'

'You think Harte thinks the way you and I do?'

'I don't know,' she replied quickly. 'I honestly don't know, but it isn't beyond the bounds of possibility—not in this particular case. All the same, don't count on his support—he has enough on his mind as it is. We all have to solve our own problems in the end, I suppose.'

'Problems!' Gernsbach looked grim. 'Sometimes I feel we ought to solve them the drastic way.' He laid his hand on the file. 'Eliminate them—wipe them out!'

Sylvia smiled. 'Do you really see everything in black and white—yes or no, obey or die, love the Jews or hate them? You're wrong, Rolf. You can coax the truth out of people and trick them into behaving humanely.'

Evening roll-call took place at 1900 hours. It was a purely numerical check held in accordance with Standing Order No. 3 of 4 July 1945, one of the earliest regulations to be laid down.

The inmates of all three blocks were obliged to muster in the inner courtyards of their respective barracks by 1900 hours precisely, silent, at attention, and drawn up in squares of a hundred—ten men wide and ten men deep, three clear paces between each square. Perfect dressing was insisted on.

Parading by 1900 hours meant starting to turn out by 1830 at latest. No one could tell where the American in charge of roll-call—normally Sergeant Popper, the provost-marshal—would turn up first. The sequence varied almost daily. Popper generally began with Block A, but he might equally begin with

Block C. He had also been known to start with B and comb the sick-bay before moving on to the two remaining blocks.

If the sergeant was taking the count on his own, things tended to go quickly. If Lieutenant Colman was counting, anything could happen. Colman usually had all the time in the world to spare. He also had great staying-power.

Block seniors issued a warning order at approximately 1815 hours. The order was relayed via corridor seniors who functioned as company commanders, to their platoon commanders, or room seniors, and woe betide the room senior whose men had not vacated their quarters within eight or ten minutes.

Leaving the dormitory did not, however, mean going straight to the parade-ground. There was a general stampede for the latrines at this time, and long lines of fidgeting internees formed in front of the latrine walls.

Hauser, who had deliberately stationed himself just behind Laffrentz, said, 'Would you wait for me outside when you've finished?'

Laffrentz was more than a little surprised at Hauser's sudden familiarity. The significance of the request escaped him, but he nodded all the same and shuffled off to wait for Hauser outside the lavatory door. Internees streamed past him, clattering along the corridor through the swing-doors, and down the stairs to the courtyard. A moment later, Hauser appeared.

'Laffrentz,' he said, 'I know we've had a few misunderstandings in the past, but these things happen. No hard feelings?'

'Of course not,' Laffrentz replied magnanimously.

'That's my boy.' Hauser gladdened the civil servant's heart by falling into step beside him. 'What you told me earlier came as a shock. Don't get me wrong—it wasn't the news itself but the fact that everyone knows about it.'

'That's life,' said Laffrentz.

Hauser held the swing-doors open for him. 'Can you give me any details?'

'Details?' Laffrentz lingered over the word. 'I could, but I don't know if you could take it. I wouldn't want to put you under an unnecessary strain—it wouldn't be fair.'

'You're welcome to my bread ration tomorrow morning.'

'No, no, I couldn't accept it.'

'Why not? I never expect something for nothing.'

'Well, all right—if you can spare it.'

'I can.'

'In that case . . . After all, I don't see why I shouldn't do you a favour.'

They reached the courtyard, where the milling throng was arranging itself in orderly ranks ten deep. The room seniors reported to the corridor seniors and the corridor seniors conferred with the block senior. Heads were put together and well-thumbed sheets of paper covered with columns of figures.

Meanwhile, subordinate commanders were chivvying the block's thirteen hundred inmates into squares, ten men wide and ten deep. Laffrentz and Hauser stationed themselves side by side. Dressing was checked for accuracy in each direction until the courtyard finally contained thirteen complete and clearly defined squares, each of one hundred men, plus a fourteenth incomplete square.

'Well,' Hauser said in an undertone, 'how much do you know?'

'Everything,' Laffrentz replied with the complacency of the well-informed.

'How did you find out?'

'Connections.'

'American connections?'

'What do you think? I wouldn't ask a Yank for the time of day!'

Hauser squinted sideways at his fat informant. Laffrentz looked as if he was asleep on his feet, but he talked incessantly, pouring out a stream of innuendo, suspicions and suppositions. Hauser wondered how much he really knew about Brigitte.

'All right, that's enough!' called the block senior. 'The Americans are coming.'

A ripple of movement ran through the waiting ranks. Shoulders straightened and heads turned to check dressing for the last time.

'Parade,' came the shrill word of command, 'parade, 'shun!'

The internees had already brought their heels together. Now they drew themselves up. Knees were braced, chests slightly expanded, and fingers aligned with imaginary trouser-seams.

Lieutenant Colman sauntered up, followed by ABC, the orderly sergeant. Behind them came Reiter. Two American guards armed with tommy-guns escorted the procession as far as the gate, where they halted with their weapons at the port and their forefingers resting on the triggers, exactly in accordance with regulations.

At an almost imperceptible nod from Colman, Reiter approached the commander of Block C, who saluted with military precision.

'Obsequious swine!' whispered Laffrentz, meaning Reiter. 'He'll vanish up an American asshole if he doesn't watch out.'

'Block C,' the block senior reported, loud and clear. 'Thirteen hundred and seventy-eight internees: nine in sick-bay, three under arrest, one sick in quarters, thirteen hundred and sixty-five on parade.'

Reiter noted these figures down and compared them with the sergeant's list. While they were engaged in their calculations the block senior gave the order to stand at ease, coupled with the usual warning, 'Stand at ease doesn't mean permission to talk!'

'Self-important bastard,' Laffrentz whispered furiously. 'He needs demoting too.'

Colman toyed with his riding-crop and studied the barbed-wire fence with a complete absence of interest. He looked as if he might yawn prodigiously at any moment. The sergeant started to count heads.

'Stop,' Colman said sleepily. 'There's one man missing.'

'Sick in quarters, sir—high temperature.'

'Get him down here,' said Colman, glancing at his watch. He had plenty of time still. It was 1920 hours, and his girl-friend was not due to pick him up at the main entrance until 2000. He had a good forty minutes to kill.

Reiter shot an imperious glance at the block senior, who detailed two men to fetch the invalid. The other internees stood motionless.

'Looks as if he's trying to stir things up again,' Laffrentz said audibly.

'Silence in the ranks!' shouted the block senior.

It goes on for ever, brooded Hauser. He stared at the neck of the man in front of him, absently noting the irregular growth of unkempt hair, the wrinkled skin and greasy collar. His thoughts were focused on Brigitte. Like a neon sign, her name flashed through his brain again and again. What would she do? More important, what would she do for him?

The sick man was hauled across the yard and tacked on to the end of the fourteenth square. He stood there, head drooping and body swaying slightly, incapable of adopting the correct stance. His eyes glittered with fever and his fingers twitched convulsively, but he seemed to relish his martyrdom. More than a thousand fellow-internees and two Americans were watching him.

Making his way to the centre of the courtyard, Colman produced a slip of paper from his breast pocket, unfolded it, and began to read in a voice which carried to the farthest corner of the parade-ground.

'Standing Order issued by the Commandant, Camp 7:

As of now, internees are forbidden to approach the wire. The minimum permitted distance is three yards. Calling or signalling across the wire is also forbidden.

All guards have been instructed to shoot without warning if these regulations are contravened.

Signed: Keller, Captain, US Army'

Hauser felt a bitter, almost putrid taste come into his mouth, but put it down to the foul American food. Listening to the Lieutenant's proclamation with mounting excitement, he felt instinctively that the new order was aimed at him. It was not only a warning but a challenge.

Pride welled up inside him too. They took him seriously. He was someone! And Brigitte? Did it mean that she had achieved nothing, or that she had achieved nothing yet? Had the order been drafted before she could intervene in person? Probably.

'That's too much,' he muttered, half to himself but comparatively loud.

Laffrentz, ever happy to feed the flames, chimed in at once, 'An infernal liberty, like everything these bastards do!'

Colman cocked an eye in their direction and ambled over at once. He raised his riding-crop, pointed at Hauser, and said to Reiter, 'Take his name.'

Unfortunate, thought Reiter as he automatically pulled a notebook from his breast pocket—unfortunate that it had to be Hauser. It might make things extremely unpleasant for him, especially as the Americans were already showing intense interest in his record. He was glad not to be in Hauser's shoes.

Reiter opened the notebook and raised his pencil. As he did so his eyes fell on the fat and bloated figure of Hauser's immediate neighbour, Laffrentz—the impudent, malicious, underhand, scheming bastard who coveted his job.

Without stopping to think, Reiter yielded to a sudden impulse and wrote 'Laffrentz' in his notebook. Then he tore out the sheet and handed it to Colman.

Colman glanced at the name and said, 'Funny, I thought his name might be Mussolini.' He guffawed.

Everything would be all right as long as Colman left it at that, thought Reiter. His fears were almost groundless, in fact, because Colman never said more than the bare minimum and sometimes not even that. Laffrentz could kick up as much fuss as he liked in the commandant's office next morning. The Americans, who expected to be duped and deceived on principle, would undoubtedly believe the worst of him. And even if things went wrong, he, Reiter, could always say he'd made a mistake. It was easy enough to make a mistake, especially when someone waved a riding-crop and said, 'Take his name.'

Colman folded the slip of paper and put it in the left-hand breast pocket of his uniform jacket. 'Okay,' he said. 'See he reports to the commandant's office tomorrow morning.'

'That was the one romantic thing about the war, I suppose,' Sylvia said, pointing to the candles which Gernsbach had set out on his studio table. 'When they were burning in the living-room or the air-raid shelter they only lit up our immediate surroundings—our own little world.'

Ted Harte, who was lounging on the couch, sat up like a jack-in-the-box. He shook his head as he reached for the whisky bottle.

'Romantic! I can't bear the word any more, certainly not in connection with the war. I can't stand to see anything burning, either. Even a candle reminds me of the millions who went up in smoke. There were decent murderers, of course—I meet them every day. There was one who earned his victims' gratitude by closing the cell door quietly—very considerate of him. Be merciful, a Jewish mother cried to an SS man—kill me as well as my children. Being a merciful man, he did just that.'

Gernsbach carefully filled Harte's glass to the brim. 'You don't want to talk about art, romance, or war. What does that leave?'

With a sidelong glance at Gernsbach, Sylvia said, 'We could always talk shop.'

Gernsbach seized on this suggestion at once. 'Tell me, Harte, do you also regard de-Nazification as a private business venture?'

'If you think I'm going to do you the favour of asking why you said "also," Gernsbach, you're wrong,' Harte said. His tone was not especially friendly. 'Apart from that, my office hours are nine to five and you know where I work. I'm off duty at the moment.'

He took a slow pull at his tumbler of straight whisky, watching Gernsbach intently as he did so. It was almost as if he wanted to drown his mounting irritation.

'But Mr Harte,' Sylvia interposed, 'anyone is at liberty to express a private opinion on official matters.'

Harte put his glass down. 'Sure, but I'm not anyone—not here, anyway, and certainly not this evening.'

'All right, all right,' Gernsbach said soothingly. 'We quite understand. Let's talk about art instead.'

Harte laughed. 'What are you trying to do, Gernsbach—get rid of me? If you think three's a crowd, just say so. I suppose you'd prefer to have Sylvia to yourself. No, don't protest, Sylvia—why shouldn't he? I would myself, if I could.'

'Perhaps we'd better talk shop after all,' Sylvia said. 'It seems to be the safest topic of conversation.'

'In that case, I vote for art,' Harte said promptly.

'Art shouldn't be talked about,' Gernsbach said. 'Art should be created and admired, preferably in silence.'

'I admire Sylvia,' said Harte. 'I admire her obstinacy. That's the second time in five minutes she's tried to raise a subject I'm determined to avoid.'

'Why?' Sylvia demanded. 'Why do you avoid it?'

'That makes three tries,' Harte said calmly. 'All right, I'll tell you why: for the sake of convenience. You can call it cowardice, if you like, but I'm simply not interested in discussing matters which make me want to vomit. I'm opting out, do you understand? I'm tired—I need a rest.'

'I sympathize,' Gernsbach said. 'There are times when one

is overcome by a feeling of sheer panic. I often get it when I'm working on a picture—when I can't make up my mind whether there's one brush-stroke missing or one too many.'

'Precisely,' said Harte. 'Not knowing when to stop, not recognizing one's own limitations—being scared that the future may be worse than the present.'

The candles gave off a gentle light. It lay, shimmering softly, on the table-top, danced over the glasses, smoothed the lines from Gernsbach's face. Sylvia looked dreamy. Harte, lolling on the couch, was enveloped in gloom.

'What would you do,' Harte asked from the shadows, 'if you were granted a wish? Only one wish, though—a pipe-dream-come-true which would last a lifetime, stay with you for the rest of your days. Well?'

Gernsbach tried to read the expression on Harte's shadowy face, but it seemed to be wholly impassive. Sylvia stared into the candlelight, smiling.

'Would you have the courage to decide? Would you risk committing yourself?'

'Could one make a blanket wish?' Gernsbach asked eventually. 'I mean, artistic perfection, a pleasant life, success in politics—something along those lines?'

'You could,' Harte replied. There was a hint of a smile in his tone.

'Difficult,' Gernsbach said after a pause, 'very difficult. You'd have to give me time.'

'How much time? Four years, twelve years—the twelve-year duration of the Thousand-Year Reich?'

'No, much more. A lifetime.'

'What about you, Sylvia?' Harte asked. 'What would you choose?'

'Another human being.'

'Anyone in mind?'

Sylvia raised her head. Her eyes were wide and radiant. She looked first at Harte, whom she could only see in vague outline, then at Gernsbach. Her smile broadened. 'I thought we weren't going to talk shop,' she said.

Gernsbach started and Harte looked slightly taken aback. The two men exchanged a look of puzzled inquiry.

'That sounded like the fourth try,' Harte said at length. 'Why do you keep trying to steer the conversation in one direction?'

'Which direction would you prefer, Mr Harte?' Sylvia asked innocently.

'I'd prefer you to stop combining social chit-chat with official matters.'

'All right. I won't say another word, I promise you, but only on condition that you promise me something in return.'

'What's that?'

'That you get to the office half an hour early and have a talk with me—on an official matter.'

'All right, I promise. Anything for a peaceful night out. Tomorrow morning it is, but not another word about Yanks and Nazis, victors and vanquished, Jewish realism and German romanticism.'

Sylvia smiled at him. 'May I pour you another whisky?'

'As long as you're quiet about it. You're not only a persistent thinker—you can't keep your thoughts to yourself. There's a time and place for everything.'

'What I'm wondering at the moment,' she said, refilling his glass, 'is what Captain Keller would ask for if he had the opportunity.'

'Cut it out!' snapped Harte. 'That's the fifth try, Sylvia. Carry on like this and you'll find yourself out of a job. Don't start on Keller—not Keller, of all people! You must have developed a mighty soft spot for him if you can't forget him even when you're with us.'

'My father used to go bowling once a week,' Sylvia said. 'I'd go along and watch occasionally. You know how one pin can knock the rest down when it pitches the right way? Well, life has something in common with tenpins—that's what my father used to say. I'm beginning to think he's right.'

'Gentlemen,' Staff Lieutenant-Colonel Mangel announced loudly to his room-mates, 'this evening's guest speaker will be Professor Sperling, the eminent brain surgeon. He is said to have carried out live experiments on a handful of foreigners and Jews, that being the ostensible reason for his internment. I would remind you, however, that, as medical superintendent of the Clinic for Brain Surgery at Buch near Berlin,

Professor Sperling also operated on persons of the highest rank.'

Trost emitted a timid cough. 'They say he even operated on the Führer.'

'Now known as plain Hitler,' said Laffrentz.

'Adolf had a brain operation?' Wickler sounded highly sceptical. 'Out of the question—he hadn't got any grey matter to operate on.'

'Gentlemen,' Mangel said reprovingly, 'far be it from me to take up the cudgels on behalf of Herr Hitler, but I feel bound to point out that he was, for better or worse, our country's last head of State.'

'Last is right,' said Wickler. 'He was the bitter end.'

Mangel ignored this remark. 'Professor Sperling's lecture will officially commence at 2000 hours, which means, in practice, ten or fifteen minutes after that time. The site of the lecture will be the area around the large table. I assume that every gentleman in Room 29 will wish to attend.'

'Count me out,' called Laffrentz.

'Not interested,' said Hauser.

'I,' Wammenberg proudly proclaimed, 'have a prior engagement. Sergeant Popper has invited me to play my accordion in the American canteen this evening—a recital entitled "Folk Music from Many Lands".'

'Attendance at such lectures is purely voluntary, of course,' Mangel hastened to explain. 'On the other hand, I had hoped for a little more esprit de corps.'

'Me too,' Hauser growled belligerently.

'I'll be in my pit from 2000 hours onwards,' Laffrentz announced. 'If you've got any esprit de corps at all you'll let me sleep in peace.'

'What's all the fuss about, Laffrentz?' asked Wickler. 'Come to the lecture and you can sleep all you want. It'll be as good as a pill.'

'Although criticism of a guest speaker's lecture can hardly be prohibited,' Mangel said, 'it does seem rather arrogant to ram one's own prejudices down other people's throats. In any case, those gentlemen who do not wish to attend are requested to go for a walk or keep to the window alcove. Any conversations conducted there should be of moderate volume only.'

Laffrentz retired to the window alcove at once and waited

for Hauser to join him. He was smoking a small pipe. Carefully concealing the bowl in his hand, he inhaled the smoke with relish and blew it straight out of the window.

'What have you got in that pipe?' asked Wickler.

'Tea,' Laffrentz replied sullenly.

Wickler came closer, sniffing. 'Hm,' he said, 'seems a funny kind of tea to me. I've never smoked tea in my life, but I wouldn't mind trying some of yours.'

'None left,' growled Laffrentz. 'This is my last pipe of the day—just used up my ration.' Caustically, he added, 'You'd do better to listen to a lecture on brain disorders. You'll get more out of it.'

'Exhibitionism, that's all these lectures are,' the architect said firmly. 'I couldn't care less how many geniuses there are walking around in here, slavering for recognition. As far as I'm concerned, it's a waste of time.'

Lectures were the one great and enduring form of evening entertainment in camp. They were held in numerous rooms, and lecturers varied the scene of their performances nightly, like itinerant preachers. A former ambassador to the Balkans lectured on the diplomatic niceties of dealing with backward nations, a general specialized in Frederick the Great and the battle of Leuten in particular, a playwright expounded his version of *Faust*, a Gestapo man expatiated on murder in the furtherance of theft, an academic explained the subtleties of alliteration and the conventions observed by medieval poets.

'A load of hot air,' Laffrentz agreed contemptuously. 'I could give a lecture on the systematic breeding of racially superior children if I wanted to, but I don't. I've got better things to do.'

Professor Sperling, the eminent brain surgeon, entered the room. Sperling was a small man who looked as if he had spent a lifetime behind a desk. His jacket was frayed at the cuffs, his greasy collar two sizes too big for him, and his manner so jerky as to suggest that he was propelled by a series of brief but violent electric shocks administered at irregular intervals.

Mangel conducted Room 29's guest speaker to the place of honour, and one or two internees pulled up stools, chairs and benches.

Hauser stood beside his bunk, mechanically tidying his few

possessions. His face remained entirely without expression even when he caught sight of his wife's photograph peeping from between the folded blankets.

Hauser's impassive gaze rested briefly on the photograph, then travelled past the footboard of his bunk to the men round the table, who were waiting for the lecture to begin. Finally, he glanced at the window alcove, where Laffrentz was still puffing away at his alleged tea. The fat man was clearly ready to talk about Brigitte, but Hauser's enthusiasm had waned. He felt calmer now, and had done ever since the strange incident after evening roll-call. Reiter had buttonholed him and said, 'Don't worry about Colman. I naturally didn't take your name.' That was what he had said, word for word, before walking off with an enigmatic smile on his face.

Hauser weighed the possible reasons. What had induced Reiter to do such a thing? He obviously sensed that there were better times ahead for him, Hauser. Was Brigitte's influence taking effect? Brigitte, Keller, Reiter, Hauser—that was the sequence, or might be. Why should a cunning bastard like Reiter stick his neck out unless there was something in it for him?

'Gentlemen,' said Mangel, 'we welcome into our midst this evening a German scholar of the highest calibre: Professor Sperling, the authority on cerebral research.'

Nineteen heads nodded in unison, a gesture which Professor Sperling acknowledged with a grave little jerk of his own bird-like cranium.

'Thanks to his vital research,' Mangel continued, 'Professor Sperling's reputation now extends far beyond his own specialized field. His operations have earned him universal recognition. It is a special privilege and pleasure to be able to welcome him as our guest speaker tonight. Gentlemen, Professor Sperling!'

Hauser made his way quietly across the room to the window corner. Laffrentz winked amiably and proffered a small wallet.

'Have some tea?' he asked in an undertone.

Hauser nodded. Shaking a little tobacco on to a pre-cut sheet of newspaper, he began to roll himself a cigarette.

A reedy voice came from the direction of the table, 'The brain has been a passion of mine since childhood. As a boy I used to split open animals' skulls and examine the exposed interior. I thus familiarized myself with the basic structure of the brain at an early age.'

'Ah, brains,' mused Laffrentz, sucking at his pipe. 'Quite a delicacy, brains are, especially when they're fried.'

He forgot to blow the smoke out of the window. The scent of tobacco drifted across the room until it reached the nostrils of Wickler, who gave a resentful sniff.

'He's smoking like a chimney,' the architect said audibly. 'Not a trace of community spirit.'

The brain specialist produced a home-made diagram from his breast-pocket and spread it out on the table. 'The best way to acquaint oneself with the structure of the brain,' he piped, 'is to deep-freeze it and slice it into sections one-tenth of a millimetre thick.'

'You promised to give me some details,' Hauser said in a low voice.

'By all means,' Laffrentz replied promptly, 'by all means, if you feel strong enough. Better think it over first, though—in fact why not forget the whole business? Nothing lasts for ever. Women are like lavatory paper. You take them, use them, and throw them away. *C'est la vie.*'

'It may well happen,' pursued Professor Sperling, 'that only isolated parts of a brain continue to function. In fact, surgeons have succeeded not only in identifying individual centres but in de-activating them by artificial means. Exposed areas of the brain can be operated on virtually as required.'

Hauser shouldered Laffrentz into the corner. 'Tell me all you know. Don't keep anything from me, not even the smallest detail. It might be important.'

'All right, if you insist, but remember this: I'm giving you the facts. Don't blame me if you put the wrong construction on them.'

It was late the same night when Reiter called on his friend Mangel. He pressed half a bar of chocolate and two crumpled cigarettes into his hand and told him, confidentially, that he was worried.

The lieutenant-colonel could understand this. He was worried too—permanently worried. And no wonder, with things as they are.

Side by side, the two men strolled along the central corridor of Block C. As they were passing Room 29, Baron von Hagen emerged and joined them. He too was worried.

'That man Hauser is an unknown quantity,' observed Reiter.

'He always was,' the Baron said discreetly. 'They entrusted him with special missions in my area and in those of some of my colleagues. He carred them out, too—without our co-operation, needless to say. We even lodged protests, though mainly of an unofficial nature. You do understand, don't you? We could hardly be expected to risk our necks.'

Reiter understood. Mangel, who was endowed with a strong sense of fair play, showed equal understanding. 'Certainly not,' he agreed. 'People can't be held responsible for things which they never wanted and seldom knew anything about.'

The Baron turned to Reiter. 'Where Hauser is concerned,' he said, 'you can count on the limited support of my friends and myself. Like you, we regard him as a universal threat. It is our duty to avert that threat.'

'And Laffrentz?'

Mangel gave a tortured grunt. Reiter looked expectantly at the Baron, who said in measured tones, 'Herr Laffrentz, late of the Ministry for the Eastern Territories . . . A Party member with a career to match. Would you like us to take a closer look at his record, Herr Reiter?'

'It might be advisable, under the circumstances,' Reiter replied. 'I deplore the necessity, but we've no choice. It's a question of personal survival.'

Darkness enveloped the small mountain resort on whose outskirts Camp 7 stood. The snow-capped peak of the Zugspitze gleamed softly against the luminous purple of the night sky.

'I hope we don't run into the military police,' Sylvia said, just for something to say. 'It's way past curfew time.'

'No need to worry about that,' Harte replied. He leaned towards her a little and noticed that she did not move away. The streets of the small town were dark and deserted—not a glimmer of light anywhere. Snatches of jazz drifted to their ears from the American officers' mess. Somewhere in the distance a drunken American soldier bellowed, '*Komm mit, Baby —mak snell!*' His voice died away, to be followed by a woman's scream.

Harte laughed softly and laid his hand on Sylvia's arm. Again, there was no detectable movement on her part.

She said, 'What a glow there is in the sky!'

'That comes from the camp,' Harte said. 'Look over there, to the east. Twenty searchlights illuminating the barbed wire, each searchlight manned by a guard with a machine-gun, and four thousand internees vegetating in the middle—very romantic!'

They walked on slowly through the silent and deserted streets, hemmed in by narrow houses. Their footsteps reverberated through the gloom.

'It's all very strange,' Harte went on, 'especially the stillness. I don't know if you'll understand this, but nearly every night of my life seems to have been filled with noise. I've lived in big cities, camps, barracks—places where I was almost always surrounded by noisy people. War makes a barbarous din.'

'But the war has been over for months.'

'Officially, yes. That's what the papers say, but our kind of war can't be switched off from one day to the next. We'll feel the effects of it for the rest of our lives.'

'I can't believe it—everything inside me recoils at the thought. Nothing is totally pointless, however horrible. If we didn't believe that, how could we go on living?' She looked at him searchingly. 'Admit it, Ted—even you can find masses of ways of reconciling yourself to the present situation.'

'Like losing my temper, working too hard and drinking too much?'

'Why not give people the benefit of the doubt sometimes?' she asked gently.

Harte slipped his arm beneath hers, again without encountering resistance, and they walked on side by side.

'I've had a lousy life,' he said, 'thanks to Germany. I've used up my last reserves of strength, self-confidence and naïvety, and now I spend my time trying to be fair to licensed killers. It's enough to get anyone down.'

'You ought to put it out of your mind.'

'Just what I'd like to do.'

'But I'm no help?' she asked softly.

Harte's arm suddenly tightened on hers, drawing her close to him.

'I've forgotten how to treat women,' he said. 'I'm all right with cattle dealers and criminals—even soldiers. But women . . .'

'You'll never get me to believe that,' Sylvia said, almost gaily. 'A man like you was designed for women—I sensed that the first time I saw you.'

Harte stopped in his tracks. 'Don't talk nonsense or I'll end up by believing it myself—what with the starlight, my Jewish sentimentality and that bottle of whisky we drank at Gernsbach's. You're sticking your neck out, girl.'

'Maybe I want to—now, at this moment. Maybe I won't feel that way so quickly again.'

'Sylvia!' Harte gripped her hard by the shoulders and looked into her eyes. In spite of the darkness, he could see that they were wide and shining. 'What sort of person do you really think I am, Sylvia?'

'I don't know yet.' She tried to disengage herself.

Harte took his hands off her shoulders and stepped back. 'Don't give me any more encouragement,' he said awkwardly. 'You may regret it.'

Sylvia hesitated. 'That remains to be seen.'

He saw her move slowly towards him. Her hands came out, seeking his. Her face was very close now, so close that he could clearly see her tilted chin and full, slightly parted lips.

At that moment the darkness round them was annihilated by the beam of a spotlight mounted on a jeep parked in the side-street opposite. There was a bellow of laughter.

Harte and Sylvia started back, blinking helplessly in the glare. The laughter increased in volume.

'What the hell are you playing at?' Harte shouted, shielding Sylvia with his body.

The spotlight was dimmed and two tall figures approached. They were wearing white steel helmets.

'Military police,' Sylvia said dully.

One of the men walked up to Harte and said, 'Pass.'

The other grabbed Sylvia roughly by the arm. 'You come along with us.'

'Hold it!' Harte snapped. 'Let go of the lady at once.'

The military policemen glanced at each other and grinned. It was a familiar line. They heard it whenever they caught a fellow-soldier with a German prostitute, which was three or four times a night.

Sylvia made a violent effort to shake off the restraining hand on her arm. Harte went up to her captor, a fellow the size of a tree, and started to push him away.

'Easy, buddy,' the man said, raising his rubber truncheon. It was a cautionary sight. The MPs had their orders and wasted little time in carrying them out. Anyone who resisted got badly beaten.

Harte pulled out his pass. Having examined it laboriously by the light of a torch, the military policeman produced something akin to a salute and handed it back.

'Now let go of the lady,' Harte demanded.

'Sorry,' the man replied. 'We have our orders. All civilians have to observe curfew regulations. If they don't, they go to jail. In addition, civilians found in the company of members of the armed forces are obliged to undergo a medical examination. I'm sorry, but orders are orders.'

Sylvia's face was chalk-white in the beam of the dimmed spotlight. Harte said quickly, 'This young lady is Captain Keller's secretary. She works for the American authorities.'

One of the policemen laughed raucously. 'Sure, we saw her at work just now. Sorry, no exceptions.'

The other man's manner was considerably more polite. 'Do you have a pass, Fräulein?' he asked.

Sylvia shook her head. 'Not with me.'

'Then you'll have to come along—to the MP post, to begin with.'

Things sorted themselves out quickly at the military police post. The lieutenant on duty knew both Harte and Sylvia. He apologized to them with a knowing grin, bawled his men out, and offered his visitors a drink. Harte declined the invitation with thanks.

'No need to explain,' the lieutenant said, winking. 'Don't let me keep you.'

Outside in the silent street, they stood and looked at each other.

'I'll take you home now,' Harte said. 'No detours this time. I don't want you to go through that routine again. Come on.'

'It wasn't your fault,' she said.

'Yes, it was. All local military police regulations were submitted to me for approval. I approved them, including the one we sampled just now. How was I to know that you'd make me behave like a human being—me, behave like a man in this country?'

'You sound bitter, Ted.'

'I'm sick of it all.'

'But you're not prepared to do anything about it, not even if I help? I'd be quite ready to try.'

'Sleep well, Sylvia—if you still can. Try to forget everything that happened tonight.'

'Everything?'

'Good night, Sylvia.'

The night wore on.

It was a night whose hot and heavy breath enshrouded the soaring mountains and, in the valley beneath, the little town and the barracks now known as Camp 7—last stop for the élite of the Third Reich.

That night, the self-styled Pole called Slembeck sat at a table in the DP camp under the harsh light of a naked bulb. He had removed his jacket and rolled up his sleeves.

He and his companions—five 'Displaced Persons'—had been playing pontoon for hours. Eating, drinking, gambling and womanizing were the DPs' way of enjoying their American-sponsored freedom. They didn't want to return home yet, ostensibly for political reasons.

Slembeck was having a run of bad luck. He lost, lost, and lost again. The wad of crumpled notes in his trouser-pocket dwindled steadily, but still he went on gambling.

He took a card. It was an ace. 'A hundred,' he said, slapping a note on the table.

'Okay,' said the man opposite, a melancholy-looking individual with bleary eyes. He had lost everything—wife, children, money, property, health and hope—but he was only one among thousands. It was a comforting thought.

Slembeck glanced at his second card. It was a seven. 'Buy for a hundred,' he said, producing a second crumpled note. The third card turned out to be a queen, which put him back where he started. Eighteen points was a modest hand, but he decided to stick rather than risk going bust.

The mournful holder of the bank dealt with the other players, then turned his own cards up—a seven and a three. The next card was a king.

'Twenty,' he said, mournful as ever. 'Pay twenty-ones.'

Slembeck pushed his two hundred marks across the battered table. His luck had been bad lately, persistently bad, but it was going to change. What was more, he knew how to give it a nudge in the right direction.

Ted Harte was sitting up in bed, turning over the pages of a book. The bedside lamp cast a broad swathe of light on the brown and discoloured paper.

One of his few boyhood friends, Heinz Kroger, had shot himself in the head with a rifle in 1932 because he had lost the will to live. Beside him, soaked in blood, lay the book he had carried around with him during his last days—Ernst Wiechert's *Die blauen Schwingen*.

Now, almost thirteen years later, Ted Harte was beginning to understand his friend for the first time. Kroger had been like one of the characters in the book, someone who went through life with his head in the air even though he stumbled occasionally, someone who wore his heart on his sleeve until the day he lost it. Then someone trampled on it, and blood mingled with the dust.

'I can't go on living with these people,' Kroger had said, 'not with these people.' Only hours later he was dead. On one page of the book he had underlined the word 'yearning' three times, then crossed it out.

Harte laid *Die blauen Schwingen* aside and stared into space for a long time. These people, he thought—people whose very existence was a threat to life . . . Sylvia wasn't one of them, though—she couldn't be. Even if everyone in Germany was directly or indirectly guilty, there were a few exceptions: émigrés, political prisoners, the men and women of the Resistance, children . . .

Sylvia was a challenge, but where was she trying to lead him?

'That boy has got class,' declared Sergeant Popper.

He regarded Arthur Wammenberg with a growing benevolence. 'Hitler's Butler' was seated on a platform in the camp canteen with his accordion on his lap, radiating eagerness to please.

'Play your signature tune, Arthur!'

Marty Popper was surrounded by his cronies: Sergeant ABC on his right, the quarter-master sergeant on his left, and, in the background, the NCOs responsible for delousing, discipline, and detention—the *crème de la crème* of camp society.

Wammenberg launched into *Who's Afraid of the Big Bad Wolf*?

'He's terrific,' conceded ABC.

'You're telling me,' Popper said. 'We're going to break into the big time with Arthur. Nazi folk-songs from a sort of barber-shop quartet, a poet chanting hymns to Hitler—think of it, a genuine thoroughbred Nazi burlesque show! The boys'll pay good money to see it. We'll tour every base in the whole goddamned army. What do you say, Arthur?'

Wammenberg nodded vigorously. Words failed him—the prospects were too overwhelming. A vision took shape in his mind: cartons of cigarettes, tins of coffee and mountains of canned food, all piled up like the advertisements in *Life* Magazine. His mouth watered.

'Gentlemen,' he blurted out, 'you can rely on me—and a lot of others like me. We're all for burying the hatchet. Why, I know one or two people who've always had a weakness for America. Even the Führer . . .'

'Shut up, Arthur,' Popper said kindly. 'More music.'

Gernsbach could not sleep. His studio was still pervaded by a faint aroma of cigarettes and whisky—that and a trace of the perfume worn by Sylvia Meiners.

He threw back the bedclothes and got up. The candles were still in their original position on the table. He lit them and retired to his chair.

The couch where Harte had been sitting was deep in shadow. The chair with the curving back, where Sylvia had sat, was bathed in candlelight.

Her face seemed to hover in the room—the face of an inquisitive child and intelligent woman, not exceptionally vivacious but never immobile. Her big eyes were full of expression, simultaneously challenging and appealing, stimulating and soothing.

Gernsbach picked up his sketch-pad and began to draw

rapidly. Leaving a large blank area in the centre of the sheet, he shaded the edges heavily and added vignetted borders—spidery doodles which told of his doubt and uncertainty. Only then did he tackle the face—her face—but it eluded him just as everything seemed to elude him these days. He knew her face but he was incapable of conjuring it up on paper.

Despairingly, he tossed the pad aside and stared into the candlelight. His gaze travelled past the candles to the chair with the curved back, once warm from the touch of her but now empty.

There was emptiness all around him, an emptiness so complete that it threatened to drown him.

Their bodies were hot and slippery with sweat. Their hands roved tirelessly over each other's skin.

'What are you thinking about?' asked Frank Keller.

'Nothing,' Brigitte Hauser replied. Her voice sounded a little husky in the darkness. 'I don't have any ulterior motives, Frank, I promise you.'

'That's all right, then.'

'I'm only a woman, and sometimes that's all I want to be. Nothing else counts with me when I feel like that.'

'Does it happen often?'

'There haven't been many men in my life. I can't give myself to anyone—it isn't in my nature. I only lose my inhibitions when I'm really in love, and I'm in love now. I've proved that, haven't I?'

'You're unique,' he said, bending over her.

'This is only the beginning,' she told him. 'A good beginning.'

It promised to be another hot day. The sun climbed quickly, turning the mountains to molten metal. The lingering freshness of the night vanished from the streets of the little town.

The ring of searchlights around Camp 7 was switched off and a thin haze seemed to rise above the buildings like the steam from a thousand perspiring human bodies.

A new day began.

Sylvia stood in front of the mirror in her bedroom, putting the finishing touches to her appearance. She tucked a strand of hair behind her left ear to see if the change of style suited her, but decided that it exposed too much of her face.

There was a knock. Sylvia deftly restored her hairstyle to normal and called, 'Who is it?'

The door opened a fraction and the landlady's smiling full moon of a face appeared round the edge.

'There's someone waiting for you downstairs.'

'I won't be a minute.'

The landlady withdrew. Sylva continued to examine herself in the mirror. Then, obeying sudden impulse, she tucked the strand of hair behind her ear again. Was it all right? She smiled at herself and decided that it was.

Ted Harte was waiting outside the front door. His eyes lit up when he saw her. He took her hand and said, 'You've done something to your hair, Sylvia. It suits you.'

Sylvia felt baffled. Harte was unpredictable. She had expected anything—a vague apology, a friendly dig, a caustic remark, a provocative statement. Instead, he commented on her hair.

'This is a new departure,' she said.

'What, my noticing your hairstyle?'

'No, coming to pick me up.' Quickly, she added, 'I hope you won't make a habit of it.'

'Fräulein Meiners,' Harte said solemnly, 'I'm merely keeping my promise. We agreed last night to meet half an hour earlier than usual. You expressed a wish to speak to me on an official matter. Since you're generally in the office by eight-thirty, you must leave the house at about eight. That being so, I arrived half an hour before the usual time.'

'I meant your usual time, not mine.'

'You know perfectly well I never stick to a fixed schedule. I always act on impulse, and in this case my impulse was to set my clock by yours.'

'You had a good night's sleep from the sound of it.'

Harte feigned astonishment. Me—a good night's sleep? What makes you think so? Obviously, you've never heard about my debauched habits. I spent the whole night on the rampage, drinking whisky and making slanderous speeches. I mean, what else could I do after all those sermons I had to listen to at Gernsbach's?'

'I wouldn't put it past you.'

'You see, you do know me after all. You wouldn't put anything past me and I wouldn't put anything over on you—just the sort of unfair arrangement that would appeal to a woman!'

Sylvia was a little taken aback. Harte seemed to have forgotten all about the events of the night before, possibly because he wanted to. Even so, there was something reassuring about him—something which invited trust.

She said, 'Are you ever serious?'

'Yes, for my sins.'

The streets of the little town had not begun to stir. They were the streets of the night before, but everything looked different in the light of morning.

'Do you feel up to discussing something important?' Sylvia asked.

'I don't seem to have much choice. All right, fire away, but make it interesting. I'm not easily impressed.'

Harte walked along beside Sylvia, listening in silence. They had left the town behind and were heading for the internment camp. The long straight avenue stretched ahead of them, bordered at regular intervals by trees and benches.

All the benches were deserted but one, and on that one, as Harte perceived from far off, sat Slembeck. Slembeck was waiting, and Harte thought he knew why.

He slowed his steps. Then he said to Sylvia, who had been talking at him without a break, 'Why are you telling me all this? You must have a reason.'

'Can't you guess?'

He avoided her eye. 'Are you asking me to believe that your motives are pure and lofty, or do you admit that you're simply out for your own interests? If so, what are they? And in case you're wondering why I want to know, there's an easy answer. I can't forget, even for a moment, that we're in Germany.'

'Don't you trust me?'

Sylvia's gaze was direct, but he looked away. 'I distrust everyone in this country until I'm proved wrong,' he muttered.

'But your distrust doesn't extend to Captain Keller?' Sylvia's tone was gently sarcastic. 'Just because he's your boss?'

Harte did not reply at once. He stared at the solitary figure in the distance. As though to gain time, he said, 'Keller isn't really my boss. We work together, but the jobs we do are completely different.'

'Perhaps, but he takes over from you whenever he feels inclined.'

'Keller makes my work easier. I ought to be grateful to him for worrying about my spiritual salvation. Why should I object?'

'You don't object because you're too weak!' Sylvia spoke without thinking, dominated by a momentary urge to hurt him.

Harte stopped in his tracks and slowly turned to face her. Looking at him, she could not tell whether his expression was sad or derisive, weary or indifferent, patient or resigned.

'Weak?' he repeated, smiling at her. 'Why not? Weak, exhausted, uninterested, disgusted, revolted—take your pick. For months I've done nothing but try to pin crimes on other people. You think I enjoy that sort of thing? I used to deal in cattle, refrigerators and soap. Now I deal in filth. Who ever thinks of asking what we'd really like to do? It doesn't matter who or where we are, all we amount to is human flotsam bobbing around in a sea of blood and barbarity.'

Sylvia suddenly felt embarrassed and unsure of herself. She suspected that she had offended him deeply and forgot everything in her anxiety to show him how much she regretted it.

'Please forgive me, Ted.'

'There's nothing to forgive,' Harte said, 'on either side. I'm not a judge—I wouldn't even presume to sit in judgment on myself, though I think I'm pretty well qualified to do so. As for judging others, I feel less and less well-equipped to do that every day.'

He saw Slembeck bearing resolutely down on them.

'Look,' he said to Sylvia, 'the world is full of challenges. Here's one now.'

'Good morning,' Slembeck said. 'May I speak to you?' Receiving no answer, he added, 'It's about that man Hauser.'

'No,' Harte said flatly.

Slembeck refused to be shaken off. 'I'm sorry to bother you, Mr Harte—you too, Fräulein. Would you prefer me to wait until we're alone, Mr Harte?'

'Not at all. Fräulein Meiners works for us—she knows the case as well as I do.'

'Quite so,' said Slembeck. 'An important case.'

'Not to me.' Harte set off again with Sylvia on his right. After a moment's hesitation, Slembeck caught up and fell into step on his left. The man was clinging like a burr, Harte reflected. He clearly intended to start the ball rolling.

'Don't think I enjoy pestering you,' Slembeck insisted. 'It's no fun waltzing into your office twenty times for the sake of a few marks. You asked me to find some war criminals for you, and I did. Why haven't my statements been taken down in writing—signed, sealed and all the rest of it? Don't you think my evidence is important? If not, what is?'

'It isn't my job to put your statements on record, Slembeck—not any more. As to whether they're important or not, that's for Captain Keller to decide.'

Noticing that Slembeck was suitably thrown by this revelation, he came to a sudden halt. 'Well,' he demanded, 'do I look like Captain Keller?'

Slembeck could not find a suitable reply.

'Very well, then. Go and see Captain Keller. He's the man for you—just the man, in my opinion.'

Slembeck's furrowed brow betrayed mental exertion. His mouth opened a little and his eyes, normally bright and foxy, went blank and expressionless.

Harte was struck by a sudden idea. 'Tell me, Slembeck, what are you really after?' His hand came up and fastened on the man's coat collar. 'I think I know what you're after,' he said sharply. 'A platinum and ruby bracelet—isn't that it?'

Slembeck made a feeble attempt to free himself. He shook his head, glanced briefly at Sylvia, then looked back at Harte again. Harte's eyes were narrowed and two thin lines had appeared on either side of his mouth.

'I'm right, aren't I?' he said, almost triumphantly. 'It's the bracelet you're after.' He pushed Slembeck away.

Slembeck staggered back a few paces but stepped forward again immediately. 'All right,' he said, 'what if it is? I only want what's due to me. I want my property back.'

Harte started to laugh. 'What's that, Slembeck? Are you laying claim to a platinum bracelet?'

'Yes, I am,' Slembeck replied doggedly. 'The law's the law, and what belonged to me before belongs to me now. Otherwise what are you here for—not to protect Nazis, surely?'

Harte seemed to find the situation highly entertaining. He

laughed at Sylvia, who stared back at him uncomprehendingly, then at Slembeck, whose eyes had regained their sly, foxy expression.

'Congratulations, Slembeck. You've put your finger on it. This is a free-for-all, with everyone scrambling madly for a share of the loot and the American authorities playing pig-in-the-middle. Some people regard them as avengers of the dispossessed, others as shrewd businessmen working for the highest possible percentage.' He slapped his slightly bewildered victim on the shoulder. 'Tell Keller that, Slembeck—it'll tickle him to death. He'll welcome you with open arms.'

Slembeck deemed it advisable to try the respectable tack. 'My claim is justified, Mr Harte, believe me. You wouldn't try to do me down, would you? After all, who's more likely to be telling the truth—me or a Nazi?'

'I only know this much: there's something fishy about the whole business. If you want my advice, get lost before I start taking a closer interest in it—and you.'

Harte turned his back on the dumbfounded Pole and gripped Sylvia gently by the wrist. 'Come on,' he said, 'try and take my mind off things a little, even if you find it an effort.'

He set off in the direction of the camp, drawing her along with him.

'That's the way it goes, Sylvia,' he said thoughtfully. 'Opportunity knocks whenever times change or property changes hands. That man calls himself Slembeck, but if the bracelet really belonged to him his name would have to be Patocki. He talks about justice, but he's really talking about getting his hands on an article of value. What about you, Sylvia? You talk about justice and human rights, but what do you really mean? What do you understand by the words? Everyone's a prisoner of his own personality, even you.'

'I don't compare you with Keller. Why compare me with Slembeck?'

Harte's mood seemed to darken suddenly. He removed his hand from Sylvia's arm.

'Who are you really in love with?' he asked quietly. 'Me, because you show you trust me? Keller, because you're so obviously jealous of his red-headed girl-friend? Gernsbach, because you take his side all the time?'

'We're on the same side,' Sylvia replied. 'So are you,' she

added quickly. 'Leave principles out of it. All I want is a little decency and goodwill.'

'And you don't credit Keller with either?'

'I didn't say that. His objectives may be the same, but he uses some odd methods. Keep an eye on them—I beg you. You're the only person who can.'

'I will,' Harte said. 'I don't seem to have much choice. I'll speak to Gernsbach about it.'

'Right away?'

'If it's that urgent.'

'It is.'

'All right.' He shook his head ruefully. 'The things one does for the sake of friendship! It's an expensive commodity these days.'

'Gentlemen,' said Staff Lieutenant-Colonel Mangel, rising solemnly to his feet, 'I sincerely regret any inconvenience I may be causing, but I feel, on mature reflection, that it was imperative to invite you to this private exchange of views.'

The internees of Room 29, Block C, sat facing their elected room senior with an air of expectancy. Communal breakfast was over, and the room, which had been swept comparatively clean by the internee on duty, was charged with tension. The occasion was one of the general discussions which Mangel considered so essential to the welfare of his small community.

'Gentlemen,' Mangel reiterated, 'force of circumstance compels me to claim your attention for a few minutes, at the end of which time a decision will have to be made. Subject to your agreement, the purpose of our discussion will be to establish where—to put it mildly—mistakes have been made. We may even be forced to issue a stern reprimand to one of our roommates. Much as I deplore such a course of action, it seems unavoidable. I sincerely trust that you understand my position.'

Looking around, Mangel was relieved to see a circle of approving faces. Laffrentz actually called out 'You're right!'—a comment which seemed to puzzle Mangel for a moment but then elicited a faint smile.

'I can assume, then,' Mangel continued after a suitable pause, 'that I have your general approval.'

The internees looked grimly determined about something—quite what, they skilfully left in doubt. The Hitler Youth lieutenant said sharply, 'There are rotten apples in every barrel. One doesn't publicize them, though. It isn't in the interests of the community.'

These sentiments were vigorously applauded and debated. The only nonparticipant was Hauser, his nerves frayed by a sleepless night. He felt a violent tremor in his fingertips. This latest development must be aimed at him—he was convinced of it. Ever since the previous morning, or so it seemed to him, he had been a centre of attention, focus of attack, victim of circumstance. Everything that happened seemed to have a bearing on him.

Meanwhile, the internees were failing to reach agreement. They started to perspire. Their dominant urge was to remove their jackets, but they sensed that this sort of informality would not be consistent with serious debate.

'Gentlemen,' Mangel said, surveying his audience regretfully, 'you appear to find it impossible to reach a decision at this stage. I therefore suggest that we adjourn these proceedings until midday.'

One or two people nodded gravely. Trost said, 'I suppose you're right,' and the Hitler Youth lieutenant declared pompously, 'This sort of thing requires thorough consideration. Even the most trivial matters can affect the destiny of Germany.'

'I object!' cried Laffrentz. 'I've had enough of these crude delaying tactics. Why all this palaver? Why dodge the issue? Let's get at the truth! Nobody's afraid of the truth unless he's got a bad conscience.'

Jerked out of their twilight state, the internees stared at him in some dismay. It was surprising to hear Laffrentz champion the cause of righteousness so loudly.

Mangel was equally astonished. 'You insist?' he asked incredulously. 'You, of all people?'

'Of course,' said Laffrentz. 'Me, if anyone. My sense of value is still very much alive, thank you.'

Mangel sat down. 'Very well,' he said resolutely. 'Since the demand for clarification comes from you, Herr Laffrentz, I see no reason to prevaricate.' He adopted a sphinx-like pose, chin raised and forearms flat on the table.

'Gentlemen, the subject under discussion is our daily bread ration. As you all know, each internee is entitled to one hundred and twenty-five grammes. Every morning we are issued with a quantity sufficient for the twenty-two men accommodated in this room, or two and three-quarter loaves, each of one kilo. These loaves are regularly collected from the cellar and brought here by one of our number, namely, Herr Laffrentz. Subsequent distribution is supervised by me. Just recently, it struck me that corners had been broken off the loaves delivered to me. At first I attributed this to damage sustained in transit. However, my inquiries elicited the assurance that two complete loaves and three-quarters of a loaf, all completely intact, had been handed to our collector. This morning, having personally satisfied myself of the truth of this assertion, I again discovered that two corners were missing. How do you account for that, Herr Laffrentz?'

Laffrentz, who had grown extremely restive during Mangel's speech, started to wriggle in his chair. 'This is an outrage!' he protested.

'You can say that again,' Wickler agreed drily. 'Well, Laffrentz, did you or did you not filch the missing bread?'

'How dare you!' screamed Laffrentz. Red blotches appeared on his pendulous cheeks. 'I resent that deeply.'

'We resent it too,' Wickler replied with unruffled calm, 'just as deeply.'

Laffrentz started to bluster. 'How dare you! How dare you make unfounded allegations against me! This is a fine way to treat a friend. I insist on a fair hearing.'

Wickler grinned. 'The evidence must be half-digested by now.'

'This is a foul conspiracy,' trumpeted Laffrentz. 'A dirty trick, that's what it is. I won't stand for it. I don't care what happens, you're not going to pin anything on me.'

The door opened to reveal a sheep-faced policeman from the German camp commandant's office. He peered round the room, squinted at a slip of paper in his hand, and asked, 'Does Internee Laffrentz bunk here?'

'Yes,' replied Mangel.

'Internee Laffrentz,' the policeman announced importantly, 'is instructed to report to the administration block at 1000 hours. He will present himself at C Gate fifteen minutes before time and be escorted from there.'

'Yes, but why?' wailed Laffrentz. He suddenly felt as queasy as a land-lubber in a force ten gale. 'What am I supposed to have done this time?'

'Not a clue.' Duty done, the sheep-faced policeman folded his slip of paper and departed.

'Perhaps they're going to offer you a special appointment,' suggested Wickler. 'Either that, or they want a little chat about your trials and tribulations during the Hitler era. What an opportunity for you to present your case!'

The corridor in the administration block was agreeably cool, though its flagged floor magnified the sound of every footstep.

Harte encountered Gernsbach near the swing-doors leading to the stairs. The two halves swung to and fro, then came to rest. Gernsbach was carrying a slim bundle of files under his arm.

'Glad we bumped into each other,' Harte said. 'I have to speak to you.'

'Have to, or want to?'

'No question of wanting to in this case, my dear Gernsbach. I need some information, and I may as well tell you right away that my reasons are personal, not to say private. Will you give me some answers?'

Gernsbach smiled. 'Let's hear the questions first.'

They walked along the corridor to the administrative offices. Here, the flagstones were covered with a strip of green carpet.

'Herr Gernsbach,' Harte began, 'yesterday afternoon, if my information is correct, you were more or less officially instructed to draw up papers transferring the White Horse to Frau Hauser. Am I right?'

Gernsbach gave a tense little nod.

'Well, what have you done about it?'

'Nothing. Nothing would induce me to prepare the necessary documents.'

'You refuse?' Harte looked half-incredulous.

'Point blank,' said Gernsbach. He sounded as if his decision needed stating clearly, as much for his own benefit as anyone else's. 'I've thought it over, Mr Harte. Captain Keller has absolutely no right to insist on my complying with his order. In fact, everything in my files argues strongly against such a transaction.'

'Gernsbach,' Harte said gravely, 'have you considered what it might cost you to refuse?'

'My job as head of the Special Branch,' Gernsbach replied. 'However, I won't give it up without taking all the measures I consider necessary.'

'Measures, did you say? What sort of measures, Gernsbach? If there really were any, are you sure you could take them? We've already had to imprison tens of thousands of people in Germany. Nobody would notice if we added one more to the list. Don't you realize what it means, direct contravention of military government regulations? They could lock you up on those grounds before you could utter a word in your defence.'

'Captain Keller will think twice when he knows what I've decided to do. And if the worst comes to the worst—well, he doesn't have the final say.'

'Yes he does, Gernsbach, certainly where you're concerned. He appointed you and he can dismiss you without consulting higher authority. Don't be such an innocent, Gernsbach. You're up against an occupying power, not a constitutional government.'

'I don't care. I intend to keep my self-respect.'

'Self-respect isn't worth a dime when you're dealing with people who are stronger and more ruthless than you are. Self-respect only produces broken men and martyrs—one martyr to every million broken men, and only one martyr in ten acknowledged as such.'

It seemed to Harte as if the corridor in front of him had become infinitely extended, and there in the distance, scarcely recognizable, lay a shapeless bundle which had once been a human being. The name didn't matter—it could be Gernsbach, Harte or Hauser. Life-blood was seeping into the cracks in the floor.

'Measures, Gernsbach? Don't make me laugh! I went through a batch of files the other day—files on what our own troops did in the process of liberating this country. And all for the sake of rooting out undesirables—to use the official phrase.'

Harte knew that only one case in a hundred was ever recorded in writing. A few lines—that was all that remained of these excesses.

There was the German schoolmaster whose identity card

described him as a 'non-Christian theist'. They beat his theism out of him and—the record stressed this—knocked him down without hitting him below the belt. Then they kicked, hosed and slapped him until he declared himself converted to Christianity.

There was the gardener who had been unwise enough to call some prostitute a 'Yankee whore'. They came for him. Two hours later he was bowing, kissing the Yankee whore's hand, and spitting blood. He spent the next four weeks in hospital.

Then again, there was Corporal Copland of Camp 7—a nice cheerful youngster from Texas before the war got him in its clutches. The war had pursued Copland as if bent on proving that the world was full of filth and brutality. The invasion had barely been in progress for twenty-four hours when Copland spent a night under heavy bombardment in the company of a screaming woman who was bleeding to death in childbirth. Some drunken German soldier had apparently beaten her husband to death and then raped her. Only two days later, Copland saw his brother's stomach ripped open by a German grenade. He staggered three miles to the nearest dressing-station without realizing that the man on his back was a corpse. A week later Copland made love for the first time in his life. A counter-attack threw his company back, and when he next saw his French girl three days afterwards, she was lying dead in a barn. Later still, Copland had been present when the first concentration camp was liberated. What he saw there put the finishing touches to his education.

Finally, there was Ted Harte himself. He hardly dared to read his own score-card. His father: dead. His mother: dead of a broken heart. His sister: vanished without trace after serving in a forced labour camp. His uncle, the art expert: gassed. His best friend, the actor: a refugee in Vienna, then Czechoslovakia, then France, where he was arrested and deported to Auschwitz. His schoolmaster, a leading authority on the languages of the Near East: first committed to a forced labour camp, then employed as an adviser by the High Command, then—after the tide of war had turned—sent to work in the mines, and finally, by then classified as non-Aryan, shipped off to Poland, where he suffocated to death in an overloaded cattle-truck.

Gernsbach's voice broke in on his thoughts.

'People will come forward to testify on my behalf.'

'Don't talk crap, man,' Harte said indignantly. 'Testify? What for and who against? Do you really think anyone in the world today is panting to fall on Germany's neck in brotherly love? Are you an anti-Fascist? All right, Gernsbach, I accept that. I do, but a number of people would say that anti-Fascism is little more than a vogue—opportunism, more often than not. Give it a year or two and you'll have a job to find an anti-Fascist at all. As for people who'll testify on your behalf! Do you think they'll testify for you and against the top dogs—against the Kellers of this world? I know witnesses can be bought by the truck-load these days, but remember this: everyone around here has got more money than you, Gernsbach. They'll outbid you with ease.'

The visions that had tormented Harte were gone now. The long corridor stretched before him in sharp focus, bare and unadorned. He saw things as they were, and reality was seldom pleasant. People lied too much. Anyone who didn't lie ran the risk of being misunderstood, but to voice the ultimate truth about the world—just occasionally—might be the shock treatment Gernsbach so patently needed. The man didn't have enough strength to finish what he had started. He, Harte, might be stronger, but a trial of strength was not one of his intentions.

Outside, a jeep braked sharply.

'Who's going to speak up for you, Gernsbach—me? Why should I? I'll never oppose any action taken by the military authorities against a foreign national—you'd better resign yourself to that. These things may be regrettable, but war makes them unavoidable. As for Sylvia, she's only an employee. Keller can fire her whenever he likes. She may know what goes on around here but it's got nothing to do with her officially. That goes for you too, so you'd better trim your sails to the wind.'

Brisk, firm footsteps could be heard on the stairs. The double doors swung open and Keller appeared.

'Good morning!' he called as he hurried towards them, radiating vitality and good humour. 'How are you, Ted? Had a good night's sleep?'

'I never sleep well in Germany.'

Keller turned to Gernsbach.

'Just the man I wanted to see. How's that paperwork coming along? All ready? I need the stuff urgently, so bring it to my office right away.'

'It isn't ready, Captain.'

Keller came to an abrupt halt. The smile froze on his face. 'What do you mean?'

'The permits you asked for—I refuse to issue them.'

'You refuse?' Keller repeated, looking dumbfounded.

Harte cleared his throat. 'Herr Gernsbach has just been explaining the situation to me.'

'I see,' Keller said coldly. Then, with unmistakable menace, 'May I ask you to accompany me to my office, Herr Gernsbach?' He glared at Harte. 'What about you? What do you propose to do now?'

'I'll head for my office too, if you've no objection. I hope it doesn't bother you that we share the same premises.'

'Not in the least.'

'I'm not so sure,' retorted Harte. 'However, we'll soon see.'

Keller hesitated for a moment. 'I've a suggestion to make. What do you say we start the day in the canteen, the two of us? Herr Gernsbach can think it over for a while longer while we discuss a couple of things. Okay?'

Harte nodded. 'But don't be too optimistic. Our friend appears to be suffering from an attack of principles, and you don't cure those in a quarter of an hour.'

So far, at least, Sylvia could see the sun without feeling its heat, bask in the light of day without being reminded that daylight has terrors of its own.

Lieutenant Colman was the first person to enter the outer office that morning.

'Morning, Fräulein,' he said in a loud friendly voice. He paused just inside the door and looked round in a leisurely fashion. Then he jerked his thumb in the direction of Keller's office and said, 'Anyone at home?'

'The Captain isn't here yet.'

Three gargantuan strides took Colman to the place where he usually waited, an alcove furnished with two arm-chairs and a small table. He perched silently in the middle of the table and spread his lanky legs with an air of patient resignation.

Some time later the door leading to the corridor opened and

Keller came in, followed by Harte and Gernsbach. They all made for the commandant's office in obvious haste.

Colman slowly got to his feet, but Keller didn't even notice him. Sylvia picked up a bundle of files and was about to speak when Keller waved her aside.

'No interruptions, please,' he said, and disappeared into his office with Harte and Gernsbach in tow. The door clicked to behind them.

Unhurriedly, as ever, Colman resumed his seat. He gave Sylvia a meaningful wink and relapsed into bored silence.

The next person to enter the room was Brigitte Hauser, clad in a figure-hugging white linen dress. Her arms were as tanned as the firm flesh of her bare legs. She held her small, spirited head at a jaunty angle which emphasized her strong jaw-line.

Colman drew in his legs and slowly sat up. The grin on his face was frankly admiring.

Sylvia grasped the picture at once. Brigitte Hauser's self-assurance had turned into condescension overnight. From the look of her, she had gained her primary objective.

'I'd like to speak to Captain Keller.' Brigitte smiled across at Colman as she spoke—the quick, bright smile of someone very much in command.

Sylvia realized instinctively that the new situation lay right outside the scope of normal camp procedure. Brigitte Hauser enjoyed privileged status now—there was no doubt about that.

'I'm very sorry,' she said eventually. 'Captain Keller can't see anyone for the moment. He's in conference.'

Brigitte Hauser was shrewd enough to smile at the girl. She said, 'Then I'll wait for him.'

Lieutenant Colman started to get up, but Sylvia forestalled him. 'Would you mind waiting outside on the balcony?' she asked.

With a curt gesture of invitation, she led Brigitte across the corridor to a glass door. This she pushed open to reveal a spacious balcony which offered a view of the Zugspitze and the Olympic ski-jump.

Brigitte looked round, then walked over to the most comfortable deck-chair. 'I'm sure I shan't have long to wait,' she said with a smile.

Irritably, Sylvia returned to the outer office. Colman was now sprawled in one of the arm-chairs with his long legs at full stretch as usual. 'Some broad!' he said admiringly. He hauled himself slowly into a standing position, produced a piece of paper from his uniform jacket, and tossed it on to Sylvia's desk. 'For the commandant,' he said. 'Can't hang around any longer.'

When the barber reached Room 29 just before half-past nine, it was Laffrentz who stubbornly insisted on having his hair cut first.

He justified this demand by quoting his appointment with the American commandant—that 'swine of a prison governor'—and pointed out that he didn't know when he would be back. The barber might have moved on to another room by that time.

'Who knows?' Wickler said drily. 'You may not come back at all.'

Laffrentz subjected the architect to a threatening glare. Every vestige of friendliness vanished from his fat face.

Mitscher, the barber, had set up a stool near the window. 'Please bring a towel with you,' he called. 'A clean one, preferably.'

Laffrentz sat down ponderously, held up his off-white towel, and said, 'Nicely tapered, please, as usual.'

Mitscher, whose swift rise within the local ranks of the Party had surprised no one more than himself, smiled. His hairdresser's tact forbade him to point out that it was virtually impossible to carry out a perfect styling job on Laffrentz's balding pate.

Laffrentz settled his bulk on the stool and stared moodily into space. He felt a persistent pressure in the region of his stomach. It came from eating his bread too quickly that morning—he had crammed it down his throat in chunks instead of chewing it slowly. What appalling conditions these were! A man couldn't even eat his bread in peace. His so-called friends jealously watched his every movement, counted every mouthful he took. They were small-minded, unintelligent nobodies. If they only staked everything on helping him become German camp commandant they would be able to stuff their bellies full to bursting-point.

Laffrentz's grubby towel became dotted with snippets of hair. Head bowed, he surveyed his room-mates. They deliberately avoided his eye, but he consoled himself with the prospect of revenge. He'd make them pay! Nobody could cast suspicion on a man of his calibre and get away with it.

Take that hypocritical bastard Mangel, who sat there scribbling away at his railway lines like the personification of loyalty and integrity. The question was, loyalty to what and whom? Mangel probably smelled better days ahead. To think that he had the cheek to sit in judgment on everyone else when he always ladled the biggest lumps into his own bowl at meal-times!

The architect pulled up a stool and sat down beside him. 'You've no idea what they're trying to pin on you,' he whispered. 'All that fuss about the bread just now—that wasn't accidental, you know. It was part of a plan.'

Laffrentz looked sceptical. 'You think so?' he said dubiously.

'I know so. Mangel's pally with Reiter, and Reiter's no friend of yours—not that one can blame him. Know what they're doing, those two? Taking out insurance, that's what. If you start making trouble up in the commandant's office, they'll simply say you're suspected of stealing from your room-mates.'

Laffrentz was shaken by a spasm of fury. His stomach heaved and a red mist shrouded his eyes. Wherever he looked he saw filth, pure and unadulterated filth. The other internees seemed to be eyeing him balefully, like a troop of malevolent baboons.

'The deterioration of army departments which had been diluted with civilian personnel,' Mangel was just saying to Trost, who was listening intently, 'pales into insignificance beside the appalling inefficiency of the civil service, which was riddled by incompetent Party functionaries. If only more heed had been paid to my memorandum of 12 February 1943, in which I recommended that civilian ministries should be entrusted to experienced staff officers, and if only . . .'

Something snapped inside Laffrentz. 'If, if!' he screamed. 'If you weren't such a pathetic fool, Mangel, I'd have left my boot up your ass long ago!'

Silence descended on the stuffy room. Mangel struggled for words and Trost looked profoundly shocked. All activity ceased—even the busy chatter of the barber's scissors. Laffrentz's broad countenance registered satisfaction.

Mangel adopted a still more rigid pose. Then, forcing himself to speak with iron composure, he said quietly, 'Our fellow-internee, Senior Administrative Adviser Laffrentz, is noted neither for his tact nor his team spirit. We would all do well to bear that fact in mind.'

'Windbag!' shouted Laffrentz. 'How dare you cast aspersions on the civil service!'

'I was merely trying to explain . . .'

'. . . that you and your bone-headed army friends would have won the war if the home front had functioned better—in other words, us. You'll pay for that, Mangel!'

Mangel turned puce and mumbled something about a misunderstanding. The Hitler Youth lieutenant, supported by a usually taciturn regional Party commissioner and a racial purity expert, who happened to be visiting Room 29, took Laffrentz's part.

'Men,' the lieutenant said sharply, 'anyone who lets the side down deserves to suffer.'

'The future of Germany is at stake,' proclaimed the racial purity expert. 'It takes a crisis to sort the sheep from the goats.'

'But . . .' stammered Mangel. 'I only wanted to . . . I was misunderstood.'

'I also incline to that view,' the Baron said.

'Misunderstandings undermine solidarity,' said the Hitler Youth lieutenant, who tended to speak in slogans.

'I demand a proper hearing,' Mangel insisted, 'an inquiry.'

'Request granted!' called Laffrentz. 'We'll thrash this out just as soon as I get back.'

Murmurs of assent were heard. The temperature dropped rapidly, and a few moments later it was as if nothing out of the ordinary had occurred in Room 29.

Laffrentz rounded on the barber. 'What's the matter with you, Figaro? Gone to sleep, or do you always earn your extra rations by standing around in a daze? Get cracking, man—the commandant's expecting me.'

Mitscher, deeply offended by the snide designation 'Figaro', decided to avenge the insult after his own fashion. On either side of Internee Laffrentz's head—or thereabouts—he cut a number of the unsightly patches known among apprentices to the hairdressing trade as 'moth-holes.'

By so doing, he turned the senior administrative adviser into a comic figure—a transformation which was to have surprising results.

Captain Keller sat down behind his desk and waved Gernsbach into a chair with studied curtness. Harte leaned against the far wall, outwardly indifferent. The room was pleasantly cool, the atmosphere chilly.

Keller sat erect with his arms slightly bent and his palms flat on the desk. He looked like a beast about to pounce.

'Herr Gernsbach,' he said, striving to sound reasonable, 'you've now had half an hour to sort out your ideas. I'm prepared to forget what you said earlier. Either you hadn't thought things over properly or I misheard you. I'm ready to give you the benefit of the doubt.'

'I'm sorry,' Gernsbach said firmly. 'There's been no misunderstanding, Captain. I stand by my decision.'

The hands on the desk became fists. Keller forced himself to breathe evenly and avoided looking at Harte, though he sensed that the CIC officer was watching him closely.

'I have the highest regard for you, Herr Gernsbach,' he said coldly. 'That's why I should be genuinely sorry if you misunderstood me. You were given a job which presented you with an opportunity of righting wrongs committed by your fellow-countrymen in the past. You seem to forget that you owe that opportunity to the American military government.'

Keller paused for a moment and glanced briefly at his watch. Then he went on, 'Here, in this establishment, I represent the American military government and issue orders on its behalf. You have had a completely free hand until now. I would remind you that I have always approved your recommendations, not only because I agreed with them but because I had full and unqualified faith in you personally. But this is a special case. The decision that has to be made is mine alone, and I bear sole responsibility for it.'

Keller removed his hands from the desk-top and transferred them to the arms of his chair. Quietly, almost casually, he said, 'I therefore order you, Herr Gernsbach, to produce the necessary documents without further delay.'

Gernsbach sounded a little hoarse, but the determination in his voice was unmistakable. 'I cannot comply with your order, Captain. My conscience forbids me to.'

Keller stared straight ahead, his eyes seemingly focused on something in the far distance. Then he leant back in his chair and looked down at his hands.

'Very well,' he said evenly, after a short pause, 'I'll accept your reservations in spite of their personal bias. You have my permission to hand over the case. Someone else in your department can deal with it.'

'That doesn't change anything. The responsibility will still be mine.'

'I've already told you, Herr Gernsbach—I absolve you of all responsibility.'

'But I refuse to be absolved of my responsibilities.'

Keller adopted his announcer's voice, cold, remote, and totally detached. 'In that case, the military government will have to dispense with your services. You're relieved of your post. I'm dismissing you.'

'You can't do that.'

Keller clasped his hands together tightly. 'I see,' he said with sudden venom, 'so in your opinion I'm not at liberty to kick you out when I feel like it. Who the hell do you think you are, Gernsbach? You don't wield absolute power over the liberty and property of ex-Nazis. You're just a side-kick employed by the American forces of occupation—one among thousands. I'd only have to waggle my little finger to replace you.'

Harte, who was still lounging against the wall, said quietly, 'May I make a suggestion, Captain? Let's not rush things. We could all use a little more time for reflection, especially Gernsbach. Give him until noon—that ought to be long enough!'

Nobody answered, so he went on, 'All right, Gernsbach, we'll send for you in due course. Finish off your paperwork. If your answer is still no, you'll have to find plenty of convincing reasons for your refusal.'

Keller and Harte remained behind in the office. Silence reigned between them for a long time after Gernsbach's departure.

Keller went through the mail which Sylvia had laid out on his desk, watching Harte out of the corner of his eye.

'Well?' he said irritably. 'Why do you keep on playing for time? I've given that man enough rope as it is.'

Harte, who had gone to the window and was looking across at the mountains, said, 'My dear Keller, I didn't engineer this adjournment for Gernsbach's sake. He doesn't need it. You do.'

Keller glanced at a slip of paper he was holding and then replaced it on the pile of correspondence. 'Listen, Ted,' he said, man to man, 'I told you yesterday that I was taking sole charge of the Hauser case. Okay, I'll handle it, but in my own way and with all the resources at my disposal.'

Harte left his place at the window and walked over to Keller, collecting a chair on the way. He swung it in a gentle arc and deposited it close beside Keller's desk. Then he sat down, propped his elbows on the desk, and subjected Keller to an inquiring stare.

'I don't know what your motives are,' he said thoughtfully.

'Ah,' Keller replied. 'In that case, why criticize them?'

A look of weariness passed over Harte's face. He tried to smile but failed. 'Look at me, Keller—you think I'm a smart cookie, don't you—a smart Jewish cookie?' The half-smile turned into a broad grin, but there was something wry and tormented about it.

'A little over ten years ago, here in Germany, I was a tattered bundle of flesh, blood and bones. They beat me to a pulp and told me to kneel in front of a piece of bunting—a flag, they called it. When I refused they carried on beating me until I went down on my knees anyway. They called me a Jewish pig and told me to shout Heil Hitler, but I wouldn't. At the time, I suppose I thought it was braver or more dignified not to, but I was wrong: it was sheer suicide. I only realized that when the blood was pouring out of my mouth, nose and ears. After that I did as I was told. I shouted Heil Hitler over and over again—just as loudly and often as they wanted me to.'

Keller shook his head as though trying to clear it of this distasteful picture. 'What are you driving at, Ted? What's the inference?'

'There isn't any. I'd just like you to spare an occasional thought for what I've told you. Why use old methods to found a new age for the people of tomorrow? It's paradoxical.'

'You're wrong! Our job is to bring the people of yesterday to justice, if necessary by applying the methods of yesterday.'

Having spoken, Keller sat back as if physical distance would help to establish the personal dissociation he craved. 'Know your trouble, Ted?' he said. 'You're hamstrung by your past.'

Harte slid forward on his elbows until he was as near Keller as before. 'Can you tell at a glance whether someone belongs to yesterday or today? Is everyone in this camp really so guilty that he has to be treated like a criminal? Can you weigh guilt like a bag of candy? Is a woman who appears to have a completely clean record bound to be innocent as a new-born baby?'

'Of course they're criminals!' Keller snapped. 'Hauser is, that's for sure.'

'Ah!' Harte exclaimed quickly. 'So that's why his wife gets preferential treatment.'

'Hauser and his wife are two different people. She isn't like him.'

'Maybe, maybe not, but any favours done to Hauser's wife may benefit Hauser himself, if not immediately, then certainly in the long term. This could just be the thin end of the wedge. Anyway, why pick on the Hauser woman? There are masses of more deserving cases.'

Keller, who felt that he had gained the upper hand at last, gave a fleeting, slightly sarcastic smile. 'What if I can assure you that Frau Hauser has earned her preferential treatment?'

'Earned it?' Harte retorted belligerently. An angry glint came into his eyes. 'How? By sleeping with you? Well, I suppose that's one way of buying a hotel.'

Keller turned pale. 'You've no right to make filthy insinuations like that,' he said in a harsh voice.

Harte recoiled. He sensed that he had gone too far, but it only intensified his anger. Rising abruptly, he said, 'That woman is corrupting you. You ought to get rid of her.'

'What if I'm in love with her?' Keller asked quietly.

'You call that love? Anyway, where does the White Horse come into this? Just a token of your undying affection, is that it?'

Keller did his best to smile. 'What do you know about my plans?'

'Listen, Frank,' Harte said, 'I'm not given to moralizing and I'm pretty sure I've come up against most sides of human nature, but your line of argument leaves me cold. I'm getting worried about you and what this chaotic country is doing to you. If you want a piece of friendly advice, stop playing with fire. Germany is like a mass grave. People fall into it and nobody even notices.'

Keller smiled. Harte's abnormal and almost obsessive earnestness gave him a feeling of superiority. 'Don't worry, Ted. I know exactly what I want.'

'Possibly, but do you know what other people want out of you?'

'Let me worry about that. My objectives are quite specific, even if they're lost on you, and I'm going after them in my own way. This is my case, don't forget. You handed it over to me, so it's no concern of yours any more.'

Keller seemed determined to end the conversation. He picked up the slip of paper lying on top of his mail. 'A report from Colman,' he said. 'An internee named Laffrentz behaved insubordinately during roll-call yesterday evening. Deal with him for me. That's all.'

'Keller,' Harte said, taking a step towards him. 'I beg you in all seriousness to think it over again—carefully.'

'I see no reason to,' Keller replied. 'As far as I'm concerned, the matter's closed.'

'Boys,' Sergeant Popper proclaimed confidently, 'You're heading for the big time. I've already got five dates lined up. The US Army is crazy to see you in action.'

Heading the concert party on the gymnasium stage was Arthur Wammenberg with his accordion. Beside him stood Otto Faust, the SA poet, and behind him a male voice quartet consisting of an operatic tenor, a Party dignitary, a Gestapo inspector, and a State Theatre actor from Munich named Wagner.

'Once more from the beginning!' exhorted Popper.

He had brought along a captive audience in the shape of his twelve German generals, who squatted on their stools, watching the performance with due solemnity. A supply of cigarettes helped to keep them in the right mood, and seven of them greeted every number with obedient applause.

The quartet opened with *You're Driving Me Crazy*, after which Wammenberg played and sang *Who's Afraid of the Big Bad Wolf*? three times in succession.

Wammenberg then embarked on his first group of Hitler stories, e.g., 'It's a lie that he used to bite the carpet. He only bit genuine Astrakhan rugs, and they weren't always available. It's also a lie that he only changed his pants once every seven days. He changed them regularly once a week, usually after his Sunday bath, though I couldn't check on that personally during the last few months. That shows you what a Spartan life he led.'

Next came Otto Faust, whom Wammenberg had recommended for inclusion in his select band of performers in return for an agent's fee of fifty per cent. The SA bard stepped forward and recited a panegyric dedicated to the Führer.

'Lead us on to glorious heights,
Thou who dwellest in our hearts
And art our one true faith,
Thou, the elect of God.'

'Terrific!' Popper exclaimed delightedly. He gave his twelve generals a nod and nine of them applauded.

Sylvia Meiners was checking the daily reports submitted by subordinate departments. These consisted mainly of dull-looking columns of figures relating to US Army personnel, detainees, and supplies. Another file was reserved for the written records of interrogations and investigations. Keller liked these to be submitted neatly arranged but without comment. However, it was one of Sylvia's jobs to go through the columns of figures carefully, check them against the average which Keller had worked out in advance, and notify him at once of any abnormal discrepancies. Although deviations from the norm were not easy to detect, it struck Sylvia that the returns from the supply department had remained constant for several weeks. Obviously, someone was operating a racket of some kind. She wondered whether to draw Keller's attention to it.

The door to the corridor slowly opened and Slembeck sidled in with a sly grin on his face.

'Is the Captain in?'

'Yes.'

'Can I have a word with him?'

'Not at the moment. He's busy.'

'When will he be free?'

'I've no idea.'

Slembeck's manner became insolent. 'Look, Fräulein, I'm not here because I want something. Your bosses want something out of me, got it?'

'I'll naturally inform the Captain that you called.'

'What do you mean, called?' Slembeck thrust his hands deep into his trousers pockets. 'I'm here, Fräulein, and I'm staying. Where can I wait?'

'Not here, anyway,' Sylvia said. 'This is a private office, not a public waiting-room. There are confidential papers lying around in here.'

'All right,' Slembeck replied sullenly. 'Where do you suggest, then?'

'Go and wait where you always wait—downstairs in the guard-room.'

Slembeck flounced out, sulking. He felt sore. These long-haired bitches opened their legs all night and their mouths all day. And his kind? Articles of merchandise, that was all. Fair enough, why shouldn't he sell himself if the price was right?

Harte emerged from the commandant's office. He paused for a moment and grinned across at Sylvia—a slightly wry grin, she thought. 'Lovely firm we work for,' he said, obviously just for something to say.

Sylvia sensed that he was angry and trying to cloak his anger in sarcasm. If only the gleam of irony would vanish from his eyes just once, she thought, the emotions he constantly strove to conceal would come to the surface. She couldn't bring herself to believe that anyone could be as unemotional as he pretended to be.

'Where's that man Colman?' Harte asked.

'I expect he's in the gym.'

Harte's grin broadened. 'Ah, so he's undergoing cultural indoctrination from Popper, is he? I must take a look. I'll probably need a large Scotch afterwards, so you'd better take a note of my schedule: first the gymnasium, then the officers' mess, the table in the left-hand corner of the bar—either at it or under it.'

'Don't you have anything better to do?'

Harte waved the question aside, noticing as he did so that he had a slip of paper in his hand.

'Quite right, I'd forgotten about this. Internee Laffrentz of Block C has to report to me. Phone Reiter and tell him to get the man taken straight to the gym.'

'Is that all?' Sylvia pleaded. 'Are you really going to duck out?'

'I'm merely bowing to higher intelligence, senior rank and better connections.'

'But Frau Hauser is here already. She's waiting for the Captain.'

Harte paused in the doorway. 'Where?' he asked.

'On the balcony, enjoying the view.'

'Very appropriate,' said Harte. With an edge to his voice, he added, 'Surely you don't begrudge our beloved commandant his little pleasures? Do you know what some people might call that, Sylvia? Sour grapes, and they don't suit you.'

'When are you going to stop treating the world like a children's playground?'

Harte turned the handle of the door leading to the corridor. 'Maybe when I get the feeling that someone loves me.'

'But love isn't a one-sided thing, Ted. It takes two people to make it work.'

'Exactly, that's just what I meant. Think it over some time.' Harte almost slammed the door behind him in his hurry to get out of the room.

Sylvia stared at the closed door. She could still see Harte's slightly stooping figure, his shrewd face with its almost invariably sardonic expression, his melancholy eyes and the fine lines round the corners of his mouth.

Keller came out of his office, radiating the sort of self-assurance which springs from contentment. 'Anything special, Fräulein Meiners?' he inquired.

'Frau Hauser is waiting outside on the balcony.'

'Good. Anything else?'

'Herr Slembeck would like a word with you.'

'Fine, I need him, but not for the moment. Was there something else?'

'No, Captain, nothing urgent or important—just routine matters.'

'All the better. Apart from Slembeck, I shall want to see Gernsbach and the German camp commandant—Internee

Hauser, too. Postpone the rest of my schedule and keep everyone else off my back. I don't want any interruptions today.'

'Gentlemen,' Baron von Hagen announced in a subdued voice, 'in view of certain confidential information received by Lieutenant-Colonel Mangel from the German camp commandant, it seems imperative that we should reach a decision.'

'What decision?' demanded His Excellency, Ambassador von Weissänger. 'We are, of course, prepared to conform with Herr Reiter's suggestions in principle. He enjoys our trust, though present circumstances forbid one to trust anyone unreservedly.'

This particular ambassadorial conference had been convened at short notice. The participants did not seem unprepared, however. They not only knew the subject but had discussed it thoroughly among themselves.

Kernitz-Weibel of Budapest, once known as a successful gentleman rider, still retained much of the youthful élan which he had always been prudent enough to curb. He said, 'We must lay our cards on the table, gentlemen—the situation demands it. Further silence on our part might be misconstrued, and that could be dangerous.'

Baron von Hagen bowed his handsome grey head and folded his hands in an attitude of prayer. 'Men like Hauser merit our sympathy,' he said. 'Men like Laffrentz merit our understanding. Personally, I balk at passing judgment on them in a way which might have far-reaching and, from our point of view, quite unintentional repercussions.'

'None of us would wish to do that.' The Foreign Office expert on diplomatic co-ordination in occupied territories, Herr Axel-Albrecht von der Lanken, usually a man of few words, stared mournfully at the ground. 'As I see it, however, all that is required of us in this instance is to try, by virtue of our special knowledge, to shed light on certain facts which would inevitably come to light in the long run.'

Ambassador von Weissänger cleared his throat. 'Senior Administrative Adviser Laffrentz of the Ministry for the Eastern Territories may have been a thoroughly conscientious civil servant—we must concede that. Unfortunately for him, he got tangled up in the cogs of government. He did what I always declined to do—you too, gentlemen, I feel sure. He signed, initialled, or caused his department to transmit, movement orders relating to the racial purification programme—in other words, to the extermination of our Jewish brethren.'

Von Weissänger paused for effect, then went on, 'We took violent exception to such policies at the time and registered vigorous protests among ourselves. Are we now to give the impression that we sanctioned them in silence?'

All present nodded gravely. The lengthy hush that ensued was broken by someone who expressed what they were all thinking:

'We ought to let the Americans know, with all due discretion, that we are not averse to collaborating with them on a basis of mutual trust. After all, the future of Europe—indeed, the Western world—is at stake.'

Brigitte Hauser heard steps approaching the balcony door. She drew a deep breath, forced herself to look relaxed, and closed her eyes. This was the moment to present an alluring picture.

Keller went over to her. She slowly opened her eyes and smiled at him, then held out her hand. The smile was tender and the gesture childlike—artfully confiding and sweetly mischievous.

'How are you?' Keller asked.

'Fine, and you?'

'Never better.'

He pulled up a chair and sat down close beside her. His fingers gently fondled the nape of her neck.

'How do you feel now?' he said, leaning over her.

'Better than ever.'

His fingertips slid upwards through her silky hair. She shut her eyes and opened her mouth a little—just far enough to reveal her gleaming teeth and the tip of the tongue that glided delicately over them. She breathed deeply, and the rise and fall of her breasts seemed to invite his touch. He bent lower over her and brushed her lips lightly with his.

The countryside sweltered in the sultry morning air. The sky was becoming glassy and the mountains were enveloped in a tremulous heat-haze. The fields beyond the barbed wire looked bleached and faded, but the surrounding peaks—Zugspitze, Wetterstein and Waxenstein—had the genteel beauty of a picture postcard.

Keller drew away from her, breathing hard. His face glistened with sweat.

'Shall we get down to business?' he asked.

'That's why I'm here.'

She sat up and tidied her hair with a series of deft, rapid movements. Her eyes sought his.

'I'm sorry to disappoint you, Frank, but I haven't got the bracelet.'

Keller felt as if someone had dealt him an unexpected blow in the solar plexus, but he retained his composure with an effort.

'Why not?' he asked.

'It was hidden, as I told you yesterday. I went to fetch it from its hiding-place this morning but it wasn't there any more.'

'Stolen?'

'I doubt it. My guess is that he hid it somewhere else just before your people took him into custody.'

Keller sat back in his deck-chair. 'This creates an entirely new situation, doesn't it? I suppose you'll be wanting to speak to your husband now.'

Brigitte swung round abruptly. She rested her elbows on the arm of her chair and leant towards him. 'It's the last thing I want, Frank. I've got nothing to say to him—in fact I wouldn't mind if I never saw him again. Don't blame me if that sounds hard—blame yourself. I don't seem to have any alternative, though. I'll just have to speak to him—unless, of course, you've lost interest in the bracelet.'

'No,' he said quickly. 'The bracelet was part of our bargain.'

Brigitte leant ever farther towards him. 'You still insist on having it?'

'Of course,' he replied firmly. 'You didn't think I'd ditch our agreement just because of last night, did you?'

Brigitte's eyes narrowed and her lips became a hard line. She slowly drew away from him. 'I didn't hear that remark.'

'I'm sorry—I didn't mean it like that. Please try to understand.'

'It's all right.'

'No,' Keller said fiercely, 'it's not all right. What happened between us had nothing to do with what we discussed earlier. I need that bracelet.'

'Won't you tell me your reasons?'

She gazed over the edge of the balcony, past the mountains and into the hazy blue sky. She heard laughter in the distance, then the sound of a jeep starting up. The engine coughed a couple of times and burst into throbbing life. Brigitte could also hear, coming from the direction of the gymnasium, the strains of a male voice quartet extolling the merits of wine, women and song. She could hear nothing of the man beside her, not even the sound of his breathing.

'You don't trust me much,' she said eventually.

'The bracelet and my—my love for you are two completely different things. You've got to believe me, Brigitte. I beg you to.'

He didn't move, but Brigitte had the feeling that he had drawn closer to her again.

She said quickly, 'I haven't the slightest desire to speak to my husband—not after all that's happened between us, Frank—but I will if you insist. I don't see how else you're going to get hold of that bracelet.'

Keller hesitated. 'Neither do I.'

'Will I be left on my own with him?'

'Hardly.'

'But he won't give anything away in front of an outsider. You know how he is. He's suspicious as hell.'

Keller tore his eyes away from her and looked down at the heavy pre-cast slabs that formed the balcony floor—massive blocks of concrete capable of withstanding anything but a direct hit.

'So you think you could persuade him to tell you how to get hold of the bracelet?'

'Yes, but only if I speak to him alone.'

'And that's your only motive?'

'What else?'

'I want to trust you, Brigitte, but it isn't easy.'

'Will you tell me one thing?' she asked. Without waiting for an answer, she went on, 'If you manage to get your hands on the bracelet, will it have any effect on my husband's case? What I mean is, if the bracelet did turn up, could he be convicted on the strength of that alone? Please be honest.'

Keller got up and walked to the edge of the balcony. He stared down into the forecourt. A few of his men were sitting in the sun, playing cards with Slembeck. Turning round, he leant against the balustrade and looked at Brigitte. Her lovely face was as smooth, sleek and inscrutable as ever.

'So you're still in love with him,' he said. 'You want to protect him.'

Brigitte shook her head almost imperceptibly. She seemed genuinely distressed.

'You know who I'm in love with, Frank. I just don't want to add to his troubles.'

'His case is quite straightforward,' Keller said firmly. 'The bracelet won't make any real difference, I promise you.'

'Why do you set so much store by it, then? I wondered about that for ages, Frank. I can't banish the idea that I might be supplying you with a vital piece of evidence. I may not love Manfred but I don't want to put a noose round his neck.'

This shaft went home. To disguise the fact, Keller turned away again and rested both hands on the railing. He wondered how to dispel her suspicions, what had to happen before he got his hands on the bracelet—what he had to do to convince her.

He stared down into the courtyard. The GIs were still being initiated into forbidden games of chance by Slembeck. Of course, that was it! Slembeck was the answer to all his problems.

'I don't need any tangible evidence, Brigitte,' he said, turning to face her again. 'I've got a witness whose testimony will be quite enough to convict your husband.'

'You mean that?'

'I'll introduce him if you like. Have a talk with him. That ought to set your mind at rest.'

'I'd like that, Frank. I want to be absolutely clear in my mind before I speak to my husband.'

'And I want you to feel that what really matters is you and me. Everything else is secondary—bracelets and hotels included. After all, we both know what we want, don't we?'

'Yes,' she replied with a radiant smile, 'we both know what we want.'

Ambition had caught up with Lieutenant Colman at last—a fact which infinitely surprised all who knew him. Even Sergeant Popper, who thought himself shockproof, found it hard to believe his eyes and ears. Colman cherished cultural pretensions.

What had provoked this was the provost-marshal's plan for a Third Reich concert-party, which had quickly earned widespread popularity among the local troops. Colman, too, had heard them perform.

'Not bad, not bad at all,' he said in a slightly condescending tone. 'Not exactly edifying, though—no re-educational value.'

Popper bridled. 'Anyone who doesn't feel re-educated after hearing my boys in action is beyond help.'

'I was thinking on a more international scale.'

'You don't say!' Popper looked genuinely astonished. 'I didn't know you had it in you, Lieutenant.'

'I may not look it,' Colman retorted, 'but I'm a goddamned musical person. You want culture? Okay, I'll give you some.'

And that was how Gershwin came to Camp 7. The gymnasium soon rang to the strains of *Rhapsody in Blue*, arranged for four hands and interpreted by internees whom Colman had recruited with Reiter's assistance and placed under his artistic direction. The prelude to this new venture was a protracted audition.

It had not been unduly difficult to round up a number of self-styled artists, and after combing the canteen premises of the former school of mountain warfare, Colman had managed to find two decrepit uprights. The pianists selected to belabour them were Internees Hügler and Flöte, the one a librettist and leading member of the Reich Chamber of Music, the other a talented amateur whose playing was said to have enthralled the inmates of several concentration camps. Precisely what had induced them to covet political laurels as well as artistic acclaim, neither man could quite remember.

'Tickle the ivories, boys!' Colman adjured them.

The lieutenant considered himself musical to the core. His sister owned an extensive record collection and he had been to three performances at the Metropolitan Opera, including two of *Rigoletto*. He didn't even object to Wagner, and dismissed Hitler's predilection for him as an unfounded rumour. Colman admired everything that his pocket encyclopedia termed genius.

He sent for music by the German classical composers, most of whom, he discovered, began with the letter B. Scores by leading American composers followed, notably Gershwin. The latter's music struck him as particularly suitable for performance on two pianos, one playing the solo part and the other standing in for the orchestra.

Colman had to tread carefully here. It was soon borne in on him that artists were goddamned touchy and goddamned ambitious. Before long, the two internees were wrangling bitterly over the distribution of labour, each convinced that he was better qualified to take the solo part.

Colman grinned suddenly as an idea struck him. He commanded each competitor to play a test piece in turn and listened intently, trying to decide which man played loudest. The loudest player got the orchestral part. It was a judgment worthy of the late King Solomon.

Harte sauntered up to Colman from the back of the hall and sat down beside him. 'Are they making music or just going through the motions?' he inquired.

Colman looked hurt. 'That's Gershwin,' he explained.

'Never mind,' Harte said indulgently.

Colman not only resented the interruption but felt that he had been deliberately misunderstood. He said, 'You can't be very musical.'

'Maybe not.'

'Hard luck.' Colman's toes tapped the floor in time to the music. 'Know what's missing here?' he asked eventually. 'The goddamned clarinet cadenza.'

'The what?' Harte raised his eyebrows.

'It's no good without the goddamned clarinet cadenza.'

Colman went on to explain that Paul Whiteman's definitive rendering of *Rhapsody in Blue* was specially noted for its introductory clarinet cadenza.

Harte, who felt an almost irrepressible urge to yawn whenever Colman took himself seriously, was bored to tears by the lieutenant's long-winded exposition. He withdrew discreetly and strolled back the way he had come. The long hall was in shadow, but the heat of the day beat down on its wooden roof. A fine layer of dust adhered to the whitewashed walls, and the paint on the steel beams had peeled off in places, revealing rich brown patches of rust. The notes of Gershwin's *Rhapsody* cascaded from the rafters.

The glass door at the back of the gymnasium opened and a member of the German camp police appeared. He was followed by a short stout internee who came bouncing across the threshold like a rubber ball.

Ah, thought Harte, my victim! He leaned against the wall and waited for the two men to form up in front of him.

The camp policeman snapped to attention. 'Internee Laffrentz, Block C, reporting as instructed,' he announced. His voice resembled the hoarse whirr of a clockwork motor.

'Very well,' Harte said. 'You may go.'

The camp policeman turned about, parade-ground fashion.

'Hey!' called Harte. 'I said you could go. I didn't order you to dismiss.'

'Yessir,' barked the policeman. He marched off in high dudgeon, marvelling at this latest example of American barbarity.

Turning to Laffrentz, Harte found himself looking into a jowly face and a pair of quick, darting eyes. The man resembled a giant hamster. His girth did not seem to have been reduced by months of internment. Since the camp was anything but a health farm, this revealed a talent for survival and a measure of ingenuity.

Suddenly, Harte's face broke into a broad grin. Laffrentz, standing sloppily at attention, scented goodwill. His little eyes widened and their sparkle intensified. His last traces of subservience swiftly vanished as it dawned on him that Harte might not be such a bad fellow after all.

What Laffrentz did not realize was that Harte's grin was directed at the 'moth-holes' that so conspicuously adorned his head. Put Laffrentz out in the rain or under a shower, Harte reflected, and the little man would look like an over-fed Dalmatian. In the nude, he would have made an admirable model for Rubens or Goya.

'Well,' said Harte, suppressing his amusement with difficulty, 'and what have you been up to?'

'Nothing,' Laffrentz assured him innocently. 'At least,' he hastened to add, 'nothing I know of.'

'You mean your presence here is a big mistake?'

'I didn't say that,' Laffrentz replied, eager to please. 'However, I strongly suspect so.'

Harte chuckled. 'So do I.'

Laffrentz told himself with relief that his luck had not run out. Harte promised to be easy meat.

'So you've no idea why you're here?'

'None at all. I'm not aware of having done anything wrong, really I'm not. Someone must have got his wires crossed.'

Harte couldn't understand why the commandant's office should have been bothered with an internee who had been fidgeting or whispering in the rear rank. The case was probably quite trivial—something to be dealt with summarily. The thought of aggravating Colman's thirst for Scotch by making unmusical remarks appealed to him far more.

'What exactly happened at evening roll-call, Laffrentz?'

'At roll-call? What makes you ask? What is supposed to have happened?'

Laffrentz was genuinely surprised. He had examined several dozen possibilities during the past hour, dredged his muddy conscience repeatedly and brought a lot of silt to the surface, but he would never have hit on evening roll-call—never. He heaved a sigh of relief, and an expression of sublime innocence settled on his fat face.

Harte immediately sensed that his reaction was authentic. Perhaps the whole thing really was a mistake.

'I see,' he said, determined to settle the matter in double quick time. 'You definitely deny having spoken on parade?'

'Certainly I do,' Laffrentz replied with conviction. 'Who-ever it was, it wasn't me.'

Harte stuffed the slip of paper into his pocket. The case was straightforward enough, but what was he supposed to do with Laffrentz—kick him in the pants, put him in solitary, enter a black mark on his conduct sheet? He contemplated depriving him of a few days' bread ration but dismissed the idea as ridiculous. The man was a walking advertisement for the high standard of camp cuisine.

'I see,' Harte said again.

Instinct told Laffrentz that he was out of immediate danger. 'No,' he repeated, unbidden, 'it certainly wasn't me. I expect they got me mixed up with Internee Hauser.'

Harte, who had turned to go, stood rooted to the spot. 'What did you say? Who did they mix you up with?'

'With an internee named Hauser. We bunk in the same

room. It's possible that the lieutenant pointed at him and Reiter wrote my name down by mistake.'

Harte eyed Laffrentz intently. 'That,' he said, 'is extremely interesting. We must have a little chat about it.'

Keller walked across to the gate which separated the internees' compound from the administration block. The camp policeman on duty received some instructions from him and doubled off smartly.

The courtyard was deserted. There was no sign of the GIs who had been playing cards with Slembeck. Brigitte knew enough English to have gathered that Keller reprimanded them, first for gambling at all, second for gambling in the open, and third for gambling with a foreign DP. The GIs vanished into the guard-room, cursing under their breath.

Keller then said a few words to Slembeck. They sounded like an order—an embarrassing order which was best given quickly but brooked no refusal.

Next, Keller presented Slembeck to Brigitte with the words, 'Tell this lady everything you know about an SS officer named Hauser.'

'Everything?' Slembeck asked.

Keller nodded. 'Every last detail.'

He turned to Brigitte. 'I won't be long, baby, I've got a few arrangements to make—you know what I mean.'

Brigitte nodded and said, 'I'm grateful, Frank.'

So it was Frank and baby now . . . Slembeck grinned wickedly to himself. Frank and baby . . . Not much doubt about what was going on. He couldn't quite see what it all had to do with Hauser, but that didn't matter. The main thing was, the woman and the captain were on intimate terms, so he'd better tell the former what the latter thought she ought to hear.

'Well, lady, what would you like to know?' he inquired.

He gestured to the bench in front of the administration block, but the lady declined to sit down. All right, Slembeck told himself, if she wouldn't, she wouldn't. At least he had been as polite as it was advisable to be to a lady who addressed the commandant by his Christian name. Now that he had done his duty he was at liberty to sit down.

He did so, fished a pack of cards out of his coat pocket and started to shuffle them with mechanical expertise. 'I'm listening,' he said politely. 'Fire away.'

'So you know an SS officer named Hauser?' Brigitte's tone was tentative.

'Know him?' Slembeck looked up, still shuffling. 'You don't know people like him. I saw him, though—saw him in action with my own eyes. There was blood spurting all over the place. I lost everything—my family, papers, possessions, valuable mementoes—the lot. The whole place went up in smoke. He owes me something, that man.'

Slembeck deposited his cards on the bench and cut them. 'Can you swear that Hauser was there?'

'Not only there but in charge. He had a gun in his hand—smoking, it was, just like something out of a cowboy movie. Mowed down anyone who got in his way and loved every minute of it. Sent for a gasoline can, splashed gasoline all over the place, put a match to it—that's Hauser for you.'

He turned up the top card and slapped it down on the bench: the knave of diamonds. The next card was the ten of diamonds, the one after that the queen. 'Diamonds mean money,' he observed, scrutinizing the three cards. 'Yes, Hauser's quite a specimen.'

'I'm his wife,' Brigitte said.

Slembeck paused in the act of turning up a fourth card. His hand rested on the pack for some seconds, then slowly withdrew. He raised his head and stared at her keenly.

'So you're Frau Hauser,' he drawled. 'Very interesting, very interesting indeed.'

He picked up another card and looked at it—the king of diamonds. 'Not bad,' he said. 'I could have cleaned those Americans out if we'd still been playing poker. They're generous—they pay in dollars and we settle up in lousy paper marks.'

'If I understand you correctly, you're prepared to give evidence. What exactly do you hope to gain, Herr . . .?'

'Slembeck,' he supplied amiably. 'You ask what I hope to gain by my evidence? Well, that remains to be seen, I suppose.'

'It does, doesn't it?' Brigitte gave him a cold smile. 'You don't look like a fanatical upholder of the truth. You want to cash in and I don't blame you.'

She watched, half-mesmerized, as he deftly spread the pack into a fan. 'What do you hope to get out of this?'

Slembeck ran his fingers delicately over the backs of the cards like a blind man reading Braille. He picked out a card with thumb and forefinger and flipped it over: the ace of diamonds.

'Royal flush,' he observed. 'Now listen to me, lady. You keep asking what I hope to get out of this. Why? Haven't you ever heard of a sense of justice?'

'I've heard of it, Herr Slembeck, but I'm not sure I believe in it.' She started to swing her handbag gently—a sign of impatience which was not lost on Slembeck. 'I take it, then, that you're one of the witnesses for the prosecution.'

'One of them, lady? I'm the best prosecution witness they've got—in fact I'm the only one. I'm unique, lady, and that makes me a pearl beyond price.'

He spread the cards across the surface of the bench with a single sweep of his hand. Then, after brief deliberation, he picked out four cards and turned them up one by one. They were the four deuces, one from each suit.

Brigitte was suitably impressed by this performance. 'Be honest, Herr Slembeck—what's your evidence worth?'

'You want to buy?'

'Let's assume so.'

'It isn't that simple,' Slembeck said slowly. 'It wouldn't be cheap, either.' He turned up several more cards, all of them diamonds. 'You've got a generous face, lady, but I'm not sure you've got the assets to go with it. There's a lot at stake here, you see—valuable family heirlooms, lovely bits of jewellery . . .'

'A platinum and ruby bracelet, for instance?'

Slembeck dropped the card he had just picked up as if it had scorched his fingers. 'How did you know that? Who told you about it—Harte, Keller, or who?'

He brushed the cards aside and edged towards her. 'Tell me, lady, do you have the bracelet in your possession? Do you know where it is? Could you get hold of it?'

'What if I could?'

Slembeck slid back again, knocking some of his cards to the ground. He stooped to pick them up and wiped them carefully on his sleeve. 'If you do have the bracelet you'll have to give it back to me. It's my property, lady. That's why I'm here.'

Brigitte sat down beside him. 'So that's why you're here and that's why you're prepared to testify. Are you sure it'll do you much good?'

Slembeck's eyes gleamed. 'I must have that bracelet, lady, and I'm going to get it too—you can bet your life on that.'

Brigitte rested one hand on the back of the bench and gave him an encouraging smile. 'Think carefully, Herr Slembeck. You're sure you want the bracelet?'

'Dead sure.'

'And that's the only reason why you're prepared to testify against my husband?' Slembeck nodded. 'What if the only way you could get the bracelet was by not testifying against him? Think it over. It's worth considering.'

Slembeck ran his thumb across the edge of the pack. The cards fluttered through his fingers with a sound like a flock of birds taking the air, then came to rest.

'Are you trying to bribe me, lady—me? All right, hand over the bracelet and I won't say a single word against your husband, not a word. The whole story's forgotten. It never happened. I don't remember a thing.'

Brigitte smiled, scenting victory, and Slembeck's eyes shone with satisfaction. Brigitte was suddenly overcome by an urge to prick his bubble of self-assurance and assert her own superiority. She said, 'Wouldn't you find it hard to reconcile that with your Polish patriotism, Herr Slembeck?'

Slembeck's only reaction was an artful grin. 'Polish patriotism, you say? Does it worry you? All right, you can think of me as a good German if you prefer—someone who's ready to help his fellow-countrymen by putting one over on the Americans. Just to set your mind at rest, I was born in West Prussia and worked in Poland. That's no disgrace, lady. War excuses a lot of things, especially as I can prove that I did my bit for final victory.'

'What if I revealed the whole of our conversation to Captain Keller?' Brigitte felt betrayed, somehow. She could not resist making the remark because Slembeck's complacency was almost more than she could stand.

Slembeck merely shrugged off the threat. 'You wouldn't be stupid enough to stick your neck out like that. Don't forget I'm registered as a displaced person—a bona fide DP. That puts me under the protection of the military government—hallowed be its name! As for you, lady, your husband is a war criminal —or could be on my say-so. I bet you're not such a shrinking violet yourself, you certainly don't look like one. Everything's against you, so think twice before you spill the beans about me. You and your kind don't carry much weight any more— you had it too good these last few years. It wouldn't matter what you said, lady, no one would believe you.'

Baron von Hagen requested Internee Mangel to notify the German camp commandant without delay that he and several of his colleagues would be willing to hold an 'informative discussion' with a senior representative of the American authorities.

Mangel's pleasure at this news was soon tinged with concern by an encounter with fellow-internee Professor Heidenstamm, the eminent legal theorist.

'Gentlemen,' Heidenstamm said sternly, 'people in our predicament should not concentrate on the purely legal aspect, which I regard as highly debatable and shall be examining at length in the course of my next evening lecture. No, we are subject, whether we like it or not, to an ethical and moral code which has been imposed upon us by causal factors whose chief characteristic is to induce an indirect transposition of values.'

Nobody understood this except Professor Heidenstamm himself, but he was wise and charitable enough to elaborate. 'In other words,' he said, 'compulsory internment may be justified and legally admissible for some of us but not for others. However, since the same coercion has been applied to all of us indiscriminately, we are all in the same basic position. In other words, circumstances have welded us, willy-nilly, into a community. We must face this fact with fortitude and act as befits our companions in misfortune.'

'Bravo!' exclaimed the Hitler Youth lieutenant, highly elated to have heard his own views couched in such authoritative and professorial language. 'Someone had to say it sometime.'

Mangel was genuinely moved by Heidenstamm's powers of persuasion. On reflection, he decided to inform von Hagen that he could not dissociate himself from the general feeling of solidarity. He had just made up his mind to advise most strongly against any form of contact with the Americans when Wickler intervened.

Whether prompted by a spirit of adventure or eager to amuse himself in his own way, the architect drew Heidenstamm aside.

'A quick word with you, Professor,' he whispered. 'This business about community spirit, companions in misfortune, and so on . . . There's quite another way of looking at it, isn't there?'

Heidenstamm frowned. 'For what my opinion is worth . . .'

'Five smokes,' said Wickler, cupping the cigarettes in the hollow of his hand. He had, without scruple, abstracted them from Wammenberg's private cache.

Heidenstamm pocketed them. 'Of course,' he said, 'I only touched on one aspect of the situation so far.'

He at once proceeded to acquaint his attentive audience with the other aspect of the situation. 'On the other hand,' he concluded, 'if we are not to surrender our individuality, this common basic position cannot and must not be allowed to lead to intellectual conformism and spiritual regimentation. As individuals, we have the right and duty to safeguard our own interests—in other words, to dissociate ourselves from base and unworthy members of our community.'

'Thank God for that!' sighed Mangel, much relieved, and hurried off to get in touch with Reiter.

Keller walked slowly towards Brigitte and Slembeck.

The instructions he had issued at the inner gate set a number of camp policemen in motion. Hauser was summoned and Reiter told to hold himself in readiness. Keller did not intend to let the grass grow under his feet.

He turned to Brigitte. 'Well, was your conversation enlightening?'

'Very,' she replied, and Slembeck added:

'I told the lady the whole story, frills and all.'

'That's good, Slembeck. Kindly remain on call. Inform the guard commander where you can be reached—I'm bound to need you later.'

Keller led Brigitte back across the gravelled expanse of the forecourt. They did not look at each other as they walked slowly, almost gingerly, towards the inner gate.

'Do you think he's a reliable witness, Frank?'

'Don't you?'

Brigitte's steps grew more hesitant. 'Has he signed a written statement yet?'

Keller peered along the camp road. Far away in the distance, a German policeman had just opened the sidegate to Block C. A figure emerged, possibly that of Hauser.

'Written statements are a pure formality,' he said, 'especially in a case like this. No, we don't have one yet, but even if we had I could cancel it by snapping my fingers. Are you ready to talk to your husband?'

Brigitte came to a halt. 'Does he know I'm here?'

'I told them to warn him—said I was giving special permission for an interview. You can only have a few minutes, but that ought to be enough.'

Brigitte tensed herself, clenching her hands to stop them trembling.

'So he knows I'm here. Does he know anything else?'

'About us, you mean?'

'I wasn't thinking of that. That's our business—for the time being, anyway. No, does he know why I've come? Has he any idea what I want?'

Keller's silence prompted her to look at him. She followed the direction of his gaze. Knowing that her husband would come from the third block, Block C, if he came at all, she stared along the road. Two men were approaching. One of them, tall and powerfully built, looked like Manfred.

'He doesn't know anything for sure,' Keller said. 'You can take it for granted that he's made some guesses, though. He can put two and two together. What's more, he's an expert on camp procedure. All he's been told is that you asked the commandant for an interview with him and that the commandant granted your request. He's also been informed that, in view of the exceptional circumstances, I insist on being present at the interview.'

'You're going back on our agreement,' she said. 'He'll never discuss anything important if you're within earshot.' Her eyes never left the tall, square-shoudered man who was walking slowly down the road.

Everything round her seemed to melt away—the barbed wire encircling the framework of the gate, the slabs of dirty grey concrete, the stretches of trampled grass and the men swarming ant-like across them. Nothing existed for her any more—only the figure she knew so well.

'It's against our agreement,' she repeated. 'You promised to leave me alone with him.'

'He knows the rules in camps like these. If I leave you alone together from the start, he'll smell a rat. Don't worry, though. I've arranged to be called away after a few minutes.'

'That's all right, then. Do we have to talk here at the gate?'

'There won't be any interruption. You can have ten minutes.'

Hauser was getting close now. Brigitte went up to the bars of the gate and looked through. Keller remained standing nearby.

Hauser lengthened his stride as he covered the last few yards. 'Hello, Brigitte,' he said with a broad smile. He put his hand through the barbed wire, grasped hers and squeezed it hard. Then he stood back and looked her up and down.

'You haven't changed,' she said brightly.

He glanced down at himself. 'My uniform's seen better days,' he replied. 'Never mind, give it time. You're looking fine, anyway.' He eyed Keller, who was doing his best to look detached.

'Sorry, Hauser,' Keller said. 'I'm afraid you're stuck with me.'

'Pity.'

'It can't be helped.' Keller lit a cigarette with unusual deliberation, turning round to face the administration block as he did so.

A deep furrow appeared on Hauser's brow. He moved towards Brigitte again and laid his hand on hers, which was grasping one of the bars of the gate. 'So you're all right, are you?'

'As well as can be expected, yes.'

He stroked her slender fingers. They were moist with heat and excitement.

'You really haven't changed,' he said. 'I didn't expect you to, of course. You never adapt yourself to circumstances—you always make sure they adapt themselves to you.'

'Nothing leaves much of a mark on you, Manfred. You haven't changed either.'

'I've lost seven pounds, but that's about all.'

Scrutinizing him closely, she noticed that he was ill-shaven. It lent him an air of grim determination—a sort of ruggedness which enhanced his masculinity.

'How's business?' he asked. 'What about your parents' inn? Do you still own it?'

'Nobody's given me any trouble so far.'

'Maybe not, but I bet they're keeping an eye on you.'

The smoke from Keller's cigarette drifted between them. Brigitte said, 'The preliminary inquiries into your case aren't complete yet. No decision about me and my financial resources can be taken until they are. As long as nothing can be proved against you, the same goes for me. I've always said you were innocent and taken it for granted that you'll be classified as an ordinary prisoner of war.'

'You're damned right I will,' Hauser said firmly.

Sylvia Meiners leant out of one of the windows in the administration block. 'Captain Keller,' she called, 'you're wanted on the phone, urgently. It's Colonel Cord.'

'All right,' Keller called back. 'I'm coming.'

He turned to Hauser. 'I'll have to leave you to yourselves for a few minutes. I don't need to tell you how unwise it would be to try anything rash.'

'Don't worry,' Hauser replied. 'I know the rules in camps like these. Making trouble for you means making trouble for myself.'

Keller hesitated for a moment, then beckoned one of the guards over and gave him some whispered instructions. The only words that could be distinguished were 'ten minutes'. The soldier nodded casually and stationed himself a few yards away.

'I won't be long,' Keller said. 'Make the most of your time, but don't take advantage of the favour I'm doing you. I'm sure we understand each other.' Then he walked off.

Internee Laffrentz was in high spirits. Interrogation officer or not, the man beside him was excellent company. They had been chatting like old friends for half an hour, comfortably seated on a rolled-up mat in the gymnasium.

Not that Laffrentz was allowing the man to pump him—far from it. Laffrentz always played it safe. First, he got Harte to confirm that the roll-call business was over and done with.

After that they started to chat in an easy-going, fundamentally innocuous way, man to man. They swapped gems of worldly wisdom, practical tips, personal experiences—nothing of any significance.

One thing seemed clear—Harte had no intention of squeezing anything out of him. That was reassuring enough in itself. Laffrentz decided to work on the American by slow degrees until he had him safely hitched to his wagon. Harte wasn't the commandant, admittedly, but he was the second most influential man in Camp 7.

Harte proffered his cigarettes with the informality of an old crony.

'Much obliged,' said Laffrentz, promptly helping himself to two. 'One for now and one for this afternoon, if you've no objection.' He inserted one of the much-prized and financially desirable articles between his blubbery lips and stuck the other behind his right ear.

'Why not take another—for this evening?'

'Very kind, I'm sure,' said Laffrentz. He reached for a third cigarette and put it behind his left ear. 'I've got pockets too,' he added, piggy eyes a-twinkle.

'We'll have to see about that,' Harte replied amiably. 'There's plenty of time to kill, so let's do it as pleasantly as possible. And while we're on the subject of killing time, how do you find life in camp? Are they looking after you properly, or do our arrangements leave something to be desired? Any comments or complaints?'

'Far too much free-wheeling,' replied Laffrentz, 'if I may be allowed to speak frankly, Mr Harte.'

'By all means. Speak as frankly as you like.'

'Well,' Laffrentz went on, 'in my opinion, the German and American authorities are out of step. I know what I'm talking about, too. Lack of organization creates bottlenecks and wastes time. For instance, personnel selection is based on personal connections, not professional experience.'

'Can you be more specific?' Harte prompted courteously.

'Well, take the German commandant.'

'Do you know him well?'

'I certainly do. He used to bunk in my room.'

'The same room as Hauser, if I remember rightly.'

'Don't remind me!' Laffrentz exclaimed. 'That man makes

me see red. He has the same effect on some of the others, too. Just imagine, Mr Harte, he tries to lead his own life—a man with his record! That's Hauser's sort all over, though—blind to reality. Me, I'm different.'

'So I've noticed,' said Harte. 'I suppose that's why we get on so well.'

Laffrentz beamed. 'I'm glad you feel that.'

Harte had Laffrentz ticking over nicely now. All he had to do was open the throttle and his newfound ally would go chugging off at full speed.

He said, 'We seem to have the same ideas about the German commandant. No problem there, but what about Hauser?'

'Your suspicions are correct,' Laffrentz replied. 'You must have a pretty clear picture of him from your files. Have you seen his wife?'

'Possibly, but where?'

'Going around with Captain Keller, maybe.'

Harte pricked up his ears. The fat man seemed to know a great deal about the things that interested him. But if Laffrentz knew, why shouldn't Hauser know too? It couldn't have escaped Hauser that his wife was up to something, but what was the inference? Camp gossips obviously kept their ears closer to the ground than Harte had suspected.

'Yes,' Laffrentz went on, 'that's the way things are. Still, one shouldn't jump to conclusions, I suppose. There may not be anything to it—just good old-fashioned friendship, maybe, or a straightforward business arrangement. Yes, that's the way people ought to look at it.'

'But they don't?'

'Far from it, Mr Harte, far from it! The place is seething with gossip—people thrive on it. You can see what I mean about changing the atmosphere in here. Some short-sighted types actually pretend to commiserate with Hauser—tell him how sorry they are and ply him with sham sympathy. And why? Because the place is run by weaklings. You need a real man in charge here.'

Harte was finding it oppressively hot in the gymnasium. The two pianists at the far end had removed their jackets and rolled up their sleeves. Colman was drinking ice-cold beer. Harte's mouth watered with longing at the sight, but he was enthralled by his portly companion's capacity for gossip. Almost involuntarily, he began to realize that the case which he had thought of as closed could not be allowed to remain that way.

It would be only too easy to yield to his natural inclination, which was to call it a day and have Laffrentz taken back to Block C. Alternatively, he could continue doggedly and perseveringly: first a few red herrings, a few generalities about women or the weather, then a few more cigarettes to loosen Laffrentz's tongue still further, and, finally, back to the subject of Hauser.

On the other hand, why get involved—why not remain aloof? It was nothing to do with him, officially. All he wanted was a little peace and quiet.

Despite himself, he said, 'How about it, Laffrentz—shall I send for some cold beer? Feel like keeping me company a bit longer, or can you think of something better to do in this lousy heat?'

'I'd be delighted, Mr Harte. Cold beer sounds like a good idea—a really excellent idea.'

Hauser stood facing his wife through the bars of the gate. He glanced at the American guard, who was staring into space and evidently didn't understand German—a stroke of luck which Hauser decided to exploit.

'Tell me,' he said to Brigitte, 'do you know that man Keller well?'

'Why should I, Manfred?'

Hauser's hand tightened on the barbed wire. He stared fixedly after Keller until he disappeared into the administration block. 'Why did he give you permission to speak to me? It isn't usual.'

'I put in a request and he granted it.'

'Yes, but why? I know Keller. He's an unscrupulous bastard—never does anything unless he's certain to gain by it.'

Brigitte reached for the hand that was grasping the barbed wire. 'It's hard for you to judge, Manfred, cooped up in here like this. People get wrong ideas in prison, and I don't suppose you're any exception.'

'Oh, no!' Hauser retorted excitedly. 'I'm simply putting two and two together. Keller not only grants us permission to speak—and that's probably unique in the annals of this camp—he even leaves us alone. He must feel pretty sure of himself. I wonder why.'

Brigitte did her best to interrupt this train of thought. 'You're letting your imagination run away with you,' she said, withdrawing her hand petulantly. 'Obviously, there are some people in this camp with nothing better to do than brood about women. It's infectious, Manfred. I can see hundreds of them staring at us, and I can just imagine what they're saying to each other.'

Hauser felt a stabbing pain in his palm. He opened his fingers and saw that the barbed wire had made a long tear in the skin.

'Imagination?' he scoffed. 'Come off it, Brigitte, there's nothing the matter with my thought processes. Why did he leave us alone, that's what I'd like to know.'

'Pure coincidence. He was called away.'

'It was a put-up job, and a goddam obvious one at that. Why the hell should some colonel want to speak to him at this precise moment?'

'These things happen. You ought to be glad—I know I am.'

'If he'd wanted to check on our conversation he'd have left a German-speaker here. For some reason or other, he didn't. Don't give me that stuff about coincidence, because I don't believe it. I'm not a complete fool.'

Brigitte looked angry. 'All right, maybe he did leave us alone on purpose. What are you grumbling about?'

'But why?' The deep cut in Hauser's palm was burning like fire and the sun dazzled him. 'Why did he do it? Are you sleeping with him?'

'What if I were?'

Hauser closed his smarting eyes against the sun, which seemed to sear his face. There was sweat everywhere, streaming down his cheeks, trickling into the corners of his eyes, running over his lips and on to his tongue, plastering the clothes to his body.

What if she really had slept with Keller? All right, the next question was: why? A human life was worth any gamble.

'What if I am sleeping with him, Manfred? What then?'

'If you are,' he said brusquely, 'the only thing that interests me is what I'm likely to get out of it.'

'I'm on my own so much.'

'All right, all right. If you're lonely, console yourself. I've no objection—you know that. You can go to bed with anyone you like as long as it doesn't hurt my chances.'

'You're not being very considerate, Manfred.'

'I never was—you never expected me to be. Ours wasn't a teen-age romance, Brigitte. We always kept our heads and behaved accordingly. Life wasn't like the movies. It was a straightforward piece of arithmetic. As long as things went right for me, you were all right, too. We've reached an in-between stage now, but it won't last much longer. As soon as this post-war farce is over we'll start where we left off.'

Listening to him, Brigitte rediscovered the old Manfred. He really hadn't changed. Stick to the facts—that was his motto and always had been.

'Aren't you slightly oversimplifying the situation?'

'It is simple! Anyone with a grasp of reality can handle anything that comes along. It's the name of the recipe that changes, not the ingredients or the way you mix them. It won't take long for me to get a job. As soon as I've found one I'll be making an income—the sort of income I deserve. I've organized soldiers up to now. In future I'll organize workers or political illiterates. Meanwhile, you've got the income from your parents' inn. Have fun and enjoy life.'

Hauser wanted to convince. Unable to dominate her physically, he wanted to impose his will on her, infuse her with his optimism, determination and strength. He not only needed her; he had to be able to rely on her.

'Are you so sure of my love?' she asked.

'Sure of your love?' he scoffed. 'Stop talking like a woman's magazine! I'm relying on your intelligence, not your love. Sex comes and goes—it's like washing your hands. One or two things happened while we were apart during the war. No, don't pretend otherwise, Brigitte—things happened on both sides. I took it for granted then, so why should I worry now? Anyway, who am I supposed to worry about—that arrogant lout of an American or a couple of dozen like him? Who gives a hang what you do with them? All that matters is what they can do for you.'

Studying Brigitte intently, Hauser was relieved to note that she seemed impressed.

She said, 'Well, now I'm here I'd like to discuss one or two business matters.'

'Go ahead. I'm always ready to talk business.'

'It's about the White Horse,' Brigitte said crisply. 'There's a good chance of picking it up cheap.'

'Excellent. The White Horse is far the best hotel in the district. What about the Americans, though? Aren't they raising objections?'

'Frank—I mean Captain Keller—will deal with those, but I didn't want to make a final decision without consulting you.'

'Good for you,' Hauser said admiringly. He magnanimously ignored the reference to Keller. 'The White Horse could be a goldmine. This is the ideal time to buy, but can you raise the cash?'

'If I realized everything—sold the inn and my jewellery as well—yes, I think so.'

Good girl, thought Hauser. Knows what she wants, thanks to my tuition. 'I'm all in favour,' he said. 'Our liberators are selling off the whole country dirt cheap, but that's their privilege. Good luck to them.'

Brigitte laid her hand on his. 'There's just one snag,' she said softly. 'I need something else before I can clinch the deal.'

'Like what?'

'That platinum bracelet you brought back from Poland. I've got to have it.'

'Not a hope,' Hauser replied. 'Completely out of the question.' After a brief pause, he added, 'Why do you want it, anyway?'

'It's Keller,' she said. 'He insists on having it.'

Hauser backed off and stuck his hands in his jacket pockets. 'No deal, Brigitte. I'm only thankful I stowed the thing away in a safe place in time. You don't think I'd be stupid enough to put a noose around my own neck, do you?'

'I'm sorry you take that attitude,' she said quickly. 'It's short-sighted of you, Manfred. You've obviously forgotten how to take a long-term view of things—I'm surprised at you.'

Hauser's hands drove deep into his pockets so that his fists showed through the cloth. 'Let Keller get his paws on that bracelet? That's just what the bastard would like. He can't pin anything on me without it. Suspicions aren't worth a damn on their own. As for his so-called eye-witness, give me a reasonably efficient lawyer and I'll cut him to ribbons in front of any court, however pig-headed. Nobody can prove a thing against me—nobody!—not unless you've heard a corpse give evidence. But produce that bracelet, my girl, produce that indispensable platinum and ruby bracelet, throw in a witness and the odd affidavit, and I'm a dead man.'

Brigitte shook her head. 'Keller seems very anxious to get hold of the bracelet, I grant you, but you're wrong about his plans for it. You regard it as a piece of evidence. He sees it in quite a different light. It would probably fetch fifty or sixty thousand dollars. That's what it represents to him.'

Hauser stiffened. 'A bribe, you mean?'

'Don't you think he'd take one?'

'Of course,' he said firmly. 'I wouldn't put it past anyone.'

'After all, what would your conviction mean to him? Just another name on a long list. The bracelet would be worth a small fortune to him, and that's all he cares about. He's a typical American. War is just a business, nothing more.'

Hauser saw the force of this argument. Bribery took many forms—women, money, medals, titles, publicity, ovations, public banquets. You could dazzle people with words, buy their silence with a cheque, corrupt them with title-deeds. All these were commonplace ways of purchasing a man's credence, conscience or conviction.

'All right,' he said, 'let's buy ourselves an American. Getting out of this place would be worth a bracelet, especially if Keller throws in the White Horse as well.'

'Where is it?'

'I'll tell you that as soon as we've settled the details. One thing at a time. First, I want a gilt-edged guarantee that I'll be released and you'll get your hotel. Then I'll deliver—on the nail, too. Drop him a hint that the bracelet is underpriced at fifty thousand dollars. That ought to egg him on—you too, I hope.'

Internee Laffrentz's spirits had soared to Olympian heights. His face radiated contentment like a beacon.

Life was worth living again, thanks to a substantial intake of ice-cold beer consumed straight from the can. Ice-cold American beer, brewed for the army of occupation and quaffed by a senior administrative adviser of the Third Reich—it all seemed so natural.

That man Harte was a real friend. You could twist him around your little finger. Four cans of beer, Harte had sent for. Each of them should have drunk two, but Harte—his friend Harte—had sacrificed half his second can on the altar of friendship. Quart cans they were, too, and a quart was even more than a litre.

He had been recognized at last, taken seriously, nodded at and patted on the shoulder, addressed as 'my friend'. He counted for something at last, even in this place. Yessir, even in this place he counted for something. Recognized, that's what he was.

Beside him marched the sheep-faced policeman. Sheep-face was escorting him back to Block C, as instructed. Camp regulations demanded his return, but for how much longer? It might not be long before the regulations ceased to apply to him altogether. He would issue the regulations then, issue or cancel them at whim.

Laffrentz blinked. His surroundings had gone blurred and out of focus. It was suffocatingly hot, walking along the camp road, like trudging through an inferno.

The beer was taking effect. Of course, that was it. Two-and-a-half beers was nothing. In the old days he could have drunk five. Five? Ten, more like. He used to soak it up like a sponge in the old days. It was the talk of the ministry.

And now, two-and-a-half beers and he felt slightly tight. It would never have happened in the old days—never. He was out of practice. Better start training, because this was only the start. There'd be more beers to come, now he was friends with Harte.

Great chap, Harte. Who cared if he was a Jew? Educated people overlooked that sort of thing these days. Liberal, that was what they called it, and he, Laffrentz, was as liberal as the next man. Christ Almighty, Jews were human beings, weren't they? Yessir! They were part of the human race again and would remain so until further notice.

The road through camp was filthy. Dust and bits of paper everywhere. Ought to be swept, and swept properly. How those idiots behind the barbed wire were staring at him. Anyone would think he was Santa Claus. Somebody ought to light a fire under them. They got silly ideas when they weren't kept busy.

Laffrentz strutted across the courtyard towards the main entrance of Block C, which seemed to sidestep as he advanced on it. He grinned mechanically to disguise the fact that his head was pounding like a steam-hammer.

A fellow-internee got in his way. Grandly elbowing him aside, Laffrentz propelled his corpulent frame upstairs and along the corridor, throwing the swing-doors wide.

Outside Room 29 he paused for a moment, panting a little, then flung the door open. Without bothering to close it, he steamed into the room.

Wickler, who was watching Mangel at work on his latest railway network, muttered something about Laffrentz having been born in a barn.

'See to it for me, Trost,' Laffrentz said majestically, and the meteorological adviser to the German High Command closed the door without a word.

Laffrentz was highly gratified by this reaction. That was how force of personality asserted itself. It was like the theatre: a wave of the hand, and whole empires collapsed.

His other room-mates reacted in a far less gratifying way. Laffrentz had expected his return to cause much more of a stir. Their indifference was a downright affront to his dignity. They cut him—him, the man who had just informed the chief CIC officer what was really wrong round here. He had two-and-a-half cans of beer under his belt, but these bedbugs didn't even notice.

Laffrentz peered round the room. He was the one who had been drinking, but they were the ones who seemed to be drunk. They weren't taking any notice of him—not the slightest bit of notice.

All right, he'd give them a psychological kick up the ass if that was the way they wanted it. Two-and-a-half beers! They didn't appreciate real merit when they saw it. An hour's concentrated discussion with one of the American bigwigs, and they showed no interest—just ignored him and went on day-dreaming. Never mind, he'd soon wake them up.

He turned to Baron von Hagen. 'Well, you ossified old aristocrat, got any horse-sense left? If so, I'll bear that in mind.

Next time we get a delivery of horsemeat at the commandant's office, you can take charge of it.'

The next shaft was aimed at Trost. 'When I'm commandant I'll get them to install a private cemetery and let you pick yourself a special plot. I'm a generous soul, Trost. Carry on the way you're going and it won't be long before you need it.'

Wickler received the following tribute to his architectural ability. 'As for you, you can not only design the new cemetery but christen it. You're an impudent bastard, Wickler, but death's a great leveller.'

Laffrentz rounded on Mangel. 'Put more zip into your work in future, Colonel. Your country needs you. Types like you are essential to the reconstruction of the Fatherland, so pull your finger out. Even if you're told to cart stones, I hope you'll do it with the dignity and enthusiasm proper to a member of the General Staff.'

Laffrentz scrutinized their faces like a prospective buyer in an art gallery, but the pictures swam before his eyes. There was a sour, flatulent feeling in his stomach. Two-and-a-half beers, damn it! He wasn't used to it any more.

He felt sick, so sick he could puke. Swivelling ponderously, he collapsed on to the nearest bed and drew his legs up. He grunted, groaned, and passed out in a flash.

Wickler raised his eyebrows. 'I don't know how he managed it, but that man's drunk—blind drunk.'

Mangel folded up his diagram and stared uneasily round the room. 'Gentlemen,' he said darkly, 'I would ask you to reflect on the possible implications of this. Alcohol impairs a man's judgment. Consider who may have got him drunk. Furthermore, consider what he may have said while under the influence of drink.'

Mangel brooded for a moment. 'Gentlemen,' he added in oracular tones, 'I don't like the look of it. I don't like the look of it at all.'

Keller entered the interrogation cell to find Hauser waiting for him. There was a blithe self-assurance underlying the man's wary exterior which annoyed him intensely.

Hauser eyed him with something akin to defiance. He did not budge from his stool or draw in his legs to let him pass. Keller summed up the situation at a glance as he stepped over

Hauser's outstretched legs and took his place behind the desk, smiling disdainfully.

Hauser continued to sit there without moving. His shoulders looked unusually broad and his hands were thrust into the pockets of his jacket. He waited in silence.

Keller, now installed at the desk, drawled, 'Well, Herr Hauser?'

The response came back pat, 'Well, Captain Keller?'

'I hope you had an informative talk with your wife.'

'Very informative,' Hauser replied cheerfully. 'I'd accept a cigarette if I was offered one.'

Hauser was a non-smoker. Keller knew that from the list of personal idiosyncrasies which Harte had inserted in the internee's file. This was one of Harte's fads—at least, Keller had always considered it a fad until now. 'Doesn't smoke,' ran the notes, 'likes dirty jokes, hides behind resounding phrases, bluffs with all the expertise of a good poker-player.' Keller read these and other remarks with grudging admiration. Harte knew his business all right. His only fault was a total inability to draw the right conclusions.

Keller extended a pack of cigarettes. 'Help yourself,' he said. 'Keep the lot if you want.'

Hauser limited himself to one cigarette and asked for a light. Keller struck a match. Hauser bent over it and lit up. The stage seemed to be set for a quiet drawing-room conversation.

Hauser resumed his seat on the stool in a leisurely fashion. He took a long drag at his cigarette and blew the smoke far across the cell. 'Well,' he said, 'when can I expect to be transferred to a POW camp?'

'Is that what you expect?'

Hauser emitted another cloud of smoke which almost hid Keller from view. 'Of course I do,' he replied confidently. 'After all, I'm willing to pay a high price for my freedom.'

The smoke haze which enshrouded Keller dispersed. 'Really?' he said, lingering over the word. 'This is news to me, Hauser. What precisely are you talking about? What's the price you're willing to pay?'

'The bracelet,' Hauser explained patiently. 'It'll bring a good price in the States—a small fortune, in fact, but you're welcome to every cent. It's a wise investment from my point of view, so I'm ready to hand the thing over without any strings. It won't be easy to raise a decent slice of capital in this godforsaken country, not in the immediate future, but the White Horse is quite an acceptable basis for negotiation. As far as I'm concerned, the deal is on.' He paused. 'Well, Captain, when are you going to dismiss these ridiculous allegations against me? In other words, when do I get transferred to an ordinary POW camp—today, tomorrow, or next week?'

Keller drew a deep breath. His brain raced as he searched for an angle of attack. He ought to have spoken to Brigitte first. He wondered what could have encouraged Hauser to bank on factors which had never entered into his own calculations. What exactly had passed between Brigitte and the man opposite him? What made Hauser so certain that he would be transferred to a prisoner-of-war camp?

Even more important, how ought he to react? Ought he to throw him out, or simply terminate the conversation? Just to fill the lengthening silence, he said, 'I'm not in quite such a hurry as you are.'

'Captain Keller,' Hauser replied stolidly, puffing at his cigarette, 'I think it's time we put our cards on the table. We won't bring sentiment into this. Brigitte generally has a very good reason for everything she does. My wife and I are modern-minded people and always have been. However intimate the circumstances, I always behave like a gentleman. You'll never have any trouble from me—Never, I promise you. There's no real hurry about the POW camp either. They'll probably keep me inside for another few weeks, so you won't be disturbed either then or later—I give you my personal guarantee. Have fun by all means, just as long as you don't prejudice my position. Is that plain enough?'

Keller felt as if his temples were being compressed by an invisible pair of hands. Hot rivulets of sweat coursed down his back. It was some time before he could trust himself to speak.

'Tell me, Hauser,' he asked, 'just what sort of a corrupt bastard do you think I am?'

Hauser took a last pull at his cigarette before tossing it away. It landed in the middle of the cell, between his feet and Keller's desk.

He said, 'Do you get a kick out of striking poses, Captain? I don't think you're corrupt. Far from it. You're a shrewd operator with an eye to the main chance, that's all.'

'I suppose it hadn't occurred to you that I might be in love with your wife?'

Hauser stared at his cigarette-end, which was smouldering to death on the stone floor. 'You underestimate me, Captain,' he said. 'I was counting on it.'

Keller stood up and mashed the smouldering remains of the cigarette with his heel.

'Then get this straight, Hauser. The bracelet isn't just a means of getting me a bank-roll and your wife a hotel. Possession of it would be final and conclusive evidence that you're a war criminal. I don't have to tell you what your sentence would be if you were convicted. That would leave your wife free, Hauser—free to come to me.'

Hauser seemed impressed by this line of argument. 'All right, you've done your arithmetic. Now let me do mine. Would my conviction for war crimes be worth as much as fifty thousand dollars in the bank? Think it over, Captain—fifty thousand at least. Why pass up such a heaven-sent opportunity on my account, especially when you can have my wife anyway—for as long as it suits you? But I explained that already, didn't I?'

'You cynical bastard!' Keller burst out. He felt an urge to fling open the window but remembered just in time that it was open already. It was some moments before the choking sensation passed.

'No need to bandy compliments, Captain,' Hauser said sharply. 'We're on our own.'

Keller turned white with rage. This wasn't a conversation any longer—it was an arrogant and deliberate attempt to humiliate him. An internee—one of four thousand—was sitting there and treating him like dirt, when he, Keller, could make the whole four thousand jump through the hoop if he chose.

'You're trying to buy and sell me, Hauser,' he snapped. 'Do you really think I'd let you put a price-tag on me? Not on your life.'

He saw, to his intense satisfaction, that Hauser flinched a little at the finality in his tone. A thin smile played round the corners of his mouth as he went on, 'I don't need any bracelet to get you convicted, Hauser. We already have one witness. It shouldn't be hard to round up two or three more and put them down to occupation costs. As for the bracelet, maybe it won't even turn up—officially, that is. Maybe it'll simply disappear. I could give your wife a sizeable share of the proceeds and grant her—her personally—a permit to buy the hotel. That's another alternative. It would be one way of making sure you really didn't get in our hair.'

Hauser swore.

'Now who's bandying compliments?' Keller retorted with ill-concealed triumph. He had the upper hand at last.

'You're bluffing,' Hauser said fiercely. 'You're trying to needle me into giving something away, when you don't even know where I've hidden the bracelet—if it exists at all.'

'Don't be too sure. Brigitte and I discussed the problem in detail—I hope you don't mind my using her Christian name, by the way. She hasn't taken a thorough look for the bracelet yet, but she knows at least three places where it might be hidden. I shouldn't underestimate her if I were you.'

Hauser stared down at the hairy hands resting on his knees. They were trembling now. 'I could break every bone in her body,' he muttered.

'Don't get personal, Hauser. I thought you told me sentiment didn't come into this.'

'Is that your last word?'

'The evidence against you is complete,' Keller replied. 'That's all I wanted to tell you. You'll probably hear anything else you need to know in court, when you're indicted for war crimes. It could be any day now.'

'And you think I'm going to take this lying down?'

Keller stood up and straightened his tunic. 'You don't have any choice. What were you planning to do—assault me? You'd be shot immediately, which would be the neatest and quickest solution to all our problems. I'm a good shot, too, in case you're interested. What else could you do? Present petitions, make impassioned speeches in your defence and bore the judges with a load of conjecture? Don't make me laugh! Who's likely to believe the outpourings of a notorious war criminal in this day and age? You'd be convicted before you could open your mouth. The war crimes tribunal at Dachau is waiting for you, Hauser. Be prepared to leave within the next twenty-four hours.'

'What do we do now?' asked Colman.

'Drink,' Harte said laconically.

Colman looked dubious. 'In the admin block?'

'First we pay a visit to Sylvia and establish an alibi,' Harte explained. 'Stop smirking, Colman, that's the only reason for the visit. We'll simply ask her if anything special's come up. She'll say no. Then we can go and get stewed with a good conscience.'

'Fine,' said Colman. 'I never mind seeing Sylvia.'

They left the gymnasium. The guard opened the gate which separated the main camp from the administration block, and they trudged across the hot gravel as if they were knee-deep in water.

Colman unbuttoned the collar of his uniform shirt. 'If this heat keeps up I'll get sunstroke, like Keller.'

'What do you mean?'

'He told Sylvia I was to deal with the man.'

'What man?'

'The one I booked at roll-call yesterday evening—a cheeky bastard who talked on parade while I was there. I've been waiting for him but he hasn't turned up. What the hell does Keller think he's playing at, wasting my precious time?'

Harte looked puzzled. 'I don't know what you're talking about. I dealt with the case myself—just now, in the gym. You saw the man, didn't you? We were having a couple of beers together.'

'Never saw him before in my life.'

'You don't know him?'

'Why should I?'

Harte did his best to focus the lieutenant's gyrating thoughts on a specific point. 'But Colman, your memo referred to him by name—Laffrentz.'

'Something like that.'

'Well, what did Laffrentz look like?'

'Like an internee.'

It was hot, Harte thought—damned hot. Colman was obviously feeling the heat even more than he did, but he refused to let him off the hook. 'So that fat little man I was talking to just now wasn't the one you booked last night?'

'Forget it, Harte. Who cares?'

'Yes or no, Colman?'

'No.'

'Who was your man, then?'

'Somebody quite different. I saw him standing by the gate earlier on, talking to Keller's new girl-friend. Keller was there too—to begin with. You must have seen him yourself—a big beefy fellow.'

'And he told you yesterday evening that his name was Laffrentz?'

'No.'

'In that case, who did?'

'Nobody.'

'Then where the devil did you get the name from?'

'Reiter wrote it down for me.'

'Just a minute,' Harte said. He pinned Colman against the door-post. 'Let me get this straight. A big beefy man spoke on parade. You told Reiter to book him, and Reiter wrote the name Laffrentz in his notebook. Is that correct?'

'Absolutely correct,' replied Colman. He elbowed his way through the swing doors into the cool corridor beyond, followed pensively by Harte.

Strange goings-on, thought Harte. Things had reached a stage where everyone in camp was trying to outwit everyone else. Everyone had an eye to the main chance, and no wonder.

Colman ambled into the outer office. 'Hi, there,' he said, and slumped into one of the arm-chairs by the door.

'Hello, Lieutenant,' said Sylvia.

Following him in, Harte saw the German camp commandant waiting near Sylvia's desk, presumably for Keller. Without a word, he went over to the group of arm-chairs in the far corner and sat down.

Sylvia pretended to work. Colman tugged his collar open another couple of inches. Reiter went on waiting patiently.

Harte decided to ask Reiter a few awkward questions, but couldn't decide on the most favourable timing.

Colman said, 'I thought we came here for a reason.'

Sylvia glanced up. She could guess what was coming. Someone was going to ask her to provide yet another alibi. Colman did it all the time.

'Well,' Harte said with a grin, 'got anything special for us?'

'What if the answer's no?'

'If you haven't, we'll go.'

'Go where?' Sylvia did not trouble to hide her annoyance.

It was always the same. Harte enjoyed provoking her, and the worst of it was, he succeeded.

Harte's reply was brief and predictable. 'For a drink.'

Brisk footsteps were heard outside in the corridor. The door opened and Keller came in. He took in the scene at a glance and was gratified to note that Colman buttoned his gaping collar with uncharacteristic swiftness and dexterity.

'Well,' he said, turning to Reiter, 'have you anything to tell me?'

Reiter prepared to deliver a negative reply. It was clear that he found the prospect disagreeable. 'I'm sorry,' he said stiffly.

'Think very carefully,' said Keller. 'You can't find me any evidence against Hauser—not even a line to go on?'

Reiter shook his head. 'No, I can't.' There was a slight stress on the word 'I'.

'Very well,' Keller said. 'If you won't, you won't.'

He glanced briefly at Harte, who was studying his fingernails with every sign of concentration. Then he turned to Sylvia. 'Internee Hauser is in the interrogation room. See that he's escorted back to his quarters at once. In addition, arrange for his transfer to Dachau. Lieutenant Colman can handle the necessary arrangements.'

Before the lieutenant could plead overwork, he went on, 'Send the following directive to Gernsbach's department: all documents relating to the transfer of the White Horse hotel are to be drawn up and submitted to me for signature without delay. I shall wait for them at home.'

Harte dropped his arms and stared straight ahead. Colman unbuttoned his collar in protest against the latest threat to his leisurely existence. Reiter might not have been in the room at all. He stood there with his head bowed in deferential silence.

Sylvia said, 'You mean that, Captain?'

'Every word.'

'But if Herr Gernsbach . . .'

'If Gernsbach refuses,' Keller cut in, '—and I wouldn't advise him to for his own sake—I shall put him under arrest. Kindly inform him of that.'

Then, as if stating his position once and for all, Keller added, 'My decision is final. Anyone who refuses to obey military government directives will be severely dealt with. Notify Herr Gernsbach of that—you're the most appropriate person to tell him. Say I expect my orders to be carried out with more than usual speed.'

He walked to the door, then turned to face them again. 'Any questions?' he asked. Without waiting for an answer, he strode out. A brooding silence descended when his footsteps had died away, but the heat seemed to rustle like silk.

'Can I go now?' Reiter asked Harte after a suitable pause.

'You can as far as I'm concerned,' Harte replied. 'Before you do, though, I'd like to ask you a question—just one question, Reiter. You can give me the answer later, when I tell you to.'

'What is it?' Reiter inquired stiffly.

'Why did you mix up Laffrentz and Hauser? It can't have been a mistake. You did it on purpose, but why? I shall expect a full explanation in due course. Now you can go.'

Reiter remained rooted to the spot. Only his lips moved. He said, 'I've always been loyal—I hope you believe that.'

Harte gave a short laugh. 'I know, you're a much misunderstood man—I noticed that just now, when you said you weren't prepared to supply information about Hauser.'

'That's what I said, yes.'

'You implied that if you weren't, others were. Who, precisely?'

'A group of internees. Under the circumstances, they think it's time to clear the air a little.'

'Who are they?'

'Diplomats—former ambassadors to countries in South-East Europe. They had dealings with Hauser, and they're ready to hold informative discussions on the subject of his past activities.'

Harte did not comment for some time. Then he started to pace up and down. Everyone stared at him curiously. At length he said, 'What has it got to do with me? It isn't my affair.'

Reiter shrugged. 'In that case, I'll tell them . . .'

'Nothing!' Harte cut in. 'Just tell your seekers after truth to hold themselves in readiness. We'll see. I can't say anything more for the moment.'

Reiter left the room. He went slowly and hesitantly, as if he expected to be called back, but no one said a word.

'I don't understand,' Colman said.

'You don't have to,' Harte retorted. 'Go to the canteen and set up some beers—ice-cold. Okay?'

'Okay.' Colman grinned. 'You want Sylvia to yourself. I quite understand.'

'You're a genius!' Harte called after the lieutenant as his gangling frame disappeared through the door. 'You don't miss a trick, do you?'

He turned to Sylvia, who was still standing beside her desk, looking baffled. 'What's the matter, girl? Something on your mind?'

Sylvia's agitation was genuine. 'I don't understand what's going on round here. Why should Gernsbach get himself arrested if he refuses to draw up papers for that creature? It oughtn't to be allowed.'

'What worries you most of all, Sylvia? That creature, as you call her, Keller's behaviour towards her, or the threat to Gernsbach?'

'Your couldn't-care-less attitude. That's what really gets me.'

'Why not take a leaf out of my book?' Harte recommended. 'It might do you good.'

'Think of something, Ted. What can Gernsbach do?'

'Get those papers ready. What else?'

He saw her stare at him incredulously. Her expression clearly conveyed that she couldn't believe her ears and longed to be told that she had misheard him.

'My God, Sylvia,' he said sarcastically. 'What else is Gernsbach supposed to do? If he's hell-bent on getting himself locked up, far be it from me to stop him.'

'You intend to stand there and do nothing?'

'No, I'm going to go off and get drunk. You're welcome to come and watch if you like. The early stages are quite entertaining. I can still laugh at myself occasionally, though the joke's wearing a bit thin these days.'

'I've got better things to do.'

'Like what?'

'I know what I'd like to do at this moment. I'd like to slap your face until my hands hurt.'

'I never knew you had sadistic tendencies. Why not despise me, Sylvia? It would make things far easier all round.'

'Despise you?' she burst out. 'Is it possible to despise a man one . . .' She bit off the words abruptly, adjusted her office chair with a hurried movement, and sat down.

Harte momentarily shut his eyes. He forced himself not to supply the missing word. Later, he told himself, much later, if at all.

He walked slowly to the door leading to his and Keller's office, paused there, and turned to look at her. He might have been admiring a rare jewel.

Sylvia leafed nervously through some papers. She felt so sick at heart she could have wept like a child. A black tide of misery engulfed her. Was her only function in life to type letters, lick envelopes, instil order into a wilderness of files—dress up tyranny in official guise?

'What about having lunch together?' Harte asked. 'It might take your mind off things.'

'No.'

'Not even lunch?' Harte gave a wry smile. 'You obviously don't think much of me.'

'No. I had faith in you, but that's all over. Besides, I wouldn't want to detain you, just in case you decided to take Reiter up on his offer after all. Those internees could give you just the information you need. It might save a great deal of unpleasantness.'

'Stop badgering me,' he said harshly. 'I've had enough of your rosy dreams of justice and fair play, friends in need and knights in shining armour. Damn it, girl—don't you realize where we are?'

The lunch-pail was standing in the corridor. Block C had received its rations first today, and the residents of the corridor for which Mangel was responsible—nearly a hundred of them—were waiting in their rooms.

Taking his measuring-stick, Mangel checked it once more for cleanliness in the presence of witnesses and thrust it into the soup. The stick struck the bottom of the pail with a dull thud.

He waited briefly until the ripples had subsided and then read off the numbers. 'Forty-eight,' he proclaimed loudly. Kindly check that, gentlemen—forty-eight precisely.'

That meant forty-eight litres to be divided between ninety-three internees. Mangel produced a special table from his breast pocket and consulted it.

'Zero-point-five-three-one litres per person,' he announced.

'It gets less and less,' protested Jäger, the Reich Peasant Leader's erstwhile lieutenant. 'Thinner and thinner, too.'

'Pig-swill,' the Regional Welfare Officer chimed in plaintively.

Mangel ignored them. 'Room 29 takes precedence today,' he said. 'Kindly get a move on.'

'What?' Jäger exclaimed. 'Room 29 again? You're always letting your own people have first crack.'

Without deigning to reply, Mangel took a list from his left-hand breast-pocket and passed it round. It gave particulars of starting-times, order of precedence, number of portions, and finishing-times. The figures covered the past four weeks and were signed by himself and countersigned by the other four room seniors.

A careful inspection of Mangel's list confirmed the validity of his statement. Room 29 could parade for its rations in good order.

Wickler, who was hovering in the doorway, rushed at the pail with a tin bowl in either hand, hotly pursued by the other inmates of Room 29. Baron von Hagen and Trost brought up the rear, the former because it was beneath his dignity to run, the latter because he was too weak.

'What's this?' Jäger demanded, indicating Wickler. 'One of your men is trying to scrounge a double share.'

'What makes you think so?' Mangel said curtly. 'I must ask you either to refrain from making such charges or to substantiate them.'

'But can't you see? He's brought two bowls with him.'

Mangel put down his ladle and turned to Wickler. 'Would you be good enough to explain why you have arrived with two bowls, Herr Wickler?'

'Certainly,' replied the architect. 'The second bowl is for Hauser.'

Mangel found this reasonable. 'You see, gentlemen,' he said, turning to the supervisors, 'the second bowl is for Internee Hauser, temporarily absent for purposes of interrogation. Herr Wickler will take charge of his portion and assume personal responsibility for its safe keeping.'

There was a mounting hubbub, and craning heads protruded from every open door. The internees did not venture into the corridor yet, in obedience to house rules, but their multitudinous voices rose considerably in volume.

'What are you doing out there?' someone demanded shrilly. 'Having a nap?'

'Hurry up or the soup'll evaporate!' shouted someone else.

There was a sudden agitated cry from Faust, the SA poet, 'There's someone else with two bowls at the back. Room 29 again. One extra ration isn't enough for them—they want two.'

'Incredible!' barked Jäger, and was promptly seconded by the regional welfare officer.

Mangel's eyes travelled along the queue until they fell on Trost, who was last in line. It was true: the luckless meteorologist had also brought two bowls. Mangel shuddered at the unpleasant misunderstandings which might beset him, less as room senior than as corridor senior, but the sight of Baron von Hagen, who was standing immediately in front of Trost, gave him his cue: diplomacy.

He said, 'Many thanks for the kind thought, Herr Trost, but you needn't have bothered. Internee Wickler is already collecting Internee Hauser's portion.'

'I had no intention of collecting for Herr Hauser,' Trost replied timidly. 'I'm standing in for Herr Laffrentz.'

Mangel sought around for a suitable reply but failed to find one. He merely nodded and said, 'Ah, in that case . . .'

Just as Mangel's ladle was poised, Jäger demanded to know why Laffrentz had not turned up himself. 'It's an established rule that everyone has to pick up his food in person,' he complained. 'Otherwise, how can we keep a proper check?'

'You're right,' Mangel replied testily. 'However, there are exceptions. Herr Laffrentz . . .' Here he paused, seeking inspiration from another glance at Baron von Hagen. 'Herr Laffrentz is—ill.'

'What?' the SA poet cried in outrage. 'I've heard that story before. It's absolute nonsense. I saw Laffrentz half an hour ago. He was not only bumptious but drunk. I don't know how he did it, but he was as drunk as a fiddler's bitch. Colonel Mangel calls that being ill. I suppose it's the stock military term for men who are incapable of doing their duty.'

'Anyway,' the regional welfare officer said sharply, 'things can't go on like this. I hereby request Colonel Mangel to apply the same treatment to his own room as he does to all the others.'

Mangel's fund of answers had run out. He stood there looking somewhat embarrassed and trying to reach a decision. The nature of the decision temporarily eluded him.

Meanwhile, Mangel's charges were growing impatient. The corridor rang with a medley of shouts and cat-calls.

'Stupid bastards!'

'It's sabotage, that's what it is.'

'They're worse than the Yanks.'

'All they can do is fiddle. They're experts at fiddling—that's why they're in charge.'

Driven into a corner, Mangel gave orders that Internee Laffrentz was to present himself at once and take receipt of his food in person. Wickler and two other men vanished into Room 29 while Mangel waited nervously, watched by his eagle-eyed supervisors.

The first sound to issue from the room was that of a loud, cheerful voice. This belonged to Wickler. The low, mumbling response was followed by a muffled curse which ended abruptly in a shrill squeak of pain. A stool was knocked over and went skidding across the floor. There was the sound of scrabbling feet and splintering wood, then silence.

At last, the door opened and Laffrentz was propelled into the corridor by Wickler. His face was puffy and his moth-eaten hair dishevelled. Mechanically, he tidied his clothes and joined the end of the line. Rage smouldered in his bleary eyes.

Wickler nimbly wormed his way forward until he was at the head of the line again. 'You can start dishing out now,' he announced. 'Two helpings for me, if you don't mind.'

'Disrespectful swine,' Laffrentz grumbled furiously in the background. 'If you knew what I know you'd come crawling on your bellies to me. It won't be long now, you mark my words!'

'Mr Harte!' Sylvia called breathlessly. 'Wait a minute, Mr Harte.'

Harte, already half-way across the courtyard, stopped in his tracks. 'What do you want? I'm off to get drunk.'

Sylvia had run after him. A delicate pink suffused her cheeks and she was panting a little. She caught him by the sleeve, her eyes shining and her lips slightly parted.

'Won't you wait a moment? Forgive me for holding you up, but I've got something to tell you—I think it's important.'

'Well, what is it?'

'Captain Keller had a phone call—no, try to look interested and keep your sarcastic remarks to yourself, too. Captain Keller just spoke to Colonel Cord—that is, the Colonel rang him. He's still at the General's place, the Villa Edelweiss, ten miles away.'

'He's welcome to rot there till the next war comes.'

'Why do you always have to be so snide? Wait for me to finish. As I was saying, Colonel Cord seemed to be in a very good mood. Stop grinning like that, Ted—he can afford to be pleasant occasionally. Anyway, he made it clear to Keller that he was here on a tour of inspection, and if Dachau phoned we were to tell them that he was visiting the area for a specific purpose.'

'The Hauser case?'

'Exactly. Cord intends to call in again on his way back to Dachau, and he wants to take the completed file on Hauser with him. Keller assured him that this would present no problem—as far as he was concerned, the case was complete. In fact, if the Colonel cared to, he could take Hauser back to Dachau straight away, ready to stand trial.'

'An efficient man, our Captain.'

'Come on, Ted, let's sit down on that bench for a minute—all right? That isn't all. Sit down and stop pulling such a long face—I'm tired of looking up at you the whole time. You're taller than I am, or, rather, I'm shorter than you are. I like that, somehow.'

'Keep to the point, Sylvia.'

'I'm trying to, but you keep on sidetracking me. Please listen. Unbutton your collar if you find it too hot, it won't worry me. Come here and let me help you, Ted. Your tie's knotted so tight it's half strangling you. No one could call you a snappy dresser, but there's no reason why you shouldn't learn. Give the tie here—I'll press it for you.'

'Is that all you wanted to say?'

'Of course not! Don't be so impatient—you'll be propping

up the bar soon enough. To go on, immediately after his conversation with Cord, Keller spoke to someone else on the phone. Who do you think it was?'

'Get to the point, Sylvia. What did Frau Hauser have to tell him?'

'Nothing at all—that's the whole point. It was the exact opposite of what Keller had been expecting. You can't imagine how furious he was! He was almost speechless with rage, and later on, when he'd pulled himself together a bit, all his charm had gone—evaporated. No more sweet nothings. He didn't even call her Brigitte, just "you", and he might have been talking to one of his GIs.'

'If you don't come to the point right now, Sylvia, I'll go away and leave you sitting here by yourself. What exactly happened?'

'All right, if that's the way you want it. Keller was amicable at first—quite amicable. He reminded Frau Hauser of her promise about the bracelet and asked when and where he could pick it up. She seemed to have no recollection of any such promise. She simply pointed out that they were in love with each other. Love, that was the word she used. I'm only telling you what she said.'

'Go on, Sylvia. Get on with it.'

'Give me a chance. Well, Keller went on and on about the bracelet, sounding more and more impatient. At last she said that the bracelet belonged to them both, not to him alone. It was a joint possession which symbolized their feelings for one another—something like that.'

'Great. What did Keller say?'

'He was speechless. Eventually, the Hauser woman said—and I quote, "I'm waiting for you, darling. No two people have ever hit it off the way we do. Come over and we'll discuss it." '

'Perfect, just perfect.'

'Well, what now? Aren't you going to do something about it?'

'Yes, I'm going to get really drunk now, but not to drown my sorrows, I'm going to drink for sheer joy.'

'You ought to be ashamed of yourself.'

'Why? Everything's fine.'

'It isn't, Ted—that's just the trouble. Right at the end, after the woman had hung up, Keller said something to himself. He sounded really grim.'

'Well, what was it?'

'It's all or nothing now—that's what he said. What do you think he meant?'

Harte stood up. His eyes twinkled as he looked down at her.

'You want to know what I think?'

'Yes.'

'I think you've been eavesdropping on conversations which have damn all to do with you, my love. Apart from that, we can congratulate ourselves. Things couldn't be better. She's taken him for a ride, the clever bitch, and I hope he enjoys it. He not only needed a lesson like this—he deserved it.'

Sylvia shook her head fiercely. 'But what did he mean when he said it was all or nothing now?'

'Who cares what he meant! Let him run amok if he wants to. Why worry—unless you're worried for his sake?'

'You don't understand me, do you, Ted? Why won't you take the trouble to understand me?'

'I can't afford to,' Harte said doggedly. 'I've got a soft spot for you, Sylvia—you know that perfectly well. Please don't take advantage of it. Let me live my life in peace. I can't think of anyone who deserves to be taught a lesson more than Keller, believe me, but he'll survive. Let's keep out of it. Keller will come through all right and things will be on an even keel again before you know where you are.'

'You really think so, Ted?' She stared at him doubtfully, craving reassurance.

'There are wrinkles on your lily-white brow, Sylvia. They don't suit you. If you can't laugh, at least smile. Life's a farce—hasn't it dawned on you yet? Well, what do you say? Shall we go and have lunch together? No? All right, I'll go by myself, but you might send for Hauser first. Don't expect too much, though. I only want to sound him out.'

The gymnasium, in which Sergeant Popper seemed to have taken up permanent residence, was situated immediately on the left of the main entrance to Camp 7. On the stage at the far end lay a genuine Persian rug, nine by fifteen, and on it stood a mock Elizabethan table and a reproduction Louis

Quinze chair. The provost-marshal was taking his ease in the latter.

'There's something missing still,' he said, frowning.

Popper was preoccupied with his German concert night, which he planned to turn into a cultural feast of the first magnitude. His generals had already been assigned to various spheres of activity—seating accommodation, stage management and ushering—and were rising to the occasion magnificently.

Wammenberg, billed as 'Hitler's Butler', was also doing his bit. 'If you wish, Sergeant, I could dig up a few intimate details about the Führer—for instance, what sort of underwear he favoured and how often he changed it. That might give the audience something to chew on.'

Popper waved the suggestion aside. 'Old hat,' he declared in the tones of one who knew what he was talking about, and resumed his daydreaming.

He toyed with the possibility of engaging Monsignor Tiso, the well-nourished ex-premier of Slovakia, as a soloist, but reluctantly discarded the idea. Tiso liked to think of himself as a budding saint, a luxury which he could well afford in view of the extra rations it brought him. He had given up folk-songs in favour of choral Mass, and Mass was hardly suitable for use as a revue number.

One thing was certain: the competition from Colman's Gershwin-strumming pianists had to be eliminated as quickly and effectively as possible. It would take more than a male quartet and some Third Reich recitations to outdo them. An idea for a hard-hitting solo performance took shape in Popper's mind: a mock lecture composed in the best traditions of German scholarship and entitled 'How to cremate Jews'.

Popper decided to submit this brilliant proposal to Captain Keller. Going in search of the commandant, he buttonholed him near the main gate. 'Captain,' he said ingratiatingly, 'I've thought of a great new idea for my recreational programme. Want to hear it?'

'Negative,' snapped Keller. 'I'm not interested in your hare-brained schemes.'

'Hare-brained schemes, sir?' Popper sounded hurt. 'That's pretty rough.'

'You're wasting your time, Sergeant. As provost-marshal of

this camp, it's your job to tail the German commandant like a bloodhound.'

'A bloodhound? That's news to me, sir.' Popper sounded even more hurt. 'Can I have that in writing?'

'Knock it off, Sergeant—you're not a barrack-room lawyer. Anyway, I don't really have anything against your crazy hobbies.'

'Crazy hobbies?' Popper was so outraged that he completely forgot to add his usual mildly sarcastic 'sir'. He simply snorted.

'You'd do far better to worry about Reiter—and my instructions. This camp is a shambles, and you're supposed to be responsible for discipline. When is Reiter going to come through with the information I asked for?'

'With respect, sir, I'm not Reiter.'

'I know, Sergeant, you're the local king of show-biz and Lieutenant Colman thinks he's running Carnegie Hall. It's a lousy stinking waste of time, but you're welcome to make a monkey out of yourself as long as you note the following orders and carry them out: one, tell Reiter either he delivers the goods inside the next three hours or the commandant's job goes to somebody else; and two, take Internee Hauser into custody and make arrangements for his transfer to Dachau or possibly Nuremberg. I hold you personally responsible for implementing both those orders.'

'Yessir,' said Popper, who had regained his equilibrium. His eyes narrowed as he watched Keller climb into his Cadillac. Then, with a full heart, he said, 'Balls!'

After that he went back to the gymnasium and got the quartett to sing *You're Driving Me Crazy*.

Camp 7's chief CIC officer was standing in the middle of his office with his back to the windows. On the wall facing him, between his own desk and Keller's, hung the map of the internment camp.

Harte slowly removed his jacket and draped it over a chair. His tie followed. Thoughtfully, he unbuttoned his collar without taking his eyes off the map. He was studying the perimeter with special reference to the location of each watch-tower.

The door of the office opened and heavy hobnailed boots crossed the threshold. Harte continued to study the map with deep concentration, even when Hauser broke the silence.

'What the hell do you want this time?' There was suppressed rage in Hauser's voice, rage tinged with desperation or, possibly, the courage born of despair. Harte liked what he heard.

He said, 'Shut the door and come here, Hauser. Stand beside me.'

The heavy footsteps approached. Hauser stationed his sweating bulk a couple of paces from Harte.

'Come closer,' Harte said. 'Stand right beside me. Take a look at this map—a good look. Our security system is pretty patchy, wouldn't you say? You're an expert on detention camps, aren't you? All right, Hauser, you needn't answer that question. I'm going to give you a chance to get out of here, but it's up to you to make the most of it. Understand?'

Fresh beads of sweat erupted on Hauser's face. The hand that stroked the massive jaw was moist and slightly tremulous.

'Why get so worked up?' Harte asked softly. 'There's no need, I assure you. Take a really close look—the security precautions are quite straightforward. No doubling up, no overlapping fields of fire.'

'Why tell me all this?' Hauser brushed the sweat off his chin. 'Why tell me, Mr Harte?'

The CIC officer casually tapped the map. 'Let's assume, for the sake of argument, that this guard—No. 4—was missing. Let's assume that he was called away—by someone entitled to call him away, of course. Once his back was turned there wouldn't be anyone who had a clear view of this stretch here.' He pointed to a masked stretch of the wall near Block C. 'I reckon that's the most obvious gap in the whole perimeter.'

He ran his forefinger along the scale-line. Hauser estimated that the distance to be covered was about forty yards.

Harte was speaking again, slowly and deliberately. 'The commandant has made an error of judgment. It would amuse me to demonstrate that in practice. Well, Hauser, how much time would you need?'

There was no reply. Hauser stared at the map in stupefied silence, breathing heavily.

'Think it over,' Harte said. 'Think it over very carefully. Well, can you quote me a definite time? I'm waiting, Hauser, but I won't wait much longer.'

The answer came in a hoarse, unsteady voice. 'Five minutes—more or less.'

'That's what I thought.' Harte inserted a well-gauged pause. 'Better make it eight minutes to allow for interruptions and avoid hurrying. Eight clear minutes somewhere between two and three o'clock this afternoon. Would that be long enough?'

'I think so.'

Harte turned to look at Hauser. His eyes were veiled and there was a faint smile on his lips. 'I think so too.'

'But why? Why are you doing this?'

'Don't ask questions. Your neck's at stake, Hauser. Do something to save it.'

'Non-fulfilment,' Gernsbach said. 'That's the story of my life. What makes it worse is that I was so full of hope for the future. I always aimed too high, I suppose. That's why I never achieved anything. I used to tell myself that circumstances were to blame, but now I'm beginning to wonder how far we're to blame for what we choose to call circumstances.'

He stared at the mountains, which were shimmering in the brilliant light of early afternoon. Even mountains can tremble, he thought. He ought to paint them sometime—paint them craning upwards like men in their death-throes.

Gernsbach's view of the mountains was framed by coils of barbed wire. He was sitting on the bench outside the administration block, and beside him sat Sylvia. He could not bring himself to look at her. His eyes ached.

'Do you know what it means, a lifetime of hope and a lifetime of disappointment? Can you imagine what it's like, trying to translate your longings into paint and failing time and time again—dedicating your entire existence to the brush and nothing else?'

'You're not finished yet,' Sylvia said.

'I've run out of hope.'

'Isn't there anybody who could restore your faith in human nature?'

'I don't know,' Gernsbach replied wearily. 'I don't understand myself, so why should I presume to know anything about other people? I feel as if I'd been marooned. I've lost all sense of direction.'

'Have you lost faith in America too?'

'What's America—a producer of canned fruit and automobiles, or what?'

'I don't know either. I only know this much: Keller doesn't represent America, nor does Ted Harte—not exclusively, anyway.'

'And I don't represent Germany. I told you already, Sylvia—I don't know what I am myself, so why should I know Germany? One day we'll be gone, and nobody will miss us. People will say: they took themselves too seriously, they couldn't discriminate any longer—they were dead inside. Ted Harte said once that all Germans were guilty with the exception of three categories: émigrés, political prisoners and Resistance fighters. I belong to two of those categories, theoretically speaking, but I can't say I feel innocent.'

Brigitte Hauser stood and looked at the building. It was large, white and imposing. Running along the two wings was the seductive legend White Horse Hotel.

To Brigitte, it was as if the façade of the building had parted like a curtain to reveal the stage beyond. She saw the foyer, dining-room, library, winter garden, bar; above, like the cells in a honeycomb, sixty rooms; below, the kitchens, cellars and store-rooms.

Presiding over it all: herself, Brigitte Hauser, referred to simply—on letterheads, in brochures and newspaper advertisements—as *B. Hauser*. Her headquarters: a manager's office in glistening white and flaming scarlet. In the office: a desk for presiding at. Along the walls: shelves laden with patent files which betokened business efficiency.

Beyond the office: her private quarters, decorated in a subdued green—a bedroom which seemed to consist of one enormous bed. She would live a full life, full of work and play.

Brigitte sighed. The necessities of life remained constant; only methods changed. Bedmates varied in accordance with the current political or financial situation. Death alone could put an end to the rat-race.

Dizziness overcame her suddenly. She swayed and shut her eyes, blaming the heat. Then she straightened up and walked resolutely towards the building which bore the name White Horse Hotel. She strode inside as though it already belonged to her.

Slembeck rubbed the underside of his chin several times with the back of his hand. His skin was as raw as the flanks of a freshly slaughtered pig. He made a mental note not to shave as vigorously in future. It wasn't necessary.

So that must be the house where the Hauser woman stayed while she was in Garmisch. It didn't look much of a place, but appearances were deceptive. After all, the Patockis had hidden their family jewels in a shabby old trunk when things started to get dangerous for them.

Slembeck's face puckered in a reminiscent grin. He took his jacket off and dropped it on the grass beside him, then sat down with his back against a tree and began to watch the house. There wasn't a sign of movement. He wondered if Hauser's wife was in. It might be worth inquiring.

He dismissed the idea. There was plenty of time. He had waited for five years—six, almost. Two or three hours wouldn't make any difference.

He had to get her alone, had to have a heart-to-heart talk with the woman. A little bargain struck between two like-minded people: a bracelet for a human life. It was a fair deal—nobody could accuse him of sharp practice. No reason why it shouldn't be arranged.

Slembeck peered sleepily across at the house. His head started to droop. He was tired, and no wonder, after playing cards all night. There was nothing like a run of bad cards to exhaust a man. He'd earned a little rest—he needed it.

The heat sucked him gently downwards. His head lolled on his chest.

'Fifi! Fifi!' came a shrill voice. 'Where are you, Fifi?'

The voice belonged to an old woman, tall and withered as a barren tree. She wandered towards Slembeck with her clothes flapping and her pointed nose snuffing the air in every direction.

'Have you seen Fifi?'

Slembeck, jerked out of his slumber, said, 'Bugger off, you stupid old bitch!'—and clamped his eyelids shut again.

Then he dozed off, slid sideways and lay inert, snoring.

Captain Keller had the feeling that he was being watched. Enemies were observing him covertly but with unmistakable respect. The sensation only heightened his self-assurance.

Harte and Colman were already installed in the dining-room

of the officers' mess when he walked in. They had snubbed him, so he chose a table in the side-room. Now he was lunching alone for the first time since he and Harte had taken over this lousy internment camp. Well, why not? It was time they realized who was boss round here.

The two men next door were talking and laughing loudly. They were laughing at him—he felt certain of it.

They didn't understand him, but he had no need to explain his actions. Their job was to obey.

Discipline, that was what the army needed. Men like the two next door debated the concept of discipline all the time. They contended that it was a refined form of individualism, but individualism was hogwash. You couldn't win wars with individualism, only with discipline.

He told the mess waiter to bring him a brandy.

'Leave the bottle,' he said. The mess waiter did so.

Then he said, 'Now go to hell.' The mess waiter vanished.

Keller found the man's prompt reactions vaguely reassuring. That, he told himself, was discipline.

'Lieutenant Colman!' he called loudly. There was an edge to his voice.

The lieutenant appeared. His state of dress left much to be desired. He eyed his commanding officer with composure, barely managing to suppress a yawn.

'Lieutenant,' ordered Keller, 'get those transfer papers for Internee Hauser completed at once, and kindly stop going around like a member of a fifth-rate chimpanzee act. I'm not running a circus. And make sure my car is waiting outside in fifteen minutes. I have to pay someone a visit.'

'Gentlemen,' said Internee Mangel, 'I must ask you to rinse your food bowls later. We have something of importance to discuss.'

'May I point out,' objected Wickler, 'that the water could be turned off in the meantime?'

'This won't take long,' Mangel replied impatiently.

The grey faces of his fellow-internees were drained of expression. They always looked blank and disillusioned once they had gulped their food down. They ate twice or sometimes three times a day, but it was never enough.

They knew that their food had to take effect, be assimilated, nourish their weary bodies, but that could only come about through rest: so, they wanted to rest. On the other hand, Mangel had something of alleged importance to discuss with them: so, they waited to hear what he had to say. It was possible that the water would not be running by the time he had finished, in which case there would be no more need to wash their bowls and spoons. They could then slump on to their bunks. That had its advantages too.

Looking round, Mangel diagnosed the general silence as a symptom of approval. Spurred on by Reiter during lunch, he had fought his way to a decision. True, he had vacillated momentarily, overcome by the heat, but then he had thought of his railway battalions in the Balkans. The heat had been semi-tropical down there, but no one ever evaded an order.

In the past twenty-four hours, he, Mangel, had witnessed things which had shaken him to the core. He was determined to impress this on the others, heat or no heat. It was time to set—and make—an example.

'I intend,' he said, 'to institute disciplinary proceedings against a fellow-internee.'

For the past thirty minutes, Internee Laffrentz had been privileged to lunch in the American officers' mess. His very special friend, Ted Harte, was attending to his needs in person and gossiping about this and that.

'Take your German women,' Harte said. 'Superb specimens, some of them.'

'You could say that,' Laffrentz agreed through a mouthful of steak. He breathed stertorously as he shovelled the plate-sized slab of meat down his throat, piece by piece.

'Do you know Frau Hauser?' Harte asked casually.

'Do I! A real stunner. Her husband isn't the only one who loses sleep over her, from what I hear.'

'You do know her—I can see that.' Harte swamped Laffrentz's steak in thick greasy gravy, eliciting a series of delighted grunts from his guest. 'Frau Hauser's a woman with strongly developed senses, one of them being her business sense. She's just in the process of acquiring the White Horse.'

Laffrentz looked genuinely surprised. He dismembered a slice of white bread as thick as a man's wrist, dunked the pieces in gravy and crammed them into his mouth. 'Shall I let Hauser in on it?' he asked, speaking with difficulty. 'Is that what you want?'

'I don't mind who knows what we talk about.'

'I get it.' Laffrentz's little eyes twinkled knowingly as he chewed. 'If you want me to pass the word to Hauser, that's what I'll do. What shall I say, exactly?'

'Just tell him the sale is almost completed. The purchase price has already been deposited in the form of cash and jewellery. Frau Hauser had quite a time raising it. Could you manage some pudding?'

'Could I? Any amount, preferably with cream, and a coffee to go with it, also with cream—sugar too. Shall I tell Hauser where I got my information from?'

Harte proffered a cigar. 'There's no absolute necessity for that, Herr Laffrentz.'

'I follow you. You can rely on me, Mr Harte. There's nothing I wouldn't do for you, not now we're friends, in a manner of speaking.'

Hauser did not return to Room 29 immediately.

The corridors of Block C were empty except for the food pails which now stood forlornly on the flagstones. Isolated snores came from behind the closed doors.

The only sign of life was on the first floor, where Professor Sprenger, a former senior educational adviser to the Hitler Youth, was busily scraping traces of soup out of one of the pails. Hauser knew it must be Sprenger even though his head and shoulders were hidden from view. The professor always scraped the pails after every meal.

Sprenger's average haul was generally estimated to be in the region of an ounce or an ounce-and-a-half, despite the fact that he regularly scraped away for half an hour or more. According to precise calculations made by his fellow-internee Professor Konradt, a dietician of international repute, Sprenger's expenditure of energy far exceeded the calorific benefits he obtained.

Hauser stationed himself at the other end of the long corridor, near the lavatories. Without craning his head, he looked out of the window. He saw a stretch of trampled grass about forty yards wide, then a wall topped with barbed wire. The wall was about ten feet high.

Carefully, Hauser checked the lay-out against what he could

remember of the map Harte had shown him in Keller's office. It tallied exactly. Here, directly opposite Block C, the wall took a sharp turn, forming an almost perfect right-angle. This masked it from the watch-tower on the left.

Harte was right about the gap, but why had he drawn his attention to it? Had he been acting on orders from Keller? It was quite possible. The two men might well be in business together—a typically American set-up. Brigitte must have inspired the whole thing, but at what price?

Hauser breathed heavily. The platinum bracelet was a headache. It could hang him if it got into the wrong hands. On the other hand, perhaps the deal really was on the level. He couldn't think straight any more, thanks to Brigitte.

He became aware that someone was standing behind him. He hadn't heard him coming. Even his hearing had ceased to function properly.

'Glad I found you here,' said Reiter's voice. 'I'd like a little chat.'

'Well, I wouldn't.'

Hauser stared fixedly at the perimeter wall, the wall which stood between him and the world he must help to manipulate if he didn't want to dangle from one of the many gallows that appeared to be such an integral feature of the international scene.

'Look, Hauser,' Reiter said impatiently, 'you don't seem to realize what's going on in this place—and all because of you.'

'What's it to you? Don't tell me you want to give me a helping hand—brother officers and all that crap.'

'I just don't want any trouble, that's all.'

'Then why go looking for it?' Hauser retorted rudely.

Reiter restrained his impatience with an effort. 'You're wrong to distrust me, Hauser. Distrusting me can only harm you and everyone else—me included, of course. It must be obvious to you that I'm trying to help.'

'Well, what do you want to know?'

'Tell me what's going on. As commandant, I ought to know. Then I can adapt myself to the situation and prepare for all eventualities.'

'What eventualities?'

'Well, Keller has been acting like a mad bull since this morning. Something's up, Hauser, and I'm pretty positive you know what it is. Trust me and I may be able to help you.'

'Listen,' Hauser said firmly, 'I look after my own interests. I don't need any help from collaborators like you. Now shove off.'

He propped his elbows on the window-sill and stared down at the wall topped with barbed wire, concentrating on the point where it formed an almost right-angled salient. That was the gap, he thought grimly.

Laffrentz was the next person to show up. 'Congratulations,' he said, 'your wife has pulled it off. She practically owns the hotel already—I heard that from a reliable source. Efficient woman, your wife. Apparently she raked together everything she could lay hands on—any amount of cash and jewellery.'

'Jewellery too?' Hauser asked in a flat voice.

'Lovely stuff. Even the Americans are drooling over it.'

Hauser made no comment. He went on staring at the gap which he was now determined to cross.

'Sergeant Popper,' Harte said affably, 'I've always followed your unofficial activities with the greatest interest.'

'I appreciate that, sir.' The provost-marshal glowed with pride. 'Take my squad of generals. They're terrific. It's just a question of knowing how to use them strategically.'

Harte gave an amiable smile. 'Just what I was going to say.'

Popper launched into a lengthy account of his squad's special aptitudes. The generals were understanding, obliging, and endowed with healthy instincts. 'They know the exact difference between a pack of cigarettes and their duty to the late Führer—they've proved that time and time again.'

'If I ever needed you and your special squad, Popper, could I count on you?'

'Any time, Mr Harte,' Popper assured him devoutly.

'In every respect?'

'Of course, sir. My generals are capable of anything I tell them to do. That's Third Reich training for you. They've learned to obey under any circumstances. Just tell me what you want done and they'll do it, from planning a break to swabbing down latrines. Nothing scares them.'

Harte looked duly impressed. 'Fine,' he said. 'So if we turned them loose on someone, like hounds after a fox, they'd play, would they?'

'You bet!' The sergeant's confidence was unbounded. 'They're men of honour, sir. I've taught them that it's their honour and privilege to jump when I say jump.'

Internee Mangel was nearing the end of his lengthy discourse. 'And so,' he said in conclusion, 'I categorically demand that our room-mate Herr Laffrentz be acquainted with the universal odium aroused by his provocative behaviour. This, subject to the agreement of all present, will be a final warning. If it goes unheeded, I shall be forced to recommend stringent measures.'

The agreement of all present manifested itself in a silence which Mangel construed as approval. His horsey face became tinged with contempt as he surveyed the men around him. Not a real personality among them.

Wickler was breathing with his mouth open, Trost dozing wearily in a corner, Baron van Hagen seated in his favourite spot beside the window, staring out and looking more than usually aloof. Wammenberg was dabbling at his 'souvenirs'—crude water-colours showing him in the guise of Hitler's butler, crude but worth all of two marks. The others were squatting silently on their stools.

Laffrentz was the only one who endeavoured to take an interest. His head still throbbed with dull insistence but he was determined not to let things slide. He had no intention of defending himself. Instead, he decided to take a leaf out of Clausewitz's book and attack.

'You're talking a load of old rubbish, Mangel. Provocation—wasn't that the word you used? Typical of you to employ that sort of terminology. Communist jargon, that's what it is. Well, don't employ it on me.'

'I beg your pardon,' Mangel protested.

But Laffrentz was well away. 'Yessir,' he said firmly, 'you're riddled with Marxism, Mangel, that's your trouble. Can't help yourself, I suppose. It's like a disease.'

'This is the end.' Mangel looked genuinely outraged.

'You've said it, Colonel,' Laffrentz retorted, warming to his task. 'You're an undercover Communist, but this is the end of the line. Mr Harte will explode when I tell him. It's typical, of course. Everybody knows the way you Reichswehr officers always flirted with the Red Army—and Stalin, for that matter.

A lifelong love affair with the Communist Party—isn't that how you'd describe it, Colonel?'

Mangel was utterly disconcerted. He wondered how he ought to respond. The obvious course was to challenge the fat pig to a duel, but it was no use. In the first place duelling was impossible in camp, and in the second place Laffrentz was no gentleman.

'You haven't heard the last of this,' Laffrentz continued defiantly. 'Your Communist sympathies need thorough investigation. Mr Harte happens to be a friend of mine. He'll be very interested to hear what I've got to tell him about you—among other people.'

The guard in the watch-tower was leaning over the parapet. He lolled there like a rag doll, but he wasn't asleep.

His narrowed eyes travelled along the barbed wire to the next watch-tower, then back again until they reached the bluish tangle of wire immediately beneath his vantage-point.

The heat seemed to flow along the wire. It washed over the walls, surged across the stretches of grass, teemed down out of a sky the colour of molten lead.

There was a storm brewing, the guard in the watch-tower told himself. He was glad there was going to be a storm. A man couldn't breathe properly in this heat.

Captain Keller knew where to find Brigitte. The White Horse was reserved for the army of occupation and its dependants. Brigitte counted as a dependant.

'It's a good hotel,' she said, smiling at him. 'Sloppily run, of course, but it won't take long to cure that.'

He sat down beside her. A waiter bustled up.

'The champagne is already chilled, sir. Which mark would you prefer?'

Keller knew that he could choose between Pommery, Heidsieck and Veuve Clicquot, but he merely said, 'Mineral water.'

Brigitte said, 'I think I know where the bracelet is.'

'I'm glad to hear that, even though it isn't specially important—neither to me nor both of us.'

'Do I get the hotel?' she asked point blank. 'I want it and you can give it to me. Your signature will be enough.'

'And your part of the bargain?'

'Unchanged, Frank. Life together from now on.'

'Even if your husband forfeits his own life in the process?'

'Yes, even then,' she said softly. 'I love you, Frank. I love you without any reservations or qualifications. Let me prove it again. We'll take a room here in the hotel—our hotel. Now, this minute.'

'And the bracelet?'

'We'll get it later—afterwards.'

'I'd sooner get that over with first. My car's outside. We could drive out to your place.'

Ted Harte was virtually alone in the administration block that sweltering afternoon. He had been counting on that. The private offices on the top floor were quiet as the grave between twelve and two. People were eating or resting from their labours.

He glanced at his watch. It was a few minutes after two o'clock. The camp lay-out on the office wall loomed over him challengingly. One watch-tower—No. 4— seemed to stand out with special clarity. It caught and held his eye like a neon sign.

He went to a shelf and took down an Ordnance Survey map. Having cleared his desk with a few rapid movements, he carefully unrolled it.

The map showed the immediate vicinity of the camp, up to a radius of fifteen miles. It was an efficient piece of map-making, but slightly obsolete. The date in the margin said 1937, and no military installations were shown. Harte went to another shelf and took down a loose-leaf file full of aerial photographs: a legacy from Herman Goering's Luftwaffe, supplemented by British and American reconnaissance teams.

He was searching for the small inn which belonged to Brigitte Hauser. It was called the Crown and it stood at the foot of a mountain some distance from the main road. An idyllic spot, from the look of it. Fairly accessible on three sides and, as the aerial photograph confirmed, fairly conspicuous as well.

Taking a pair of calipers, Harte measured the distance between the camp and the isolated Gasthof. Comparison with the scale at the side of the map showed that the two points were only five miles apart in a direct line.

This was fortunate. An ordinary pedestrian could cover the

distance in an hour and a half, whereas someone proceeding with caution because he wanted to escape notice would take about two hours. Allowing for bends in the road, a car could do the same trip in fifteen minutes.

Harte tore a sheet off a memorandum pad and drew a simple sketch-map of the area: the road, the Crown itself, the near-by hill with its scattered clumps of trees, a field bordered by a stream. Neatly folding the slip of paper, he put it in his pocket. Then he closed the file containing the aerial photographs, rolled up the map, carried both over to the shelf and carefully stowed them away again.

He left the office and walked along the corridor to the stairs.

There was activity on the ground floor. The general administrative offices were kept permanently manned by day in accordance with standing orders. The air was filled with the buzz of afternoon conversation and a loudspeaker was blaring in the guardroom. Harte made for the room which housed the standby squad.

The standby squad was one of Keller's inventions. Broadly speaking, the men at his disposal were divided into three groups. One did guard duty, the second formed the standby squad, and the third supervised and carried out routine tasks. The three groups took it in turns to stand guard, stand by and perform general duties. Spare time was a luxury. The men secretly cursed Keller. Harte they tolerated.

Of all three assignments, standby duty was the least demanding and most boring. Eighteen men and two non-coms had to spend twenty-four hours in the same room on constant alert, which meant that they were not allowed to remove their clothes.

Two trucks waited in the courtyard, ready to move off at a moment's notice. Rifles, tommy-guns and two MGs stood ready in one corner of the room, considerably reducing the available space. The men contended that the internees lived like hotel guests, compared with the barrack-room hubbub and discomfort of standby duty.

Nobody took any notice of Harte when he walked in. The men continued to loll on their mattresses, flicking through magazines, listlessly reading army newspapers, or staring at the wall. They drank from Coca-Cola bottles, liquor being strictly banned by order of Captain Keller.

On the wall hung a placard which proclaimed the four freedoms. Some comedian had attached a hand-drawn addendum to the stars-and-stripes-adorned border. This read: *Be nice to the Krauts. There isn't a Nazi among them.*

The corporal sitting beside the telephone raised his hand and beckoned Harte over. It was Copland, one of the very few men who still devoted an occasional thought to the war. The gist of his conclusions was that might and right were identical.

'Are you here officially or unofficially, Mr Harte?'

'Why do you ask?'

'If you're here officially I'll stand up and salute; if not, why torpedo our afternoon rest?'

Harte grinned. 'I was curious to see the state of your pigsty, that's all. How long does it take you to turn out?'

'Depends whether you're asking officially or unofficially. Officially, I'd say three minutes. Unofficially, I would have to have a pee, the boys would take time to wake up, one of them would be in the shower, and at least three others would have lost something—socks, pin-ups, hand-grenades. Better reckon on a quarter of an hour.'

'What if something really happened?' Harte drawled.

'What, for instance?'

'Do you think this camp is escape-proof, Corporal?'

'No, but the internees are. They slink around with their tails between their legs and call Hitler a bastard on demand. They're too weak-kneed to make a break for it.'

'Three thousand nine hundred and ninety-nine of them, maybe, but what about the four-thousandth?'

'You reckon someone's going to try?'

'What if someone did?'

'We'd fill him full of holes. One burst ought to be enough.'

'What about the order which states that escaped internees are to be recaptured unhurt if possible?'

Copland's prize-fighter's features registered conviction. 'Know something, Mr Harte?' he confided. 'I think we Americans are too goddamned sentimental. We've got a pussy-foot complex. From what I hear, the SS managed things far better. They used to spring half a dozen prisoners and then let fly—like shooting fish in a barrel. At least we'd get some firing-practice that way.'

'You'd like that, wouldn't you?' Harte said thoughtfully,

squinting into the dense haze of tobacco-smoke which shrouded the room. 'Tell me, isn't this squad supposed to be commanded by an officer?'

'Supposed to be, yes—there's always one officially assigned to us. It's Lieutenant Colman's turn today, but have you ever known him to be around when he's wanted? The lieutenant values his privacy, just like Captain Keller, so that leaves us holding the baby. Don't worry, though. If there's any dirty work to be done we'll do it.'

Harte made no comment. War had taught the young Texan that human life wasn't worth a plug nickel, and now he believed it. If Copland was sent off on a man-hunt, he'd go for broke. Death didn't figure in Harte's programme, but the fear of death was something else. He could use that.

'So you'd normally take fifteen minutes to move out,' he said eventually. 'If you can make it ten, so much the better. You never can tell.' On that note he left the room.

At the entrance to the administration block he paused and looked at his watch. It was well past two already—two twenty-five to be precise.

Problems were looming up on all sides, one of them being Copland. If Harte wasn't careful, Copland would turn his operation into a bloodbath. The corporal's enthusiasm must be curbed, but how? The standby squad was part of his plan—one of the most essential items in his calculations—but he hadn't reckoned with Copland.

He went to the nearest telephone and asked for a line to the officers' mess. It was several minutes before Colman could be prevailed on to come to the phone. He sounded tired and irritable.

'You're on standby duty today, aren't you?' Harte asked.

'Always am,' Colman grumbled. 'Never is the day when I'm not responsible for something. Today and every other day it's the standby squad, but that's no problem. It runs by itself.'

'Listen, Colman,' Harte said, 'don't ask any questions and try to forget this conversation if you can, but I'd feel happier if you were on the spot today. Just in case something happens.'

'Hey, what are you driving at?' Colman sounded a little perturbed. 'What's cooking?'

'Nothing—yet, but we ought to be prepared. I'd say that

was advisable with a commandant like Keller, wouldn't you?'

Harte rang off and walked across the courtyard to the outer gate. Passing through it, he strolled along the main road past the internment camp in the direction of the Eibsee and the Austrian border.

Tower No. 1 was situated immediately beside the main entrance. Tower No. 2 was almost opposite Block A. Tower No. 3 covered Block B, and Tower No. 4 coincided with Block C.

The duties of guards on day-watch were strictly laid down. The guard in No. 1 tower had to cover the stretch of wire and wall between his own tower and No. 2. No. 2's stretch ran as far as No. 3, and so on round the full perimeter. The towers were normally double-manned at night, which meant, in theory at least, that surveillance was possible in both directions at once. In practice, boredom ensured that the standard of observation was not very high.

Opposite the guard in Tower No. 4 ran a stretch of wall about sixty yards wide. This was the stretch which included the almost rectangular salient visible on the camp lay-out, ten feet of dead ground which could only be commanded by eye and machine-gun fire from Tower No. 4 itself.

Harte carefully studied Tower No. 4 from the road.

The guard was leaning over the parapet, gazing with rule-book fixity along the barbed wire which ran past Block C. The man's attitude conveyed apathy and fatigue. He yawned.

Glancing at his watch again, Harte saw that it had just turned half-past two. He looked around, but there was no sign of life.

Briskly, he left the main road and set off through the long grass towards Tower No. 4.

The hurriedly convened ambassadorial conference was brief but informative. For once, it took place in the basement wash-room, which was invariably deserted during the afternoon. Baron von Hagen presided.

'I can't help being alarmed by the Americans' attitude,' he said uneasily. 'We offer to supply them with vital information, but they show no interest whatsoever.'

This was alarming indeed. Herr von Weissänger, late of

Bucharest, was the first to echo the Baron's sentiments, wholeheartedly supported by Herr von Kernitz-Weibel, late of Budapest. The little group hummed with dark forebodings.

'It's appalling, their total incomprehension of German affairs. How can they even intimate that there's no fundamental difference between one German and another? That's the sort of attitude which positively invites disaster.'

They were confirmed realists, these experienced professional diplomats. Decades of public service had taught them that the State was a durable commodity. Their country was far from finished. Appearances were deceiving, and today's enemy could well become tomorrow's ally. Diplomats not only knew this—they banked on it.

'Well, we won't stand for this sort of treatment,' was the general verdict, but Baron von Hagen skilfully smoothed his colleagues' ruffled feathers.

'We are not dealing with our kind, unfortunately. That will come in time, but I fear we cannot wait until then. The camp authorities seem to have an obsessive craving for evidence against Hauser, who was, after all, only a junior representative of the executive arm.'

'And one with whom we have absolutely nothing in common!'

'Precisely the point we have to make, gentlemen. Why should we delay any longer? This appears to be a question of survival, therefore a matter of the highest priority.'

Herr von Weissänger cleared his throat. 'What I know about Hauser would be more than enough to send him to the gallows, especially if you all corroborate it. If there's really no alternative, I'm prepared to testify.'

'Very commendable of you,' Baron von Hagen said thankfully. 'I only hope your decision has not come too late.'

Internee Trost, renowned for his meteorological advice to the German High Command, felt one of his dizzy spells coming on. He lay stretched out on his bunk. The roaring sound in his ears was closing in with claustrophobic insistence.

This roaring sound was growing in volume and duration day by day. Trost experienced a sense of utter helplessness. Nobody gave a damn about him. He wondered what time it was. Gingerly turning his head, he surveyed the stuffy room. Almost all his room-mates were asleep—every bunk occupied. He estimated that it must be about one o'clock, possibly two o'clock or even later.

The menacing roar seemed to engulf him. It was as if all the blood in his body had rushed to his head. He felt his stomach give a violent heave. Stifling a groan, he sat up painfully. The walls started to rotate, ballooning like curtains in a strong draught.

He levered himself off his bunk and staggered to the door. Don't be sick, he commanded—whatever you do, don't lie down and be sick. He could picture what would happen if he disturbed his friends' siesta, hear the harsh words and coarse laughter, imagine the lavatorial jokes cracked at his expense.

Doggedly, he closed the door behind him and leaned against the wall with his knees trembling. In front of him stretched the long empty corridor. Right at the far end, sharply silhouetted against the window, stood a man—the only sign of life in the whole corridor.

Trost breathed a sigh of relief. There would be only one person to witness his wretched attack of weakness. He tottered towards the window, because there at the end of the passage was the lavatory. He could be sick there and put his head under the tap afterwards.

Trost went as fast as his rubber legs would carry him. He cannoned against one wall, rebounded and cannoned into the opposite one. Suddenly, the rectangle of brilliant white light at the end of the passage rocketed skywards.

He did not hear the dull thud his body made as it hit the flagstones.

The man at the window walked up to Trost and hauled his limp form into the lavatory. Cold water cascaded over the meteorologist's head. The roaring sound which had invaded his skull receded and the mist before his eyes seemed to dissolve.

Trost became aware of a rusty drain and a strong bony hand gripping his upper arm. Raising his head, he saw a face he knew. It was Hauser's.

'Go on,' Hauser urged him, 'throw up and then hold your head under the tap again.'

'Thank you,' Trost muttered. 'Much obliged, I'm sure.'

Hauser looked closely at the pale exhausted face, yellowish eyeballs and tangle of dirty grey hair. They belonged to a man who was ripe for death.

Disgust overcame him—disgust at the thought of vegetating, of giving up without a fight. Well, he wasn't prepared to do that. There were better places to die than the scrapheap. Anything but that.

He went back to the window. If Harte came, he would have to come by the road leading past the camp, a broad and conspicuous thoroughfare which was closed to civilian traffic. Harte would then walk across to Tower No. 4 and engage the guard in conversation. The critical moment would arrive as soon as the guard's head was turned.

He would be able to see Harte from the first-floor window, follow him all the way as he walked up to the guard and distracted his attention. Down in the courtyard the view would be completely obscured by the wall, which meant that he had to keep watch from the first floor.

It also meant that he would have to run downstairs and skirt the whole block before he got to the wall, losing valuable and possibly vital minutes.

Trost, wet-haired and green around the gills, emerged from the lavatory and shambled towards him. He clutched at the window-frame for support, breathing hard.

'How do you feel?'

'Better, much better. I really am most grateful to you, Herr Hauser.'

Hauser raised his head and peered across the barbed wire. A man was walking down the main road, parallel with the internment camp. He was heading for Tower No. 4.

It was Harte—no mistake about it.

Hauser felt a thrill of excitement. He ran his eyes once more over the essential features of the scene: the wall with its almost ninety-degree angle, the forty yards of tall grass, the road, and, beyond it, a belt of undergrowth. That was his primary objective.

'Look, Trost,' he said suddenly, 'you can help me.'

'I'd be glad to.'

'You see that man coming down the road?'

'The American?'

'Yes. Don't let him out of your sight. I'll go down into the courtyard now and stand where you can see me. Now this is important: as soon as the American goes over to Tower No. 4 and speaks to the guard, give me a signal. Nod your head and wave.'

Trost could not quite gather what was expected of him but he wanted to be helpful. Even though he felt drained of energy and will-power he owed Hauser a debt of gratitude.

'I'll do it,' he said.

'Listen, though—this is really important: don't nod and wave until the American is actually speaking to the guard. The guard must have turned round. Herr Trost. He must be facing in the opposite direction, understand?'

'Yes,' Trost replied. 'I understand.'

Hauser hurried off down the passage, leaving Trost propped against the window-frame. His face was damp with sweat and his head muzzy, but the roaring sound had gone completely.

There was Hauser, down in the yard. He looked up at Trost, who peered at the distant figure of the American and shook his head.

The yard was almost deserted, and there was little activity among the few internees who could be seen. It was the time of afternoon repose, the time when men lay on their bunks or sat in the shade, brooding in silence.

Hauser stood in the full glare of the sun, staring fixedly at Trost.

Trost observed the American more closely. He recognized him now. It was Mr Harte, the camp's chief CIC officer, whose name and function filled every internee with dread. He was walking placidly down the road, looking as if he had all the time in the world to spare. Opposite Tower No. 4, he slowed down still further and glanced at his watch.

Leaving the road, Harte went up to the watch-tower and hailed the guard. The guard turned round and leaned over the parapet on the far side of the tower.

Trost gave several vigorous nods, raised his arm and waved as instructed.

Hauser, who had been staring up at him so unwaveringly, came to life with a sudden jerk.

Trost found it hard to follow what happened next. He saw

Hauser sprint across the yard, make a grab for the top of the wall and hang there with his legs dangling.

In an instant, Hauser had pulled himself up and thrown his left leg across the parapet. His right foot scrabbled against stone as he hauled his thick-set frame on to the wall. He seemed to roll over the barbed wire in one continuous movement.

Then he dropped to the ground on the far side and was lost from view.

Trost felt the blood drain from his cheeks as he stared down, aghast, into the courtyard. The handful of internees who had witnessed the incident were scurrying off like frightened rabbits.

They hadn't seen anything. They hadn't been there. Trost awoke to the realization like a man jolted by an electric shock.

It was an escape, and escaping was a punishable offence. More than that, it was regarded as an admission of guilt.

Again, anyone who had knowledge of an escape, successful or attempted, rendered himself liable to punishment if he failed to report it. He, Trost, had already rendered himself liable to punishment. Once again, he had become an accessory.

He wondered what to do: report the incident, keep mum, cover himself, feign ignorance, ask the others for advice?

There was always Mangel, of course. He could put in a report to him. As room senior, Mangel would have to decide whether to take the matter further. That was it. Mangel could shoulder the responsibility.

Trost's muddled thoughts were cut short by a sudden report. They were shooting, he concluded with a shudder, shooting at Hauser. What now?

But no one had fired. Peace still reigned over the watch-towers. Guard No. 4 was still talking to Mr Harte. A dull rumbling sound filled the air, like a car thundering over a wooden bridge.

It was the storm, Trost told himself, the storm which everyone had been waiting for. He had forecast it.

'Hi, Keller!' The cry, uttered in a powerful, high-pitched voice, came from an army jeep. 'Just the man I wanted to see. Glad I ran into you.'

'The pleasure's mutual,' Keller called back. He turned to

Brigitte, who was sitting beside him in the Cadillac. 'That's all we needed,' he muttered. 'It's Forsell, the Commander of Occupational Forces. He clings like a leech.'

They were on the outskirts of Garmisch, proceeding in the direction of Mittenwald. Major Forsell expressed the desire for a talk but Keller did his best to hedge. He was heavily—and officially—engaged.

'I quite understand,' Forsell said, leering at Brigitte. 'All the same, I'm sure you can hold out for another five minutes.'

'I told you he was a leech,' Keller whispered to Brigitte.

'Another few minutes won't matter,' she said. 'Besides, I'll be able to tidy myself up a bit—for you, Frank. I think I'll change. It's swelteringly hot today.'

'Do that,' he said. Then, to Forsell, 'You're welcome to join us for a drink if you feel like it.'

Ten minutes later the two men were sitting over a bottle of brandy in the small and countrified bar-room of the Crown. Forsell's rotund and somewhat puffy face was slightly flushed, less on account of the heat than because he had already consumed a tumbler of brandy.

Forsell was extremely annoyed. He vented his spleen on Germany, the US Constitution, and sundry superior officers.

'This country gives me a pain, Keller,' he concluded.

'Me too,' Keller said.

'Anyone would think we won the war so we could play nursemaid to these lousy people!'

Keller shrugged. 'Looks like it.'

Forsell might be a fat and overbearing slob, reflected Keller, but his brother was a three-star general, his brother-in-law a senator, and his uncle a big noise in the military government. Forsell had far better contacts and connections than he did himself, which was a fact worth remembering.

Keller might be a ruthless and ambitious young man, reflected Forsell, but he enjoyed a reputation for success. Even his uncle, T. S. Wagner, one of the most influential figures in the military government and a man not noted for generosity of spirit, had referred to Keller in glowing terms. 'He'll go far, that boy,' T. S. had said. 'Handle him with kid gloves.'

'By the way Keller, did I tell you my uncle sent his regards?'

'Yes, you told me on the phone yesterday morning.'

'Yesterday morning?' Forsell tried to furrow his fleshy and unwrinkled brow in an effort to convey pressure of work.

'Yesterday morning?' he repeated. 'No, this was since then. I called T.S. again yesterday evening. He's staying with my brother—you know, the general—here in the district.'

Name-dropping bastard, thought Keller. Forsell displayed his relations like sign-boards: my uncle, the big potato; my brother, the general; my aunt, the Secretary of State's widow. Keller smiled at him.

'Yes,' Forsell went on meditatively, 'old T.S. sent his best regards. Said he appreciated all you've done here and told me to tell you to look him up when you get back to the States.' He swallowed another tumblerful of brandy. Rivulets of sweat trickled down his face, making it look as if it had been basted with dripping.

'What did he mean exactly, Major—look him up when I get back to the States?'

Forsell smiled with infinite condescension. Nothing, he implied, was hidden from him whose brother was a general, whose uncle . . .

'T.S. wants to quit. He's flying to Bremerhaven this week and his ship sails next Monday. However, he wants to wrap up the Eastern Territories war crimes before he leaves. The Hauser case is the only major one outstanding. Get the point?'

'Of course I do, but you can tell him that the Hauser file is practically complete.'

'You mean that? T.S. will be absolutely delighted. He told Colonel Cord he was sure you'd manage it.'

'In my own way.'

'It's the only way, Keller, even if it is against the general trend.'

'What trend, Major?'

'Well, I guess it's a little hard for you to judge, without my connections. To quote my cousin, the Air Force general, we're allowing the fruits of victory to be wrested from our hands. Those were his very words, more or less.'

'Why does your worthy uncle have to quit?'

'There's no *have to* about it,' Forsell replied, his complacent voice untinged with reproach. 'He wants out. He doesn't want any part of this.'

'Any part of what?'

The major ordered more coffee and brandy. As soon as the waitress had gone he looked around carefully for potential eavesdroppers.

'Give it another few weeks—months at the most—and you'll see for yourself. You'll be expected to treat your war criminals like US citizens. I tell you, Keller, it won't be long before they start debasing all the things we soldiers fought and died for.'

Very much alive, Major Forsell meditatively tipped several spoonfuls of sugar into his coffee. 'And why, Keller? Because trade follows the flag, that's why! We fought a man's war, but all big business thinks of is money. Another two or three years and those internees of yours will be coining it—you'll be begging them for a hand-out.'

'But what about de-Nazification, Major? A lot of Germans look on us as liberators. They think we're here to help them clean up their country.'

'All balls,' Forsell replied firmly, slurping his coffee. 'Sounds good but means nothing. Just a smoke screen to blind us to the fact that we've got the world in our pocket. The world belongs to us, Keller. We've got it made, but what do we do? Back down, back-pedal, shove experts like T.S. into the background and bring nobodies to the fore. I ask you, why should we negotiate when we can give orders? Why should we let people badger us out of what belongs to us anyway? Justice is like a windmill—it operates when the wind blows. Well, we're supplying the wind at the moment, Keller, just us and nobody else, but for how much longer?'

'I'm sick of the whole business,' Keller said.

Forsell gave a polite smile. 'My sentiments exactly.'

'I'm sick of it but I'll handle it in my own way. Please excuse me now, Major. I have a couple of urgent matters to attend to.'

Ted Harte re-entered the camp on his way back from Tower No. 4.

The sentry snapped to attention. Harte casually returned his salute and headed for the administration block. He seemed to be in a hurry.

A big storm was brewing. The countryside sweltered beneath a tarpaulin of hot and treacly air. In the sky, towering banks of blue-black cloud were fitfully illuminated by vivid yellow flashes.

Lieutenant Colman was lounging in the main entrance, idly surveying the approaching storm. Harte hailed him.

'Glad to see you're still around, Colman. There's going to be a monumental explosion.'

'The storm?' inquired Colman. He made a dismissive gesture, as though brushing the clouds aside.

'No, something very different.'

'What?'

'Come with me—you're in for a big surprise.'

'Really?' Colman said. 'What's Keller done this time?'

Harte ran upstairs and pushed open the door of the outer office. Sylvia was not there, which seemed to annoy him. 'Fräulein Meiners!' he yelled.

A door opened farther along the passage—it was the door of the room where Gernsbach worked—and Sylvia peered out.

'I need you,' Harte called. He sounded resentful. 'Urgently!'

Sylvia hurried towards him. Meanwhile, Colman had also toiled his way upstairs.

'What's all the fuss about?' he demanded. 'Is the place on fire or has someone broken his neck?'

'You've got to alert the standby squad at once, Lieutenant,' Harte told him. 'Get ready to move out.'

'But what's the matter?' Colman insisted.

'Everything.'

Sylvia eyed Harte doubtfully. 'How many drinks have you had?'

'Just get on with your job, Fräulein Meiners. Make sure the switchboard is double-manned from now on. Send for Gernsbach and tell the German camp commandant to stand by.'

'What's going on?' Sylvia asked as she swiftly jotted down some notes on her pad.

Harte, who was pacing nervously back and forth, paused in mid-stride. 'What's going on? Hauser's escaped, made a break for it—pulled a vanishing act, that's all.'

Colman emitted a prolonged whistle and slumped into an arm-chair.

'How did it happen?' demanded Sylvia.

'Why ask me?' Harte retorted blithely. 'I'm not an information bureau. We'd do better to work out what's going to happen now. The war crimes tribunal will bust a gut.'

'Dachau's a long way off,' Sylvia said. 'If anyone busts a gut it'll be Captain Keller. I ought to notify him at once, but I'm not sure where he is at the moment.'

'Who cares?' Colman observed casually. 'He's got other fish to fry. Anyway, how did Hauser manage to get away in the first place? That's what I don't understand.'

'Don't you? Okay, so the army doesn't pay you to use your imagination. Come with me.' Harte walked into the inner office, followed by Colman.

The lieutenant stood in the middle of the room with his hands buried deep in his trouser-pockets and stared at the wall-map of Camp 7. He shook his head slowly. 'You mean he broke out—just like that?'

Harte nodded. 'Just like that.'

'Must have been the guards' fault,' hazarded Colman.

'Nonsense, Colman! Our security system is sketchy. Don't try and pin it on the men—they're okay, even if some of them could use more training. No, blame this on the officers.'

Colman remained obdurate. 'One of the guards must have been asleep on his feet,' he insisted.

'Whatever it was, we must do our utmost to recapture the man.'

'You take over,' Colman said. 'As long as we can't get hold of Keller, you're in charge here.'

Harte was irritated by his total failure to elicit any positive reaction from Colman, but before he could speak the lieutenant went on, 'Anyway, where did you get your information from? Who reported the escape?'

'I just know,' Harte replied. 'You'll have to be satisfied with that for the time being. If I were in your shoes, all I'd be worried about would be the best way of deploying the standby squad. After all, that's your responsibility, isn't it?'

Colman flinched. 'My responsibility?' he mumbled.

'Yes, sir,' Harte said cheerfully. 'Yours and yours alone.'

He reached into his pocket and pulled out the sketch-map he had made earlier. 'Take a look, Colman. This'll show you the location of an inn called the Crown. The Crown belongs to Hauser's wife. Hauser can have only one destination—that's obvious to anyone who bothers to figure out how his mind works. Now I'll tell you how to deploy your men.'

'Okay,' Colman said. 'If you insist, but I'd still like to know how you found out.'

It was not sound sleep that descended on the internees after lunch, but a sort of waking dream in which they were plagued by thoughts of all that had brought them to Camp 7.

They lay brooding in the sultry afternoon heat, brooding and speculating on the future. Dreadful, the way everything became magnified—all the things that should never have happened.

Dreadful, too, this eternal self-interrogation. What did you do? What can they prove against you? What papers, documents, photographs can they dig up?

There was that newspaper report of the April 20th celebrations, Hitler's birthday—and you, you idiot, were on the list of invited guests. A Gauleiter at the top, then various Party bigwigs, and, finally, you—you and a Gauleiter, indissolubly linked by lines of newsprint.

Or there was that photo of the prize-giving. You won an award, and who donated it? The Party! Who presented it? A Nazi official! That makes you a marked man. For ever? If not, for how long? Whatever you're in for, the prospects are bleak and the past has turned into an agonizing nightmare.

More self-interrogation. How much responsibility can I disclaim. Will they produce witnesses? Who will the witness be? The man who called himself my friend, drank my wine and smoked my cigarettes? The girl I picked up and dropped? A priest, a subordinate, my wife and children?

Consider the ominous significance of things . . .

What did they mean by cutting off the water? Coincidence or petty annoyance? Administrative blunder or calculated warning?

What did they mean by issuing soap? Was it a deliberate improvement in living conditions or an unmistakable sign of prolonged detention?

What categories were summoned for interrogation—war criminals, automatic arrests or security threats?

Was it the end or the beginning, procrastination or acceleration, tactics or chance? What lay ahead, death or freedom? What was happening outside?

Thoughts glided through their minds like serpents as they lay there, spying on each other through closed eyelids. What was to one man's potential advantage could be to the certain detriment of his neighbour.

A sudden bang jolted them into wakefulness—a loud, dry report, like a shot. The bang reverberated round the walls of Block C.

Wickler was the first to realize what it was. The architect sat up in his bunk and listened with his mouth open. 'Thunder,' he announced.

Nobody else spoke. The internees strained their ears to catch the second clap of thunder, but it never came. The heat seemed even fiercer and more oppressive than before.

Then the door burst open and Trost stood swaying in the entrance, his face yellow-grey. The door banged against a tier of bunks.

'Fancy making a racket at this hour, man! You must be crazy!' This protest came from Wickler, who jumped at any opportunity to escape from his melancholy musings.

'Herr Mangel,' Trost called in a choking voice, 'I've got something important to tell you.'

'But not during our siesta,' snapped Wickler.

'Can't you shut up?' Laffrentz grunted from his bunk. 'I need my beauty-sleep.'

This remark was enough to make Mangel sit up. 'What's the matter?' he demanded.

Trost closed his eyes for a moment. His lips trembled. Then he blurted out, 'Hauser's gone.'

'What do you mean?' Mangel asked in surprise. 'What do you mean: gone?'

Trost fought for breath and clutched his left side. 'Over the wall,' he gasped. 'He went over the wall.'

Silence ensued. None of the room's inmates felt any inclination to comment. They merely stared at Trost incredulously.

'Somebody give the man a chair,' the Baron said after a pause, 'and some water.'

Wickler slid off his bunk and fetched a chair. He rammed it against the back of Trost's knees. Trost collapsed on to it, then sipped greedily at the mug of water which was thrust into his hands.

'Now tell us,' Mangel said. 'Tell us the whole story.'

Trost recounted the sequence of events in detail. He hadn't thought anything of it at first, he insisted—nothing at all, they had to believe that. He was completely in the dark. His head had been aching so badly that he could hardly think straight. Hauser helped him, so he was under an obligation to the man. It was only natural.

Mangel returned to his corner without a word, looking thoughtful and more than a little perplexed. Silently, he glanced at Baron von Hagen, who slowly shook his head. Wickler was beside himself with glee. Laffrentz's jaw had dropped. The others wore an air of blank inquiry.

'Some nerve,' Wickler said with a touch of admiration. 'It must have taken some nerve.'

'But what happens now?' Trost wailed. 'We've got to do something, but what?'

Mangel, who was seated stiffly at the table, said, 'Nothing. No action will be taken.'

'What do you mean?' Laffrentz demanded swiftly.

'We don't know anything about anything,' Mangel replied in slow and measured tones. 'It would be wiser to turn a blind eye.'

Baron von Hagen gave a discreet nod.

'Out of the question,' said Laffrentz. 'We must report this at once. It's a punishable offence not to.'

'I have reported it,' Trost said. 'I've reported it to my room senior. I'm not liable to punishment.'

Mangel eyed the meteorologist with repugnance. 'Stop talking nonsense. You didn't see anything, hear anything or do anything. You know nothing about it.'

'Will that be all right?' Trost asked helplessly.

'Of course it will,' Mangel retorted. 'We simply can't afford to know anything about this business. No suspicion must be allowed to fall on us. There may be trouble ahead, but there's no point in meeting it half way.'

'Out of the question!' repeated Laffrentz. 'This sort of thing has to be reported.'

'Be reasonable,' Mangel said menacingly.

'It's going to be reported!' Laffrentz declared. 'By me, what's more. I shall inform Mr Harte.'

Mangel got up, looking grim. 'You will not leave this room,' he said. 'What happened here has nothing whatsoever to do with you.'

'We'll soon see about that!'

Laffrentz blundered towards the door, but Wickler was too quick for him. The Hitler Youth lieutenant stationed himself resolutely at Wickler's side and several of the others rose to their feet. The only non-participant was Wammenberg, who had burrowed under his bedclothes.

Lightning arithmetic satisfied Mangel that he would, if the worst came to the worst, be able to count on the majority of his room-mates.

'Stay put or we'll beat you to a pulp,' he said.

Warily, Laffrentz stood his ground. His piggy eyes gleamed with fury. 'How dare you threaten me!' he said uncertainly.

'I'm merely pointing out the possible consequences of your behaviour. We'd sooner put you in the hospital than let you sneak off to the Americans.'

'You're committing a punishable offence,' Laffrentz blustered. 'It's your duty to inform the authorities. If you won't, someone else must. There are severe penalties for failing to report an escape.'

'I did report it,' insisted Trost.

Mangel thought hard. What was he to do? Any course of action was fraught with dangers of its own. All he knew was, if a report turned out to be necessary, Laffrentz was the last person to make it.

'I did report it,' Trost repeated plantively, 'in the presence of witnesses.'

A brilliant idea took shape in Mangel's tortured mind. 'Of course the authorities must be informed,' he said with sudden decision. A faint smile appeared on his rosy face. 'Herr Trost reported the incident to me, and I shall transmit the information to the authorities—through the proper channels, needless to say. My first step will be to submit a report to the German camp commandant, having previously alerted the other corridor seniors, the block senior, the camp police commander and the commandant's adjutant.'

'But that's a ridiculous waste of time,' Laffrentz snapped.

'That,' Mangel corrected him, 'is what is known as proper channels.'

Hauser hurled himself into the undergrowth on the far side of the road when he heard the short sharp detonation that heralded the storm.

He lay there with the blood racing through his body. His chest heaved and his fingers clawed the ground. He listened, trying to make up his mind if what he had heard was a shot.

No, if they had fired at him he would have heard them calling to each other. Loudspeakers would be blaring and alarm bells shrilling. That was the signal for the hunt to begin. If it began now, he could kiss the world goodbye.

Nobody had opened fire. His nerves had let him down. The bang wasn't an ordinary detonation but the beginning of a storm.

Looking up, he saw that the sky had taken on a purplish hue, like a basinful of water stained with ink.

He debated what to do next. Satisfaction welled up inside him. He had made it to the bushes. He was a man—the only man among four thousand self-styled members of the national élite. Some élite! A lousy bunch of gutless wonders, only interested in number one. Filth, that's what they were, like everyone else today, even his wife. Yes, even Brigitte. She was all ready to sell him down the river, the dirty whore!

He banished her from his mind. There were more important things to think about, like what to do next. The first move was to get farther away from camp and out of the guards' range.

Farther away from Harte, too. Harte was a cool customer. The way he had stood there calmly, chatting with the guard but seeming to stare straight at him from thirty yards away!

No point in wondering why it had happened or why Harte had done such a thing. It was his good luck, and it was up to him to make the most of it.

He crawled through the undergrowth. Sweat poured down him, but he pressed on. Only when it trickled into his eyes and blurred his vision did he cautiously rise to his knees and peer round.

The sun had vanished behind a thick blanket of cloud. It was even more sultry than before.

His jacket, an SS tunic stripped of insignia, was soaked with sweat. It not only hampered his movements but was plainly recognizable.

He pulled it off and threw it into the bushes, then inspected himself with some satisfaction. No reason why he shouldn't be seen now. His grey-blue shirt looked neutral, like a labourer's. His trousers obviously came from army stocks and so did his boots, but everyone dressed like that today. Nobody would glance at him twice.

He stood up and looked back through the undergrowth. He had already travelled almost five hundred yards. He listened intently.

Peace reigned in Camp 7. No sirens, no raised voices, no whine of engines, no scurrying figures—just peace and quiet. He had made it!

His next objective? Not Brigitte. She had failed him—he had written her off.

He unbuttoned the front of his shirt and hurried on, striking across country through long grass which awaited the second mowing.

In the distance, beneath a clump of trees on a hill, stood a figure—a scarecrow, a bag of bones with rusty black clothes fluttering from it. If it was a woman, it certainly wasn't Brigitte.

Stumbling over hidden stones, he noted with rage that his thoughts had again turned to Brigitte.

Not Brigitte, he commanded himself. He mustn't utter her name, mustn't think of her—only of the bracelet which he had to have if he wanted to stay alive. The bracelet was his sole guarantee of survival.

A faint cry came from the figure on the hill. He stood still and listened with his head cocked. All he could hear was the rasp of his own breathing.

The old woman's voice rang out once more, shrill, plaintive and lingering. 'Fifi!' she called, and again, 'Fifi!' She raised her arm, seeming to point straight at him.

Hauser felt relieved. She was calling a dog. She wasn't shouting at him, only calling some lousy little dog.

He hurried on, almost tottering as he headed for the small cemetery which lay deserted in the middle of open country, surrounded by lush meadows and shaded by gnarled fir-trees. The mountains beyond made an idyllic setting.

Hauser pushed open the gate. The hinges squealed and the gravelled path lay before him, but he hesitated and looked round. There was no one in sight, no sound except the shrill and reiterated cry of 'Fifi!' in the distance.

A livid yellow flash of lightning plummeted to the ground, followed by an ear-splitting clap of thunder. The ground seemed to quake beneath Hauser's feet.

He rushed forward, heavy boots scrunching the gravel. With the unerring certainty of a sleep-walker, he made his way past weather-beaten crosses, dilapidated stone borders and withered flowers, until he came to the mound he sought.

The stone above it bore his father's name, *Otto Ernst Hauser*, but he did not spare the inscription a glance. Instead, he stumbled over the marble border surrounding the grave and dropped to his knees.

He might have been praying. In reality, he was digging feverishly at the loose earth with his bare hands. Suddenly, his contorted, sweat-stained face went rigid. The questing fingers stopped scrabbling and lay almost inert on the dark brown soil, empty. He had not found what he was looking for.

The bracelet was not there.

Another flash of lightning sped to the ground. The harsh glare was reflected in his sweat-stained face. His features were contorted with savage and uncontrollable fury.

'The bitch,' he said dully, 'the dirty bitch.'

There was a whisper in the distance. He listened involuntarily to the whisper as it turned into an unbroken roar.

Then the sky seemed to open and the rain engulfed him with suffocating intensity.

'The bitch!' he groaned. 'The dirty rotten bitch!'

'I always put my cards on the table,' Keller said. He eyed Brigitte gravely. 'I hope you realize that.'

'Come here,' she said, putting out her arms. 'We're wasting time.'

Brigitte lay naked on the bed. She was smiling. The rain

hissed monotonously past the windows and the balcony door, which were wide open.

'Why don't you come here?'

Although Keller felt an urge to fling himself on her and forget, he hesitated. 'I love you,' he said softly. It sounded almost like an entreaty.

'I know,' she said.

'But you aren't the only thing in the world.'

'I know that too,' she said, and her smile broadened.

'I want you, but I want the bracelet too.'

'You can have it, as long as I get that hotel.'

'It's yours, as long as I can rely on getting the bracelet. Did you find it?'

'Yes.' She sounded complacent. 'It wasn't too hard, even though he picked a pretty crazy place to hide it in. Anyway, I've got it now, in spite of him. It's here in this room. Want to see?'

Keller shook his head as he mechanically unbuttoned his tunic. 'Your word's good enough for me. That clinches the deal. As soon as you hand over the bracelet I'll give you the title deed of the hotel.'

'When, Frank?'

'Today, if you like. Later this afternoon.'

'That gives us a couple of hours, Frank. Let's make the most of them.'

Reiter appeared in the doorway of the outer office and gravely asked Sylvia if he could speak to her.

'You must be mistaken, Herr Reiter. I imagine you want to speak to Captain Keller.'

Reiter shook his head. 'No, I want to speak to you, Fräulein Meiners—you personally. May I?'

'But of course. What can I do for you?'

Reiter edged gingerly into the room. 'Fräulein Meiners,' he said solemnly, 'Internee Hauser has escaped.'

' I know.'

Reiter regarded her with unwavering solemnity. 'May I take the liberty of asking who told you?'

Sylvia, who did not know quite what to make of Reiter's earnest demeanour, said rather impatiently, 'Mr Harte told me.'

Reiter nodded. 'And who told Mr Harte?'

Sylvia raised her eyebrows at his persistence. 'Why don't you ask Mr Harte yourself? Mr Harte is deputizing for Captain Keller during his absence. He's in the office next door, supervising operations. Would you like a word with him?'

'I merely wanted to report that Internee Hauser had been seen escaping.'

'Why tell me about it?'

'So that you can pass the information on,' Reiter said meaningfully, 'always providing you want to.'

'Everyone knows already.'

'Do they know the full details, Fräulein Meiners?'

'What do you mean?'

'Nothing, nothing at all. Just as a matter of interest, though, have you any idea how Hauser managed to get away? Because Guard No. 4's attention was distracted. Quite by chance, of course—far be it from me to suggest otherwise. He was engaged in conversation by an American. From all accounts, it was Mr Harte.'

Sylvia flushed. 'Really?'

'You seemed pleased.'

'If it's true, Herr Reiter . . .'

'You can assume so.'

'Then it's simply wonderful—wonderful news, Herr Reiter.' Sylvia looked immeasurably relieved. 'My God,' she said, 'I'd never have thought it of him.'

'Possibly not,' Reiter said, baffled. 'Anyway,' he went on quickly, 'I've done my duty by reporting the incident. That puts me in the clear, doesn't it?'

But Sylvia wasn't listening to him. She turned and hurried into the commandant's office. Harte was standing beside the open window with a microphone in his hand.

'No interruptions, please!' he called, looking resentful.

'Ted,' she said sharply, 'what have you done?'

Harte feigned astonishment. 'Don't start building me up into a hero, girl. You couldn't be more wrong.'

'If you've done what I think you've done, Ted, I'm filled with admiration.'

'Kindly shut your enchanting mouth and leave me in peace. I've got to find out whether we're still in business. We could be completely bust.'

Sylvia did not move. He raised the microphone and pressed the 'send' switch. 'Big Daddy calling Gershwin,' he said. 'Come in, Gershwin.'

Colman's voice answered, sounding unusually brisk and businesslike. 'Gershwin here. Go ahead, I'm listening.'

The code-name 'Gershwin' was Colman's idea. Ever mindful of his cultural pretensions, the lieutenant had insisted on christening the whole operation after his favourite composer.

'Big Daddy calling Gershwin,' Harte replied with a swift sidelong glance at Sylvia. 'Have you taken up your preliminary positions as instructed?'

'Everything's going according to plan.'

'Anything special to report?'

'No—nothing you could call special.'

'What do you mean, Gershwin?'

Five miles away, Colman laughed so hard that Harte's radio set vibrated. 'Everything's just fine,' he said. 'Keller's Cadillac is parked outside the door. It's a perfect set-up.'

'Listen, Gershwin!' Harte called excitedly. 'This changes everything. H. must now be detained outside the building. Do you understand? H. must be prevented from getting inside at all costs.'

'Why?'

'Because anything could happen.'

'What more do you want?' Colman's untroubled laugh rang through the ether. 'This is just what some people I know have been waiting for, isn't it?'

'Gershwin!' Harte pleaded. 'Don't rock the boat—and that's an order. I repeat: H. must be detained before he enters the building—before, is that clear?'

'I don't read you,' replied Colman. Harte could hear the grin in his voice. 'Seems like we've lost contact. Gershwin will act on his own initiative from now on. H. now heading in this direction. H. will be allowed free access to the premises under surveillance. Will report further developments in due course. Over and out.'

'Be reasonable!' called Harte.

'Gershwin for ever!' Colman retorted gaily.

'Know something?' Sylvia said to Harte. 'I admire you.'

'Admire me?' Harte replied uneasily. 'You ought to commiserate with me. I've just been taken for a ride by someone called Gershwin.'

Laffrentz was giving his captors no peace. 'How long since Hauser went?' he complained. 'More than an hour, and what's happened? Nothing!'

'You're wrong,' Wickler retorted. 'It's started to rain since then.'

Mangel, apparently engrossed in his latest railway network, said, 'I advise you to calm down, Herr Laffrentz. I've done all I can. The responsibility rests with Herr Reiter now. He's the German commandant, after all.'

But Laffrentz would not be appeased. Thoughts of revenge coursed through his brain. He had them over a barrel now. What if he did sneak an occasional crust of bread? What were a miserable few ounces of bread compared with their criminal machinations? He'd teach them to try and drop him in the shit.

'Listen, Mangel,' he said belligerently, 'just in case you're in any doubt, I consider the steps you've taken to be totally inadequate—wilfully inadequate. I hereby draw your attention to the fact that I've drawn your attention to the fact.'

Mangel disliked wrangling. Apart from that, he had messed up his diagram of the goods yards at Skopje. Signal-box No. 2 was not correctly aligned with Signal-box No. 4. His nerves were on edge. Irritably, he hurled his pencil across the table.

'There's nothing more to be done,' he said. 'We can't do more than we've done already.'

'Yes, we can,' Laffrentz insisted.

'Poppycock!' snapped Mangel. 'What, for instance?'

'Let me go and see Mr Harte. We talk the same language—not that I've ever taken sides with a Yank, of course. It's just that I know how to handle him better than anyone else.'

Mangel thought this over. Things must be under way by now, one way or another. It was annoying that Reiter hadn't reported back yet, but who could tell what the Americans were up to? They were an unpredictable lot. Laffrentz mustn't be allowed to take charge, that was the main thing.

'No,' he said angrily. 'Try walking out of here and we'll break every bone in your body.'

It was uncharacteristic of Mangel to use such forceful language. The inmates of Room 29 sensed this and averted their gaze. Laffrentz pricked up his ears.

'I'll remember that, Mangel,' he said menacingly, but recovered himself at once. This was his finest hour! Reiter wasn't back yet. Either the Americans had refused to see him or he was marking time. Why shouldn't it be he, Laffrentz, who kept the Americans *au courant* instead of Reiter—not just in this particular case, but always?

Laffrentz said, 'I note that an internee has escaped. I also note that everyone in the room knows about it. I further note that the German commandant has been informed. The question is, why no action? I smell a rat, my friends. I repeat, why isn't anything happening?'

At that moment the door opened. A camp policeman stuck his head inside and called, 'Internee Laffrentz, report to the commandant's office right away.'

'Me?' Laffrentz demanded excitedly. 'Is that true? Who wants me?'

'Mr Harte.'

Laffrentz preened himself like a peacock. His sweaty face shone with triumph. 'I'm coming,' he said proudly. 'Out of my way, all of you.'

Mangel struggled to retain his composure. Fate had hit him below the belt, but he rode the blow manfully. 'Perhaps it's all for the best. I always thought we could rely on you when it came to the pinch, Herr Laffrentz. You will represent our interests, won't you, Herr Laffrentz?'

'You bet I will!' Laffrentz replied spiritedly, heading for the door.

'Don't forget your responsibilities,' Mangel called after him. 'You have a duty to the rest of us. That puts you under an obligation, Herr Laffrentz.'

'You're telling me,' Laffrentz said, and swept out of the room.

Corporal Copland was utterly unmoved by the fact that Lieutenant Colman had assumed command of the standby squad. He ignored the lieutenant and pressed on regardless.

Copland was straining at the leash. He scented blood.

Firmly convinced that live ammunition would be used in the near future, he loaded the MGs on to the truck as if they were crown jewels.

Colman slouched after him with his shoulders drooping. He gave Copland free rein, and Copland made the most of the opportunity, shouting orders in a solid stream and chivvying his men like a sheep-dog. The members of the standby squad boiled with rage but they shouldered their rifles and doubled to the duty truck without protest.

All Colman had said to Copland, when he differed with him over some point of procedure, was, 'As far as I'm concerned, Corporal, you can write me off as a moron, a cretin, or anything else you like. I couldn't care less, just so long as you remember who gives the orders around here. Okay? Right, get your men into position.'

And so there they were, deployed in a circle around the Crown, most of them split up into pairs. Radio communication had been established between them and Camp 7. It was a perfect set-up—hills, plenty of cover, and, smack in the middle, visible in every detail, the building under surveillance.

They waited. Lieutenant Colman had prudently stationed himself next to Copland. The corporal, who was checking the mechanism of his machine-gun for the umpteenth time, said, 'You really think he'll come, Lieutenant?'

'It's got damn little to do with you what I think, Copland.'

This was the sort of language Copland understood. He grinned to himself and said, 'If he does turn up, there'll be no problem. We wait until we get a bead on him and then pump him full of holes.'

Colman's eyes narrowed. 'He'll be detained exactly according to plan,' he said. 'That's an order, not from me but from the acting commandant. An order, Corporal.'

Copland relapsed into angry silence. The lieutenant was dead from the neck up. It was crazy to obey orders implicitly. Orders were a general indication at most—only fools followed them to the letter.

The rain beat down with unmitigated ferocity. It drummed on the truck and pattered on the steel helmets of the waiting men. Their uniforms were spongy with water.

'See that Cadillac down there, parked outside?' Copland asked, hoping to disconcert the lieutenant.

'Well, what about it?'

'Looks like Captain Keller's Caddy.'

Colman shrugged. 'There are plenty of models in that colour.'

'Not in this neck of the woods.'

'How would you know, Copland? Are you an auto-spotter?'

The corporal gritted his teeth. Colman was even stupider than he thought. He just carried out orders. When he radioed the camp he retired to a hollow about ten yards away. Spoke to that semi-civilian oddball Harte, and it sounded like a lot of bullshit. The only recognizable word was 'Gershwin'. Colman was a big laugh, no kidding.

The rain grew heavier, hanging from the sky in dark skeins. Some three hundred and fifty yards below them, the lonely inn looked as if it was swathed in gauze.

Copland, comfortably ensconced behind his MG, couldn't wait for Colman to make himself scarce. It was strange he hadn't given up already, considering the state of his uniform. Copland glanced at the lieutenant and grinned. Half an hour in the rain had turned him into a uniformed scarecrow.

But Colman went on standing there in the bushes, quite unperturbed. The rain had ceased to worry him. He didn't mind it any more, now he was soaked to the skin.

Copland gave him a last contemptuous look and then concentrated on the terrain in front of him. Slowly, he swept it with the barrel of his machine-gun. His sights crept across the inn from right to left: hedge, orchard, right-hand corner of the building, windows, front door, glassed-in veranda—what a target! He itched to pull the trigger and blow it to smithereens. The foresight crept on: left-hand corner of the building front garden, a path which degenerated into a rough track. He looked along the track.

And then he saw, aligned in his sights, a big man heading for the inn at a swift trot, crouching and keeping under cover as far as possible. This was it. This was the man they were looking for—Copland recognized him. The man had caught his eye at roll-call and on other occasions. This was the bastard who had kept them waiting in the mud and rain.

There he was, Copland reflected scornfully, a corporal in the US Army by the grace of God, and there below him, in the sights of his MG, was a man. If he chose to, he had only to crook the forefinger of his right hand a quarter of an inch and he would cut him in half—saw him clean across the middle.

It was just the way Laffrentz had imagined it. Harte received him like royalty. A real gentleman, Harte. Not another word about his being a Jew. It didn't mean a thing—a biological accident, nothing more. Men of breeding graciously overlooked that sort of thing.

This was a day to remember. The sheep-faced policeman—one of his future minions—had come to get him. The circle of awed faces in Room 29, the solemn progress through camp with perfect bearing maintained despite the heavy downpour, and then the outer office: the secretary—a pretty little thing, though not enough meat on her—sprang to life at the sight of him and vanished into the holy of holies through double doors leather-padded à la managing director.

Then came the moment he had been waiting for. The doors opened and Harte appeared on the threshold. He couldn't be expected to drop all formality, not in the presence of a subordinate, but he did say, 'Ah, there you are, Laffrentz. Come in.'

Laffrentz, who knew the routine, realized that this was mere convention. As soon as the double doors had closed behind him, Harte gave him a familiar pat on the shoulder, 'Well,' he said, 'who would have thought we'd meet again so soon?'

Laffrentz nodded eagerly. 'Yes, indeed. Who'd have thought it? I hoped so, I don't deny that. A certain fellow-feeling—know what I mean? What can I do for you?'

An arm-chair was drawn up for him, and what an arm-chair! Would he care for a drink? Laffrentz declined, but only half-heartedly. A cigar or cigarettes? With pleasure. Both, one for afterwards. Anything else—ice-cream, perhaps?

'It's ages since I had ice-cream.'

Harte took a can out of his locker. Producing a multi-purpose pocket-knife he prised open the can-opener and worked away.

'Here,' he said, proffering the open can. 'Try some.'

Laffrentz avidly inhaled the sweetish aroma. He dipped his forefinger deep into the can and stuck it in his mouth, then sucked with relish.

'First-class,' he declared. 'Top quality.'

Harte fetched a plate and a teaspoon and inverted the can. The unfrozen ice-cream slithered smoothly on to the plate. 'Dig in,' he said. 'I hope you enjoy it.'

'I will,' Laffrentz replied happily, and dug in.

'Right,' Harte said after a short pause. 'Now start talking. Begin at the beginning and don't leave anything out.'

Laffrentz rapidly scraped his plate clean but could not bring himself to lay it aside. Holding it carefully on his lap as a memento, he bared his soul for Harte's benefit.

First: the expression of a sincere desire to be as informative as possible about the recent escape.

Next: a brief excursion into past history, some of it already covered by the morning's conversation. Laffrentz believed that he could be especially helpful to Mr Harte in the matter of background information.

Then: an attempt to reconstruct the incident itself in every detail.

Furthermore: the reaction in immediate and less immediate circles, in other words, the reaction in Room 29, in the recreation area, at the German commandant's office—in short, the general reaction to Hauser's escape. Not vitally important, to be sure, but probably worth noting.

Finally: the unavoidable conclusion to be drawn from such incidents, to wit, that unwelcome speculation should be checked, quashed, eradicated. However, this would be possible only if new men with fresh ideas were placed at the helm. Laffrentz not only recommended this as a matter of urgency but would be happy to make himself available if so desired.

Sylvia Meiners came in to announce that the German camp commandant was waiting outside.

'I'll see him,' Harte said. 'Give me another five minutes.'

'Anything new?' asked Sylvia.

'Do you think I'd tell you if there was?'

Sylvia smiled at him. 'Any news from the standby squad?'

'None. We've lost radio contact—that's what Colman says, anyway. He's acting on his own initiative now.'

'The lieutenant usually knows what he wants.'

Harte raised his eyebrows. 'Don't tell me you've got a soft spot for that guy?'

'I've got a soft spot for a lot of things that come from America.'

'Why not sing *The Star-Spangled Banner* while you're at it?'

Laffrentz gave a familiar grin, but neither Sylvia nor Harte seemed to notice. Sylvia smiled at Harte and left the room. Harte gazed after her pensively.

'Nice piece,' Laffrentz ventured.

'Really?' Harte replied coolly. 'You think so?'

'Well, I know a good thing when I see it,' mumbled Laffrentz, who realized that he had just made a slight *faux pas*. 'I wouldn't dream of generalizing of course.'

'Listen,' Harte said abruptly. 'You're sure there's no mistake—at the time when Hauser went over the wall, an American was talking to the guard responsible for that sector?'

'Absolutely positive. Strange, isn't it? Unless the American was short-sighted, he must have seen Hauser.'

'I was the American, Laffrentz,' Harte said deliberately. 'What do you say to that?'

Laffrentz indulged in a violent attack of coughing, studiously avoiding the CIC officer's eye.

'Well?' Harte asked gently.

'If it was you, Mr Harte, I'm sure you had your reasons.'

'You mean I deliberately turned a blind eye?'

'I'd never dare suggest such a thing, Mr Harte!' Laffrentz protested vehemently.

'So you're prepared to spread any version of the affair which I consider appropriate?'

'Need you ask!' Laffrentz gave Harte an ingratiating smile. 'I told you, there's a sort of fellow-feeling between us. I'm proud of it, Mr Harte, and I want it to grow. You can count on my fullest support.'

'Corporal,' Lieutenant Colman said easily, 'stop fiddling around with that MG the whole time. Take your finger off the trigger—you've got live ammunition up the spout.'

Copland forced himself to remain calm. 'Lieutenant, why don't you take cover and leave the rest to me? I have combat experience. Besides, you'll get pneumonia if you wander around in the rain any longer, and we can't do that to your ever-loving mother.'

He had the internee named Hauser neatly lined up in his

sights. Another hundred yards and he'd be able to knock him over like a dummy in a shooting gallery.

'Come here,' Colman ordered. 'Stand up, Corporal, I'm talking to you. Get back behind the nearest bush.'

'You're spoiling my aim, Lieutenant,' Copland replied evenly. 'I've got him all lined up. Gimme another fifteen seconds and I'll blow his head off.'

'Stand up, Corporal—now!'

'Are you trying to stop me?'

'I give the orders round here, not you.'

'Crazy orders, Lieutenant.'

'Compulsory orders, Corporal. Get away from the MG or I'll turn you into a stretcher-case—you can bet your sweet life on that.'

Copland's jaw dropped. Nobody had ever treated him this way before, least of all Colman. He backed down.

'But that's the Captain's Caddy parked outside. What happens if the Kraut goes for him? Are you ready to answer for that?'

'I don't know what you're talking about, buddy. I'm just carrying out an assignment, and my orders state that the escaped internee must not be prevented from entering the building. He's to be detained as soon as he comes out again, that's all. Nobody said a word about a Cadillac or anything else, get me?'

'I get you.' The corporal looked at Colman with new eyes. 'I always knew you had a big head, Lieutenant, but I never realized you had the brains to go with it.'

Ted Harte made repeated attempts to raise Lieutenant Colman on the radio, but in vain. Colman did not reply.

'Why doesn't he answer?' Sylvia asked uneasily.

'Because he doesn't want to, that's my guess.'

'Maybe his set's out of order, Ted. Remember the weather.'

Harte shook his head. 'It can't be that. These gadgets are virtually foolproof—they function in any weather. No, I'm afraid he's decided to take the bit between his teeth. Keller's aversion to Gershwin may turn out to be expensive. I'm going to go ahead, anyway. Either my calculations are correct or they aren't. If they aren't, what have I got to lose? I can't make a bigger hash of things than I have already.'

He went off to see Gernsbach in his office.

Gernsbach did not take the slightest notice of his visitor. His face was almost expressionless, and he was drawing.

The figure of an American soldier took shape on the sketch-block. He was leaning against a post in a loose-limbed attitude which suggested the spurious calm between two bouts of fighting. The face, with its childlike eyes and hard-bitten mouth, was surmounted by a steel helmet like the shell of a tortoise.

The figure in the foreground seemed to be wreathed in barbed wire. Above and beyond it were mountains, soaring pinnacles of stone.

Harte stared at the sketch for a long time. Then he said, 'I see you're drawing.'

'Trying to, but everything I do turns out so damned morbid.'

'Have you filled out those papers for the Hauser woman?'

'Yes,' Gernsbach replied simply.

This annoyed Harte. 'What do you mean, yes? Is that all you've got to say?'

Gernsbach shrugged his shoulders and continued to draw in silence.

'Did you know that Hauser had decided to terminate his stay here? He's on the run.'

'Why should I worry?' Gernsbach said calmly.

'Why? Because there's big trouble brewing, Gernsbach, and you're in it up to your neck. Check every phase of these developments and you're bound to reach a point where you say to yourself: it couldn't have happened except for me.'

'What do you expect me to do? I did refuse, after all.' Gernsbach looked up from the sketch-block and stared at Harte with bitterness in his eyes.

'Oh, no!' Harte exclaimed. 'Don't tell me you're washing your hands of everything too. Hygienic people, the Germans—always washing their hands! So you refused until you stopped refusing. So what?'

'I protested, though!'

'Come off it, Gernsbach, no flimsy excuses. If you'd really dug your heels in and refused to issue the papers Keller asked for, the whole thing would have taken quite a different turn. I challenge you to deny it.'

Gernsbach avoided Harte's searching gaze and stared thoughtfully out of the window. The sky was a mass of blue-black cloud. 'I've been at fault, I do see that,' he said absently.

'What are you going to do about it?'

'Whatever you say.'

'Spoken like a true German!' Harte's eyes flashed with scorn. 'Here am I, send me! God Almighty, Gernsbach, don't just stand at attention with your eyes shut, waiting for orders. Open your eyes, roll up your sleeves, and get cracking!'

'Give me a line to go on,' Gernsbach said helplessly.

Harte stood up and faced him. 'I'll make it even easier on you: I'll give you an order. That's the best and simplest way of getting something done in Germany—has been for centuries and will be for centuries to come.'

'You're not being fair,' Gernsbach retorted at once. 'I'm not the heel-clicking type.'

The sardonic grin on Harte's face was replaced by a friendly smile. 'All the better,' he said. 'I'm going to give you an order just the same, but I leave it entirely up to you whether or not you obey it.'

Gernsbach nodded. 'Well?'

'Scrap everything to do with the White Horse—everything your department has done so far. Cancel the whole transaction and make sure you sink it without trace. No file copies, no records, no title deeds—nothing! Simply scrap the whole dirty business down to the last pen-stroke.'

'I'll do that,' Gernsbach replied firmly. He drew a deep breath and looked out of the window again. The mountains were almost obscured by driving sheets of rain. He said, 'You've given me back my courage, Harte.'

'Nonsense, I'm just boosting my own.' Harte patted Gernsbach lightly on the shoulder and hurried back to his own office. Reiter was still waiting for him.

'Well,' Harte said without preamble, 'let's clear the air. Are you ready to start?'

'What exactly do you want, Mr Harte?'

'Information,' Harte replied. 'If it turns out to be the information I need, I'll do you a favour in return.'

Reiter regarded him with a comradely eye. 'I respect you a lot, Mr Harte. I expect you know that.'

Harte waved the remark aside. 'Save your breath,' he said.

'I don't want compliments. All I'm interested in at the moment is facts—facts I can use.'

'Very well,' Reiter replied. 'I think I know what you're after, but may I clear up one point first?' Harte nodded. 'Thank you. My query is, what are the authorities likely to do as a result of this escape—step up security precautions, reduce rations, cut off the lights, hold special roll-calls, impose extra restrictions, turn off the water?'

'I've no idea,' Harte said candidly. 'I can only assure you that I shall do everything in my power to prevent a worsening of conditions.'

Reiter gave a slight bow. 'Thank you, that's good enough for me. Please ask your questions and I'll do my best to answer them.'

Harte stared meditatively at the floor. 'I won't bother to appeal to your conscience, though I'm sure I wouldn't appeal in vain. You were a soldier, not a butcher. You know my theory—most of the inmates of this camp are innocents or fools—but you also know the camp contains a substantial minority of war criminals, mass-murderers and the like. You're locked up with these creatures, but that doesn't make you brothers-in-arms, does it? Of course it doesn't. Do you see what I'm driving at, Reiter? I want you to slough off this criminal minority. I want you to dissociate yourself from the murderers and criminals and hand them over for trial.'

Reiter did not speak.

'I'm only concerned with the Hauser case,' Harte went on. 'Only the Hauser case. I think you know me well enough to believe me when I tell you that there won't be any peace in this place until the Hauser case is settled. To be quite frank, my personal position depends on the outcome. You could help me if you wanted to. What do you say?'

Reiter nodded. 'Very well,' he replied. 'Have you ever heard of Operation Horse-fly?'

'What about it?' Harte produced a memorandum pad and waited.

'Horse-fly was a special mopping-up operation carried out behind the Russian Front. Check on its effects in the Bolkhov-Orel-Bryansk area and find out who was in command.'

Harte jotted a few notes on his pad. 'Good,' he said in a flat voice.

'Apart from that,' Reiter continued, 'I indicated to you more than once that several internees were prepared to make statements on the subject.'

'I didn't believe you,' Harte conceded frankly.

'Anyway, they're ready to talk. The gentlemen in question used to be ambassadors to various Balkan countries. They could make a valuable contribution to your file on Hauser.'

'Thank you, Reiter.'

Harte gave a mock bow, then walked across the room and filled his lungs with the fresh air that was pouring through the window. Rain lashed the outside of the casement as he watched inky-blue cloud obliterate the last vestiges of sulphurous yellow sunlight.

A sudden flash of lightning sliced the seething sky. Almost instantaneously, thunder exploded in clouds like a celestial bomb.

The wind rammed itself against Hauser's back as he half-ran, half-reeled towards the place where Brigitte lived, the place where he would find the bracelet.

The wind, which had sprung up suddenly, tore the sheets of rain to shreds and drove them along like a dust storm.

Hauser instinctively avoided the main roads—quite instinctively, because he was no longer capable of systematic thought. He simply chose the shortest route, which took him across fields, over fences and through undergrowth.

His legs carried him along automatically. Although he often stumbled over unevennesses in the ground, he carried on with teeth gritted and fists clenched, mentally ordering himself to keep running at all costs.

There was the inn at last. It loomed up in front of him suddenly, visible in broad outline through the streaming rain. A vivid flash illuminated the sky beyond.

Hauser staggered up to the front door and flung it wide. He might have been peering into an unlit cave, for all his eyes could make out in the gloom.

He took two or three drunken paces forwards and slammed the door behind him. It closed with a dull crash.

Hauser groped his way forward. A figure stood in his path, but he brushed it aside with one sweep of the arm.

Panting, he climbed the stairs to Brigitte's room. Tangled

skeins of wet hair gummed themselves to his forehead and festooned his face. His mouth hung open.

He blundered along the passage towards the door beyond which Brigitte and the bracelet were waiting for him—had to be waiting for him.

He threw his whole weight against the door and it burst open. It was lighter inside the room.

Brigitte was lying there, naked. She sat up and stared at him in petrified silence. But for the amazement and incomprehension in her eyes, she might have been a statue.

Slowly, he tottered towards her.

Only then did he notice the figure beside her—a man, also naked. The man was trying to pull a blanket over his body.

Hauser laughed aloud, a low, menacing sound. He moved quite slowly towards the man who was lying in his wife's bed. As he went, he picked up the first heavy object that came to hand, a massive family Bible.

'I'm warning you!' shouted the naked man in his wife's bed. He sat up abruptly. 'Remember who I am, Hauser!'

Hauser gave a twisted grin. 'I don't know you,' he said, and laughed savagely. 'All I can see is a man in bed with my wife—no uniform, no badges of rank.'

He raised the book and brought it crashing down on the man's head. The man collapsed with a grunt and lay still.

'How could you!' Brigitte gasped. She cringed away in horror, trying to put as much distance between them as possible. 'What are you doing here?'

'I want to know what's going on.'

'How did you get out?'

'Weren't you expecting me?'

She stared at him helplessly.

Hauser did not take his eyes off her. He moved towards her, still holding the book, swayed, and leaned against the wall. 'Where's the bracelet?'

Brigitte came to life again. She got up and put out her hand, but he jerked his arm away. Her face was set in a frozen smile. She did not spare Keller's motionless form another glance.

She said, 'You're soaked through. You need a change of clothes and something to eat.'

'The bracelet,' Hauser repeated in a hoarse monotone. The

pain in his legs shot upwards, constricting the muscles around his heart and stabbing at his brain.

'Where's the bracelet?'

Brigitte's smile was more a grimace than a smile. 'Where do you think it is?' she said, playing for time. 'Where you hid it, of course.'

Lightning flashed outside, momentarily illuminating the room like a revolving beacon. The window-frame looked huge and spidery in the sudden glare.

'Hand it over,' Hauser said. 'Hand it over at once.'

Receiving no answer, he moved towards her. She shrank back, but he closed in on her until she was brought up short by the wall.

'The bracelet!'

He spoke quite gently, but she went on staring at him with dilated eyes. At last she said, 'I haven't got it.'

Hauser raised his fist and smashed it into the pale oval of her face.

He did so twice more.

And then, as he stood there unmoving, he saw the pale face become suffused, saw the features crumple and subside as Brigitte slid down the wall and collapsed.

Hauser dropped to his knees beside the inert body and grabbed it by the shoulders. He hauled Brigitte to her feet, shook her, and thrust his distorted face into hers.

'The bracelet!' he yelled.

She dragged herself painfully to the table and started fumbling with her handbag.

Hauser wrenched the bag away from her and tore it open. His hands trembled as he rooted around inside.

The bracelet was there.

Still panting, he rushed out into the passage in his desperate eagerness to dispose of the bracelet. Back in the bedroom, Brigitte turned even paler, groped blindly for support, and slumped to the floor.

The bracelet must vanish, and vanish without trace—that was Hauser's one and only thought. Only its disappearance could save him.

Slembeck had not foreseen all this. His conscience was clear, in a manner of speaking. In other words, nobody could prove anything against him.

Even so, the American patrol which picked him up informed him that he was 'wanted' by Mr Harte.

This worried him. Mr Harte was no friend of his. More than that, he was a Jew, which probably accounted for a lot of things.

Anyway, what had he done that was so terrible? Just hung around outside the house where Brigitte Hauser usually stayed when she was in Garmisch. So what? He had even gone into the house to speak to her, but he had drawn a blank—he could swear to that.

Then the storm broke. That rain! It sent him scurrying for the shelter of the DP camp, where he tore off his wet clothes, put on a dressing-gown—a modest item of loot—and lurked beside the window until the Yanks arrived.

They hauled him off to see that little swine Harte, with his eternal grin, and Harte said, 'Let's talk, Slembeck.' Then he said, 'You must think I'm a complete fool.'

'What makes you say that?' Slembeck protested feebly.

'Would you like to know what I think you are?'

Slembeck shrugged.

'You'll laugh—I think you're a murderer.'

'A joke in poor taste, Mr Harte,' Slembeck said, but he did not smile.

'What about your evidence, Slembeck? Is that in better taste?'

Slembeck looked round helplessly.

'Me, a murderer?' he asked, all injured innocence. 'How on earth do you figure that out? You shouldn't make such accusations, Mr Harte. I don't deserve this sort of treatment.' He paused. 'You couldn't make it stick, anyway.'

Harte sat back in his chair. 'You're under suspicion of murder, Slembeck. You naturally claim to be the soul of innocence, but how much longer can you keep it up? Do you really think I'm such a fool? Do you really imagine I had a sudden urge to feast my eyes on your honest face?'

'Get to the point!' Slembeck said angrily.

Harte savoured the man's reaction. He rubbed his palms together. 'Listen carefully, Slembeck. A short while ago, Frau Hauser was found unconscious, pouring blood and gasping like a stranded fish. They don't hold out much hope for her. The motive? Robbery. Now comes the interesting part. What do you think was stolen? Among other things, a platinum bracelet.'

Slembeck turned pale. 'A what?'

'You heard me. A platinum and ruby bracelet—your bracelet, Slembeck.'

Slembeck's mouth opened and shut. 'What do you mean, my bracelet?'

'The finger of suspicion points straight at you, Slembeck. You went looking for Frau Hauser—there are witnesses who saw you hanging around for hours—and now this.'

'You don't seriously believe that I—I, of all people . . .'

'I don't believe anything, least of all anything you tell me. You needn't bother to put on an act for my benefit. I stick to the facts and the facts are quite enough to put you behind bars.'

Slembeck felt his legs turn to jelly. He started to plead with Harte, bombarded him with assurances that he was innocent—certainly in this particular case.

But Harte was implacable. 'Look at it whichever way you like, Slembeck, we've got more than enough circumstantial evidence to hang you. Let me spell it out for you. A bleeding, battered woman, a vanished bracelet, and you—demonstrably interested in the bracelet and demonstrably on the look-out for the woman just before she was attacked. You forced your way into her lodgings in Garmisch, traced her to the scene of the crime, and robbed her. That bracelet was your ambition in life, Slembeck. You made that very clear more than once.'

Dull rage welled up inside Slembeck. The dirty little Jewish pig had it all figured out. Harte was right. He had quite enough circumstantial evidence to send him to the gallows.

There he sat, the double-dealing bastard, grinning to himself and pretending to study his fingernails.

'Why won't you believe me?' Slembeck demanded. 'Why haven't you a good word to say for me? All you're doing is incriminating me, but why?'

Harte's eyes twinkled amiably. 'I suppose you think you're a martyr, eh?'

'All I want is . . .'

'The bracelet. I know, you were ready to murder for it.'

Slembeck felt like a man floundering in deep water. The clothes clung tenaciously to his body and waves of fever surged through him.

Harte merely laughed at him.

'Shit the bracelet!' Slembeck yelled.

'All the better,' said Harte. 'So you've made up your mind. You don't like the idea of being arrested and you'd rather make a statement instead.'

'What sort of statement?' Slembeck asked dazedly.

'You can choose. Either I get the statement I want or I have you locked up on the spot. Your next port of call would be a war crimes tribunal.'

Sweat streamed down Slembeck's face. His stomach had twisted itself into a knot and he felt sick.

'And if I make this statement?'

'Your troubles are over.'

'Do you mean that, or are you just bluffing?'

'I give you my word. As soon as you tell me what I want you can push off wherever you like—a long way off preferably.'

Slembeck drew a deep breath. Then he said, 'All right, I'm ready.'

Harte rang for Sylvia. 'A statement,' he said. 'Take it straight on to your typewriter.'

Sylvia nodded and screwed a sheet of paper into the roller. It was clear that nothing surprised her any more. She refrained from smiling at Harte, much as she would have liked to.

'Right,' said Harte. He started to pace up and down the room. 'Herr Slembeck has decided to champion the cause of justice. In other words, he is ready to testify that Hauser was present when war crimes were committed. Is that so, Slembeck?'

'Yes,' Slembeck replied sullenly.

'Get that down, Sylvia. So you're a witness, Slembeck, a witness to the fact that Hauser participated in such crimes?'

'Yes.'

'And you can also testify, in this connection, that Hauser appropriated a platinum and ruby bracelet? Is that right?'

'Yes, I saw him take it.'

'This bracelet,' Harte continued, 'was owned by the Patocki

family. You worked on their main estate, Slembeck. The circumstances of your employment don't matter, but let's assume that they were legitimate.'

Slembeck's jaw dropped at this latest evidence of Harte's omniscience. 'You knew that all the time?' he said petulantly. 'If you know it all, why bother to ask me?'

'So this bracelet belonged to Count Patocki's family?'

'Yes, but they couldn't hang on to it. They had to leave everything behind.'

Harte came to a halt. 'You see. The Patockis left in a hurry, so they didn't have time to appoint a properly attested heir—you, for instance.'

'I suppose not. Anyway, they're dead now.'

'How do you know? Did you kill them?'

'No!' Slembeck exclaimed in horror. 'No, of course not. I just heard, that's all.'

'Don't start inventing things, Slembeck. Stick to the facts and don't tell me anything you don't know for certain.'

'I've already told you all I know.'

'Very well,' Harte said. He went and stood in front of Slembeck. 'I've got what I need, anyway. You realize the implications of what you've told me? One of them is that you've no interest in the bracelet because it doesn't belong to you. There's nothing to suggest that you have any valid claim to ownership. Far from laying claim to the bracelet, your statement is an attempt to shed light on an obscure situation. Very gratifying, Slembeck, and very satisfactory from your point of view. I appreciate your co-operation.'

Harte paused for a few moments, looking more relaxed.

Sylvia got the statement ready for signature while Slembeck vainly tried to follow Harte's train of thought.

'Everything's quite straightforward so far,' Harte went on. 'Do you know what, Slembeck? I don't think there's any good reason why I should hold you on suspicion of murder. The whole idea seems absurd, on second thoughts.'

Slembeck began to see daylight. He said, 'If the bracelet doesn't belong to anyone any more, who will it go to?'

'Not you, anyway. Now sign.'

Slembeck signed. 'And that's what they call justice,' he grumbled. 'I always thought it paid a man to do things out of the goodness of his heart.'

'Slembeck,' Harte said, 'do you know what you deserve? You deserve to be thrashed. The fact that I haven't thrashed you is all the payment you'll get. Now get out before I change my mind.'

When Hauser tried to leave the Crown he found his path barred by an American officer armed with a sub-machine-gun. He recognized him as Lieutenant Colman.

'Halt,' Colman said, raising his gun. His tone was almost genial.

Colman had removed the weapon from Corporal Copland just in time and made him carry the walkie-talkie instead. Copland was furious that he, with his combat experience and his single-minded determination to show how a tommy-gun should be handled, should have been summarily disarmed by an untried lieutenant.

However, one look at Hauser was enough to revive the corporal's hopes slightly. The German crouched like a cornered beast and looked wildly around for a means of escape.

'Don't try anything, Hauser,' warned Colman, 'not with me.'

'Get out of my way,' Hauser said softly.

'Don't be a stupid son-of-a-bitch. The place is surrounded. If you get past me there are three other groups waiting to shoot you down, understand?'

Hauser bowed his head. He had understood. Quietly, he said, 'That dirty swine Harte. I might have known better than to trust a Jew.'

'I'll pass that on, Hauser. Now shut your mouth and get your hands above your head. Move, man!'

Hauser slowly raised his hands. He did not look at anyone.

'Search him, Corporal,' Colman ordered. Copland ran his hands over Hauser and brought to light a handkerchief containing an object the size of a man's fist—a bracelet. He handed it to Colman, who glanced at it briefly and stuffed it in his pocket.

'That's good enough,' said Colman. He beckoned three men over and consigned Hauser to their care.

'Get him into the truck. If he tries anything, shoot him. Corporal, you stay here with me. It's the safest place for you.'

Copland grimaced and stared longingly in Hauser's direction.

'Stop making faces and get that radio working,' Colman told him, looking amused. 'Call the camp and say Gershwin reports H. safely in the bag. Evidence affirmative, further details shortly.'

'Will do,' the corporal said reluctantly.

'After that, come inside with me. I'm curious to find out who that Cadillac belongs to.'

'Sorry,' Sylvia told Harte, 'Colonel Cord's on the line. He wants to speak to you or Keller.'

'Get rid of him.'

'It's no good, Ted. He says it's very important, and he's going to wait until he's put through to one or other of you. He points out that there's an army directive which states that a CO or his second-in-command have to be on call at any time.'

Harte looked at her inquiringly, but she shook her head. No, Colonel Cord was not to be shaken off. They both pricked up their ears as the radio emitted a sudden buzz.

Harte reported his presence and listened intently. 'Fine,' he said with relief. 'Let's have the rest of the story as soon as possible.' He turned to Sylvia. 'They've got Hauser and the bracelet.'

'Thank God for that.'

'Yes, but there's no news of Keller and the Hauser woman yet. We won't hear for another few minutes.'

Harte went over to the phone and said his name.

'Well,' Cord asked without preamble, 'what about the Hauser case?'

'It's all settled.'

Cord purred with satisfaction. 'You mean that?'

'Sewn up good and tight, Colonel. There's plenty of evidence now, good solid evidence as well as testimony.'

'Great,' Cord said happily. 'You've done a grand job. My congratulations to you and Frank Keller. You can hand over the stuff to me personally. I'll be with you inside an hour.'

'In an hour, Colonel?' Harte yelped. 'I thought you were in Nuremberg.'

'No, I'm not far away. My old friend the General is putting me up at his villa in the mountains. I'll leave right away.'

'There's no necessity for that, Colonel.'

'I'll hurry just the same. Can't wait to celebrate your success.'

That concluded the exchange. Harte slowly replaced the receiver. 'That's all I needed,' he said with a frown.

'But everything's all right, isn't it?'

Harte shook his head and stood there brooding for some moments. Then the radio buzzed again.

'Big Daddy here,' Harte said mechanically. He listened to Colman's report in silence. Then, after a longish pause, he glanced at Sylvia. 'Things sound confused at that end. Keller was hit over the head by Hauser. They don't think he's seriously hurt, though.'

'What a stroke of luck!'

'That remains to be seen. It seems Frau Hauser is dead—murdered by her husband. Those are the bare facts. What led up to them is another matter.'

Sylvia did not speak for a while. Then she said quietly, 'There's a sort of poetic justice about the whole thing, somehow.'

'What nonsense,' Harte said, with a ghost of a smile, 'charming and lovable nonsense, Sylvia, but nonsense all the same. Just wait till Keller gets here and you'll soon see. How will he react? That's the question, but I'm afraid I know the answer already.'

Laffrentz returned to Room 29 in triumph. He walked in, looked round, and said nothing. The others regarded him expectantly, but he merely raised his eyebrows and lowered them again. All he said was,

'Well, that would seem to be that.'

'Did everything go off all right?' demanded Mangel.

The only response was a wordless stare, so Mangel repeated his question in a rather more courteous tone. 'Is everything all right, Herr Laffrentz?'

'You could say that,' Laffrentz replied with infinite condescension. He elbowed aside one or two of his room-mates, who were still eyeing him as if he were an oracle, and demanded that the table where he usually sat should be shifted three inches to the left because there was insufficient room for him to get by.

Next, Wickler sidled up and inquired if the Senior Administrative Adviser would care to sit for a portrait—a large-scale pencil sketch, thirty inches by twenty.

'Very well,' Laffrentz said. 'Carry on.'

So there he sat in portentous silence with Wickler squatting opposite him, pencil in hand. The other internees clustered round the architect, feigning an interest in art, but Laffrentz preserved a sphinx-like inscrutability. From time to time he wagged his head meaningfully and said, 'That man Harte!' or 'If only you knew!'—then relapsed into silence.

The effect was telling. The others gaped at him—all of them, even that degenerate old bean-pole of a Baron, whose horsey countenance proclaimed his aristocratic pedigree like a signboard. Mangel's demeanour was that of a subordinate waiting for instructions, and Trost gazed at him like a faithful dog. Even the Hitler Youth lieutenant signalled his approval by remaining silent. As for Arthur Wammenberg, he winked confidentially and thrust a few cigarettes into Laffrentz's hand.

Let them sweat it out, Laffrentz told himself—every last one of them. They had treated him like dirt and he wouldn't let them forget it, not now that he was on the point of stepping into Reiter's shoes.

'My God,' Wickler exclaimed, lowering his pencil, 'you're an incredibly stupid-looking man, Laffrentz—like a prize cow dressed up as an internee. I could do a caricature of you, but a portrait's out of the question.'

Laffrentz gasped for breath. 'How dare you!' he snapped, but Mangel said soothingly,

'It was only a joke. Nobody would dream of saying such a thing in earnest, Herr Laffrentz.'

'You will apologize to me at once,' Laffrentz demanded sternly.

Wickler tore his sketch in half, rolled it into a ball and threw it at Laffrentz. 'There,' he said, 'use it any way you want.'

'Gentlemen, gentlemen,' Mangel pleaded in a conciliatory tone, 'what's the matter with you? Why get so hot under the collar?'

'I'm not,' retorted Wickler, 'though God knows I've every reason to be. Take a good look at that man's face—it's just asking to be punched.'

'Why not punch it, then?' shouted someone in the background.

'I'm a pacifist,' Wickler replied, and retired to the window alcove.

Mangel tried to salvage the situation. 'Don't mind him, Herr Laffrentz. It's only his artistic temperament.'

He looked round for approval, but none of the others supported his peace-keeping endeavours. They obviously hadn't grasped the extent of Laffrentz's ambitions. Laffrentz was an up-and-coming man, and quite capable of making life hideous for them all if he chose to. Mangel decided to try again.

'My dear Herr Laffrentz,' he said, 'you really mustn't take flippant remarks too seriously. Claustrophobia, bad food, uncertainty about the future—these things affect the temper as well as the digestion.'

Mangel's honeyed tones drew no immediate response from Laffrentz, who merely snorted with indignation. 'You mark my words,' he said at length, Cassandra-like, 'even impudent bastards like Wickler meet their match sooner or later.'

At that moment the door burst open to reveal Reiter standing grim-faced on the threshold. 'Where's that swine Laffrentz?' he demanded in a voice which almost cracked with fury.

The tension in Room 29 suddenly reached breaking-point. Threats and recriminations flew thick and fast. Laffrentz thought he was seeing things and Mangel felt completely dazed.

'Go to it!' yelled Wickler. 'Give the bastard what for!'

Reiter forged a path through the throng. He bore down on Laffrentz with his hands curved like talons.

'You fat swine!' he hissed. 'I'll teach you to try and pinch my job! I'll teach you to try and sell us all down the river, you ass-kissing bastard! Come here and get what's coming to you. I'm going to knock your teeth out.'

'Go on, Laffrentz,' Wickler said encouragingly. 'Get it over quickly before he thinks of something worse.'

'Just a moment,' Mangel interposed. 'Herr Reiter, am I correct in assuming that you are still the German commandant of this camp?'

'You're damned right I am! You can take that as official.'

'That's all right, then.' Mangel stepped back, looking relieved.

Reiter and Laffrentz confronted one another, three feet of stuffy air between them. The rain had stopped, and motes of dust were dancing in the watery sunshine that filtered in through the window. The two men exchanged ferocious glares, both reluctant to make the first move.

Wickler, who was standing behind Laffrentz, gave the fat man a shove which sent him cannoning into Reiter. Having staggered backwards a couple of paces, Reiter leapt forward and wrapped his arms round Laffrentz, who did likewise. The entwined pair clung to each other, straining, until somebody tripped them up. Then they collapsed with a crash and started rolling around on the floor.

'Get the table and chairs out of the way,' Wickler called briskly. 'Clear the ring for round one!'

Captain Keller said nothing. He just stood there with a face of stone. There was incredulity in the way he stared at Lieutenant Colman, even though he had already put two and two together.

'Still alive?' Colman inquired with a touch of surprise. 'I thought he might have done you in.'

Keller indicated the body lying on the floor, the small, twisted body that had once been Brigitte Hauser. Colman saw at a glance that she was dead. He went to the door and called for Corporal Copland, whom he had prudently stationed outside in the corridor.

'Send for an MO and put guards on every door. Nobody leaves or enters without my say-so.'

Keller had almost finished dressing by the time Colman re-entered the room. The captain's fingers trembled slightly as he knotted his tie. He still said nothing.

'Funny, when you come to think of it,' Colman said, nodding at the corpse. 'Husbands normally murder their wives' boy-friends. It'd be more logical if they murdered their wives, but they don't as a rule. Hauser's got brains. This is a typical *crime passionel*—quite a respectable thing to do in some parts of the world. What do you think, Captain?'

Keller avoided Colman's eye. He reached for his jacket,

which was hanging over a chair, and put it on. Then he picked up his cap but did not put it on. His head hurt and his skull felt as frail as an eggshell.

'Where's Harte?' he asked in a flat voice.

'Back in camp,' Colman replied promptly. 'We're in touch by radio. You can contact him any time. Our code name is Gershwin, if that means anything to you.'

Keller looked straight at Colman for the first time. His expression contained none of the reproach Colman had been expecting, but he still looked incredulous. He said, 'I'll take the car back to camp.'

'Any instructions, Captain? Any orders or suggestions?'

'Not from me,' Keller replied, and left the room.

For a few seconds the lieutenant stared after him with a thin smile on his face. Then he conducted a last careful inspection of the room and its contents—the rumpled bed, the upturned chairs, the strangely shrunken body of the dead woman. Ambling out into the passage, he found that Corporal Copland had gone. He heard Keller's Cadillac drive off and privately congratulated himself on not being in Ted Harte's shoes. A handful of Gasthaus employees stared at him in awe as he nodded to the sentry at the front entrance and headed for the truck.

At that moment a muffled cry came from the truck and its canvas side-walls started to shake. A moment later, a figure tumbled over the tail-board like a sack of potatoes. It was Hauser. A second figure—Copland's—hurled itself on the prisoner and began to punch him savagely.

'I'll teach you!' Copland panted. 'I'll teach you how to behave, you German bastard!'

Lieutenant Colman paused to light a cigarette. He watched the fight until it became clear that Hauser was past defending himself. Copland was more than a match for him.

'Hold it, Corporal!' Colman called sharply, tossing his cigarette away. 'Take your hands off him or I'll put you in hospital.'

'You?' snarled Copland, beside himself with rage.

'Okay, I'll get someone else to. I give the orders round here —remember?'

Copland reluctantly climbed off his victim and got up. It

began to dawn on him that he had gone too far. With an effort he said, 'He asked for it, Lieutenant.'

Colman lowered his voice so that only the corporal could hear. 'You're asking for it too,' he said menacingly. 'What's more, I'm going to make sure you get it.'

'I was attacked and beaten up for no reason at all,' Hauser gasped. 'It's a disgrace.'

'Shut your mouth or I'll shut it for you,' Colman told him pleasantly.

'Let me do it, Lieutenant,' Copland volunteered. 'I'd be glad to.'

'You stand by for further instructions,' Colman commanded briskly. 'Send the following message from Gershwin to Big Daddy: operation complete—one dead, two wounded, and one corporal under arrest. That's you, Copland. You might tell them something else while you're about it: Captain Keller's on his way back to camp.'

Keller braked sharply to a halt and left the car without removing the ignition key, without slamming the door, without even noticing that his Cadillac was standing right in the middle of a no parking zone which he himself had established.

He did not seem to see anybody or anything. Absently, he climbed the stairs and walked into his office. Here he paused.

There were three people in the room—Ted Harte, Sylvia Meiners, and Sergeant Popper, who had turned up a minute or two before—but Keller simply noted their presence and said curtly, 'I'd like a word in private with Mr Harte.'

Sylvia and the sergeant left the room at once, though not before Harte had given Sylvia a nod. A brooding silence descended on the room for some moments. The camp noises sounded muffled, even though the window was wide open.

Harte stood motionless beside the commandant's desk. After some hesitation, Keller went over to him. All the spring had gone out of his step. He halted, facing Harte.

Then, in a low but distinct voice, he said, 'Thanks, Ted.' That was all, but there was no doubting his sincerity.

Seconds passed. Harte did not move or show any sign of emotion. He seemed to be waiting for something—something which inspired him with a mixture of hope and apprehension, something which was bound to happen if Frank Keller was still Frank Keller.

Keller said, 'Yes, Ted, I'm grateful to you, but my gratitude wouldn't be complete without this.'

His fist shot out with lightning speed and caught Harte full on the jaw.

Harte felt as if some irresistible force had knocked his legs from under him. He staggered backwards, collided with the wall, and slid to the floor.

When he recovered his senses and tried to heave himself to his feet, Keller was standing behind his desk. He could see, through the pink haze that still veiled his eyes, that the captain was doing his best to smile.

'Come here,' Keller called invitingly.

Harte got up and started to straighten his clothing, but it needed little attention.

'I've got something for you,' Keller continued. He was holding a bulky file in his hand. 'All the dope on Hauser. It's your case again from now on. Deal with it as you think fit.'

The CIC officer massaged his chin. 'As I think fit?' he said incredulously. 'Did you really say that?'

'Sure,' Keller replied, proffering the file.

Harte made no immediate move to take it. He said, 'You know what this could mean?'

'Of course. I've had enough—I'm quitting.'

Harte took the file. 'Okay,' he said simply. 'I'll handle it, but I'll handle it my way. No more interference from you, whatever I do—is it a deal?'

'It's a deal,' Keller replied. The commandant of Camp 7 went over to the window and stared out, not down into the compound but up at the mountains. They were all he seemed to see.

'Balls,' said Lieutenant Colman, as he walked into the commandant's office. The remark was addressed to himself, not Keller or Harte. Casually, he tossed the bracelet to Harte, who glanced at it briefly and put it in his pocket.

'What's your trouble?' Harte inquired.

'This lousy weather. It rained all the time I was out. Now I'm inside it quits.' Colman stripped off his jacket and shook it.

Harte watched him intently. 'Well, what else?'

'I told you—it isn't raining any more.'

'Nothing special to report, Lieutenant?'

Colman gave an amiable grin. 'Yes, I've got one hell of a thirst.'

'You can attend to that later. First, let's get the picture straight. As I see it, the whole thing was quite simple. An internee escaped and you recaptured him with the help of the standby squad. The credit's all yours—in fact they'll probably pin a medal on you. Anything else?'

'The man killed his wife.'

'Nothing very exceptional about that,' Harte said unemotionally. 'Maybe you disagree?'

'Me? Why should I?' Colman looked from Harte to Keller and back. 'Seems to me we've all got the same basic idea,' he drawled. 'You can count me in, anyway, just as long as I get my little request.'

'What's that?'

'Gershwin and the rest of the classics—I'd like to hear a bit more of them in this place. Do I get a free hand?'

'That's for the commandant to decide,' Harte said. He turned to Keller. 'Okay, Frank?'

Keller nodded. 'Okay.'

'In that case,' Colman said, rubbing his hands delightedly, 'everything's hunky dory. I'll issue the necessary instructions right away.' And he hurried out.

'What was all that about?' Keller demanded brusquely.

'Don't underestimate people's feelings,' Harte advised. 'It doesn't matter what sort of feelings they are. You can do a lot with them if you steer them in the right direction. That's what I'm doing for you.'

'As a friend?'

'I don't know what you mean,' Harte said, almost coldly. 'No, Frank, as an American. You may be irritated by the idea but it's true. Try and accept it.'

'Right,' said Harte. 'Get Corporal Copland to bring Hauser in. I'd like the following people to be present: Captain Keller, Lieutenant Colman, and Fräulein Meiners—the last-named for the sake of the record.'

'Do you insist?' Keller asked.

'I'd prefer it.'

'Very well.'

'One more thing, Frank. Please leave the talking to me. Don't butt in whatever happens. If you feel the necessity to comment, favourably or otherwise, leave it till later. Can I rely on you?'

Keller nodded.

'Good,' Harte said. 'To continue. The following will hold themselves in readiness in the outer office, Herr Gernsbach, Herr Reiter, Internee Laffrentz, and the man known as Slembeck. In addition, Reiter is to bring along a couple of his Balkan ambassadors—he'll know the ones I mean. Meanwhile, Sergeant Popper will get the camp ready for Colonel Cord's arrival. I want the colonel welcomed by a choir at the main entrance.'

Sylvia went off to transmit the CIC officer's instructions. Harte cleared his desk, deposited the Hauser file neatly on top, and pulled up two chairs—one for himself and the other for Hauser.

Keller watched these preparations with a hint of uneasiness. 'I hope you know what you're doing,' he said eventually.

'I've a pretty good idea.'

'What happens if your plan misfires?'

'You foot the whole bill. That's what you expected me to say, isn't it, or have you started to trust me at last?'

Keller did not reply. Harte opened one of his desk drawers and produced a bottle of whisky. He removed the cap and took a long pull. 'Medicine,' he said. 'My gum's bleeding—must have bumped into something hard.' He offered the bottle to Keller, who shook his head.

'No, thanks. Later, maybe.'

Harte nodded sympathetically. At that moment Sylvia came back into the room, so he took another ostentatious swig.

'Medicine, I suppose,' Sylvia said with a smile. 'Everything's ready.'

Harte retired behind his desk. Keller went over to the window and leaned against it with his back to the light. His shadowy face was almost unrecognizable. Lieutenant Colman ambled in, grinning expectantly, and made himself comfortable in a corner.

Hauser appeared, escorted by Corporal Copland. The faces

of both men exhibited bluish-red bruises and there was a broad strip of adhesive tape across Hauser's chin. 'Go on, buddy,' urged the corporal, 'keep moving.'

Hauser looked round, blinking. As soon as his eyes fell on Harte he went straight up to him and said, 'You're the smartest bastard I've ever met.'

'Don't waste your compliments, Hauser.' Harte gestured to the chair facing his desk. 'Flattered as I am by your opinion, I'm afraid I must qualify it. A good routine job—that's all it was.'

Hauser sat down stiffly opposite Harte. 'All right, fire away, but don't imagine I'll fall into the same trap twice.'

'Your wife is dead. You know that, don't you?'

Hauser's square head drooped for a moment, but there was a glint in his eye when he looked up again. 'I'm sorry—I didn't mean to kill her, of course. I acted on impulse, after catching her in bed with a man.' He refrained from glancing at Keller. 'It was manslaughter, and I'll prove it in court as soon as I'm given a proper hearing.'

'That would suit you fine, wouldn't it?' Harte said sarcastically. 'You'd welcome a nice cosy conviction for manslaughter if it stopped you from being tried for mass murder.'

'Just a minute!' Hauser blustered. 'Don't try to hush up the circumstances, because they stink to high heaven.'

'What circumstances?' Harte inquired pleasantly.

Hauser drew a deep breath. 'Well, for a start, stop acting as if you didn't know who was in bed with my wife.'

'Who was it? An American? The beds in this part of the world are littered with Americans, and very welcome they are, for whatever reason. Finding one in bed with your wife wasn't so exceptional. I'd call it more of a general rule—a sign of the times. Anything else?'

'Yes, a whole lot of things,' Hauser replied grimly. 'I've been brutally maltreated.'

'By me, you mean?' Copland intercepted an encouraging glance from Harte. 'You attacked me and I defended myself. I can swear to that.'

'And I can confirm it,' Lieutenant Colman said laconically from his corner.

The corporal looked surprised and grateful. 'What the lieutenant says goes,' he said solemnly. 'The lieutenant's word carries a lot of weight round here. Ask any of the boys and they'll tell you the same.'

Keller regarded the others with bewilderment. He wondered what had got into them. Things were happening which contradicted all his preconceived ideas. Colman and Copland, who usually did nothing but snarl at one another, exchanged a meaningful wink.

'What's all this?' Hauser demanded furiously. 'Don't try any more tricks on me, Mr Harte, because they won't work. What do you think'll happen when I tell everyone how I managed to get out of here?'

'Cut it out, Hauser. You couldn't make it stick, especially as I can prove you were planning a break days ago. I've got witnesses. Herr Laffrentz is ready to make a sworn statement to that effect, and he isn't the only one.'

'Laffrentz is a dirty bastard,' Hauser bellowed, 'and that goes for most of the others. Laffrentz is a liar, Keller tried to make a deal with my wife, and you helped me to escape.'

Keller gripped the window-sill convulsively and Lieutenant Colman sat up with a gleam of anticipation in his eyes. Copland clenched his fists and Sylvia jumped to her feet, but Harte sat back in his chair and laughed, loud and long. Everyone stared at him in surprise.

'You're talking crap,' he said eventually, 'unconvincing crap, at that. Every accused man tries to incriminate prosecution witnesses, undermine their reputation, impugn their credibility —it's one of the oldest and most ineffective tactics in the book. What do you hope to gain by it? Take note of the following: point one, we regard Herr Laffrentz as a reliable witness; point two, whether or not Captain Keller tried to make a deal with your wife remains to be proved. Only a statement from your wife could decide that, and she's dead—you killed her. Herr Gernsbach, the public trustee, is not in possession of any documents relating to the White Horse which mentions the names Hauser or Keller, and he can testify to that any time you like. He's waiting in the outer office. Shall I ask him to come in?'

Hauser glared wildly round the room. 'This is a conspiracy!' he blustered.

'I haven't even started yet,' Harte assured him, opening the file on his desk. Abruptly, he asked, 'Ever hear of Operation Horse-fly?'

Hauser blinked momentarily, then looked Harte full in the face. He did not speak, but edged one foot sideways as though he were about to jump up.

Rage welled up inside him—rage mingled with frustration and despair. He could have wept, raved, bellowed like a bull, but he did none of these things. He had to reckon with the possibility that Harte was bluffing again. Or did the CIC man really know something about Horse-fly?

'How green is your memory, Hauser? What about Bolkhov, Orel and Bryansk? Nice goings-on behind the lines, and all organized and led by you, Herr Standartenführer. Cattle-trucks full of candidates for the gas-oven, blazing houses with people inside—subhuman elements, in your terminology—and a whole series of mass graves. Detailed affidavits on the subject have already been sworn and signed.'

'Who by?'

'A number of people.'

'A number of lying bastards!'

'I'd prefer to describe them as contributors to a good cause, however unwitting or unintentional their help may have been. There are far more of them than you probably imagine, by the way. For instance, I also have statements referring to your activities as an official transporter of subhuman freight in Belgrade, Bucharest and Sofia.'

Hauser bowed his head in silence. He clenched his fists and looked round like a hunted animal, but all he could see was a circle of indifferent faces.

'And you think that'll be enough?' he growled. 'I'll tear your so-called witnesses to shreds. I'll show them up as a bunch of Nazis who'd swear to anything in order to save their own skin—rabble, unprincipled swine, scum who are ready to renounce their own country for the sake of survival. Even an American ought to feel sick at the thought of using them.'

Ted Harte felt in the pocket of his uniform jacket and brought out an object the size of a man's fist. He deposited it in the exact centre of the desk and pushed it towards Hauser.

'A ruby bracelet,' he said. 'A work of art of international repute, formerly owned by the kings of Poland and later presented to a Countess Patocki. Remained in the family's possession for several centuries—until October 'thirty-nine, when it changed hands. That was when all the surviving Patockis were exterminated—an operation directed by you, Herr Hauser. Name of witness: Slembeck. He's next door too, waiting to give any evidence required of him. You had this bracelet on you when you were detained by Lieutenant Colman, Hauser. That completes the chain of evidence.'

Hauser said nothing. He got to his feet and stood there swaying like a wounded man. His chest rose and fell. Then he turned to Corporal Copland and yelled, 'I want to get out of here! Get me out of here!'

'With pleasure,' said Copland.

'The war crimes tribunal at Dachau will welcome you with open arms,' Harte called after him. 'You leave tonight.'

The internee choir organized by Sergeant Popper broke into a four-part rendering of *Home, Sweet Home.*

This was the prearranged signal which meant that Colonel Cord had arrived at the main entrance—not too soon, fortunately. Keller gave Harte a nod of appreciation and gratitude, but his expression seemed to say: what now?

Cord climbed out of his exalted cousin's Rolls-Royce and inspected the German choir, which was clad in an assortment of cast-off US Army camouflage jackets. His eye softened slightly, for he too was a lover of the arts. As a teen-ager, he had played string bass in a high school band known as the Big Five.

'Thank you, Sergeant,' he said, returning Popper's salute. He extended his hand and the provost-marshal shook it vigorously.

While the internees continued to extol the merits of home in strongly accented English, Keller and Harte hurried out of the administration block to greet the colonel, followed at a leisurely pace by Lieutenant Colman. Cord hailed them enthusiastically.

'Good to see you again, boys! This camp is like an all-American oasis in the middle of a desert.' He shook them warmly by the hand. 'You represent all that's finest in America, and you ought to be goddam proud of yourselves. You may be too modest to admit it, but I'm proud enough for the lot of you.'

Keller made no comment and Harte smiled politely, but Colman said, 'You'd have been proud if you'd seen me in the rain this afternoon, sir.'

Cord did not grasp the meaning of this remark but made no effort to fathom it. In his eyes, the lieutenant was an insignificant link in the chain of command, and such men had a logic of their own—a senior officer had to accept that. Quickly, he turned back to the people that mattered, Keller and Harte.

'Have you really cleared up the Hauser case?'

'Once and for all,' Harte assured him.

'He escaped,' Keller announced with dangerous candour.

'What was that?' Cord demanded, aghast. 'Did you say escaped?'

'Yes, but he was recaptured two hours later,' Harte amplified quickly. 'The credit for that goes to Lieutenant Colman.'

Colman looked modest. 'I only carried out Mr Harte's instructions. Besides, a lot of credit belongs to my men, especially Corporal Copland. He's developed some first-class methods of dealing with the Hauser type of German. I can't commend him too highly.'

It had taken a bare minute for Colonel Cord to grasp the situation and rise above it. 'Boys,' he exclaimed with an endearing smile, 'I congratulate you. You've shown you can handle any problem that comes along, which is the way it ought to be. I suggest we drink to that.'

He strode off towards the administration block, leaving the others with no choice but to follow. Every salute Cord received from passing members of the camp staff was returned with comradely warmth.

'Boys,' he declared as they climbed the stairs, Keller on his right, Harte on his left, Colman bringing up the rear, 'we live in an age in which every individual is required to make momentous decisions—almost hourly, in our own case. These decisions have to be made regardless of opposition, misunderstandings and outside factors—results are all that count. We won the war. Why? Because we were better, stronger? Friends, that isn't the point. The truth of the matter is, our cause was just. That's what I told a relative of mine, a Senator who's well in line for the Presidency or Vice-Presidency, and that's what I'm telling you now.'

'You needn't worry, Colonel,' Ted Harte assured him. 'Everything has turned out just the way you wanted.'

Cord paused in the corridor with an air of relief. 'I didn't expect anything else. However, as I told you a few days back, the Hauser case has acquired a sort of key importance, so watch your step.'

'Hauser's finished from every angle,' Harte said. 'We've even managed to effect a change in the climate of opinion here. One or two internees are actually prepared to co-operate with us.'

'Congratulations!' cried the Colonel. He avoided looking at Keller, but placed a friendly arm round his shoulders. 'A glimmer of light in the darkness, eh? Well, press on with the good work—keep your eye on the ball.'

They entered the outer office. The various people who had been summoned to attend Hauser's interrogation—unnecessarily, as it turned out—were still there. Harte presented them to Colonel Cord one by one.

'Herr Gernsbach, active member of the Resistance and head of our civil department. An artist by profession.'

Cord was wholly indifferent to this information, but he favoured Gernsbach with a benevolent nod. The next person to be introduced was Slembeck.

'Herr Slembeck has made a vital contribution to the Hauser case,' Harte explained. 'He claims to be a Polish patriot. We ought to give him an early opportunity of returning home.'

'There's no hurry,' Slembeck said hastily, taken by surprise. 'I feel quite at home here. Besides, I'm not really Polish. I come from West Prussia, which makes me a sort of German Pole. Best of all, I'd like to become an American.'

'Good for you,' Cord purred. 'However, if Mr Harte thinks you belong back in Poland, that's where you'll go.'

Slembeck was elbowed into the background by Laffrentz, who took the liberty of introducing himself. 'My personal adviser,' Harte explained with a twinkle in his eye.

Cord grasped the implication. His intuitive powers were remarkable. He saw through the whole affair but disguised the fact. His admirable imitation of a guileless uncle was designed to short-circuit any complications that might have arisen.

He nodded to Laffrentz. He also nodded to Reiter, and gave orders that both men were to be regaled at his expense. His concluding words to them were, 'Men, this is an exceptional situation—not of my choosing, but one that has to be accepted. We must all make the best of it.'

To Baron von Hagen, who was the next to be presented, he said in a semi-confidential tone, 'You're a diplomat and a public servant, Mr Ambassador: I'm a soldier. We both know from experience that everything is relative and nothing lasts for ever. Apart from that, we're humane people, people with a sense of purpose and an awareness of the things that matter. Am I right?'

The Baron concurred with alacrity. 'Absolutely, Colonel. Thank you for being so understanding. I trust that your sympathetic attitude will be matched by an increment in our rations.'

'It shall be done,' Cord assured him promptly. 'It's time we made a distinction between notorious criminals and conscientious administrators who have had the misfortune to be shamefully exploited by an unscrupulous régime.'

'This country is a sewer,' Captain Keller said dully. 'Spend any length of time here and you end up smelling like all the rest.'

The Colonel was surprised and disconcerted by this uncharacteristic remark, but Harte's cheerful laughter saved the day. Cord joined in and swiftly retired to the inner office, where he greeted Sylvia Meiners with a relieved smile.

'You're a sight for sore eyes, my dear,' he told her. 'You're also a woman and women aren't as introspective as men.' He glanced at Keller. 'We males have a tendency to think too much.'

So saying, he sank into an arm-chair, folded his hands, and surveyed the men standing round him, Keller, Harte, and Colman.

'Colonel,' the lieutenant said invitingly, 'I've scheduled a Gershwin concert in the gym in your honour.'

'Great!' exclaimed Cord, keeping his eyes fixed on Keller. 'I can see you don't neglect the cultural side of things in this camp. I like that, Lieutenant. It illustrates the scope of your responsibilities here, but it must be quite a strain on the constitution. Anybody who bears a heavy burden of responsibility deserves a little relaxation now and then—you, for instance.' He nodded at Keller. 'You're welcome to a little furlough, my boy.'

'Thank you, sir,' Keller said stiffly. 'I'd like to be relieved of my command.'

'Sure, sure, nobody deserves a rest more than you do. Request granted. Consider yourself on furlough as of now—Mr Harte will deputize for you. A reliable man, Mr Harte, I feel sure. Now let's celebrate.'

Reiter, still wearing his commandant's arm-band, stood waiting for Harte at the inner gate. He did not have to wait long.

Harte said, 'The internees aren't going to be subjected to any increased restrictions. That's quite an achievement, Reiter, and a lot of the credit goes to you.'

'I don't feel particularly pleased with myself.'

'Stop brooding, man! You've no reason to feel guilty. All you did was to give me the tip about Horse-fly. Several thousand people died in that little operation, so why shouldn't one more bite the dust? And don't start talking about retribution, because that's all nonsense. If this country had to pay every last one of its debts I don't suppose it would ever get on its feet again.'

'It really isn't easy to be a German,' Reiter said quietly.

'There are good Germans, just as there are good people in every part of the world. What they mustn't do is join forces with narrow-minded individuals who claim exclusive rights for their own nation and dismiss the rest as foreign bodies which ought to be exterminated at the first opportunity. Is that what you want?'

'No, for God's sake! No!'

'Then do something about it.'

Frank Keller was packing his bags. Nobody had offered to help, nor would he have welcomed any such offer.

Sergeant Popper was standing by the door, watching him. He said, 'It's a lousy world, Captain.'

'You can say that again.'

Popper gave a reassuring nod. 'But how did things get this far?'

'I've asked myself that, and I'm afraid I know the answer.'

'Well, I don't get it,' Popper went on, frowning. 'What does Lieutenant Colman hope to achieve by plugging Gershwin like that? You shouldn't have given him permission, Captain. That's what started it all.'

Frank Keller glanced up from his work in surprise. He stuffed some shirts carelessly into the suitcase and dropped three books on top—a Hemingway novel, a collection of Lincolniana, and a volume on psychological warfare. Then he said, 'This camp deserves a new commandant.'

'I don't see who's going to improve on you, Captain,' Popper said plaintively. 'You knew we had a dirty job to do and you did it. No one can blame you for that.'

Rolf Gernsbach was rolling up his canvases and arranging his sketches in piles.

'I've had it,' he told Sylvia Meiners, who was standing motionless in the middle of the room. 'I've failed all along the line. I can't paint any more, and that means I'm three parts dead.'

Sylvia shook her head. 'You mustn't give up. You ought to regard the things that are happening or have happened here as a transition—a half-way house to something better. All that matters is what comes afterwards.'

'Sylvia,' he said, 'do you know what I am? I'm a man with no one to lean on. I'm alone. What's more, I'm a German.'

'Please,' she said gently, 'please don't ask me for something I can't give you.'

Rolf Gernsbach gave a nod of resignation. 'When Goethe was seventy-five he tried to work out how much real happiness he had been granted in his life. Not even a month's worth—that was his estimate, and I'm afraid even that was an exaggeration.'

'I'm very fond of you, Rolf.'

'I know, like a sister.'

'That's saying a great deal.'

He smiled. 'Sisterly love is fine in its way but it isn't enough, not in this country. Goethe had some bitter things to say about our people, but even his God-given imagination couldn't extend to Nazi Germany and its consequences. Well, we've experienced them at first hand. That's why we must realize that we're done for—unless you believe in miracles, of course. Have you got the courage to believe in a complete transformation, in fresh starts and new beginnings?'

Internee Laffrentz lay on his bunk and groaned. His groans were music to the ears of his room-mates, not that they knew why he was groaning. He had simply over-eaten. Apart from that, Harte had officially described him as his personal adviser, so his groans were not unalloyed with satisfaction.

'We must adapt ourselves,' declared Wickler. 'If there's one lesson we ought to have learnt by now, it's that.'

Wammenberg gave an approving grunt. He had been saying the same for days now. He knew how to consort with conquerors. His Führer and late employer had trodden the paths of glory for years and brought Europe to its knees while he, Wammenberg, was running his bath-water.

'We shall never give up,' cried the Hitler Youth lieutenant, 'never! Guts and staying-power, that's what we need. The real Germany will never die.'

'Oh, my God,' gasped Trost. 'I can hardly breathe—I'm dying. Won't anyone help me?'

Nobody helped him, secure in the conviction that he would outlive them all. While they were busy trying to save their necks, Trost, the meteorological miracle man, would doubtless be released from internment and return to the bosom of his family.

Lieutenant-Colonel Mangel wound up his current railway scheme. Tomorrow he would start on Belgrade junction and later concentrate on Sofia. He had enough projects to occupy him for months to come.

The Foreign Office interpreter prayed. The regional commissioner doggedly continued to amass grounds for his speedy release—he had written two articles for *Das Reich* and signed at least three more of an embarrassing nature, but he could prove that he had saved four or five Jews from certain death. The regional welfare officer sought to allay his uneasiness by recalling that he had known a general who played a not inconsiderable part in the 20th July plot against Hitler.

'We're victims of circumstance,' he said, 'every one of us.'

Baron von Hagen hastened to agree. 'Whatever our attitude to the former régime, circumstances were to blame. It's time people recognized that. Why all this talk about overcoming the past? We must tackle the present, otherwise we shall never get to grips with the future.'

They were alone in the big room. Harte was leaning across his desk, smiling at Sylvia and admiring the way her hair caught the light. His face was very close to hers.

'Well, Sylvia, what about us?'

'What would you like me to tell you—that I understand you or that I admire you? You wouldn't be rash enough to get involved, would you? If I know you, you'll never forget what country we're in.'

'Is that all you've got to say?'

'What more do you want to hear?'

The light had gathered in her eyes now. They were wide and clear, and their radiance was meant for him alone.

She smiled. 'I do have something else to tell you, as a matter of fact. Don't drink any more whisky today. I like my men sober.'

'Good,' said Harte. 'In that case, everything's all right.' He felt himself beaming like a child with a new toy, but it didn't matter. He could afford to smile now.

'What are we going to do later on,' Sylvia asked dreamily, 'when this is all over?'

'Raise cabbages,' Harte replied, 'clean boots, carry bags—anything at all, as long as it doesn't help to put people behind bars.'

'I love you,' Sylvia said.

Famous War Books in Fontana

Reach for the Sky Paul Brickhill *35p*
The unforgettable story of Douglas Bader, the legless fighter pilot of World War II. 'This is a handbook of heroism . . . there is no medal yet for courage such as his.' *The People*

Bridge on the River Kwai Pierre Boulle *25p*
One of the finest war novels ever written—the famous story of three remarkable men who survived the hell of a human slaughterhouse.

The Phantom Major Virginia Cowles *30p*
The astonishing exploits of David Stirling—commando hero of the desert war. 'A thrilling story of openly dramatic triumph.' *Daily Telegraph*

Send Down a Dove Charles MacHardy *35p*
'The finest submarine story to come out of either World War.' *Alistair MacLean.* A British sub in the closing years of World War II fights off mines, the Germans, and a mutiny below decks.

Carve Her Name with Pride R. J. Minney *30p*
The story of Violette Szabo. 'A vital, vigorous woman, brimming with fire and scorn.' *Evening Standard*

The Tunnel Eric Williams *30p*
'No wartime thriller has more successfully explored the motives and emotions of the prisoner-of-war.' *Spectator*

The Wooden Horse Eric Williams *25p*
'A tale which deserves to rank with the great adventure stories of all time . . . Vivid, exciting and tense.' *Queen*

More Escapers Eric Williams *40p*
'In this sequel to *The Escapers*, Mr Williams has lost none of his verve. The reader is likely to find each of these escapes more enthralling than the last.' *Times Literary Supplement*

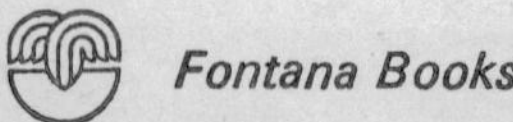

Fontana Books

Fontana is best known as one of the leading paperback publishers of popular fiction and non-fiction. It also includes an outstanding, and expanding section of books on history, natural history, religion and social sciences.

Most of the fiction authors need no introduction. They include Agatha Christie, Hammond Innes, Alistair MacLean, Catherine Gaskin, Victoria Holt and Lucy Walker. Desmond Bagley and Maureen Peters are among the relative newcomers.

The non-fiction list features a superb collection of animal books by such favourites as Gerald Durrell and Joy Adamson.

All Fontana books are available at your bookshop or newsagent; or can be ordered direct. Just fill in the form below and list the titles you want.

FONTANA BOOKS, Cash Sales Department, P.O. Box 4, Godalming, Surrey. Please send purchase price plus 5p postage per book by cheque, postal or money order. No currency.

NAME (Block letters) ____________________

ADDRESS ____________________

____

____

While every effort is made to keep prices low, it is sometimes necessary to increase prices at short notice. Fontana Books reserve the right to show new retail prices on covers which may differ from those previously advertised in the text or elsewhere.